THINGS UNSEEN

THINGS UNSEEN

THE ISAAK COLLECTION

DAVID T. ISAAK

Things Unseen

Published by Utamatzi Inc.
Huntington Beach, CA 92646
www.utamatzi.com

Professionally edited by Shavonne Clarke
Cover design and art by Jeff Brown Graphics

ISBN 978-1-958840-08-5 (Hardback)
ISBN 978-1-958840-09-2 (Paperback)
ISBN 978-1-958840-10-8 (Electronic)
ISBN 978-1-958840-11-5 (Audio)

*Now, faith is the substance of things hoped
for, the evidence of things unseen.*

*Through faith we understand that all the worlds are
framed by the Word of God, so that those things which
we see are made of things which do not appear.*

*The Epistle to the Hebrews, 11:1 and 11:3
(freely rendered)*

INTRODUCTION TO *THE ISAAK COLLECTION*

My husband, David Isaak, and I first met in January of 1969, in ninth grade world history class. When I saw him walk into class, I immediately decided we needed to be the best of friends. He had similar feelings. Our first date was to an Iron Butterfly concert in February of that same year.

David and I were together for over fifty years, ever since that first concert, and I thought we'd have lots more time together. That was not to be. He was only sixty-seven when he died—he turned sixty-seven laying in a hospital bed after a massive stroke. He died three weeks later, and did not come home to me. However, he left behind a treasure: five glorious novels. I won't judge you if you feel like I may be biased. I am. His novels *are* great, though. Here is what a fellow author, Terry Cooper, says about the third of the novels, ***Things Unseen***:

> "Having been acquainted with David Isaak for over twenty years and having enjoyed his previous notable works, I approached his first foray into the murder mystery genre with high expectations. To my delight, he adeptly navigated the genre, infusing it with his distinctive mixologist twist of flawed human relationships, supernatural elements, and the heart-wrenching world of drug trade amidst the desolate backdrop of southern California's Mohave-to-Joshua Tree wasteland. ***Things***

Unseen is a captivating novel, enriched by Isaak's profound knowledge of the area's geology, delving into the intricate dynamics of relationships, the drug trade, and, of course, murder. Throughout the story, Isaak employs a mystic flair to explore the depths of human nature and raises thought-provoking societal questions as relevant today as they were in 2002. This clever and riveting murder mystery not only captivates but lingers in the mind, leaving readers contemplating its insights long after the murderer is revealed."

—Terry R Cooper, author of *Orange Detention*
and *Privacy Wars. www.terryrcooper.com*

My mission in life now is to ensure that this literary treasure is David's legacy. We did not have children, but David encapsulated some of his fine mind in the form of these thought-provoking, amusing, diverse, passionate stories.

These five books form **The Isaak Collection**. In addition to the metaphysical-tinged murder mystery of **Things Unseen**, the collection includes: **Tomorrowville** (dystopian science fiction), **A Map of the Edge** (a coming-of-age story with some dark elements), **Earthly Vessels** (magical realism, with the forces of light and dark battling on Earth), and **Smite the Waters** (a political thriller with a twist).

Here, in David's writing, you can hear the voice of a man who is now silent, but whose words will live on—reaching across time. Words that speak loudly of David's passions, of his sense of social justice, and of his appreciation for other humans and the complex relationships we have with one another. Please join him—and me—as he continues his journey.

Thank you.

David's wife, Pamela Blake
Huntington Beach, CA
July 2022

1

When they took me in for the formal identification, my first impulse was to deny it was her; she looked different somehow. Yet it had to be Claire: the tiny diamond-shaped scar that just touched the left of her upper lip was unmistakable.

She'd carried the scar more than thirty years. Dad had been beating our older brother with a belt, and seven-year-old Claire tried to grab his arm. The backswing caught her on the lip with the beltbuckle. I'd like to be able to report that seeing blood oozing from his daughter's mouth made Dad remorseful; if so, he hid it well.

Over the years the pale diamond of skin matured into an ornament of sorts, a strange beauty mark that stood out against Claire's tanned skin. Or had before—with this pallor the contrast lessened, as if she were a fading photograph of herself. Her eyes hadn't been closed completely, and it looked as if she peered out through her eyelashes, glancing a little to the side.

The left cheek showed a florid bruise. Her neck was ringed with uneven purple marks, garish under the fluorescent lights; but beneath these wine-dark blotches was a black tone that seemed to go deep into her flesh.

Naked under nothing but a sheet—it was impossible to believe she didn't feel the cold.

After answering their questions, I sat in the row of hard plastic chairs lining the hospital hallway, the kind of chairs you find in bus stations. I stared at the floor. If you looked just right, there was some kind of pattern in the blotchy tiles. I pushed my glasses up my nose and squinted. If you just barely closed your eyes and peered through your eyelashes the way Claire had, you could almost see a design lurking in the linoleum.

The deputy sheriff had left after the formalities, taking pains to ensure I understood Detective Bolles wanted to see me later in the day. The orderly stayed behind. He stood there in the hall and watched me with what must have been concern, a burly, ponytailed man with a golden name tag. *Leo Janus—Pathology.* A bright tattoo started in the soft flesh between his thumb and knuckles and swirled up to cover the whole thickness of his left arm, the hallucinatory colors disappearing into the sleeve of his green scrubs. I wondered how far it continued and why he had done it. Doesn't life leave enough marks on its own?

I felt Leo lower his bulk into the seat to my right. We sat quiet together in the hall. The faint sound of riotous laughter came from a television far away.

They insisted on giving me a tranquilizer and driving me back to my hotel. In my room at the Yucca Valley Inn, I sat on the corner of the bed. What was I supposed to do next?

Mourn? I wasn't sure how. My parents would have prayed, loudly and ostentatiously, but I wasn't a believer. Claire probably wasn't either—at any rate, I was pretty sure she didn't believe in the austere Lutheran God of our mother and father. What would Claire do if our positions were reversed, and I was under a sheet in the morgue?

I had no idea.

I wasn't even sure what had happened. All I had learned over the phone was that she had been found two days ago, murdered—strangled—in her home. The sheriff's department was stingy with the details. Perhaps I didn't press them very hard.

I'd driven up from San Diego, checked in just before dawn, and then headed straight to the hospital. Everything was still in the suitcase. It seemed wrong to unpack, somehow disrespectful, but what else was there to do? I've always been a reasonable, methodical person: waiting to unpack wouldn't change anything.

I'd brought enough clothes for three days; I folded these neatly into the top two drawers of the dresser. Toothbrush, toothpaste, and unwaxed dental floss I lined up to the left of the sink, but then I realized with annoyance the only place to plug in my electric razor was also on the left, so I had to move all my dental items to the right. No matter how you clean an electric razor there are always little whisker fragments, and I tried to make sure they stayed out of my toothbrush. I hardly needed a razor in the first place: I only used it to keep my beard trimmed and to shave about three square inches on my cheeks.

I found myself standing at the foot of the bed and looking at the empty suitcase. I didn't know how long the authorities would want me to stay out here, so I had brought plenty of work—and I had a conference paper that had to be e-mailed off in three days.

I unzipped the computer satchel, unloaded the stacks of papers and reprints, and took out the laptop and opened it atop the small desk. Motels all have tiny little desks, as if travelers never write anything more ambitious than postcards.

No reason not to knock off a few paragraphs right now.

I booted the computer, started the word processor, and brought up the conference paper, "Unconformities in Tertiary Sediments of the Sheep Rock Wilderness: Evidence for Post-Erosional Volcanism." I scrolled to the bottom. 'Despite what Everson postulated in 1943, there is'

There is. There is *what?* I must have known what I meant at the time I wrote it.

I turned to the stack of reprints on my left. On top were my bionotes for the conference, with a poorly reproduced photo of me at the head of the page. Everything about the picture was gray.

L. Walker Clayborne, PhD, is Ashford Professor of Geology and Geophysics in the Earth Sciences Department of the University of California, San Diego, and is considered one of the leading authorities on volcanic landforms of the Southwest. Dr. Clayborne completed his undergraduate studies at the University of Arizona—inexplicably my vision was blurring as I read—and received both his MS and

PhD at Stanford University. After postdoctoral studies at the Hawaii Institute of Geophysics—my throat tightened, and it became hard to swallow—he took a position with USGS to develop a new emergency preparedness program—I could hardly breathe, an eon of tears seemed dammed up inside me—for major seismic and volcanic events in the Western states—oh God Claire I'm sorry, I'm so sorry, I'm so sorry—

I lurched to my feet and the chair fell over behind me. Blind, I stumbled to the bed, my fingers fumbling at my glasses, and threw myself down. I couldn't remember the last time I had cried, it had been years and years, even when Elizabeth and I divorced there were no tears on my part...

There were no tears now, either. I trembled on the verge. My whole body shook with the force of it, and I had to fight for each shuddering breath. My eyes burned. Part of me watched from a distance and noted the tranquilizer must finally be kicking in.

My trembling gradually subsided and I lay on my side somewhere between waking and sleep. Over on the desk my laptop gave a few urgent beeps, signaling that the battery had run low. When no one came to plug in the transformer, it shut itself down with a long electronic sigh.

I woke just before three in the afternoon. I took the time for a quick shower and trimmed my beard; at forty-four, there was already more gray than brown. I pulled on fresh khaki Dockers and a pressed shirt, topped this off with my old tweed jacket, and stepped out of the room.

I searched the parking lot for my Jeep before I remembered it was still at the hospital. My room was at the back of the motel, so I walked around to the front office. It was a stunningly clear desert afternoon, almost too warm for a coat. The parking lot and the front of the motel were decked out in full Christmas attire, the giant metal snowflakes and prancing reindeer bizarre against the backdrop of bare rock and Joshua trees.

As always in California it took a long time for the cab to come, but it was good I'd taken a taxi—the driver bothered to look at the card the officer had left. I would have driven to the County building over in Joshua Tree rather than the new sheriff's annex in Yucca Valley. This turned out to be a low-slung, concrete-block building with no architectural pretensions. As with most county buildings in the high desert, it was clear the designer had been told to build it fast and build it cheap.

Someone once said you know you're getting old when the policemen start to look young: the officer behind the counter was preposterously adolescent and blond. I explained I was there to see Detective Bolles; he replied politely that Bolles was with someone, but would be out in a few minutes. Would I take a seat?

I would. The waiting room was big, perhaps thirty feet wide, mostly empty concrete floor. The whole room seemed to have been designed to be as unwelcoming as possible. Were they afraid if they put in halfway-comfortable chairs that people would decide to hang out there and drink coffee?

Police radios crackled behind the desk. About ten feet away, a teenaged couple sat together. The boy leaned back in his chair, his body stiff, his arms crossed tight with his hands locked under his armpits; the girl had both feet up on the seat of her chair, and her arms hugged her knees to her chest. In the corner a middle-aged Hispanic man in well-tailored clothes sat rocking slowly in his seat, his gaze fixed in midair. I desperately wished I had brought something to read.

We all looked up as the heavy door by the front counter opened and a figure stepped through. It was obvious immediately it wasn't a police officer. The first impression was of a girl, short, slight, and seemingly lost in her dark, floor-length coat. The narrow, almost pointed face that stared out angrily between cascades of straight ebony hair corrected the impression—this was a grown woman, probably in her mid-thirties.

She stopped with her hand still on the door and stared at me as if in recognition. She looked straight into my eyes; her own were so black they seemed to be nothing but pupil. For a moment it seemed she was going to say something; but if so, she changed her mind, and instead tried to slam the door behind her.

A hand blocked the door with an outthrust palm and shoved it back open. Despite the blue suit and bolo tie, the man who stood in the doorframe was clearly a cop. He had a big, tight smile on his face, and he pitched his voice high to carry across the room. "Drop through whenever you feel like telling the truth, Mandy."

"Screw you, Rick!" she shouted back over her shoulder. She straightarmed the front doors open with surprising strength, and disappeared into the parking lot, her coat flying behind her like a cape.

The blond desk officer caught my eye and nodded toward the man in the doorway. I stood and walked toward him.

"Can I help you?" the man asked, wary.

"Detective Bolles? I'm Walker Clayborne." I held out a tentative hand.

"Oh…oh, yeah." He reached out and shook my hand, a single hard clench and pump. "Rick Bolles. Sorry about that. Having a bit of a hissy fit in the back there." He consulted his watch, then drummed on its face with the fingers of his free hand. "Is there any chance you could come back in an hour or so?" He lowered his voice, as if confessing some character flaw. "With one thing and another, I haven't had anything to eat since about five-thirty this morning, and I have a meeting in a couple of hours that'll run right through dinner… Or, if you want, we could grab a bite to eat together…"

"Sure." I didn't care where we talked, and I suddenly realized I hadn't eaten all day either.

"Okay. You just hang here for a second, let me grab a couple of things, and we'll go."

He came armed with a thick manila folder and a notepad, and ushered me out a side door labeled *Emergency Exit Only—Alarm Will Sound*. The sensors on the doorframe had been silenced by duct tape.

On the way across the parking lot he said, "Let me just say how sorry I am about your loss. It isn't easy to lose somebody, and losing them to murder is as hard as it gets." I made some noncommittal noise. The words sounded rehearsed, and I wondered how many times he had said them before. He didn't seem insincere, but there was an incongruity between his sympathetic words and his hyperkinetic body language. Even though he was probably five foot six and slender, he seemed as if his skin could barely contain him. His dark-brown hair gleamed with some sort of gel or spray. "I want to let you know we'll do everything we can. Claire was a nice person."

I was surprised by this. "You knew her?" For me, police detectives were people in movies or newspapers, not people you knew personally.

Bolles looked over at me without breaking stride. "Sure. Well enough to say hello, at any rate."

I felt foolish without being sure why. More to make conversation than out of real interest, I asked, "What was that woman back there so angry about?"

"Interesting you should bring that up. Means I don't have to." We arrived at a car, unmarked, one of those nondescript, oversized V-8s. Bolles looked at me across the tan roof of the car. The tip of his tongue came out and batted the center of his upper lip as he considered me. "You aren't by any chance acquainted with that woman, are you?" he asked. "Or, maybe, you remember her from somewhere?"

"No," I said, "why would you think that?"

"I don't. Just a passing thought." He tossed the keys up and caught them, and opened the driver's door. I heard a clunk as the door on my side unlocked.

The glove box on the passenger side had a large sticker pasted on it: Smoking Prohibited in This Vehicle by Order of the San Bernardino County Sheriff.

"Buckle up," he said. He backed the car out of its parking place, shifted, and then pulled us out onto Highway 62, headed east. "'That woman' paid us a visit to offer us information about your sister's murder." Bolles had very blue eyes, and every so often he widened them to underline his words. This showed the whites all the way around the blue and made him look slightly manic. "Problem is, you see, she claims the 'information' she's got came from a dream." He swung the car over into the fast lane, powered on past a pickup truck. To my annoyance, he lit a cigarette.

"A dream?" I was baffled. "So it's some kind of prank?"

"No, nothing so simple. She does have some facts—facts she shouldn't by rights know. Now, I pretty much doubt she got it from a dream—"

"What kind of facts?" I discreetly cracked the window.

"Now, Dr. Clayborne, you gotta understand I can't really give you details. In a homicide investigation, we try to hold back a few things, things only someone involved would know. Our friend Mandy knows some of those things. For starters, she knows what the murder weapon was." He accelerated us back into the right lane and gave a chuckle of exasperation. "The number of people who are supposed to know what the murder weapon was can be counted on my fingers, and I'd still have my thumbs left over. So either she really knows something about who did it; or, more likely— Shit, hang on a second here."

He braked quickly, just short of making the car skid, and pulled us up behind a patrol car. Two sheriffs were on the sidewalk arguing with a gaunt, bearded man dressed in Army fatigues. Bolles jumped out, threw his cigarette to the ground, slammed the door, and hustled over. All three of the other men towered over him, but there was no doubt he was in charge. The voices were indistinct, but Bolles talked loud and fast, pointing back and forth between the men, gesturing back over his shoulder with an outstretched thumb. He threw his hands in the air as if beseeching the sky, and then pointed at the patrol car. He gave a terse order and then stalked back to our car. As Bolles slid back onto his seat, I saw the sheriffs ushering the man into the patrol car, but doing so courteously enough.

"Christ on crutches." Bolles turned the key and pushed the accelerator. The engine roared, and we moved back into traffic. "Arresting pedestrians for public drunkenness? I wish we could get all of the drunks out of the cars and *onto* the sidewalks."

"Where are they taking him?"

"Home, if they know what's good for them." He drove in silence for a few moments, driving skillfully but a little too fast. He blew out a hard breath, pursing his lips. "Okay. In any case, either Mandy knows something about what happened, or, more likely, somebody in my shop or in the coroner's office has been talking out of school." He snorted.

"Of course, let's not forget the possibility God Almighty revealed it to her. Take *that* to the DA and see what it gets you."

"So are you going to arrest her?" I felt lighter already. Maybe this would all be resolved quickly. "If she knows so much, maybe she's the murderer."

"Whoa, slow down. For starters, I know Mandy; she's not a killer. A little strange, but we'd be in big trouble if that were a crime around here. On top of it, women don't strangle people to death. Just don't happen. Check the statistics." Bolles thumbed open a tin of mints on the car seat, tossed one into his mouth, and offered the tin to me. I shook my head. The detective sniffed, and snapped the tin shut. "Chances are she's banging some blabbermouth in the coroner's office. But if not, we can learn more by keeping an eye on her than by locking her up. And what are we gonna lock her up for? Obstruction of justice? A half-assed charge if I ever saw one, and it never sticks anyway. Look at Nixon. Look at Clinton."

We wheeled into the dirt-and-gravel parking lot of a small diner on 62. More dirt than gravel: the dust rose up and clouded the windows when we parked. "Hop out." He opened his door. "By the way, I don't take just anybody to such nice places."

Faux farm kitchen layered over with Asian knickknacks and several posters of American flags. Bolles behaved like a regular, grabbing menus from behind the cash register and leading us to a table before the waitress made it out from the kitchen.

I ordered breakfast, a safe bet anywhere. Bolles requested a health-plate lunch special that included cottage cheese and a soy patty. Our server, whose name tag read, *Ng*, flirted with him while she poured our coffee.

Bolles took a drink of scalding coffee and sighed with gratitude. "I appreciate your getting here on such short notice; I understand you were just leaving on vacation."

"Actually, I was just leaving on a sabbatical."

Bolles made a noise which could have meant he didn't know what a sabbatical was, or that he didn't see any significant difference between that and a vacation. "Well, let's start by getting some background."

"Of course," I said, "but I really don't think I know anything that will be useful to you."

"Well, you might be surprised. Despite what the TV has this country thinking about 'random violence,' ninety-nine times out of a hundred the murderer is somebody who knew the victim. Suppose you just start telling me about your family, about Claire's life—friends, acquaintances, boyfriends…especially boyfriends."

Ever try to summarize the history of your family to a stranger? The fact my audience was poised to take notes made it even harder.

We ate, and I told him what I could. Our childhood in the suburbs of Phoenix. Our parents, both dead now, conservative and religious. Three siblings: Edgar, the oldest, brilliant in every way; me, in the middle, not nearly as smart as Edgar; and Claire, the baby, the rebel.

Edgar had sailed through school in theoretical physics, first at Johns Hopkins, later at Berkeley; for the last fifteen years, he had been happily ensconced at Cambridge, and showed no signs of wanting to move back to the US. I, on the other hand, had more or less trudged through college, smart enough to get good grades and acquire a decent transcript, but never able to mimic Edgar's effortlessness. Intellectually, if Edgar was a figure skater, then I was a guy scrunching along in snowshoes.

Claire was another story entirely. Her interests were wide-ranging and seemingly erratic. Starting in junior high school, one week it would be anthropology, the next, Pythagorean philosophy. One day she was a committed communist; the next, an Ayn-Rand libertarian. In the early days, her enthusiasm was infectious; even if you thought her latest theories ranked with the belief that the moon was a wheel of brie, the force of her conviction was somehow thrilling.

As she reached her late teens, however, things turned ugly. Edgar and I were both closet atheists by the time we were in high school. (Well, actually Edgar calls himself an agnostic; he claims anything else is unscientific. After all, he says, atheism is a belief too.) But both of us kept our opinions pretty much to ourselves—is there anything more pointless than arguing with someone about religion?—and we even went through catechism and confirmation without a murmur of dissent. Claire just wasn't built to keep anything to herself, and she fought ferociously with my mother about religion and faith. Edgar and I were away at college for most of this, but we received constant telephone reports from the warring parties: my mother's tearful complaints and worries about Claire's soul, Claire's scornful accounts of our parents' hypocrisy.

I could agree with most of what Claire said about our parents' faith, at least in principle, but I might have been more sympathetic to her side of the story if she had not adopted weird beliefs of her own. At first I thought this was just to antagonize Mom—it was no doubt pretty aggravating to have a Hindu, a Scientologist, a Lord-Knows-What under one's roof. But as time went on, it became apparent to me that Claire had a genuine mystical bent she wasn't likely to outgrow.

She finished high school early, with a spotty transcript, and promptly stage-managed a fight that neatly resulted in her expulsion from our parents' house. She spent a thoroughly disagreeable—for both of us—week sleeping on the couch in my Tucson apartment, where she quarreled with me about everything from God to socialized medicine; and, although her intellect was undisciplined and scattered, I came to the uneasy realization that maybe *both* of my siblings were a lot brighter than I.

I saw her only occasionally over the next few years. Mom and Dad almost never saw her. She was in and out of colleges (all second-rate schools), and seldom stayed long in one place. I received cryptic postcards from the most unlikely of towns, ranging from Tulsa, Oklahoma, to Port Moresby, Papua New Guinea. I had a few flying visits from her, and she managed to drop in on Edgar a few times; eventually, of course, there was Mom's funeral. She didn't come to Dad's.

She laughed when I said I was getting married, and didn't come to the wedding, though she did send a carved Senegalese fertility charm; when Elizabeth left me two years later, Claire observed she was surprised it had lasted more than six months—the implication being, I think, that it was my fault. Claire's day-to-day life was vague to me; I had the impression of men, a lot of them, and probably drugs of some sort. Somewhere along the way, she buckled down and finished her BA, and eventually received some kind of graduate degree or license in social work, but she never seemed to find full-time work—or, if she did, she never stayed long at the same job. She often borrowed small sums from me, but seldom repaid them.

She had been in the Yucca Valley area for about six years—some sort of record for her, I imagine—and it seemed she might stay in the High Desert permanently. She once even steered a conversation around to the subject of loaning her money for a down payment on a house; I had quickly squelched this idea, and now I felt a little ashamed.

Bolles had listened quietly to my monologue, making a few notes, but toward the end I caught him glancing at his watch. "Can you fill me in on the rest on the way back to the station? I need to head out pretty soon here."

We each paid our own check, Bolles keeping up a steady stream of pleasantries with Ng.

Bolles had just popped the locks on the car when his eyes focused somewhere over my shoulder, and he froze like a bird-dog on point. "Do me a favor," he said in a conversational tone, eyes still staring past me, "get in the back seat and just play it cool."

"Cool?"

"Just— Oh, don't say anything, and act like a cop." He put his fingers in his teeth and whistled, a nasty, loud shriek. I started to look over my shoulder, but the slightest shake of his head told me not to do so. He pointed his index finger over my shoulder in a double thrust—*you, you*—and then jabbed it down at the passenger-side door—*there, there.*

Act like a cop? I opened the back door, slid in, and shut the door behind me. Out the window I saw a scruffy man in his mid-thirties, hesitating by the crosswalk that ran across Highway 62. The man shook his head, but some gesture Bolles made must have changed his attitude. His eyes searched the highway as his palms rubbed up and down the sides of his grubby jeans. He shot one last look across the road, and then ran to within a few yards of the car. His voice was shaky. "Hey, man, this is really fucked up."

Bolles opened the driver's-side door. "Get in the car, Jesse." Bolles climbed in and pulled the door closed.

Jesse hesitated, and then made a dash for the passenger-side door. He opened it, glanced side to side, then ducked in and slammed the door. He couldn't have been more obtrusive about the whole thing if he had been wearing bells and safety orange.

Jesse's eyes widened when he saw me in the back seat. "Who the hell is this?" Jesse demanded in a whisper. "I don't know this guy."

"Let me worry about who he is. This guy's got nothing to do with it."

Jesse continued to stare at me. Even from the front seat, he smelled of stale alcohol, the kind that sweats from the pores of heavy drinkers on the morning after. "What the hell you calling me off the street for? Can't we get in my car instead?"

"Oh, good idea Jesse. That wouldn't look suspicious at all. There's a dozen reasons I might have made you get in this car. How would you explain my being in your car?"

"Well, what the fuck is so important?"

"Gee, I don't know. Seems to me maybe you didn't show up the last two times you were supposed to see me—don't call—don't return my calls. Basically seems like you've been hiding from me."

Jesse hunched forward. "Look, man, Joop and his bunch keep talking about how somebody's gotta be giving you guys stuff. It's like they're saying it around me just to spook me and see if I'll say something. I'm scared pissless."

Bolles made a so-what gesture with his hands. "They probably *are* trying to spook you. They know something hinky is going on, so they're probably trying to spook *everybody*. Don't be so paranoid."

"You don't understand, man. I get these phone calls, and there's somebody there, but they don't say anything; they just breathe for a while and then hang up."

"Probably a secret admirer. Maybe you should get caller ID."

Jesse patted his jacket pockets, found a pack of Camel Lights, and tilted one out.

"Hey!" Bolles snapped. Jesse jumped. "I know you're not the shiniest ornament on the Christmas tree, but can't you read?" He pointed at the no-smoking decal above Jesse's knees. "No smoking in this car. It's the law."

Jesse stuffed the cigarette into a jacket pocket without bothering to find the pack again. "Listen, I'm scared of Joop, he's fuckin' nuts. I need to get out of this shit."

Bolles lifted his hands, and for just a moment I was sure he intended to shoot his arms out and grab Jesse by the throat. Instead, he leaned across the seat, as if telling a secret. He draped his arm across Jesse's shoulders; Jesse jumped at the contact. "Jesse. You're scared of Joop?" His voice became very quiet. "You should be a lot more scared of me, you little fuck. Those disability payments you're scamming off the State? You're gonna need'em for real if you screw this up. You want your PO to violate you on something? You want to bounce back with half a dozen new charges on top of it?" He leaned in closer, widened his eyes, and smiled. "Try me," he whispered, "just try me."

Jesse started to say something, but Bolles used his comradely arm around the shoulder to pull him closer. "Nobody else is on your side, Jesse. Try to be a little more cooperative." His voice was calm, reasonable, like a school counselor who is a little disappointed. "Try and be a little more productive. And try not to piss me off. Above all, when I set a meet, we meet. Right?"

Jesse mumbled placating things, and he left in a hurry, tugging his jacket around him.

Bolles leaned back against the driver's-side door, apparently at ease. He lit a cigarette. "Children, dogs, and horses," he said. "You have to use language they understand. Sometimes I hate this pissheaded job." He gestured for me to come up into the front seat and then started up the engine.

I asked if he could drop me at the hospital so I could pick up the Jeep. On the way, he quizzed me about Claire's friends, lovers, involvement with drugs. I couldn't help much. Even though my field work brought me out to the area frequently, I didn't see much of Claire when I passed through.

Bolles' voice stayed even, but I imagined I could hear growing exasperation. "Did she mention any other men you can remember? Was she living with anyone?" He glanced over at me, and I shrugged my shoulders helplessly. "Was she involved with any kind of religious cults or groups?"

"If there were any out here, then the chances are pretty good she was involved with them," I said. "I don't know anything specific."

"Did she mention anything about anyone she might have had contact with at the prison?" Bolles asked.

My astonishment must have been plain. I tried to envision Claire as—as what, a prison guard? A prisoner?

Bolles pursed his lips. "You didn't know she worked part time as a counselor at Eagle Mountain?"

I shook my head. "No…she never said anything about it."

"Ohh-kayy, then." He braked, and I realized we were in the hospital parking lot. "Think things over; call me if anything comes to you that might be useful." His voice said he'd decided I was a dead end. He handed me two business cards, even though I already had one of his. "The other card there is Wilson, our evidence guy; he'll be in touch with you regarding your sister's personal effects and other arrangements."

I thanked him for the ride and opened the door, but before my feet hit the pavement he added, "Oh. Appreciate it if you could give me your brother's phone number in, England, was it? I'd like to give him a call."

And why not? There was every reason to suppose somebody who lived halfway around the world knew more about Claire than I did. "I'll have to look it up and phone you; I have it on my computer, I imagine." Close family. "Umm—maybe I should stay around for a few weeks in case I can help with the investigation or something…?"

"That won't be necessary," Bolles answered. "Fact of the matter is, I'd discourage it. Just make sure we have your numbers."

The winter sun had already dipped behind Mount San Jacinto by the time Bolles dropped me at my Jeep. The long shadows pointed east, and I followed them a dozen miles to the entry gate at Joshua Tree National Park. I needed to spend time somewhere familiar, to stand on firm ground.

About seventy million years ago, huge stretches of California experienced a massive episode of intrusive volcanism. Rocks were sucked down toward the hot fault lines, melted, and then pushed up to form gigantic bulges just beneath the surface. When the blanketing soils eroded away, they exposed giant blocks of white, grainy stone which can still be seen from the Sierra Nevadas down to Joshua Tree.

I pulled over to the edge of the road and stepped out. The sun was gone now, but the rising moon provided plenty of light against the bright rocks and gravels. It had turned chilly, and I pulled my arms in close to my body as I crunched across the sand.

Claire once remarked that when night fell in the desert, you could immediately feel the cold of outer space seeping in. I had pointed out that in reality the Earth was reradiating its stored heat into the clear sky; there was nothing above the atmosphere from which to "seep." Tonight, though, I could see her point; it did feel as if a chilled fluid were leaking down from the black sky.

At the first large jumble of rocks my feet picked their way up the easiest surfaces, avoiding any paths that would require me to remove my hands from my coat pockets. Sixty million years ago, these had been sharp cubes and towers, like gargantuan building blocks. When I was still working on my dissertation, Claire had visited me out here. She had been in awe of the weird beauty of the place, and had spoken passionately about the strange power that had sculpted the rocks around us.

I'd explained that everything she saw was the result of low temperature—rather ironic, I suppose, for a desert landscape. When night falls, the moisture in the air accumulates on the rocks, especially on any sharp edges, and hydrolyzes the rocks to a kaolinite clay. Clay expands when moist, and this chips away at the rocks, and removes the corners and edges first, forever rounding and softening the shapes, like an ice cube held under a running tap. The real sculptor here was the cold.

She laughed and told me I was describing the chisel, not the sculptor.

I knew so little about her, really. Maybe it's like that with relatives; because we grow up around them, we don't have to get to know them. With friends, there's a process of discovery, as we accumulate facts and insights; with family, it now seemed to me there were mostly assumptions and prejudices.

Atop a large boulder I stared out at the rising moon. All alone here in the darkness, but with the glow of Los Angeles in the sky over the mountains. No wife, no children, both parents gone, my brother on the other side of the Atlantic.

I suddenly needed to understand Claire, to know her; maybe in some strange way, to make it up to her. I needed to know what her life was about, how she lived, what drew her to this place. I knew the contours of the High Desert better than I knew the curves of my own face; but, for the very first time, I wanted to see them through someone else's eyes.

And I wanted to know what had really happened to her.

2

Monday, December 30th, just over two weeks since Claire's murder. During that time I had rearranged my sabbatical plans, selected a mortuary back in Phoenix, and organized and attended the funeral—a very sparsely attended funeral with so many of our relatives already gone on Christmas vacation. I'd been back and forth between Yucca Valley, my apartment in San Diego, and the mortuary in Phoenix so many times that I'd exhausted the small stash of CDs in the car. One more Mozart string quartet and I would start running mazes. Across much of the Salton basin I'd been reduced to tuning in to mariachi stations.

A few days ago the evidence people had given me the contents of her purse, including the keys to her house. Supposedly they had pulled down the crime-scene tape yesterday, but when I'd arrived in Joshua Tree the previous night I'd opted for a motel.

I had never visited Claire's house, but Wilson, the forensics specialist, had assured me that the address on her driver's license was current: 145 Ironwood Road, Joshua Tree, California.

The northern flats of Joshua Tree are a jumble of dirt roads, clusters of houses scattered across empty desert. Few of the roads go through to anywhere, and they connect in a seemingly random fashion. The whole affair is like a labyrinth, but one with only a foot-high wall; it is perfectly possible to see a house a hundred yards away and yet not be sure how to drive there without going cross-country. Some of the roads literally go nowhere; they plunge off into the sand for a mile or two with no apparent goal, and then end abruptly for no apparent reason.

It looked simple enough on the map, but I took several wrong turns before I found Ironwood, a graded dirt roadway that dead-ended after a quarter mile, a half-dozen houses strewn along its edges. Few homes had any plants other than the native mix of low brush, yuccas, and the occasional Joshua tTree: no ironwoods visible anywhere. Some of the houses had chain-link fence around their "yards," but there was seldom anything to distinguish the ground inside the boundaries from the ground outside.

I passed 165 Ironwood on the north side of the road, but the next address after it was 130 on the south. It seemed impossible to miss an address on such an empty street, but I'd managed it. I turned around and drove back toward 165. The house was a modest stucco affair, probably two bedrooms. This time I noted there was a cottage about forty yards behind the main house, a small white clapboard structure with its own rough driveway cutting in at the west edge of the main house. Sure enough, there was Claire's car, an aging Honda. She must have driven carefully every moment on these roads to avoid getting stuck in the sand; even her driveway was a little treacherous.

I pulled in next to her car and shut off the engine. The hush of the noon desert settled on me. I left the car as if trying not to wake a sleeping child and walked up to the front door, fumbling at Claire's key ring.

I opened the door and stood in the doorway, reluctant to step inside. I was obscurely embarrassed, as if I was invading Claire's privacy, and, despite the brightness of the morning, I felt a tremor of unease.

The cottage was small, perhaps a thousand square feet. The front door opened into a large single room. Facing me was an ugly blue sofa that divided the room front-to-back. The front half was a living room containing two unmatched armchairs and a coffee table, clearly secondhand. Beyond the couch to the left was a kitchenette, to the right a dining area Claire had converted to a study.

On the left wall were two doors. The first stood open: a bathroom. The second, presumably leading to the bedroom, was closed.

The police had told me precious little over the previous two weeks, but one of the things I knew for sure was that Claire's body had been discovered the morning after the murder, when a neighbor brought by a UPS package and discovered the front door open. Claire's body had been found sprawled against the couch. The neighbor must have stood here, where I stood now, and looked straight in at Claire's body leaning back on that blue sofa.

Imagination is worse than any crime-scene photo.

I stepped into her house.

In the same way primitive parts of your brain recognize someone by their cough or their footsteps, I recognized the room as distinctively Claire's. It could have been her bedroom back home grown older, as if her possessions and decorations had aged and developed along with her. Slovenly, bookish, bohemian: unframed posters thumbtacked to the walls.

A quartet of wilting houseplants hung above the back window. Beneath the sill stood a pair of cheap dual-drawer filing cabinets, flanking brick-and-board shelving filled with clutter. The right wall of her study area held a small desk with overflowing bookcases to either side, books that didn't fit pushed in sideways atop the others.

To my surprise, she had a computer on her desk; I would have predicted Claire would be a technophobe.

I opened the door to her bedroom, a shockingly dark room nearly filled by a king-sized bed. The shelves of the headboard were stuffed with books and papers, and the window above it was half-filled by an air conditioner. This must have been her refuge in the summer months; by July the High Desert heat comes down every morning like some huge febrile bird settling onto its roost.

An odor of rot. The morbid side of my mind leapt to the conclusion it was the smell of death; but I followed my nose to a sink full of unwashed dishes. I gagged, and opened the back door, gulping fresh air.

I stood there, unwilling to confront the sink. Behind the cottage there was a clearing for additional parking, but beyond that at least a half-mile of untouched desert stretched away to the north.

I spent until the early afternoon cleaning and getting situated. The smell from the sink was bad enough that I had to take frequent breaks outdoors; I left the doors and windows open to air things out. The inside of the refrigerator was a garden of mold, and after some exploratory sniffing I dumped everything into a trash bag, pulled on rubber gloves, and scrubbed the whole interior with baking soda and water.

I sat in a living-room chair with a cup of tea, steeling myself for the process of cleaning the bedroom. I realized I had avoided sitting on the couch where Claire had died. Ridiculous.

I stood up and moved over to the couch. Just as my hips touched the cushion the phone jangled and I spilled tea on my lap.

I put the cup down and picked up the handset after the third ring. "Hello?"

"Hi." A woman's voice. "Ummm—Jared?"

"No Jared here. You must have the wrong number."

"Oh. Isn't this Claire's?"

"Yes, but—"

"Who's this, then?"

"I'm not used to being interrogated by strangers, but this is her brother. May I ask who *you* are?"

"Oh, sorry, I just—that is, this is her friend Kirsten Benninger. I was calling 'cause I thought Jared might be over there fetching the UWI stuff."

"UWI?"

"You haven't heard about the hassles with Universal?"

"I haven't the slightest idea what you're talking about."

There was a pause before she said, "Look—is there any chance you could come meet me right now? I'm only going to be here for another ninety minutes before I head off for LA, but there's some things you ought to hear about…"

Kirsten's directions took me through Twenty-Nine Palms. East of town was a dirt road with a sign declaring, *Wild Desert!* Beneath the sign, a banner flapped: *Sorry, We're Closed. Will Reopen January 2.* At the end of the long drive I saw a compound: high chain-link fences covered with creepers, the perimeter softened by clusters of desolate smoke trees and a few transplanted palms.

Kirsten was younger than I expected for a friend of Claire's; Claire had been approaching forty, but Kirsten was the age of one of my undergrads.

Our picnic table was centered in a fenced rectangle a stone's throw across. To our left was an exit in the fence; beside it a dismounted turnstile lay atop sacks of cement. This section of the compound was mostly bare earth, but several palos verde saplings lifted their chartreuse limbs by the table, and asphalt pathways had been laid down, meandering across empty space.

Behind Kirsten was a prefab office not unlike a schoolroom. To our right, the pathways converged and led into well-shaded walkways, wandering between the zoological displays. I heard far-off shouts, and caught the musky scent of caged animals.

I studied her as she went through her condolences. Beneath a head of glossy brunette curls her blue eyes were flecked with black and gold. Her skin was deeply tanned yet freckled, the freckles spreading out from her nose with decreasing density, like stars whirling out from a galactic center. It was a moment before I realized she had asked a question. I begged her pardon, and she said, "So you don't know anything about UWI and the Uber-dump?"

"The Uber-dump?"

"Claire's term for it, *Das Uber-Dumpen.* Universal Waste—great name, huh?—is trying to build this massive landfill out here. We were all involved in trying to stop it—the site's right over one of the main aquifers—and there was this fire out at their site office, and now they're suing everybody they can think of who was an officer of *Stop*

The Dump—they had Augustus picked up by the police on some kind of ridiculous charge—"

I held up a finger. "Sorry. Too much, too quick. You called looking for someone named Jared. Why would he be at Claire's? And who's Augustus?"

She was bright, but her explanation was disjointed. I gathered that Jared and Augustus were members of organizations opposed to the UWI development, as well as being Claire's friends. "Jared's also the local steward for the Desert Wildlife Fund, and he's practically a lawyer. I thought he might be over at Claire's picking up some of her files on the dump—Universal has been seizing everybody's records on the basis of some kind of warrant."

"Wouldn't he call first? And how would he expect to get in?"

Kirsten shook her head. "We all knew where she kept her key. And there was no reason to expect anyone would be there—I mean, we didn't even know about you." She looked down at the table. "We didn't really know you'd even been here, and then Claire's body got whisked off; we couldn't— We didn't even know about the funeral." She blinked back tears.

"I'm sorry."

She nodded, still looking down.

"I would have invited all of you if I'd known. It all happened so fast, and I didn't know who any of her friends were…"

She rubbed her eyes with the base of her palms. "Doesn't matter. We had our own little observance." She sniffed. "So how long are you staying?"

"I don't know. I at least need to pack up Claire's things, or give them away. But I'm on sabbatical, and it doesn't really matter where I am for a while. I thought I might stay until…"

"Until?"

"Until I figure some things out, I guess."

She stared at me, big blue eyes with red rims. "You should. You should make sure they find out who did this."

"Hey, I'm not a detective. I just—"

A high-pitched squeal of fury cut me off. To our right, at the far end of the compound, three men held up a long piece of netting and advanced slowly on the largest javelina I'd ever seen, almost three feet high at the crest of its hoglike back.

"Shit," Kirsten said, "Brutus got out."

Javelinas, even big boars like this one, aren't usually dangerous unless they're panicked, but something had set this one off: his little eyes rolled in terror. He gaped his mouth, displaying his huge incisor tusks, daring the men to move forward. One of them took a step and the animal charged. All three of them jumped back, the middle fellow stumbling and pulling the net down on top of himself.

Brutus swerved short of the fallen man, hooves scrabbling hard to turn his muscular bulk, and bolted for the other end of the fenced compound. Kirsten was already on her feet and running hard for the open gateway. But there was no gate—what could she do even if she headed him off?

I found myself starting after her, yelling, "Don't! Let him go!"

About five feet from the gateway, Kirsten grabbed the handle of a galvanized trash can and used all the leverage her body could manage to swing it into the opening. She slammed it down just a few seconds before Brutus thundered up, skidding in the dirt.

His way blocked, the boar turned his wrath on her, his jaws ready to lunge. Kirsten's eyes darted side to side, and she seized the edge of the trash can and vaulted straight up, landing with both feet inside the container. Brutus took a sideways bite at the can, his massive head denting the metal, but the keepers had arrived on the run and neatly entangled him in the net. He screamed in frustration and fear, and then thudded down onto his side.

His squeals grew louder as they secured the netting, and Kirsten pulled herself back out of the can, crying, "Stop it! Careful! You've got his leg caught—!" She knelt down in their huddle and helped them make adjustments, and the squeals subsided to an exhausted panting.

Two of the men stayed with the animal while one went to fetch an electric cart. Kirsten knelt a moment longer, stroking Brutus's flank, and then she came back to the table and sat down. "Poor guy was so scared. He wouldn't have lasted an hour outside this place—would have probably squared off with a pickup truck." She sniffed the air, and then looked down at her feet. "Gack. Garbage all over my shoes."

I sat down across from her. "That was amazing."

"Yeah, he's something."

"I meant you. I meant amazingly brave."

She gave a thin laugh and held out both of her trembling palms. "You're crazy. I was scared out of my mind."

"That's what I mean. It isn't brave unless you're scared, is it?"

She gave a weak smile. "You sound like Claire."

"*I* sound like *Claire?*"

"She always said you two were a lot alike."

"She said that?" It seemed unlikely.

"Well, what she actually said is that you two were basically a lot alike, but that you—" She stopped and blushed.

"That I what?"

"Nothing."

"No, come on."

She shrugged. "But that you never got around to pulling the stick out of your ass."

That sounded more like Claire. "And what else?"

"That she was your anima."

"Anima?"

"Your shadow side. Said she was living out the side of your life that you keep buried." She glanced at her watch. "Oh, hell—I need to get out of here." She stood, and swung a backpack up from beneath the table.

"Wait—I still need to talk with you about a number of things…"

"Didn't you say you were staying out here for a while?" I nodded. "I just have to run over to Santa Monica for the night, say bye to some visitors at my parents' place. I'm trying to get back tomorrow for New Year's Eve—though I may not get in until late." She fished paper and pen from her pack and scribbled her name and phone numbers. "We'll call each other when I get back…maybe on the first? And I need to remember to call Jared, too, and let him know you're at Claire's."

I stood. She hefted the backpack onto one shoulder and headed toward the prefab office. At the door she turned and said, "Walker? It's good that you've come."

3

After I left Kirsten I stopped for dinner at a Mexican place in Twenty-Nine Palms. I'd left the house without a book, and spent the meal pondering, fruitlessly, about Claire. Why hadn't Bolles mentioned her legal problems? Was Claire involved in arson? What sort of people were her friends?

I left half my dinner sitting in its pool of corn oil, and went shopping to fill Claire's empty refrigerator.

In December dusk speeds across the High Desert, and I needed the Jeep's headlights by the time I arrived back at the cottage. I had two armfuls of groceries; I supported one with an uplifted knee while I worked the key in the lock. I gently shouldered the door inward.

I was groping for the light switch with a grocery-laden arm when there was a noise in the shadows. Something rushed forward and slammed against me, and groceries flew in all directions. I just glimpsed the outline of a large, rough-clad figure before a blow to my midsection doubled me up.

I fell to my knees, my upper body curled protectively over my stomach, and choked, fighting to hold down my dinner. The attacker kicked me hard in the face with a booted foot and the force of it threw me onto my side, crashing against the open door. He jumped over my body and ran outside. I heard footsteps run to the rear of the house, the slam of a car door, the roaring protest of an engine given too much gas.

A smarter, tougher man than I would have at least rolled over to try to get a glimpse of the car and driver, but I was still busy gagging onto the carpet. I listened to the crunch of tires on the dirt driveway as the car raced away.

Nothing had been broken, but my gut ached, and I had to force a large roll of gauze up one nostril to control the bleeding.

Bolles arrived with Wilson and a small forensics team. They dusted for prints—and took mine for comparison—while Bolles quizzed me. Did I have any kind of description? No. Had anything been moved or taken? Yes—the contents of Claire's filing cabinets were strewn across the floor. The lock on the back door had been forced—did I have any idea why someone would break in? None whatsoever.

After the rest of the team packed up and stowed their gear in the cars out front, Bolles stayed inside with me. I sat on the couch, but he remained standing, his hands clasped behind his back; he rolled up onto the balls of his feet, and then rocked back and forth, making himself alternately taller and shorter. He studied me without speaking, as if he suspected there was something I wasn't telling him. Fair enough: I doubted he was being forthright with me. "Well," he said at last, "if I were you, I'd clear up my business as soon as possible." He glanced at some of my luggage. "And I'd certainly stay in a hotel room rather than out here. A murder and an assault in the same house in less than three weeks—I wouldn't call this a safe place to be." He gave me his peculiar eye-widening expression and then left.

Once they were gone I cleaned up the blood-spattered bathroom sink and then searched Claire's medicine cabinet. There were three Percodan, past their expiration date, and I washed all of them down with water from my cupped hand.

I'm not brave, and never have been. Oh, I can be pretty outspoken at a meeting of the faculty council, and I have spent many a week in backcountry fieldwork, days from the nearest road. But the last time I'd been in a physical confrontation was when I was twelve—if you discount the dish that Elizabeth had flung at my head two days before she filed for divorce.

It isn't that I don't admire bravery: Kirsten's thoughtless battle with the javelina earlier that day, saving it from itself, evoked my deepest admiration. It's just that courage isn't one of my virtues.

What I lack in bravery, however, I make up for in stubbornness. As a kid, I never got to see the inside of Claire's clubhouse because I refused to say the secret password: "Stupid boys." After bitching and moaning, most of the other boys gave in and joined Claire and her friends in the old paintshed in the backyard. By all accounts it was a classy place, with carpet on the floor and snacks scavenged from every kitchen in the neighborhood, but I never saw the inside; I sulked alone in our ramshackle boys' clubhouse, down in the mesquite-covered arroyo, muttering "stupid boys" to myself, but refusing to say it to the girls.

This stubbornness made me miss out on some fun over the years, but it served me well in other ways. What else is a PhD about, other than doggedness? It's different under some of the European systems, but in the US the dissertation process is about showing up and slogging your way through the regulations, the references, and the endless carping of your committee.

As a kid, one of my favorite lines in film was from James Coburn in *The Magnificent Seven*: "Nobody throws me my own guns and says, *Run*. Nobody." Now, realistically, guns make me nervous; and if Eli Wallach had told me to run in that mean Mexican accent, I would probably be running still. But the fact that Bolles seemed to want me out of here made me want to dig in my heels and stay, any way that I could.

I moved the Jeep around to the back of the house; there didn't seem to be any point in announcing I was here. I parked in the middle of the flat space at a cockeyed angle to prevent anyone else from parking back there, out of sight.

I did indeed chain the back door, but before I did so I searched the area behind the cottage for some means of protection. There were a few rusty tools leaning against the wall. The one with the most heft was actually a garden rake, but I couldn't picture defending myself with a rake. The shovel seemed more threatening, so I lugged it into the house with me.

I iced my nose by wrapping a few cubes in a towel and holding the makeshift icepack against my swollen nostril. With my free hand I searched through the cupboards until I found a stash of liquor.

I'm not much of a drinker. Even in high school, when it was almost mandatory, I never got drunk. At parties as an adult, I take a beer or a glass of wine to fit in, but little more.

Tonight, however, it was a medicinal matter. Even if I had gone to the ER, the War on Drugs has made it almost impossible to get a decent painkiller prescribed unless you are terminally ill, and there have even been articles written by experts wringing their hands over the fact that some dying cancer patients are spending their last days addicted to morphine. I didn't think three Percodan and a handful of extra-strength ibuprofen would be enough to let me sleep.

I was looking for something strong; even with the ice dulling the pain, my nose throbbed insistently. Claire had a few bottles of wine, some kind of melon liqueur, a container of peppermint schnapps shaped like a Christmas tree, and a bottle of Southern Comfort. Of the possibilities, the latter somehow looked the strongest—and Comfort was what I sought.

It's hard to do much when one hand is clutching your nose. I managed to drop a few cubes of ice into a tall glass. I held the bottle against my side with my elbow, and then arched my forearm and wrist up and back like a swan's neck to twist off the bottle cap. I eased the bottle down onto the counter, set down the bottle cap, and filled the glass. I sat down in the desk chair and took a tentative sip.

It wasn't bad. I was expecting something rawer, like the few tastes of whisky I'd ventured. It was warm, even a little hot, but also surprisingly sweet. I used it to swallow two more ibuprofen.

I sat there for some time, rocking in the desk chair and sipping my drink. Slowly the tension eased out of me, so quietly that I didn't see it go; it fell away like the tiny bits of skin that constantly rain down from our bodies. I heard once that if you saved up all of the skin you shed in your lifetime, it would fill—what? A dozen trash bags, or a swimming pool, or something ridiculous. There was a whole invisible ecology that lived on our dead skin, little skin mites and the things that preyed upon them; our beds and carpets teemed with these things, like microscopic Asian cities buried in the folds of the fabric. After I read about that I had started changing my sheets frequently, and vacuumed the mattress each time I did. My ex, Elizabeth, had been weirdly annoyed by this when we were still together, even though I did all of the work myself.

Claire's study was arranged so that everything was in reach from the chair, excepting the higher shelves of books. I swiveled the chair around, pushed with one foot, and spun in a circle, holding my drink carefully so as not to spill it. Bad idea: the inner ear of adults doesn't take kindly to spinning. I steadied myself. It felt cozy there.

I eventually realized I was inebriated. Not falldown, drooling drunk, maybe not even over the legal limit, but drunker than I had ever been. I had downed three-quarters of the glass, and Percodan and pain, tension and tiredness all ganged up with the alcohol to make me feel—what?

I wasn't sure. Different. Ah, Claire, if you could see me now, your brother, drunk and lost and a little wet-eyed, always on the verge of tears nowadays but never really weeping, sitting in your study afloat in that great sea of darkness that still reigns between Palm Springs and Las Vegas…

I sat the glass down on the desk. I turned off the lights in the living room, but left the light on over the kitchen sink in case I needed to find my way in the dark. I saw the shovel leaning against the sink, and laughed stupidly; defending myself with a shovel was preposterous; defending myself at all was preposterous. As I had demonstrated earlier today, anyone set on doing me harm could do so before I realized what was happening.

I nonetheless dragged the shovel behind me into Claire's bedroom and leaned it against the open door. I sat on the corner of the bed and let myself fall backward. It felt good to lay there.

I must have heard noises in my sleep, because I woke with all of my senses alert. My vision was never this sharp on awakening: it seemed freakish until I realized I'd fallen asleep with my glasses on.

For a moment there was nothing, and then an indistinct metallic sound came from the front of the house. I held my breath and listened, hoping to convince myself it was only an animal, or perhaps the wind. But there was no point in pretending. Someone was scrabbling at the front doorknob.

Why had I stayed here? What was I trying to prove? Dial 911— No. Too late for that.

I picked up the shovel and crept into the living room. I hefted it up above my shoulder like a baseball bat. To my horror the door swung in.

I know I gave some weird cry as I jumped forward, but before I lashed down with the shovel I realized the figure in the doorway was a woman. I clumsily diverted the blow and clanged the shovel against the floor.

It was Mandy, the woman I'd seen at the sheriff's station. She screamed as I leapt at her, but she also acted. Her hand flew to her coat pocket, whipped out, and sprayed me direct in the face with a blast from an aerosol can.

I dropped the shovel and clutched my hands to my face. I was protected from the worst of it by my glasses, but I howled in pain, stumbling to the side.

"Stay there! You just fucking *stay there*!" I couldn't see, but her voice told me she was more than ready to give me a second shot. "Who the fuck are you? What are you doing here?"

"I'm Claire's brother! I have keys!" I pulled off my glasses and tried to rub the sting away from my eyes, but this seemed to make it worse.

There was a pause while she decided whether to believe this. "Okay. Stop touching it. Don't rub it! Sit down and let me help you."

I squatted and felt for the couch, managed to sit down on it. I heard her off behind me, opening and slamming cupboards and drawers.

She knelt in front of me and used an oily washcloth to dab at the flesh around my eyes. It was all I could do to keep my hands on the seat next to me. "Why'd you do that?" I asked in my most pitiful voice.

"Jesus! You were about to brain me with a shovel. Stop moving!"

I couldn't really argue the point. "What is this stuff, Mace? Am I going to need to go to the emergency room?"

"It's not Mace, it's pepper spray, and you only got a light dose, and no, you aren't going to need to go to the hospital." My vision was still blurry, but that was to be expected with my glasses off. She picked up a kitchen towel and drenched it with liquid from what looked like a bottle of cooking oil. "This cleans up pretty good if you know what you're doing. The oil picks up almost all of it. It's just capsicum, the hot stuff from peppers. All natural. Maybe even organic." She dabbed close to my nose and I sucked air through my teeth. She ignored me and continued rubbing.

"What are you doing here, anyway?" I asked, gritting my teeth as she touched my bruises. "Why are you breaking into Claire's house?"

She set the towel on the floor and moved back into the kitchen. "I could ask you some of the same questions, couldn't I? Shit, if she has rubbing alcohol, where would she keep it?"

She came back across the living room and I heard her voice from the bathroom. "Well, to answer your questions, first of all, I wasn't breaking in, I have a key to the place. And when I saw there was a light, I *did* knock, you know. Second of all, now that the place isn't ringed with yellow tape, I thought I might water the plants—doesn't look like *you've* bothered—or even take them home… Plus she still has some books of mine… Ah-hah!" She emerged from the bathroom, an indistinct silhouette holding up a bottle in either hand. "Total victory! Rubbing alcohol to pick up the rest of the oil, witch hazel to soothe the sting. Oil, alcohol, witch hazel—I believe the anarchists call this a 'Seattle cocktail.' Lay down and close your eyes for the rest of this."

I lay back. "So you knew Claire?"

"No, I creep into strangers' houses and water their plants. Don't you? I've known her for about three years—stop peeking! You don't want this in your eye."

She doctored me and asked about the injuries on my face. I told her about the break-in earlier, about the police investigation; I even found myself telling her about the last two weeks, the funeral, my urge to come here and find out what had really happened to Claire…

It was comforting to lie with my eyes closed and talk while someone tended to my wounds, even if some were wounds she had inflicted. The adrenaline rush had worn off, and I felt heavy and warm.

I'm not sure when I fell asleep.

4

"So you're the geologist brother?" Mandy asked.

I nodded. "Geology and geophysics, actually—G&G—but, yes, that's me."

"Claire used to refer to you as 'The Rock Star.' Your brother the cosmologist she always called 'The Space Case.'"

We sat by the front windows of the Water Canyon Coffeehouse, a gathering place in Yucca Valley, down on 62. It was much larger than I expected; we had chosen a table in the front, amidst armchairs and bookshelves, but the seating area wrapped around in a long *L* toward the coffee bar far in the rear. A stairway by the espresso machine led up to a high, railed loft that looked down on us from ten feet or more. The café was designed in a southwestern motif, but the dreamcatchers in the windows and the bulletin boards hawking yoga, massage, and alternative healing somewhat undercut the antique effect. Old West meets New Age.

In the calm light, Mandy looked very different. Her features were a little too angular to be called beautiful, but she was pretty enough when she wasn't slamming through doors or assaulting people with pepper spray. The thought made me self-conscious. With fifteen minutes' work and copious amounts of cold water, I had removed the cylinder of gauze and hardened blood from my nostril, but my nose and the side of my face were bruised, my eyes pink and swollen. I'm not handsome under the best of conditions; today I wasn't sure I should

33

be seen in public. Still, when I woke this morning I had found a note with her cell-phone number, and the chance to quiz her about Claire—and about her preposterous claim of "dreaming" Claire's death—was irresistible.

The problem was to find a diplomatic way to raise the issue, not just to avoid challenging her, but also because Bolles had told me about her supposed dream in confidence. Or I thought he had—but when I considered it, I wasn't sure. I decided to bide my time. "The sarcasm definitely sounds like Claire. She seemed to spend most of her time angry about something or another."

"Angry? Claire? A little sarcastic, yeah…" Mandy frowned. "I don't think anybody around here would describe…would have described her as angry." She crooked a finger back at herself with a smirk. "*This* is the girl most people would describe as angry and sarcastic."

The Claire I knew had anger as her leitmotif, echoing whenever she appeared as if Wagner had scored her life. I decided not to head further down that road until another time. "So if I'm The Rock Star, what did she call herself?" I asked.

"'Danger Rangerette.'" She saw my blank expression. "It was a comic strip." Mandy tasted her coffee—Dante's Blend—winced, and reached for a packet of sugar. "You know, we haven't really been introduced, you and I, despite our little get-together last night. I'm Amandinea Cicerone—not Amanda, please note; thanks a lot, Mom—but pretty much everybody calls me Mandy. They call you Lionel?"

I nearly spit out a mouthful of coffee. "That's what Claire called me?"

"When she wasn't referring to you as The Rock Star. Isn't it your name?"

"Technically. I go by my middle name, Walker. My brother Edgar uses his middle name, too. I got off relatively easy; his first name is Julius. The only people who use our first names are the other siblings, as a way of teasing." Suddenly I felt desolate; only Edgar would call me Lionel now.

Mandy either didn't notice or decided to rescue me by keeping the tone light. "Wow. Julius and Lionel. In some states, I think your parents could be prosecuted for child abuse. So was 'Claire' a middle name too?"

"No, it was her first name. So if we wanted to badger her, we had to call her by her middle name. Prudence."

"Prudence. Ouch." She glanced at her watch. "I'm going to have to take off pretty soon. I had sort of figured you might call a little earlier in the day."

The coffeehouse had only a sprinkling of other customers, but now the bell over the door jingled. Three big men filled the entryway—bikers, to judge from the heavy boots and scruffy denims. The first one through the door had a face as big and round as the moon, curiously smooth and childlike.

They began to take a table in our section, but one of them, a tall, immensely fat man with a beard that ended halfway down his chest, noticed us. "I sense the presence of the evil one." It was hard to tell from his tone whether he was joking or not; his delivery was unnatural and self-conscious, like something from a high-school play.

"Oh, nice Christian charity, Billy," Mandy said. It was clearly intended for them to hear, but she didn't bother to look in their direction.

"Let us seek somewhere with cleaner air," Billy said to his friends. The other two turned and headed back toward the coffee bar. Billy also left the section, but thudded his mountainous bulk close to our table as he did so. "'Thou shalt not suffer a witch to live,'" he intoned solemnly.

"What have you got on there?" Mandy demanded. "Denim, leather, wool vest…"

"Huh?" He glanced down at his swollen belly and frowned.

Mandy imitated his preaching tone, tilting her chin down and making her voice lower. "'Thou shalt not wear a garment of diverse sorts, such as of woolen and linen together.'" She sipped her coffee, and reverted to her normal voice. "Deuteronomy chapter twenty-two, verse eleven."

Billy was briefly taken aback, but not chastened. "Jesus freed us from all that." He sat down hard on the first syllable, *JEE*-zuss, the second syllable almost an afterthought: the pronunciation of a Southern Baptist, tossed in amidst standard Californianese. "Those are the rules God gave to the Jews. But Jesus said, 'I bring you a new covenant.'"

"Did he also say, 'But, hey, guys, feel free to nose around the Old Testament and kinda pick and choose?' Did he say, 'Go ahead and be a self-righteous prick about some things, but just ignore anything you don't feel like obeying? Stomp on homosexuals, but eat all the bacon you want?'"

This whole exchange made me nervous. Billy looked like he argued with his fists, not his wits, and I saw muscles squirming beneath all that fat like snakes in a tub of pudding. Mandy seemed completely serene, and didn't even bother to look up. Fine for her. If he punched anybody, it would probably be me.

With an obvious effort of will he calmed himself, and reverted to what he must have thought of as his pious voice. "In the Bible it says, 'Even the Devil can quote Scripture for his own purpose.'"

Mandy shook her head, and spoke in a softer voice. "Oh, Billy, I don't know who told you that, but it's not from the Bible. That's *Merchant of Venice*: 'Mark you this, Bassanio...'" She looked up at him. "Maybe you should spend more time reading the Bible, and less time listening to those television preachers. Don't you know if those guys on TV had their way, you and your friends'd be some of the first ones up against the wall?"

Billy shook his head and seemed ready to say something, but he reconsidered and shambled off instead.

Mandy shouted after him, "And spend more time with the Gospels, and less with the rest of it." She lowered her voice back to a conversational tone. "Sad thing about it is, it doesn't even say thou shalt not suffer a *witch* to live."

"Really? I've certainly heard the phrase often enough."

"The Hebrew there was *chasaph*, which means 'poisoner.' King James changed it because he wanted biblical authority for all his witch-hunting. I need more coffee. You?"

I shook my head. She scurried off to get a refill and I studied her as she went. She was trim, and her hips jutted out sharply from her waist, too wide for conventional beauty. Five feet tall, maybe five-one at best, yet she took strides that would have done a basketball player proud.

When she returned she resumed as if she hadn't left. "The world is filled with people who call themselves Christians, but they almost never seem to quote Jesus. You'd think the words of their Messiah would take precedence over anything else in the book, but no, they'd rather quote the Old Testament—or if they decide to quote the New, it's almost always Paul, some misogynistic Jewish bureaucrat who never even met Jesus. Dimwits."

"Who were those guys?"

"'Shackles Torn Asunder.' Do you *tear* shackles? I would have thought you shattered, broke, or burst them. At any rate, it's a group of lowlife Christians; most of 'em are former speed-freak bikers. Billy's got more teeth and more viable brain cells than most of them. There's quite a few groups like that around, and it's not entirely a bad thing—most of the members were really dangerous fuck-ups before they got religion."

She doctored her coffee, and when I said nothing, went on. "The problem is, once they join up, suddenly they think they know everything. 'Look at how this has improved my life!' Well, shit—anything up to and including euthanasia would have been an improvement; most of these guys had hit bottom and then started digging. Born-again Christians, new AA members, and people who just quit smoking: there should be a law that none of them can have opinions for at least three years after they convert."

"So you're religious, but not—not what? Fundamentalist?"

"I'm not religious, I'm spiritual. Do you know what religion means? I mean, literally, at its root?"

Much scientific terminology is based on Greek and Latin roots, but this one stumped me. "No, I confess that I don't."

"It's from the same root as 'ligature' in surgery, when you tie off a bleeding vein. 'Religion' means binding together, tying up. Closely related to 'fascia,' which are the elastic tissues that bind muscles into bundles and also the things that held together the bundle of rods Roman emperors used as their scepter—that's where 'fascism' comes from, by the way. Both of them are about organizing people in power structures, and neither of them are about you or your soul." She sipped her coffee, licked her lips.

I know it was arrogant of me, but I seldom expected anyone outside the academic world to be both articulate and passionate about ideas. Physically, Mandy and Claire were very different, but when Mandy talked about things she cared about, the words might have been written by Claire.

Mandy mistook my musing for disapproval. "Wow, listen to me. And I thought I needed more coffee! I'm sorry, ignorance plus self-righteousness is just a combination that lights my fuse."

"No, don't apologize. It's just that you reminded me of Claire for a moment there."

"Oh." We sat silent for a few moments. Happiness is easy to share, like a public fountain, but sadness is a private little pond. "So you'll be staying a few more days?"

"Actually, I thought I might stay a few weeks. I'm taking a sabbatical, working on a textbook. I thought I might stay at Claire's place, if I could find out who the landlord is."

Mandy watched me. At length she said, "That's easy enough; the owner is named something like 'Givens,' and she lives in the house out front." She added a half-packet of sugar to her coffee and stirred. "That's why you're out here? To write a textbook?"

"Well, I thought I might—might spend some time finding out more about Claire…" I felt pressure from those dark eyes. "I mean, doesn't make much sense—"

"Hey, it's okay. Makes sense to me. Might make more sense to me than it does to you." Her watch alarm beeped and she shut it off. "I really have to go. I have a meeting with some people to wrap up a course design for next semester."

"You're a teacher?" I hadn't even thought about how she supported herself. Did people like Mandy need jobs?

"Not as a career. I'm a programmer. A consultant, which is a term we use for 'expensive but mostly unemployed.' I also teach a web-design class out at Copper Mountain, the community college. Not exactly a UC, but it helps pay the bills."

"This is a strange part of the world for computer consulting." I was reluctant to let her leave.

"Not that strange. A lot of the work nowadays is arranged online; they don't care where you plant your butt. Plus there's some interesting work locally, requires a computer whiz." She took a gulp of cold coffee. "I really *do* need to get moving here."

"I—I'd like to talk to you some more; I have a lot of things I'd like to ask you."

"I bet you do. Are you doing anything tonight?" I shook my head. "No date on New Year's Eve? Pathetic. Give me a ring on my cell later, after six. I'm going to a little get-together with a few friends—friends of Claire's, I might add—and you're invited. Okay?" I nodded my assent, although I wasn't sure I wanted to go to a party. She laid a slim spray can on the table: pepper spray. "Housewarming present. I have a spare." She started to rise.

The Shackles-Torn-Asunder crew were on their way out, and Mandy hesitated, obviously preferring not to crowd through the exit with them. Ten feet from the door, Moonface spilled a whole cup of hot coffee down his pants, and yelled, "Shit!"

Billy turned on him and actually wagged his finger: the world's fattest, scruffiest first-grade teacher. "Profanity is one of the easiest traps to fall into."

Mandy stood up. "Actually, it's probably just fine. Where does it say that vulgarity is wrong?"

"Now *that's* in the Commandments!"

"Nope. Says you shouldn't take the Lord's name in vain. So no misuse of 'Jehovah,' or any of his other names, and by extension probably not 'Jesus,' and, having been raised a good Catholic girl I would have to argue no fooling with Mary or the Saints. *Shit-piss-fuck* is okay—vulgar, yes, but not profanity." She strode over to the door and pushed it open, the little bell above tinkling. She stood in the doorway and smiled at the three of them. "On the other hand, 'golly,' 'gosh,' and 'goldarn' are all derived from people substituting some similar sound for the name 'God,' and are therefore probably best avoided. At least, if you worry about such things." She looked back at me and waved. "See ya."

The door shut and all three of the bikers turned and frowned at me. I adopted a silly what-can-I-say expression. Moonface chewed his lip. Billy narrowed his eyes and peered closely. Then, as a flock, they left the coffeehouse.

5

The first thing I did after I left the coffeehouse was drive to K-Mart and buy a baseball bat. Even with Mandy's pepper spray in my pocket, a clublike object seemed like good additional insurance.

There were plenty of locksmiths in the Yellow Pages, but only four in the immediate vicinity. The first number I tried had been disconnected, and the second took me to a recorded message informing me Don McKinney would be on vacation from December 22nd, returning the 5th of January.

The third number took me to a standard your-call-is-very-important-to-us message, and I left Claire's number. The fourth simply rang, a dozen or more times.

I dropped the handset back in the cradle and noticed that a red light was blinking on the adjacent answering machine. I pressed *Play*, heard a loud beep, and then a long pause where I could hear someone breathing. A man's voice: "Dr. Clayborne? Sorry—it was just weird hearing Claire's voice on the recording... This is Jared Huizinga. Kirsten told me you were staying out at Claire's until we can get to the bottom of this. Listen, something important has come up. Call me as soon as you can—" He rattled off a number and said goodbye.

I dialed his number and immediately was transferred to a recorded female: "You have reached the mobile voice messaging box for..." And then, in his voice, "Jared Huizinga." I left a short message with both Claire's number and the number of my cell.

Phone tag, the new American sport.

I stood amidst the papers the intruder had heaved out of Claire's filing cabinets, reluctant to start sorting through them.

I moved to her computer instead. I roved through her directories, opening files at random. A lot of them seemed to be memos for organizations she must have been involved with: a couple of environmental groups, a free clinic, a local yoga center, some kind of neighborhood anti-drug organization, and, to my surprise, a couple of churches. I didn't open every file by any means, but nothing I found during my prowl seemed to help.

I scanned her bookshelves. The titles were obscure; they gave me no clue as to content. A set of magazines entitled, *The Entheogen Review: The Journal of Unauthorized Research on Visionary Plants and Drugs.* Shelf after shelf of arcane hardbacks: *The Cube of Space. PiHKAL. Faces In the Clouds. The Origins of Consciousness in the Breakdown of the Bicameral Mind. Sefer Yetzirah.* I flipped this last one open at random and read. *As explained earlier (1:9), however, the Breath associated with Keter is not graspable, since this Sefirah represents a level above the intellect. The only place where this breath can become manifest is in the lower Sefirot. Therefore, even though it is on a level above Chokmah and Binah, it is only manifest on a level that is below them.* I couldn't even discern the topic under discussion, much less the point.

I started to push *Sefer Yetzirah* back into its slot on the shelf, but a packet of some sort was blocking its way. I pulled it out: an envelope of pictures from a one-hour photo developer.

Most of them were just shots of the desert, but a few were taken near water, probably on the banks of the Colorado River. They weren't particularly well composed; in the artistic sense these were snapshots rather than photographs. But suddenly, there was Claire, flanked by a red-haired woman and a balding man. The other two were laughing. Claire wore a smile, but stared frankly into the camera.

The next shot showed Claire by herself, with the river as a backdrop. She had on cut-off jeans and a blouse unbuttoned and tied across her diaphragm, leaving her tanned belly bare. Her brown hair was cut off just below the ears. Unlike Edgar and me, who both had Mom's ice-blue eyes, Claire's brown eyes matched her hair color note for note; Edgar used to claim we had adopted her from a Tijuana orphanage.

Claire was never fashionably slim; when puberty hit, her body changed shape like one of those sponge toys you drop into a glass of water. She was never overweight, but she worried that she was; seeing her posing proudly with her midriff bare was a surprise. Her hands were on her hips and her feet were planted wide apart, solid on the ground. Her face was faintly amused, but open, confident, and, well, sexy.

Sex wasn't something our family discussed, and thinking about the sexual lives of my family members was something I always preferred to avoid. But once Claire discovered sex, she owned it in a way which couldn't be ignored. I remembered a time when I was twenty-one, and had just arrived, somewhat reluctantly, for a family Thanksgiving. I had driven straight through from Palo Alto to Phoenix, and came up the walk lugging a duffel. I fit the key into the lock and kneed the door open.

Claire was on the living-room couch. Her blouse was open. Both of her nipples were aimed at the ceiling, but as she lolled her head sideways to look toward the door, one breast rolled with her and pointed at me. Her Indian-print skirt was hiked up around her waist and her legs were lifted and spread. Between them, the frightened face of a teenage boy looked up, spotted me, and vanished back out of sight.

I stood in the doorway like a misplaced lawn ornament. My first urge was to turn and go; my second, to demand an explanation; my third, to make light of it—my, we've grown up, haven't we? Instead of any of these, I pulled the front door shut behind me, hefted my bag, and crossed to the hallway without a word.

I couldn't resist a backward glance as I left the living room. Claire had both hands on top of the boy's head, pressing his face between her thighs. She looked straight into my eyes. Her cheeks were blotchy, but with a flush of arousal, not embarrassment; her look was not one of apology, but of triumph.

I looked through the rest of the photos. They seemed to be nondescript shots of the desert, taken in places where it was seen at its worst: places where a handful of rundown houses and trailers were surrounded by rusted-out car bodies and refrigerators with the door ripped off. One picture showed a strangely familiar service station, probably 1930s vintage, with a few boarded-up buildings out back; a couple of modern cars were parked in front, and a handful of men stood around talking. If these were meant to be Southern California Gothic, like a western version of the famous pictures of the families and homesteads displaced by the TVA dams back in the Depression, they didn't succeed.

Claire's phone rang, and I fumbled for the extension on her desk.

I expected Jared, but it was K.R. Lansky, Locksmith, returning my call. I asked if he'd be able to come repair a broken lock and fixture that afternoon—a little carpentry on the doorframe might be required.

He hmmmed a moment. "Not too much of the day left, and I already have one appointment… Where you located?"

"Joshua Tree, off of Sunfair Road."

"In that case, I might be able to squeeze you in, my appointment's over there. What's the address?"

"One-forty-five Ironwood. It's a little—"

"Whoa, hold it. I've already got you scheduled for three-thirty."

"What?"

"This is the sheriff's department, right?"

"No, this is the occupant."

"Hang on a sec." I heard papers shuffle. "Uh-huh. Faxed order from the sheriff's department."

I rubbed my forehead. Had Bolles arranged for someone to come fix the door?

"Yep, got a work order, warrant number and everything—but the order is to 'facilitate entry into an unoccupied residence.'"

"I don't understand."

"Means that they have a warrant for me to open the lock and stand by while they enter the premises and do something. Formality, really. Any sheriff's deputy can jimmy a lock, but the law won't let 'em most times. More money for me, I suppose."

"There has to be some sort of confusion here. The police have been in and out of the premises for the last three weeks. I want a lock *fixed*, not opened."

"Hey, you're right—there's plenty of confusion here. But it ain't my confusion. I'm gonna be out there at three-thirty: if I'm supposed to jimmy a lock, I'll jimmy it, if I'm supposed to fix it, I'll fix it. Hell, if you guys want me to fix it and then jimmy it, that's what I'll do. Just try and sort it out before I get there."

I steeled myself to spend the rest of the afternoon digging through Claire's papers. It was hard going, and I felt like I had only removed a dippersworth from a deep well. Most of the papers had been flung about when the intruder had ransacked her filing cabinets, but they were clearly an eclectic mix in the first place. I tried to sort them into logical categories, but some of the content defied classification, at least to my untutored mind. What, for example, was a reprint entitled, *The Concept of Plants as Teachers Among Four Mestizo Shamans of Iquitos, Northeastern Peru*, and with what manner of other things should it be grouped?

There was a lot of material about counseling and the prison system: the Eagle Mountain Correctional Facility Employee Handbook, dozens of papers on counseling of inmates, assorted memos from the warden. There were also a scattering of pay stubs from the contractor that ran the prison; it looked like Claire's time there varied from week to week, usually no less than ten and no more than twenty hours.

Interleaved with all of this were memoranda and spreadsheet printouts for the High Desert People's Clinic, apparently a nonprofit organization based in Yucca Valley. Some of the pages appeared to be budgets; others were clearly minutes of a board meeting. There was what looked like an outline of a grant proposal.

There were many articles on addiction counseling, as well as flyers for conferences on substance abuse. It wasn't clear to me if these belonged in the Eagle Mountain pile, or in the People's Clinic pile, but it soon became clear these merited a stack of their own.

There were folded Xerox pages bunched together in the piles, with front pages printed on colored paper. The titles were puzzling at best (*Sound and Color*, *The Great Work*, and *Seven Steps* were examples), and they were labeled as being lessons in a sequence. On the back of the colored front page, it read, *Copyright 1961, Builders of the Adytum.*

A few glances through the interior pages left me no wiser, but I took the trouble to grab Claire's *Webster's* and look up *adytum*: "the innermost sanctuary of a temple open only to priests: SANCTUM."

There were also flyers for a bewildering array of organizations and meetings. The Church of the Rock was prominent among the flyers, as were the far more intimate notices announcing meetings of the Eleusinian Circle.

Mixed in with all of this were photocopies and reprints of articles that seemed to me to fit no sensible pattern at all. Archaeological studies of particular cultures; reviews of neurology and brainwave patterns; a clump of scholarly articles on beermaking in Sumeria and medieval Germany; a series of papers on the Renaissance use of something called "memory palaces;" a handful of papers on Bell's theorem and some other speculative areas of quantum physics.

At last I found several thick folders labeled *Uber-Dump*: material on UWI. But these contained mostly contracts, BLM lease forms, annual reports and SEC filings...nothing that told me anything important.

I took off my glasses and massaged my eyes. Was all this simply a sign of Claire's wide-ranging interests—or did these all lock together in some important way? Did this all add up to a pattern or a governing passion, or was this pointless, like trying to synthesize someone's love for both baseball and Brahms into a grand theory?

I was undecided, but what I found next seemed like Claire's answer to the question. It was a pocket-sized "blank book" she had filled with quotes, and on the first page I read:

The steps a man takes from the day of his birth until that of his death trace in time an inconceivable figure. The Divine Mind intuitively grasps that form immediately, as men do a triangle.

— Jorge Luis Borges

The Mirror of Enigmas

I had the peculiar feeling Claire was speaking to me through the quote, as if she had somehow maneuvered the book into my hand in time with my train of thought. A ludicrous idea, what the psychologists call "magical thinking," something we outgrow in early childhood. Preposterous; but it felt true.

Maybe I should see a psychiatrist. Perhaps the shock of Claire's murder had upset my brain chemistry, and I needed medication. Possibly I ought to join a support group, or find an Internet chat room for the bereaved. I was sure no one, neither friend nor mental health professional, would tell me that staying out here, trying to climb inside Claire's head, was healthy or productive.

My face was tender and my nose still throbbed. I decided to take a break and see what was on TV. I struggled up from the floor and ground my fists into the muscles on either side of my lower spine as I stretched. My back problems seemed to be returning.

To my consternation, I realized there was no television set. For a brief moment, I jumped to the conclusion it had been stolen, but after looking around the room I changed my mind. It was clear that the layout of furniture had never been designed to accommodate a television; when a television is part of a room, all the seating is arranged to focus on the screen, as though it were a speaker's podium.

There was a pair of chairs and a small table in front of the cottage. I fixed a cup of tea and went out to sit for a while.

The day was cool but blindingly bright. I could hear cars, the shouts of children, and some kind of a small motor—surely not a lawnmower, there were no lawns—but these all seemed to come from a great distance, no more than a murmur. Underneath it all, the silence of the desert almost seemed to breathe.

My talk with Mandy hadn't gone as planned. I had hoped to coax her into explaining her real connection with the murder, minus the nonsense about dream revelations. At some level, I had been prepared to dislike her. I had failed in both respects. She had dominated the conversation, not letting me steer her in the least, and I had found her combative intellect charming—in an overbearing sort of way.

She hadn't bought the idea that I was staying out here to write a textbook, but it wasn't clear what she believed instead. To be honest, I myself wasn't sure why I was here or what I hoped to accomplish.

I would describe myself as focused. What I may lack in native talent, I make up for in self-discipline. I have always been good at choosing goals and working toward them. My recreational time was parsed out carefully: some time with the TV here, a movie there. At the end of the day I needed to tally up my achievements and see that I'd moved forward. This approach carried me through school, protected me through my dissertation, and ultimately rewarded me with tenure, a full professorship, and an endowed chair.

So what was I doing now?

It was easy enough to say I was spending time trying to get to know my sister's world, but something about the statement rang false in my ears. Any kind of close scrutiny made me uncomfortable; Bolles and Mandy both had a way of looking at me and making me feel as if I were lying, or at least evading the truth.

Someone—Roger Sperry, I believe—did some experiments at Cal Tech many years ago where severe epileptics had their brains split in two, right down the corpus callosum. This was the origin of the whole right-brain/left-brain paradigm, which has since degenerated into what looked like a lot of New-Age nonsense to me. But one part of the research was intriguing. When they showed the left eye a funny picture or cartoon, so that only the nonverbal side of the brain could see it, the person would laugh. When they asked the person why they were laughing, of course, only the verbal side of the brain could answer— and it couldn't see the funny picture.

The interesting thing about this research is that the verbal side didn't confess, "I have no idea why I'm laughing." Instead, it invented something. I'm laughing, therefore something must be funny. The subjects claimed something was tickling them, or that the doctor looked amusing, or that they had suddenly recalled a hilarious joke.

I wasn't sure what I was doing or why. For the first time in my life I was doing something that had no clear explanation and goal. And, as if my brain were split in two, I was making up reasons.

The telephone rang and I dashed inside.

"Dr. Clayborne. Jared." Agitated breathing.

"Walker, please."

"Fine, Walker then. Sorry I didn't get back to you sooner, I'm bailing somebody out of jail. I think UWI is headed over to your place—typical—they're hitting everybody over the holidays—"

"I talked to a locksmith who said he's coming here at three-thirty to open up the house for the sheriff's department."

"Shit. Yeah, that's them."

"What does the sheriff's department have to do with it?"

"If it's anything like what's been going on here with Augustus, they have some kind of warrant to direct the sheriff's office to seize evidence for their suits, and impound anything valuable against any possible RICO judgments. They don't get to just charge in, though—not yet; they get to point at things, but it's the sheriff that has to seize them."

"What difference does it make if they seize some of Claire's stuff?"

"From talking to Kirsten, I figured you were trying to get to the bottom of all this. That's going to be hard if they take all her files, her computer, all her stuff—"

"I take your point."

"They're only doing this to torment her, make life difficult. They may not even know she's dead."

"Surely the sheriff's office is aware of that."

"Detective division and the errand boys who deliver subpoenas are different crews. The right hand knoweth not what the left doeth…" He pulled his mouth away from the phone, yelled to someone, "Yeah, I'm on it!" and then said to me, "I'm headed out there as quick as I can wrap up. If they get there first, stall them; lock the door, claim you're the resident, and refuse to let them in. Gotta go. Bye."

"But—"

I spoke to a dead line.

Three-fifteen. I sat in front of the cottage and nursed my second cup of tea, waiting: waiting for Jared, or the sheriff, or the locksmith.

An old Impala drove slowly down Ironwood Road, dust boiling up in its wake, and pulled into the driveway of the house out front. The building blocked my view, but I heard car doors and indistinct voices, the casual commotion of a family.

The back door of the main house opened and two children appeared atop the steps. They spotted me and without hesitation hurtled down the stairs and ran across the yard in my direction: a boy and a girl, both in jeans, both golden-haired. When they were about ten feet away, they stopped short as if there were an invisible fence. They looked to be about six or seven, but it was impossible to tell who was older; they might have been fraternal twins.

"Who are you?" the girl asked.

"This is our cottage but we rent it out," the boy said.

"We're not supposed to be back at the cottage but our yard goes all the way to where I'm standing so it's okay."

"The police were here and it was all covered with yellow tape and nobody could go here without being a sheriff."

"How come *you're* here?" the girl asked.

"The lady who used to live here got killed."

"Slow down a little," I said. "My name's Walker. Claire was my sister, who used to live here. I'm staying for a few days to straighten things out."

"She was your sister?" the boy asked.

"You must be sad."

The back door opened again, and a woman in a housedress looked out. She saw the kids talking to me, scurried down the steps, and then crunched toward us. "Can I help you?" she called from the middle of the yard. It was a challenge, not an offer of assistance.

I rose, and the children backed up a few feet. I had to speak loudly. "If you're Mrs. Givens, I've been hoping to meet you. I'm Walker Clayborne."

"He's Claire's brother," the girl pointed out as her mother neared.

"He's straightening her things," the boy said.

The woman stepped between the two children and put a hand on each blond head. "Whyn't you two get back to the house?" the woman suggested, and used her hands to turn them around.

"Can't we stay?"

"Aw, c'mon, Mom."

"Back to the house. Now."

The kids ran back. Their mother crossed her arms and asked, "So what can I do for you?" I could see her frown as she examined the bruise on my face and my swollen nose.

"Deputy Wilson should have mentioned I'd be dropping by to take care of Claire's things and make arrangements…" The children had taken a liberal interpretation of getting back to the house; both stood on the bottommost step and craned their little bodies in our direction.

"I haven't heard from him. But we been gone, and we don't got an answering machine."

"Oh. Well, I'm sorry to surprise you. I've been hoping to contact you."

"About what?"

"Well, Claire's things are kind of in disarray, and there's a lot of things that need to be straightened out, and"—lying now—"I need to be in the area to help with the investigation, so I was wondering if it might be possible to rent the house for a couple of months…"

"What'd you say you do?"

"I'm a professor of geology at the University of California in San Diego."

From the slight softening in her expression, I gathered that she considered this to be a respectable job. Not everyone does. She uncrossed her arms and nervously twirled a strand of her drab brown hair around her finger. Would the bright gold on her children's heads fade to that someday? "Thought for a minute you was one a them lawyers was coming through here bothering Claire."

"Lawyers? Why were lawyers looking for Claire?"

She gave the tiniest twitch of her shoulders, as if she were too worn out to shrug. "Guys in suits, couple months ago. Came by two or three times wanting to find her. Must of found her or give up, cause they stopped coming by." She eyed me suspiciously as something else occurred to her. "Say, if you work in San Diego, how you goin' to stay here for a couple of months?"

"I'm on a sabbatical—I'm taking time off to complete a textbook."

"Hmm." She considered. "I've got to start off by telling you Claire owed rent for this month—she usually paid on the fifteenth. Let her move in with no deposit, so we're shy a month's rent with nothing to back it up. Not that I blame her, poor thing. And what's more, she still had three months to run on her lease…"

"How much was her rent?"

"Four-thirty-five a month. Water included, which is no small thing around here."

"Well, Mrs. Givens, I seriously doubt I'll stay out here for three months, but I'd be happy to write you a check for the full period of the lease. I certainly plan on covering all of Claire's debts."

She studied me through narrow eyes. I could tell the offer seemed generous to her, and that to her mind this meant there was a hidden catch lurking somewhere. Finally she nodded. "That would be fine. Save us tryin' to rent it out again right away; might not be too easy to do seeing as there's been a murder in there."

"Let me get my checkbook." I hurried inside and reappeared with checks and a pen. "So that would be four-thirty-five for three months—"

"Four months. She owed for this month too."

"Four months, then. So that would be, umm…"

"Seventeen hundred and forty dollars."

I was astonished at how quickly she supplied the total. Either she was faster than I at multiplication without pen and paper, or she'd been working it out for a while. I scratched out the check, noted the amount in the ledger, and passed it to her.

She examined it carefully, folded it in half, and held it tight in her hand. "Well, I thank you, Mr. Clayborne. This has been a shock to us all, and I been worried about how we'd ever get money for this month and how we'd find another renter." She shuffled her feet a little, and said, "I am truly sorry for your loss. It's a terrible thing. Claire was a good woman, everybody around here liked her. Now, she had people coming and going all hours of the night, but they was always well-behaved—no loud music or big parties. Not like some." She lowered her voice. "I've got to tell you, I been nervous ever since, it's just me and the kids out front. We just got back from a week at my sister's, I couldn't stand another night here with the police swarming all over everything… I keep a shotgun in my bedroom, but I still wonder what might happen if some crazy got into our place of a night. I confess it's gonna be comforting to have a man staying out here for a while."

I was glad she had a shotgun, because I found it unlikely that any crazed killers would be daunted by my presence. I also realized she probably didn't know there had been a break-in yesterday. I saw no reason to mention it—it might alarm her, and make her reconsider the wisdom of renting to me.

"Well, Professor, I guess I should let you get back to your work." Behind her the children had become bored with watching us talk, and had invented a game which involved hopping up and down the back steps. "You need anything, you just give a holler." She turned and started back to the house.

"Mrs. Givens—"

She stopped and looked back.

"Were you the neighbor who found my sister?"

She revolved to face me. "I was." She chewed her lip, feeling she owed me something, either because of my kinship or my check, but then shook her head. "I just can't talk about it. Maybe later, when it's not so fresh in my mind. Already keep seein' it as it is. I been over and over it—"

We both turned at the sound pulling up the drive: a long white BMW sedan, streaked tan with dust, followed by a sheriff's patrol car. I backed over to the front door and locked it.

They came all the way down the drive. My Jeep and Claire's Honda were already there, so they double-parked behind us, the BMW on the inside.

A woman in a suit pulled herself from the driver's side of the Beemer and bumped the door shut with her hip. She glanced down, grimaced, and dusted the side of her skirt. She looked like she had stepped right out of an executive conference room, but when she came around the car with a confident stride I saw she had skipped pumps in favor of running shoes. Smart, given the sand.

A thirtyish man swung out from the passenger side. His dark hair was gelled up into modest spikes, and his sunglasses were perched high on his forehead. He slammed the door, and, with a practiced motion, jerked his chin down, hard, so the glasses snapped down onto the bridge of his nose. The effect was spoiled by the fact that they landed too low and off-center, so he had to reach up with a finger to push them into place.

Mrs. Givens sidled beside me. "He's one a them as was here before," she whispered.

If the pair were trying to look like lawyers, they had done a solid, central-casting job.

They stood by their car, both with their hands on their hips, staring at the patrol car. I could faintly hear the sound of a police radio. The woman eyed the man, and then, unobtrusively as possible, rotated her hands on her hips so that her thumbs pointed backwards instead of forwards, mirroring his position.

At last the door of the patrol car opened, and a young deputy sheriff made a wide circuit to come over to stand by the lawyers. The woman tossed her head—a strange maneuver for someone with her hair in a bun—and gestured toward us without turning our way. "Deputy—do you think you could clear out these onlookers? We don't need an audience."

He trundled over to us, and I glanced at his name tag: Forbes. "I'm afraid I'll have to ask you to leave the property," he began.

Mrs. Givens stepped forward and looked up into his face. "I'm thinking you must be mistaken. This is *my* property we're on."

The woman glanced over. "Oh? And where exactly is the property line between your house and the residence in back?"

Givens crossed her arms. "Ain't any. I own all of it. And two acres out back, and the lots to either side. So unless those papers the deputy is holding are to evict me from my land, I'm stayin' right here." For no apparent reason, her maternal radar kicked into gear, and she glanced over her shoulder at her back steps, where the children watched wide-eyed. "Hey! Both of you get inside…I mean now!" She turned back and faced our three visitors, the barest trace of a smile on her mouth.

A pickup rattled down the drive, *A-1 Locksmith* painted on the side. "Grand Central Station ain't in it," Givens muttered. The truck braked to a halt, and the lawyers moved farther in our direction as the dust cloud drifted toward where they had stood.

A sunburnt man in a Raiders cap—presumably K.R. Lansky—opened the driver's door and stood on the running board, looking across the cab at the five of us. "So. We decide what work needs to be done here yet?"

"We need a lock repaired," I said, and Givens shot me a curious glance.

"We need the front door of this cottage opened," the woman corrected.

"If you need the front door opened, whyn'tcha just ask Professor Clayborne here?" Givens asked. "He's got the keys."

"Clayborne?" the woman asked.

"Claire Clayborne's husband, I assume?" the man asked.

"No," I said, "her brother."

"Well, if you have keys, you can save us all a lot of trouble by just opening the door," the woman said.

"Is there a reason why I should?"

"The deputy is holding a warrant to search Claire Clayborne's residence for certain items pertaining to a civil suit regarding arson and conspiracy. You can let us in, or we can have the locksmith do so instead. Either way, you have no legal standing in this matter whatsoever."

"This isn't Claire's residence anymore."

"Since?"

"Since her death. Are any of you aware she was murdered a couple of weeks ago?"

The deputy looked stunned. The lawyers exchanged glances I couldn't read. "Ms. Chiarella?' the deputy asked. "Were you aware of this?"

She hesitated. "No. No, I wasn't, but it doesn't affect anything. The warrant is for her residence, not her person."

"But this is *my* residence at the moment," I said.

"*Your* residence?"

"I'm staying here. And I've paid for a four-month lease."

Mrs. Givens toyed with my folded check.

Chiarella said, "Let's just get this over with. We have a decent warrant, a specific warrant, and I—"

Deputy Forbes shook his head, looking down at the papers in his hand. "I'm outta my league here. I do subpoenas and evictions. I'm not a judge."

"Do you know Detective Bolles?" I asked. "Wilson, from forensics?"

Forbes considered me. "Sure."

"Last night—not even twenty-four hours ago—they were here, taking forensic evidence, dusting the place for prints... I'm not even sure they're done with the place yet. I certainly don't think you should let a bunch of lawyers poke around inside without clearing it with them first."

"That's completely irrelevant—" Chiarella began, but then we all turned our heads to look at a car that hit the bump at the edge of Claire's drive so hard that, for a moment, it was airborne. An old gray Datsun, from the days before *Nissan* was used in American marketing, sporting rust spots around the edges of the passenger door. It raced up the drive and came to a jerking halt behind the locksmith's truck.

This time the cloud of dust was too big to move aside from, and we all held our breath and fanned our eyes as it blew across us.

Jared was a thin man in his early thirties. His wiry hair parted on the side, but it swelled up in front to make an impromptu pompadour. He scanned all six of us—me, Forbes, the two lawyers, Mrs. Givens, and K.R. Lansky—and settled his gaze back on me. "Walker?"

I nodded, and he came over and stood close to me. "Have they been in yet?" he whispered. I shook my head. "Have you seen the warrant?" I shook my head yet again. He raised his voice, addressing Forbes. "Can we take a look at the warrant in question, please?"

Chiarella marched over toward us; her partner slouched against the car, unaware or uncaring that he was covering the back of his nice blue suit with a thick coat of High-Desert aeolian dust. "Who's he, and how is he a party to any of this?"

"I'm Jared Huizinga, and I'm the executive director and steward of the local office of the Desert Wildlife Fund."

"Ah. The turtle people."

"Tortoise."

"Whatever. Are you also a lawyer? More specifically, are you retained as an attorney for either Mr. Clayborne—"

"*Doctor* Clayborne," Jared said.

"—or for—for the owner of record of this property?"

"I am not an attorney, though I narrowly escaped such a fate, praise God, and I don't represent any of these people."

"Then I don't see any reason we should show you this warrant."

Jared shrugged and turned to me and Givens. "Nonetheless, I imagine both of you might like to take a look at it…?"

"I *would* like to see it, at this point," I said. I held out my hand, and, after a slight pause, Forbes presented me with a thick sheaf of papers.

"Mind if I read over your shoulder?" Jared asked.

From over by his pickup, Lansky said, "My charge is sixty-five dollars for the call, and eighty dollars an hour for the labor. That includes all the time standing around since I first got here."

"Go around back and do whatever you need to do to fix the back door," I said.

"Now just a minute," Chiarella said, "we may need you right out here…"

Lansky hefted a toolbox out of the rear of his truck. "I'm gonna start on the back door. You decide you need the front door jimmied, you gimme a shout."

Jared was reading the front page of the papers I held, and he snorted. "Officer…"

"Deputy Forbes."

"Deputy Forbes. This is a mighty specific warrant here, and it's for the residence of someone who no longer has a legal residence…" He whispered in my ear. "Did Claire have a will?"

"No." That much I was sure of.

"Furthermore, the person in question died intestate, so there are huge potential questions about who 'owns' any of her property. Not to mention that what used to be her property is intermixed with the property of the current resident—"

"That's ridiculous!" Chiarella said, leaning in at Jared. "The warrant is very specific—"

"The warrant is vague as hell—'documents and/or records in any form whatsoever, including but not limited to paper, electronic, and magnetic storage media'—that could be anything including cuneiform tablets or people's memories—"

Forbes was nodding steadily. "You're right. I'm not saying this warrant isn't valid, but it certainly was issued under different circumstances than what was presented to the judge…"

"Are you refusing to execute this warrant?" Chiarella demanded.

Forbes lifted the papers from my hands. "Not at all. If the office tells me to, or, better yet, if a judge tells me to, then I'll be happy to do my duty. But I'm not going to make a legal judgment about all of this. I'm not a lawyer." He headed back toward the patrol car.

"Well I *am* a lawyer," Chiarella shouted at his back, "and I'm telling you that there are consequences for failing to execute a properly constituted warrant in a timely manner…"

Forbes ignored her with aplomb, settled into his patrol car, and backed down the drive, veering two tires off into the sparse brush to avoid the locksmith's truck and Jared's Datsun.

"How'd you like to face charges for practicing law without a license?" Chiarella asked Jared.

"I'm not accepting fees and not holding myself out as an authority on legal matters."

"Well I *am* an attorney, and I think you're over the line here."

"You're welcome to try to prove it. But we have attorneys too, and ours are doing it because they're right, not because someone has taken a lease on their asses."

Chiarella started to say something, but her partner, still leaning on the BMW, called out, "Hey. Dr. Clayborne. Can I have a word with you? In private?"

Jared leaned in close to my ear. "I wouldn't talk to any of these UWI people without witnesses."

I was more inclined to trust Jared than the UWI reps, but I wasn't ready to trust anyone just yet. "I think it'll be okay." I walked over toward the man in the blue suit, and he stood up.

He spoke softly. "Dr. Clayborne. What kind of doctor, if I might ask?"

"PhD. Professor at UC San Diego."

"Professor, then. I don't know how much you know about this situation, but if I were you, I wouldn't get too close with that guy over there, or any of his friends. They're a bunch of doper anarchists, and the law is going to bring them all down some day soon."

"Your opinion is noted."

"Furthermore, we're a big company. We have influence in DC; and we have lots of juice in Sacramento, where your boss lives. So don't end up on the wrong side of this."

"Are you threatening me?"

"Not in the least. I'm just trying to keep you from wandering into the middle of a shitstorm without a hat and slicker. That guy and all his friends: Losers."

Including my sister, I supposed.

He pitched his voice at Chiarella. "Hey, counselor—we ready to roll?"

Chiarella and Jared were standing in sullen silence, watching us. She gave an exaggerated sigh. "Sure. Let's go through the whole thing again, and then come back." She started toward the car. "You remove anything," she said to me, "we'll have you up for obstruction of justice."

"You won't get a second warrant," Jared said. "Pulling this shit over the holidays was cute, but our people are all caught up now. You should already expect malicious prosecution, harassment, and frivolous filing suits from the Hapgood crap you pulled."

"Acting as an attorney again?" she asked, and opened her car door.

"Hey, pal," Jared said to the other attorney, "you have dirt on you."

The man looked down and swatted at the dust marks on the back of his slacks.

"No," Jared said, "I didn't mean on your suit."

The man stared, and then opened the car door and slid in. "Fuck you," he said, and slammed the door.

"Witty," Jared said to me.

Chiarella gunned the engine, cut the wheel sharp, and swung it back around again, following the path of the patrol car down the edge of the driveway with impressive skill.

"Well," Mrs. Givens said. "Guess it's time to go start dinner."

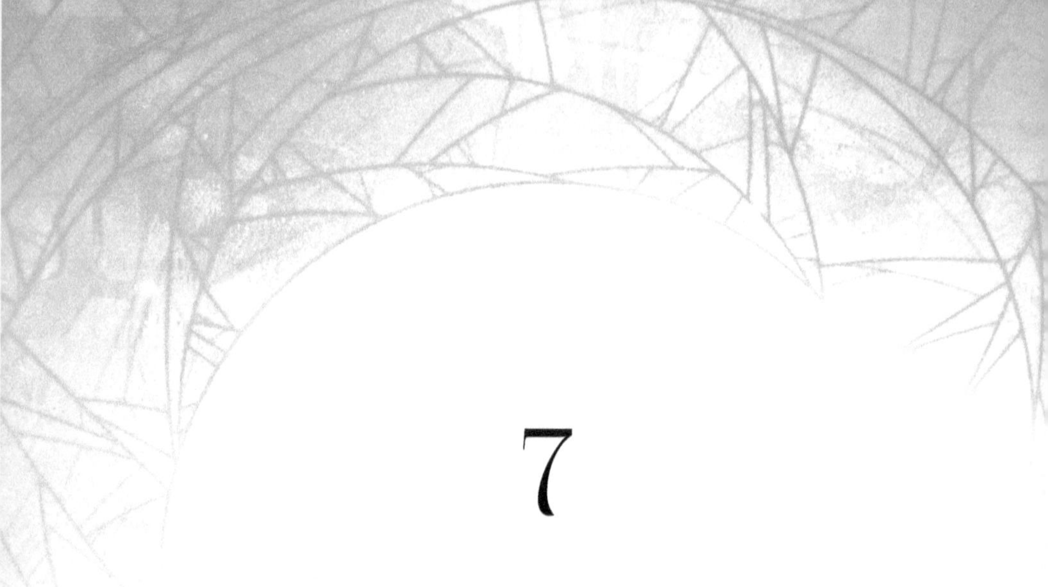

7

Jared wanted to head back to his office. "We have all kinds of papers to file if you don't want those idiots coming back here in the next couple of days. We were already in the middle of filing a pile of the same on behalf of Augustus; this should mostly be a matter of changing the names in the blanks."

"Tell me about UWI."

"Big rich company that doesn't give a shit about anything but money. Bunch of back-East thugs in suits. Hated Claire and Gus because they pretty much had the goods on their project—all kinds of environmental problems with the aquifer."

"Such as?"

"Not my area. I just watch things like the way they hire people to sneak out and dig up tortoise burrows, move the tortoises somewhere else. At least we hope they move 'em. Maybe they just kill them and put them in one of their many dumps. Anyway, Claire's thing was about the stability of the site and contamination of the aquifer. Geological stuff. You'd have to talk to Gus."

Geological stuff? Claire? "And how do I find him?"

"I'm hoping that they're letting him out of jail today. If not, soon. They still have most of his papers and reports tied up, though—carted off every filing cabinet in the place…" Jared darted a glance at his watch. "I really have to go." He started to turn away.

"Wait. Do you think UWI has anything to do with what happened to Claire?"

He stopped, took a deep breath, and thought about it. "Part of me wants to say yes. I'm sure they aren't going to be too broken up about it, but I don't think they'd take the risk. She's small fish by their standards—somebody to drag down in a legal morass."

"A dispassionate assessment, indeed."

Something changed in Jared's eyes. "Hey, man—I loved Claire. But you asked."

I felt myself flush with shame, though I wasn't sure why. "Who do you think is responsible, then?"

"I don't know. A couple of her old boyfriends were sort of creepy, in my opinion. A lot of her drug-rehab clients were real lowlifes… I've gotta go." He turned and ran to his car.

"I'd like to get together with you some time," I shouted after him, "talk this over a bit more…"

He paused with the car door open. "Mandy said you were coming with her to our little observance tonight. Why don't we talk then?"

I went inside the cottage and used the phone to hunt for Sam Drexler, a fellow professor at UCSD; he specialized in corporate economics, and I thought he could fill me in on UWI. He was probably off somewhere over the break, but I left a trail of phone messages urging him to call me on my cell or at Claire's home number.

I spent the next few hours poring through Claire's papers, until Mandy finally arrived at eight, driving a dark Saturn equipped with extra-wide sand tires. We spoke little as she drove us into Yucca Valley, navigating the erratic holiday traffic; everyone in the area seemed to be on their way somewhere else. The car's CD player whispered out strange music, to my ears a kind of tribal drumming mixed with a string quartet.

We passed through most of the long strip of town, and then she turned north off of 62 and began to climb the low hills that ringed the west end of town. Houses were close together here, by desert standards, but the neighborhood had developed over many years, and '70s ranch-style houses were mixed with bungalows dating back to the '20s. The house where she stopped must have been one of the earliest in the area, but it looked as if it had been updated by a series of owners until it could not be said to be in any particular idiom. It must have started as a Craftsman-style bungalow, but the front porch had been completely enclosed to form a room. The home perched just above a major outcrop of dark gneiss, and a small deck ran from the side of the house out onto the rock.

Light bloomed as Mandy opened the door and said, "Hello!—you guys here?" Without pausing she stepped inside and gestured for me to follow.

"Mandy!" A tall man with brownish hair and a goatee stooped down and hugged her. He was in his late twenties, dressed in a lavender T-shirt and loose cotton pants. When he released his embrace, a blond woman slid neatly between the two of them and took his place.

"Chad, Melanie, this is Walker that I told you about—Claire's brother." I held out my hand, but to my surprise Chad wrapped his arms around my shoulders and hugged me. I was uncomfortable with this, my face pressed against his chest, but he showed no signs of letting loose; instead, he rocked slightly, and I found myself returning his embrace.

He released me and held me by my shoulders at armslength. "Man, I am so sorry."

Melanie hugged me too, her long, sweet-smelling hair brushing across my lips. Her touch was remarkably intimate; her body was pliant against mine, without any of the usual tension when strangers touch—at least not on her part.

They took our coats and brought out mugs of hot spiced wine. The vapors from the wine penetrated my sinuses on the first sip, a heady, relaxing sensation. I took a seat in an overstuffed chair; Mandy sat crosslegged on the floor. Chad and Melanie faced us on the couch against the back wall. What had once been a commodious porch had been turned into a living room; the original front door of the house was still visible in plastered-over outline behind the couch. The décor was a combination of thrift store and Pier 1 Imports, with a lot of Indian cotton prints draped on the furniture. Abstract batiks mounted on wooden frameworks served as wall art. It smelled nice, a faint hint of incense overlaying a clean, scrubbed odor.

We made small talk. Chad was a freelance magazine writer who described his specialization as "new-agey travel pieces." When I asked, Melanie described herself as an occultist.

"Is there much money in that?" I asked.

She laughed, and the whole room seemed warmer. "None at all. But it's where most of my time and energy go. When I'm not working the world of esoterica, I'm a librarian at the county branch library. A little esoteric itself." I studied her as she talked. Objectively there was nothing remarkable about her looks, but I was becoming aroused just by watching her. She wore her body like a garment she had thrown on for fun. When Chad reached over and touched her with the familiarity of long acquaintance, I felt a little nudge of resentment.

When I admitted to being a geologist, Chad wanted to know why the white boulders of Joshua Tree stopped so abruptly, being replaced by the darker, sharper rock outcrops at this end of the valley. "The rock that our deck is built onto—it's almost black."

"That's just on the surface—it's a weathering product called desert varnish. The real rock underneath is light gray. But these rocks are the main surface exposures all along these mountains; the isenbergs in Joshua Tree are only seen because all of the cover has eroded away…"

Melanie tilted her head, bemused by the jargon. "*Icebergs?*"

I smiled. "*Isenbergs*. German for 'rock islands.' They're made of monzogranite that welled up under the surface. When the rocks on this hill erode away, it will quite likely look like Hidden Valley underneath."

"I assume that won't happen right away," Mandy said.

"Unless it gets a lot rainier in these parts, we're probably safe for another twenty million years or so."

My pedantry was cut short when a car pulled up outside. Melanie uncoiled off the couch to open the door. I stood as Kirsten and Jared came in, followed by Dawn, a blond woman of about my age, dressed in hospital scrubs.

Chad, Melanie, and Mandy scuttled off to the kitchen, declining all offers of help. More hot spiced wine was distributed. After the inevitable, uncomfortable sympathy about Claire's death, we chatted; when I found Kirsten hadn't told them about her encounter with the escaped javelina, I told the tale.

I then attempted to ferret out more information about UWI. Kirsten and Jared were full of strong opinions about the company and its project, but short on facts; exactly what I would have expected from Claire's friends.

The conversation turned to a portfolio of Jared's photographs which he'd brought along. Many were the usual silver-gelatin prints of stark rocks rising from the sand, but his forte seemed to be the desert plants that forced their way through cracks and crevices in the geology. As far as my untrained eye could judge, he was good, and I said so. He confessed photography was what he would do fulltime, if only he could make any money at it. Our conversation about the difficulty of making a living in the arts was interrupted by a summons to dinner.

The dining room was paneled in weathered wood, possibly salvaged from a barn, which had been sanded and varnished with great care; the irregularities and unevenness had been preserved. Once we were in our seats, the room just contained the table and the guests, with barely enough room to edge behind someone else's seat. Chad sat at one end of the table, Melanie at the other. I was on Chad's right, across from Mandy, and next to Dawn. Jared and Kirsten managed to squeeze in on Mandy's side; the table wasn't really large enough for seven, and I felt a little out of place.

"Shall we sit for a moment?" Chad asked. I had no idea what he meant, but the others all closed their eyes. For a moment I thought they were going to pray, but if they did it was done silently. Kirsten put the palms of her hands together in the standard prayerful attitude, but raised them and touched her thumbs to her forehead. For me it was a long and uncomfortable pause before eyes opened and dinner began.

The food was surprisingly good despite being strictly vegetarian, and much of the light conversation centered on the individual dishes. I ate much and said little. It was pleasant to sail along on the waves of other people's chatter, propelled by yet another glass of wine. I was surprised to hear Melanie say "Well, do the police know anything yet?"

Chad asked, "Do we really want to talk about this now?" From the incline of his head I could tell he was signaling Melanie to be aware of my feelings.

"It's fine," I said. "I'd like to know what's going on myself."

Chad shrugged. "It seems to me it's got to be somebody from the prison. I mean, isn't that the most likely? Talking with convicts every day, she probably attracted the attention of some freak. Not to mention the way Kirsten and Claire were on their 'clean up our town' campaign for a while; Claire was pestering every speed connection she had from the prison."

Melanie shook her head in disagreement. "It sounds good, but it doesn't really make sense. Eagle Mountain is a minimum-security prison. It's for dopers and people who forge checks, not killers."

"Killers forge checks and do dope too."

Dawn leaned in to join the argument. "I think it's more likely some religious nut. Claire hung around some of the offbeat church groups here. Some of them are pretty damaged. And most of them hate anybody who doesn't share their exact set of beliefs."

"They're loud and obnoxious," Chad replied, "but they aren't really violent."

"Oh? Just last year one of the supposedly saved almost beat somebody to death in a parking lot. I was on duty when they brought the poor guy in."

"One case. It's rare."

"I'm not so sure. People calling themselves Christians have a pretty scary track record. Look at the Inquisition, look at all of the wars between different Christian sects, look at abortion-clinic bombings. Look at Kosovo: most of the Serbs claim to be Christians."

"What about Universal Waste?" I asked. "Could they have anything to do with it?"

"I wouldn't put it past them," Chad said. "They act like they're connected with the Mafia or something."

Melanie shook her head. "Don't Mafia types threaten you first? If she was getting threats, she would have told us. And anyway, I thought they usually did something to the brakes of your car or something."

Chad was about to respond, but Jared jumped in. "Personally, I think it was an ex-boyfriend. Claire had pretty lousy taste in guys. All of the last three have been psycho."

Melanie said, "Oh, you just think that her taste in men was atrocious because she never got interested in you."

"Oh, give me a break. Remember the kickboxing instructor? He'd be my first suspect."

"He was cute."

"And demented."

"Nobody's perfect, Jared."

"I think you're all thinking about this too hard," Kirsten offered. "It doesn't have to make a lot of sense. It was probably just some junkie or stalker—"

"But Mandy says he took something from her house!" Dawn said. "Does that sound like some random killer?" She shivered. "Sounds more like a creep to me."

"Well do you think some junkie or speed freak is going to break in and *not* take something?" Kirsten tugged her short curls back until the skin of her forehead was taut. "Makes my skin crawl just talking about it. God, Mandy, I'm glad I didn't have to see it…"

At long last, my chance. "Did you *see* something?" I asked Mandy.

She looked down at her plate for a long time, and everyone else fell silent. At last she said, "Let's go for a walk, Professor."

"Dessert first?" Chad suggested. "Coffee?"

Mandy stood up. "Maybe when we get back."

The night had turned cold but the air was still. We walked along the road that hugged the hillside, hunched forward with hands thrust into our pockets, not ready to speak. It was the dark of the moon, and the lights of the city below us were reflected and multiplied infinitely in the swirl of the galaxy above.

Mandy turned on Mohawk Trail and our steps crunched onto dirt road. Far away the occasional pop or scream of fireworks reminded me it was the eve of the new year. "Let's go to the park," she said.

I had a passing acquaintance with Desert Christ Park, Antone Martin's surreal contribution to the High Desert. A religious sculptor of the 1950s, Martin had covered a large sandy cove on the hillside with biblical scenes. Originally more isolated, the park now abutted an expanded church. The figures stood taller than human, made of a brilliantly white, hard casting plaster. On moonlit nights, or when the floodlights illumined them, dozens of figures could be seen from the highway.

We had to watch the ground as we walked to be sure of our footing. Tonight the park wasn't lit, but the figures loomed out of the darkness like ghostly pillars, showing the general shape and contour of the main path. Without looking up or breaking stride, Mandy said, "So you're set on playing detective."

My first instinct was to deny it. "No. I'm just trying to get inside Claire's life a little bit. It feels like I owe her that, somehow."

"Sounds like detective work to me. It's okay, I'm not making fun of you. You want to get to the bottom of this, I'm with you all the way."

"I'm sure the sheriffs are more capable than I in that regard."

"Capable, maybe. Willing, I'm not so sure. Rick Bolles is a weird guy."

"What do you mean?"

"I'm not sure what I mean." She sighed. "It's just that Rick probably should have been Wyatt Earp, back in the Old West. He has his own theories about what laws need to be enforced when. Sometimes he comes down hard over something minor. Other times something major slides."

"Are you saying that Bolles isn't trying very hard in Claire's case?"

"No. No, I'm not saying that." We walked on a few steps. "I'm just saying that I don't always trust him."

We reached the easternmost edge of the park, and the path arced back around, leading us up the hill and then back to the west. I took a deep breath and dove in. "Tonight Kirsten said something about how you 'saw' something connected with Claire's murder." She didn't respond. She seemed engrossed in the scrunch of our steps on the loose-packed trail. I persisted. "When I talked to Bolles, he said you claimed you'd seen something in a dream, that you had actual details of the murder… I'm prepared to believe you know something important, but I'm not going to believe you saw it in a dream. I don't believe in that sort of thing."

We walked for several moments before she answered. "You're right, it wasn't a dream. That's just what I told Rick."

I nodded to myself. Now we were getting somewhere. "Then why did you tell Bolles it was a dream? To protect someone?"

"No. It was just pointless to tell him the truth."

"Which is…?"

"That it was a vision. Plus I was stoned."

"What!" I stopped. "Oh, that's wonderful! You took some kind of hallucination to the police?"

"It wasn't a 'hallucination,' it was a vision, and I saw it in detail." Her voice quavered. "It was horrible, okay? So don't fucking treat it like something you can fucking laugh at!" She marched off down the path, her head pulled down toward her chest.

I stood there in confusion for several moments. Dark hair and long dark coat: I could hardly make her out up ahead. "Mandy. Wait. Wait a minute, I didn't mean…" I jogged off after her.

At the upper edge of the park the sculptor had built a stone façade representing the front of a church. The centerpiece of the stonework was a large bas-relief of Leonardo's *Last Supper*. Mandy leaned her back against this and looked out across the town. When I came closer I saw the city lights reflected in her wet eyes.

I leaned on the wall next to her. The heavy stone still radiated the heat it had stored during the day. A few blocks down the hill a roll of firecrackers went off like a machine gun. The distant, crackly sound of the loudspeaker on a sheriff's cruiser: *"All fireworks—are illegal—in San—Bernardino—County."*

"Mandy, I was only trying to say—"

She sniffled. "Just shut up for a second, okay?" I did as I was told. After a long pause, she said, "Alright, now say what you were going to say."

"I wasn't trying to offend you. That really…wasn't my intention. But I'm having a problem here. Bolles tells me you know some key facts about the murder; you tell me that they came to you in a—a vision or something. I'm a scientist, Mandy. I just don't believe in such things. So I either have to conclude that you somehow guessed at some of the facts, or that you're—that you're not being completely honest about how you got the information."

"You're not being completely honest either," she said. "I've had plenty of science training. There aren't very many laws about what can and can't happen. Talk about unscientific—unscientific is when something happens and you refuse to look at it because it doesn't fit with what you already believe. If I grew wings and flew into the air, I'm sure you'd question your sanity rather than your theories about what's possible."

"Probably true."

"Well, it's stupid."

To my lasting surprise, she kicked me in the shin. Hard. I gasped.

"What was that for?"

"What was what for?"

"You kicked me!"

"How do you know? Prove it."

I could see where this line of argument was going, and considered it sophomoric. Still rubbing my shin, I said, "That's a really specious line of reasoning. I know kicking is possible; I felt you do it; and tomorrow I'll have a bruise as evidence."

"And *I* know certain other kinds of things are possible, from experience, from many, many experiences, and *I* feel them happening, and when they happen *I* have evidence too, in the form of things I couldn't know about otherwise."

"I'd have to see a lot more data. I'm by nature a skeptic."

"Well goody for you. Do you think I give a shit about your belief systems? Is it my job to convince you of something? If you care, then get off your butt and find the facts." She paused, giving me an opportunity to talk. I didn't. "James Thurber—of all people—once said, 'Skepticism is a useful tool of the inquisitive mind, but it is scarcely a method of investigation.' You're not *gathering* evidence, you're ignoring it."

I waited for a moment to regroup my thoughts and try to get the conversation back on a rational footing. "You're saying you saw something without being physically present? Give me a mechanism. Tell me how such a thing is possible."

She took a deep breath. "You know, I don't really care how or why these things work. It's something that's happened to me my whole life—I sense things or see things or get weird impressions from people. If you want to know *why*, you should talk to Ettenmoor, not me—I'm just trying to live with it."

"Ettenmoor? You mean Ronald Ettenmoor? The physicist?"

"Sure. You know him?"

"No. But I've certainly heard of him. You mean he believes in all this stuff?"

"Do you have any idea how snotty you sound? 'You mean *he* believes in all this stuff?' Could you be just a little more insulting about this? 'You really believe that? And, ohmigosh, you mean somebody *intelligent* actually believes it too?'" She wiped her eyes with the sleeve of her coat. "I don't know what Ron Ettenmoor believes, but he's at least exploring things, trying to find out what they mean. He's a real scientist; you treat science like some kind of fucked-up religion."

"How do you know so much about Ettenmoor?"

"I do consulting work for him. He lives out here during the cool part of the year."

This was getting too complex for me. "And does he know about your—your vision, with Claire? Is he part of your, uh, crowd?"

"I'm not sure what you mean by 'part of my crowd.' We know a lot of the same people. Does he know about me seeing Claire's murder? Yes. I talked to him right afterwards."

"And what did he say?"

"What did he say? He tried to be comforting. He was sorry for what I'd been through. He was sad about Claire. What you'd expect from somebody who cared." She shivered. "I'm getting cold. We should start walking."

We headed toward the west end of the park. Backyard fireworks still rattled and shrieked across the valley; their frequency seemed to be on the rise as it grew later.

After a long pause, Mandy began talking again, quieter now, and I found myself leaning over toward her as we walked. "Even when they're lighting firecrackers out here, it's still all lost in the immensity of the place…that's why I moved out here. I used to work in Silicon Valley. There were so many people around, so many vibes flying at me all the time, it was like living in a radio tuned to static…it was like everybody's internal lives were banging on my door. There were holes punched in me and everybody just leaked in."

We reached the far end of the park, where there seemed to be a cave with a slab leaned to one side of it. The stone rolled away, perhaps? We turned and started a long curve back to the entrance. Mandy seemed lost in some sort of reverie, and it surprised me when she resumed: "I'd be in a grocery store and I'd get pieces of some woman's worries about her teenage son, or I'd be at work and I'd see that a guy I worked with would be diagnosed with cancer that afternoon. I'd sit in meetings, and suddenly I'd see all of the things the people in the room felt about each other, all of the anger and fear and desire, all the weird sex stuff." She groped through her pockets for a tissue and then blew her nose. "By the time I left the Bay Area, it was getting to where I'd make eye contact with someone in another car on the freeway and there'd be this rush of stuff, things that had happened to them, things they were thinking about, things that were going to happen. Just this wave of disorganized crap. Sometimes it got bad enough I could hardly drive."

It sounded like serious mental illness to me, but I wanted to try and get back on friendly terms, so I asked, "And that's what made you move to the desert?"

"Yeah. Over the ages, lots of mystics have gone to the desert to open themselves up. For me it was more like trying to shut things down and patch up all the holes."

By this time, we were headed back down Mohawk Trail. The number of pops and screeches in the valley accelerated, and were joined by spoons banging on pots, car horns, and what sounded suspiciously like gunshots. We stood still and took it in; some of the sounds seemed to come from many miles away. It crested after a few minutes and then tapered back to random bangs and whistles.

We resumed walking. "Happy New Year, I guess," Mandy said.

"Happy New Year."

We turned west, back onto asphalt. I didn't know what to think. What Mandy was telling me seemed insane; her description of her state of mind back in the Bay Area seemed like enough to get her committed. But she seemed sane enough walking there beside me. "I— Look, I'm sorry about how I approached things back there. I didn't want to fight with you. Would you be willing to explain things to me, if I promise to keep my mouth shut and not ask questions?"

"I might try. And you can ask questions if you want—you just can't ask nasty, mean questions. I'd really appreciate it if you didn't call me a liar, directly or indirectly."

"Agreed."

"I'm not sure where to begin. The High Desert is filled with offbeat people—occultists, religious groups, UFO abductees, hermits—and I guess it has been ever since the first prospectors set up shop. The Indians thought it was a power place too." She gave me a look. "And don't start telling me how it's just a matter of geological forces, either… Anyway, there's a group of us who have sort of a loose organization for self-exploration. We call it the Eleusinian Circle."

"I saw some memos or something about that back at Claire's place. Was Claire a member?"

"Sometimes. It wasn't a very formal organization."

"What does the name mean? It's sort of familiar."

"Have you heard about the Eleusinian Mysteries?" she asked. I made a noncommittal noise—it sounded like something I might have heard about in college. "Are you acquainted with Eleusis?"

"Umm—a place south of Athens, in ancient Greece?"

"Right. We named our group after a ritual that was celebrated there for centuries…it had a lot in common with what we are doing. Most important, it had a potion, called the *kykeon*, that opened you up to all kinds of things. We have our own *kykeon*—not the same one the Greeks used, mind you; ours is from the Amazon. Our goals and tools are similar, but not identical."

"You take some kind of potion to 'open you up.'" I hesitated. I was on thin ice here. "I thought one of the things you came out here for was to keep from being opened up."

"I see what you mean. It's hard to explain. Spending time in those spaces under safe conditions sort of strengthens my psychic muscles, lets me cope better the rest of the time. Usually."

Headlights appeared behind us, and we cast long ectomorphic shadows that looked like Dali's Don Quixote. The car moved slowly. Loud music played, muffled by the closed windows, so only the thudding bass notes carried through the air. "Off the road," Mandy whispered urgently.

"What?"

"Off the road!" She shoved me hard and I crashed upslope into a creosote bush. I heard the scream of tires as the car hurtled by. She flew through the air and landed on top of me. Bits of gravel fountained up from the street and rained down. The car didn't slow or pause, but continued to accelerate. I heard the squeal of a skid as it turned a corner, and I listened as it became more remote and gradually mixed in with the traffic sounds from Highway 62.

"Are you okay?" I asked.

Mandy rolled off of me and sat on the sand, knees bent and legs wide apart. She leaned her torso and head down between her knees.

I pushed myself up onto my elbows. The bush cradled me like the nest of a giant bird, and its strong, almost chemical scent rose up around me. In the distance a string of firecrackers went off.

"Are you okay?" I asked again.

Her voice was muffled. "I'm not injured."

I lifted myself out of the bush and sat next to her. "What was that?" I asked at last. "Were they trying to hit us?"

"I don't know." She lifted her face. "Maybe they were just drunk kids, screwing around."

"But they *would* have hit us if we hadn't moved."

"Yes."

We worked our way back to Chad and Melanie's place. We wasted no energy on talk; our ears were busy probing the night for danger. At one point we heard the sound of a car coming up the hill, and we both stood still, waiting. It turned and disappeared off to the east.

Inside the warmth and light of the house, Mandy detailed what had happened on the road. There was a general susurration of dismay as all five of the others encircled us and picked fragments of creosote bush from our clothes. Did we see the car? Get a license number? Who would do such a thing?

We sat and let the exclamations and conjectures run their course, like a flock of birds settling down after a panic. At last there was a long pause, broken when Kirsten said, "I think maybe Dawn's right after all. Maybe somebody *is* after us."

"Let's not get carried away," Chad objected. "How would anybody know Mandy would be out there for a walk?"

"Maybe they were looking for *any* of us. Maybe they were watching the house…"

Dawn leaned over and put her arm around Kirsten's shoulders. "Hey, hey, you're taking my theory way too far. I said I thought some nut might have come after Claire. That's a long ways from some big conspiracy to kill all of her friends, too. Take it easy."

Kirsten nodded. "Okay. No conspiracy. But can I sleep at your house tonight anyway?"

Dawn smiled. "Are you really worried, or is this just a tricky come-on?"

"You can take it however you want, so long as I don't have to go back to my apartment tonight."

It was after two in the morning by the time Chad and Melanie saw us off. Mandy waited while Jared's car pulled out. Her hand held the keys in the ignition, but instead of turning them, she leaned her forehead on the steering wheel.

She straightened up, started the engine, shifted into reverse. As she looked over her shoulder to back up, she said, in a matter-of-fact voice, "I'm scared."

She turned off the CD player and we drove in silence as far as Sunfair Road. As we turned north onto the flats, she said, "When we take the potion, we go someplace isolated to do it—someplace you have to hike in to. Get as far from civilization as possible. Cuts down on the mental static, and it also keeps anybody from messing with us."

She slowed down and turned onto the first of the dirt roads. Outside the bright beams of the headlights, the whole world was black. "The last time we did it, we were way up in the wilderness west of Death Valley. Jared was there, and Dawn, and a couple of other people. I was feeling weird. I almost decided to sit the whole thing out. But I drank it down anyway—stupid of me, really. After about an hour I was feeling uneasy, but it makes most people nauseated, so I tried to ignore it. What could I do anyway? Once you swallow the stuff, you've jumped off the bridge—it's too late to plan anything." She turned the wheel and we rose over a hump; I realized we were in Claire's driveway.

She pulled all the way back to the cottage, stopped, and killed the lights. The only illumination was the faint glow from the dashboard. The motor purred in the empty night. "I know you've probably seen cheesy movies of people on LSD and all kinds of hallucinations. Hollywood loves that shit. But it's nothing like that; you don't see things that aren't there and think they're real. It's— Well, it can't really be explained, but you don't see giant flowers blooming and giraffes dancing and rooms full of dwarfs."

"But that night I was getting more and more agitated. Everybody was really tuned in to me, and they were all getting freaked out, and then all of a sudden I got this flash that something was wrong with Claire—and then something really fucked-up started happening." She swallowed. "Really fucked-up. I was here, in the cottage, and I was looking at Claire but it wasn't me looking at her, it was like I was a camera looking out through somebody else's eyes, and she was yelling at me, really mad, and then I—he—whoever—hit her in the face, hard, with this big gloved fist, and knocked her onto the floor against the couch."

"He—he took out a chain, and wrapped it around her neck, and she was looking up and fighting to get up off the floor and then she was clawing up at him and then she was just fighting to get her fingers under the chain"—Mandy sniffed, and I knew she was crying, but not angry tears this time—"and then her whole body arched and thrashed and then…she just died." Her voice faltered, and then regathered its strength. "She just died. I could see it. It was like the light just went out of her.

"He let her body fall back against the couch. Like a piece of garbage. Didn't even take the chain off her neck. He went back to her filing cabinets and dug through and took something, a fat manila envelope. Then he went back and stood over her for a little while. He took something, a small pouch or something, and threw it down by her. And then I tuned out of the whole thing.

"While it was going on I was screaming and crying and I couldn't see anything except what was going on back here. My body was up on its feet and stumbling around, and everybody was trying to make me sit down and keep me from falling into the campfire.

"I was hysterical. I knew what I saw was real, and I tried to tell the others what was happening. They mainly tried to calm me down, telling me maybe it was precognition and wasn't really happening then, maybe it was some kind of fantasy or warning or something. But I knew. I knew. And even though there was nothing I could do, I wanted to hike out, right then, in the middle of the night; I couldn't just sit there and hold all of that. But they wouldn't let me go." She wiped her palms down across her face. "Good thing. We were way out in the rocks. Trying to hike all the way out would have probably gotten us killed, even with the moonlight, even if we were straight.

"It was the worst night I ever spent, and in the morning we hiked out as best we could. When we got to the car, we tried our cell phones, but that whole part of the desert is a big blank in transmitter coverage. Jared drove fast, but it was almost ten in the morning by the time we got a signal. I called Claire, and it just rang. Answering machine turned off. I called Chad and Melanie and had them try to contact her. Eventually they called back. They drove by the cottage and saw the police were already here."

She sat and breathed slowly before she spoke again. "So. That's what happened. And I eventually worked up the nerve to go tell Bolles, but I told him it was a dream. I could tell from the way he reacted that everything I told him was right on target. But he didn't buy the dream idea. He didn't believe it—*doesn't* believe it—and I'm not sure what he thinks." She looked over at me. It was too dark to see anything but the faintest outline of her features. "Well. There it is." She waited for a heartbeat, and asked, "What do *you* think?"

I opened my mouth to speak and then closed it again. "I don't know what to think. I'm—basically I'm confused."

"Me too." She turned away, leaned her head back against the seat. "It's awful just talking about it… I'm completely wasted. I need to go home."

"Are you sure you're okay by yourself?"

"Yeah. I've had a lot of nights like this lately. And you should remember I'm the girl with the pepper spray. Are *you* okay by *your*self?"

"Of course," I answered. Because that's the guy thing to say.

"I'll call you tomorrow. But not until late."

I said goodnight and slipped out of the car. I paused at the front door of the cottage and watched her pop on her headlights and back down the drive. Waiting and watching: another guy kind of thing.

When the sound of her car had disappeared, it was just me and the night and an empty house. And I wasn't okay by myself. Even when I opened the door and turned on the lights, it felt like blackness was trying to push its way inside. Everything looked too round, too big, too present. The scene Mandy had described kept playing in my head.

I knew it was irrational. I knew it was just my subconscious mind telling me stories. But I could feel the presence of the death that had happened here.

It was almost dawn when I fell asleep. I left all the lights on.

8

Viewed from a high place, most of the town of Joshua Tree clings to Highway 62 like mineral encrustations ringing a hydrothermal vent. On the flats to the north, where it was easy to build, the disorganized residential districts might have spalled off from the road, scattered like talus below a cliff face. To the south, the crazed boulders of the park rise steeply, forming a bulwark against the spread of the city.

Except for a few hermits who planted their cabins out on solid rock and slogged in their water every week on muleback, development along the park boundary was slow. Installing utilities across acres of solid stone wasn't worth it to most of the potential homeowners. But beginning in the late 1970s, the severe beauty of the area began to attract real money, and the rock formations that weren't enclosed by the park became prime building sites.

Ronald Ettenmoor's house was wedged into a canyon formed by towering beige boulders. The house itself was built of large, apparently irregular plates of tan material that overlapped like the carapace of a beetle. The front windows were set well back, almost hidden beneath the overhang of an irregular roof. There were no power lines, no water pipes exposed on the rock surfaces. The driveway that snaked its way between the giant stone outcrops was cement with finely crushed rock stamped into its surface, so the drive itself appeared to be some freakish geological feature: an unwarranted lava flow of improbable smoothness.

The whole dwelling blended into the landscape almost perfectly. It must have been expensive to create something so unobtrusive.

I parked at the foot of the long driveway, fifteen minutes early for my appointment. Even though his work was far outside my area, I had heard a lot about Ettenmoor, one of a handful of physicists actively pursuing quantum computing. When I had called Edgar on the morning of New Year's Day, my brother had made it clear Ettenmoor's time was at a premium: "You know, Lion, Ron's quite the thing these days. Imagine he spends as much time talking to chipmakers as to colleagues. The universities all want him now, just so they can list him in the catalog. I think he's gotten quite used to having his own way." A sigh across the phone. "I could do with some of that myself."

A prima donna—no, even worse, an academic prima donna. "So I should be careful with him?"

"Not at all, not at all. He's easy to get on with, a great talker, brilliant mind, just brilliant. Not the least bit prickly—just busy." The longer Edgar stayed at Cambridge, the more his speech took on a plummy British cast. "I'll ring him up and arrange an intro, should you like…"

I told him it might be a good idea. Our conversation wasn't strained, but it was made uncomfortable by all the things we weren't saying. Only four days prior we had stood together at Claire's graveside as her coffin was lowered into the ground.

"Lie, are you okay out there? Why all this hanging about our sister's place?"

"Just trying to understand some things. Julius, is Ettenmoor interested in occultism and UFOs and all that crap?"

"You expect me to do you favors when you call me Julius, Lionboy? The answer is, I don't really know—but when you get far enough into quantum, the line between science and 'all that crap,' as you so gracefully put it, isn't terribly clear-cut."

Two hours later I received a call—not from Ettenmoor, but from a man who identified himself as "Dr. Ettenmoor's personal assistant." Ettenmoor's calendar was tight, but, it being a vacation in most of the civilized world, he had time that very day—either that, or wait for over a week. I told him the sooner the better. Would half an hour suit me—say, four that afternoon?

It did; and there I was at 3:45—though I wasn't completely sure why. Mandy's story of seeing Claire's death was vivid, and she'd convinced me she believed it really happened like that. But it was also patently impossible. I hoped Ettenmoor could give me some insight.

I called Jared on my cell, but rang through to his answering machine. I asked if he could leave a message on Claire's phone about how to locate her previous lovers. I turned off my phone and waited for a few more minutes—wanting to arrive neither too early nor too late—then started the engine and steered up the long driveway. I had driven the Jeep up many a rocky canyon, but it had never rolled so smoothly and evenly through the passing geology; this was the Disneyland version of fieldwork.

I parked and stepped up onto a porch formed by the overhanging slabs of roof. I knocked. The double doors were solid wood, polished, with faceted glass inlays.

Steps approached and the door opened. A young man in turtleneck and jeans greeted me with a smile and outstretched hand. "Dr. Clayborne? Larry Rodale, Dr. Ettenmoor's assistant. He's on the phone right now, but I expect he'll be off any moment."

I followed him into a huge, open-design space, the curved roof arching high above us. The kitchen, dining room, and living room were demarcated in the most gestural fashion; a handful of freestanding walls like monoliths poked up here and there to suggest boundaries. The floors were bleached wood, covered in only a few places by carpets. The furniture seemed Scandinavian— somber fabric clinging to wood in easy curves—but the overall sparseness gave the rooms an oriental, Zen flavor. Larry confided, "It's best if you just wait in his study, if you want to speed it up—having you there will get him off the phone faster."

At the rear of this cavernous space, a wide hallway took us deeper into the canyon. The right side of the hall was floor-to-ceiling glass that looked straight out at car-sized boulders. There was moisture in the protected depths of the canyon: a few twisted pinon pines reached out from crevices in the rocks. Jared's camera would have loved it.

Thirty feet on, the hallway opened into a substantial chamber. The rear wall was filled with sliding glass doors, giving a view of the boxed-in head of the canyon. There were pairs of doors to both sides; the first one on the left stood open, and Larry gestured for me to follow him in.

It was a study, but on a larger scale than I expected. There wasn't just one desk, but three, all piled deep with reports and papers; there were two drafting tables plastered with taped-down blueprints and Post-It notes. The desk in the center of the room was occupied; a big man leaned back in a swivel chair, his construction boots planted on the corner of his desk. A phone handset was stuffed between his shoulder and ear, leaving his hands free to unscrew a ballpoint pen. He pulled the barrel apart far enough to see the innards, then screwed them back together and freed a hand to salute us.

Larry gestured to a chair in front of that desk, and I sat. He pitched his voice low. "Can I offer you anything? Coffee, tea, Coke…?" I shook my head. He stood there, apparently unsure of what to do next. Ettenmoor pointed at the handset, rolled his eyes skyward, and then grinned; he used his free arm to shoo Larry toward the door. He made a point of catching my eye, and held up an index finger.

I studied him. He wasn't what I expected. He was pale, with reddish hair and a short, sparse beard just showing gray at the edges. He nodded his head in response to whatever he was hearing on the phone, and went back to unscrewing the pen and separating the two halves of the barrel as far as he could without allowing the cartridge to drop. He looked like a lumberjack or roofing contractor just starting to let his muscles go to fat. Those thick hands seemed made for grabbing and heaving, not for this delicate fiddling with a pen.

He laughed, not altogether pleasantly. "Bet they do, bet they do. Know what? Still isn't going to happen…yeah, yeah…because it's boring, that's why. Astro-fucking-nomically boring…"

He swung his boots down off the desk and looked at me, but his eyes then drifted to the side as if drawn back into the phone call. He shook his head, shook it again; I wondered if he thought his caller could sense these gestures. Finally he said, "*I* understand. Do they?… Oh, bottom line? Bottom line: we don't do this unless we *all* feel like it… Okay, have him call me. Make sure he has answers first." He tossed his pen down. "Nope, not your fault… Gotta go… take care…bye."

He blew out a long, factory-whistle breath and put his palms flat on the top of the desk, hands wide apart. "Man! Guy is an object lesson in how *not* to live. Person can spend all of their time and energy on money. Might even make you successful. But God punishes you by making you dull, dull, deadly dull." He leaned across the desk to shake; I stood and let him engulf my hand in that meaty paw. "I'm Ron, even Ronny to some. You're Lionel?"

"Umm—Walker, actually."

He sat back down and busied himself unlacing his boots. His head disappeared and resurfaced behind the desk every so often, like a marine mammal touching its blowhole to the air.

"Oh…sorry…could swear Edgar said—doesn't matter…" He sat up, pulled off one boot, then the other. They thudded to the floor. "So how is Edgar?"

He had spoken to Edgar more recently than I. Chances are, with conferences and professional get-togethers, he spent more hours in Edgar's company each year than I did. "Oh, he's doing well, all things considered. We had something of a tragedy in the family recently."

"Hmmph." Ettenmoor nodded. "Sorry. Your sister." When death is discussed, most people assume a somber mien, as if Death himself is present and searching our manner for sufficient signs of respect. There was none of this with Ettenmoor. "She was local, huh? Guess we had friends in common." He turned and took a few steps to one of the auxiliary desks in the room. "Edgar. One of the greats, you know."

"He's brilliant."

"Brilliant's common. No, brilliant and *unorthodox*. Field hasn't caught up to him yet… Always return *his* phone calls." He turned his back to me, and to my surprise stripped off his shirt. "Most calls nowadays are from venture-capitalist dickheads. Want to create the next Intel… I stretch out a little this time of day. Can talk while I do it." He stepped out of his pants and stood naked with his back to me. He wasn't simply pale, but actively white. "Hope you don't mind." He gave an enigmatic smile over his shoulder; he had a big, soft face that seemed wider at the bottom than at the top. "Gonna do it either way."

I mumbled something affirmative. He pulled on baggy cotton pants and tugged a sleeveless T-shirt over his head. He hoisted a roll of rubbery mat onto his shoulder, and said, "Let's see how the day's doing."

We were just past the winter solstice, so the day, of course, was pretty much over. He proceeded out of the room with a curious, rolling gait, like an animal that only occasionally rose onto two legs. I followed him into the interior chamber, and then out one of the sliding glass doors.

The canyon was already deep in shadow. A layer of cold air roiled along the ground, following downslope paths worn into the rock by Pleistocene rainstorms. I expected the chill air would change his mind, but he rolled out his mat on a table-like boulder that rose about four feet off the ground. He clambered up on it and sat, legs straight and splayed apart, for all the world like Alice's caterpillar atop the mushroom. A grunt, and he leaned forward, grabbed his left foot with both hands, and used this to pull his body down toward his leg. He groaned. "Damn. Feels good." He moved to the right side, repeated the motion, and then grabbed right and left foot with their respective hands and leaned forward to touch his chest to the mat. I was startled. He wasn't limber like a gymnast, but any suppleness was a surprise in someone so ursine.

"You're remarkably flexible," I said.

With his chest still pressed to the mat, he said, "Try to stay loose." His voice was only slightly colored by the effort, but his breathing was audible. "Mind and body mirror each other…one gets stiff and unbending, the other does too." He came up out of the pose, stood on his knees, and arched backward to grab his heels. "Go ahead"—pause for a few short breaths—"you wanted to talk about something." He arched his back, lifting his heart toward the sky. He gritted, "I'm listening."

I was chilled. I pushed my hands into my coat pockets, hugged my arms in, began to pace as I spoke. I explained as briefly as I could the circumstances around Claire's murder including Mandy's vision; when I first mentioned Mandy's name, he grunted in recognition.

He pulled himself out of the arched pose and sat on his heels. "Whoo. That's a rush." He rolled forward and brought the top of his head to the mat, his face disappearing between rounded shoulders.

I waited and walked in a small circle. One of the contorted pines brushed my face. Once I had been working up north near Ridgecrest when an ecoscience team dug up all of a desert juniper, down to the finest hairs of its roots. The trunk and branches were dwarfed by the mass and reach of the root system. Most of the tree was really below the surface.

Ettenmoor's voice was muffled. "Mandy works with me."

"Yes, she mentioned that. In fact, she mentioned you as somebody who took an interest in the, uh, the scientific underpinnings of these sorts of things."

He came up out of his curled position and sat back on his heels. To my amazement, there was a thin sheen of sweat on his face despite the cold. He smiled. "Better." He rose to his feet, stood erect, bent one knee and brought his foot high up on the opposite thigh. Balanced on one leg, he brought his hands together at the center of his chest. "'These sorts of things,'" he mimicked. "Damn. Sounds like a Victorian bringing up sex… Yeah, I research things people label 'psychic.' My hobby." He paused to lower his leg, and then performed the position on the other side.

"Is that why Mandy works with you? Because you think she's psychic?"

"She's a software engineer. Top-notch, too. Not bad with electronics, either. Never had the knack, myself. Well, except on paper… She's sensitive, sure. Not why she works here."

"So, this research you're doing: Are you trying to prove that these psychic things exist, or that they don't exist?"

He snorted. "Wow. Question's so messed up I don't know where to start." He straightened his leg and stood on both feet, heels and toes pressed together. He reached his hands above his head, palms pressed together, and arched his torso backward, his pelvis pressed forward, his head and shoulders reaching back behind him. He held this position for only a few seconds, his whole body trembling, and then slowly lifted himself erect and lowered his arms to his side. "That's enough for now. Let's go get a drink."

He swung down off the rock, rolled the mat, hoisted it onto his shoulder, and led me back into the house. He tossed the mat down, slid the doors shut, and started down the hallway toward the main house. I hustled along a pace or two behind. He didn't look back to see if I was following. "Glass of wine, I think. Red, or white?"

"Um, either is fine. Isn't drinking a little inconsistent with your yoga?"

"How so?"

"I'm not sure. I don't really know much about yoga; it just seems that most of the kinds of people who do it—"

He glanced back at me, eyebrows lifted, then plowed on ahead. "Ah. 'Inconsistent.' You mean 'non-stereotypical.' People who do yoga eat granola. Vote Democratic, maybe Green, and—"

"Well, I didn't mean—"

"—drive Volvos. Hate cigarette smoke but burn incense. Right?"

He led the way across the expanse of the main room to what must have been the dining area. He crossed immediately to a huge wrought-iron wine rack and began nosing through it. He pulled out a bottle, inspected it, put it back, and selected another. It was warm inside the house; I doffed my jacket and hung it over the back of a chair next to the dining-room table.

I wasn't sure how to answer in a way that wouldn't annoy him. "I didn't mean to imply anything. It's just that a lot of things do seem to go together…" He had peeled the foil as I spoke, and now drove a corkscrew into the cork with a few powerful twists and yanked it out with an audible pop. "I mean, isn't that how market research works? Correlating a lot of traits?"

"Bra-vo." He came over to the blonde table, three wineglasses interleaved with the fingers of one hand, a bottle in the other. "Larry!" he bellowed. "Glass of wine!" No answer came, but he poured three in any case, a red so dark as to verge on black. He handed me a glass, sat down, and drank deeply; none of the careful and considerate tasting of the connoisseur. "Sit down. Any rate, bravo. People won't admit they stereotype. Sure they do. A model. Everything's a model. But you see the problem with stereotyping." He paused, shouted, "Yo, Larry!" and then asked, "How's the wine?"

"It's good." It was, although I was no great judge. "And of course there's problems with stereotyping when it results in injustice, but—"

Ettenmoor was already shaking his big head, mouth full of wine. "Mmph-mmm." He swallowed. "Not the problem. Stuff it does to others is a side effect. Problem is it's a model—letting your model get in the way of seeing. Hurts you."

"How so?" How did we get off on this tangent?

"Pigeons. Pigeons in the park; they get this model going: *People who feed us don't want to hurt us.* Usually works. Makes it easy to trap pigeons, though."

"But detecting recurring, reliable patterns, and developing them into laws—isn't that what science is all about?"

He pointed at me. "Don't want to end up as a trapped pigeon, do you? *Not* what 'science is all about.' That's the lowest level of science. Basement science. Cellar dwellers."

Larry appeared, seemingly from nowhere, and picked up the third glass of wine. He nodded at me, but addressed Ettenmoor. "You remember that Casewell wanted to do the phone thing at six?"

"Fuck. Put 'em off again. Tell 'em I'm in a coma."

"Okay." Larry started to leave, hesitated. "How long is this coma expected to last?"

"Long time. We're talking life support." Ettenmoor turned his attention back to me as Larry disappeared. "Advice—never, never do anything that turns out to be useful to business guys." He took a big drink, refilled his glass, drank again. "Need another bottle here. Another of the same?"

"Sure, that would be fine." I wasn't done with my first glass yet.

He stood up from the table but continued talking with his back to me, busy at the wet bar. "Cellar-dweller science. All those people busy confirming what's already accepted." He came back with an open bottle, filled his glass again, topped mine up. "The real action is with things that don't fit."

"The exception that proves the rule?"

He sat back in his chair and exhaled heavily. "No offense, but, fuck, I hate that phrase. You even know what it means?"

"Well, it means that even for the most solid rule you can come up with, there's always an exception."

"Yeah. What most people think. That's why I hate the damn thing. 'Prove' there was used in its old sense, meaning 'test.' You know, like military? Like 'proving grounds.' For new weapons? Phrase originally meant: *Here's an exception—the exception that* tests *your rule. Uh-oh, your rule seems to be in pretty big trouble!* Somehow it got turned completely around: *Here's an exception. But, hey, doesn't matter! Always happens, even to the best rules!'* "

He glowered at his wineglass. I drained mine. He looked up, refilled my glass. "Sorry. A few things really get me going." He grinned. "Actually, there's a huge list. Nothing personal. So what were we talking about?"

"I came here with a lot of questions. But I believe that the last thing I really asked you was outside, when I asked if you were trying to prove the existence of so-called psychic phenomena, or disprove it."

"Right. A screwed-up question. Never set out to prove or disprove something. Lots of scientists do, usually because the government gave them money. Go reach this predetermined conclusion. Basically whores, traitorous swine. Bung'em up in barrels and leave'em by the curb on trash day." He drained his glass again. I took a big gulp from mine. "Sorry. Thought of something." He slapped at nonexistent pockets in his yoga outfit, then jumped up in frustration and stalked over to the wet bar.

He returned with a pen and a pizza-delivery flyer printed on bright-orange paper. He sat, turned it to the blank side, and scribbled. It was Greek to me, literally: Phi, the wave equation, Sigma, the sum-over-states. I recognized a few terms, but the equations were a mystery. I reflected that Ettenmoor's peculiar manner probably stemmed from having only a portion of his mind engaged on conversation; the rest was working on something else. He was completely focused now, though. There were lines around his eyes, but the rest of his face was smooth and almost pudgy, and he worked on the page with the concentration of a child learning to color.

He folded the sheet in half, sat back, and exhaled. "There. Better." He refilled my glass. "Real question here: What are you trying to do? Solve your sister's murder? Contact her ghost? Prove that there's nothing here that doesn't fit your model of the universe?"

I chuckled. "Well, I'm certainly not trying to contact her ghost."

"Might happen. Couple of years ago I lost somebody. Aggh. Hate that phrase. Fuck it, she *died*. Month or so later, things started happening. Coincidences about things we shared. Phrases of hers, popping into my mind. Eventually I could feel her presence."

Great Mind of Our Times or not, this seemed delusional. "Are you sure you just didn't *think* you felt her presence?"

I was jarred when Ettenmoor laughed outright. "You think that makes sense? Your question, I mean? What's the difference between having a feeling and thinking you have a feeling?"

"The difference is whether or not she was somehow really present."

"Present where? In my mind? In the past? In the air? In another dimension? Does it matter where?"

"Of course it matters where! If you're saying that you are sort of remembering someone who's dead, there's no real problem. If you're saying that someone who's dead is still around, then there's a big problem."

"Those the possibilities? How about this: I'm in touch with someone from the past. They're dead now. Doesn't mean they didn't exist. Doesn't mean they didn't leave their essence etched somewhere… can think of a dozen other possibilities." He leaned one elbow onto the table and made a fist, knuckles turned toward me. "Tell you two things we know from quantum. One." His index finger popped up. "Time doesn't work the way we think. Time may not even be comprehensible. Two." His middle finger joined his index in a V. "Observe or perceive the universe, you change the universe."

"Well, if you're talking about Heisenberg, sure, but that's all subatomic."

"Not just Heisenberg. And little things add up." He jumped up from his seat. "Reminds me…" He meandered across the room to a little desk, pulled open the top drawer. He came back with a thin sheaf of what seemed to be 8x10 photos. "You know cloud chamber tracks?"

"I know what they are: photos of the tracks of subatomic events taking place. But I can't read them."

"Don't matter." He sat back down, pushed a photo across at me. Two scratchy curves converged against a grainy background. "See this? Two opposite particles colliding." He pushed over another, with the two scratchy curves, and a third line emerging from the point where they touched. "Mutually annihilate, combine to form a single particle."

I just nodded.

"Okay. Now here is something interesting." A single curved line. He pushed forward another photo. "Now look just a little later." The single line was longer, and two curves intersected just at the point where it had appeared.

"I don't understand."

"Me either. But the first pictures showed what you'd expect: Two particles colliding to create a third. The second pictures showed a particle popping into existence, and then, after it's happily off to kindergarten, its two parents arrive on the scene and wipe each other out."

I shrugged. "So? I don't see the point."

"Point is, sorta jacks causality all over the place, don't it?" He shook his head. "*That's* worth looking into. Anomalous. Might get something out of it other than a nice warm feeling that we already understand everything."

"But you have hard evidence there. That doesn't mean every claim an individual person makes is worth taking seriously." The wine was beginning to make me seem profound to myself, and I pointed at him with the rim of my glass: "There's a difference between evidence and anecdotes."

"And what's the plural of anecdote?"

"Umm—anecdotes?"

"No. The plural of anecdote is *data*. We've got tons of data. What we don't have is insight."

Larry interrupted to summon him to the phone: "You really have to take this one, Ron."

I drained my glass and refilled it myself.

"You ever see an eclipse of the sun?" Ettenmoor asked as he sat down.

"Not in real life."

"Important astronomical phenomenon. Now here's the difference between you and me. Neither of us understood the mechanism, neither of us had ever heard of such a thing, and some traveler from a distant land tells us about it. I say: Interesting. You say: Nonsense."

"That's not quite fair. I just object when something stands so thoroughly outside the boundaries of science, and—"

"Oh, come on Walker! Take a quick glance at the things western science has claimed don't exist: Giraffes. The platypus. Ball lightning. Female orgasm. Deadly spiders—"

"Oh, come on, that's not really—"

"Continental drift. The ability of women to reason, the ability of women to learn math. The identical nature of chemicals in living and nonliving matter. The intellectual aptitude of nonwhite races. Germs— why, they practically burnt Semmelweiss at the stake for trying to make surgeons wash their hands!—I mean, who would be stupid enough to believe that things could be so small you couldn't see them?"

"Okay, okay." I held up my hands like he'd pointed a revolver at me.

"What's your earliest memory? What age?"

I frowned. "I don't see what that has to do with anything, but I have several memories from when I was two; some might be from a little before I was two."

"I know people who remember their birth. I know people who remember *before* their birth. But I also know a guy, bright guy, doesn't remember anything from before he was five. And here's my point: he doesn't believe that anyone else *really* remembers before they were five either."

"But that's ridiculous. The world is filled with people who can remember when they were two. And they can remember things that their family can confirm really happened."

"And how do we know they aren't remembering things they were told? How do we know their families aren't lying?"

"What reason would they have to lie about such a thing?"

"Well, why would people lie and claim somebody in a family is precognitive? Why would whole families lie about poltergeists? Skeptics don't have problems with people lying for no reason. Apply the same standards to remembering when you were two, and hey: Guess you're delusional."

I hunched forward, elbows on the table. "I don't see the analogy. And everybody accepts that there's no physical reason why you shouldn't be able to remember when you were two. But I refuse to accept that people can somehow just suddenly know what's going on a hundred miles away!"

He pointed, poking his finger at me. "Exactly. Exactly. You refuse to accept it. No evidence would make you change your mind. Bothers you a lot. Why?"

I stood up. I was tipsy. I didn't care. I grabbed my glass, took a swallow, and then gestured with the glass in my hand: "But it doesn't make any damn sense! Look—a mind just suddenly perceiving things at a distance, or in the future—it's just against the laws of physics!"

Ettenmoor gave a malicious grin and leaned back with his arms behind his head. "Oh, yeah? Which ones?"

Great. I'm arguing the laws of physics with one of the leading physicists of our time. What the hell. I gulped down more wine, and said, "Because there's no connection, there's no mechanism, there's no way for the information to travel. You can't just magically move information from one place to another without a medium and without expending any energy."

He stood up too, now. "Really? What medium transmits light, then? Moving information without energy: who said energy wasn't expended? The brain runs at about fifteen watts. Hell of a lot more than my cell phone."

"It doesn't make any sense. Where's the connection between a brain in one place and an event in another?"

"A *mind* in one place and an event in another."

"Mind, brain, what's the difference?"

"Ahhh—now maybe we're getting somewhere." He poured the rest of the bottle into his glass, frowned at the fact that it only filled it partway, and lumbered over to the wine rack again. "Suppose you're one of those people who thinks the mind has to be inside the brain. Probably even believe that the brain creates the mind."

"Well, of course."

"Evidence?"

This seemed so patently obvious that I was momentarily taken aback. "Well, if the brain gets hurt, the mind gets hurt, too. If something goes wrong with the brain's chemistry, then we get various kinds of mental illness." I was warming to my subject, now; this was a good, irrefutable line of argument. "In fact, it's a lot more precise than that. If there is an injury to the speech center, you can't talk; if there's an injury to the auditory center, you can't hear. There's a one-to-one relationship." I spread my arms wide as I declaimed this; Ettenmoor filled the glass in my outstretched hand.

He sat down. "Listen carefully, because this analogy is precise." He topped up his wine glass and sat the bottle down beside it. "By your logic, a TV set produces all of the programs that we see, because if we damage the set, the programs go away. We see Bruce Willis—I jerk out a few wires—presto, Bruce Willis goes away. Does Bruce Willis live in the TV?"

"Of course not."

"Then why be so sure brain damage proves that the mind is *in* the brain? Brain might just be a receiver. Mind could be in another dimension for all we know. "

"I don't really get the point. Fine, maybe the brain isn't the mind. So what?"

"Hey, your model, not mine. You used it to argue the mind can't perceive things that don't have a direct wire to the brain. If your model's wrong, why are you so damn sure about what is and isn't possible?"

I moved away from the dining area and sat down in one of the armchairs that ringed an island of carpet. Scandinavian-style furniture may look good, but it isn't very cozy. I realized that the rug beneath my feet was a woven reproduction of an integrated circuit, probably an Intel chip of some sort.

Larry strolled up to the table, refilled his own wine glass. "Tehranian's expecting you to call, you know."

"Hey, I'm busy pontificating. Put him off for a couple hours. No, an hour. I'll eat a sandwich on the phone. Not like he'll notice. Wouldn't notice if I laid down the receiver."

Larry winked at me and went off to make excuses.

Ettenmoor joined me in the ring of armchairs. "Suppose I told you that some kinds of ESP work—but only at certain phases of the moon."

"Well, I'd be pretty skeptical—there's not—there's no logical connection."

"There's no *logical* connection between mosquitoes and malaria either, until you know about *Plasmodia* protozoans. And think of all the times you've been bitten by mosquitoes without getting malaria: wrong kind of mosquitoes, right kind of mosquitoes but not infected."

"But at least there's a mechanism in terms of things we know…"

"But not in terms of things we knew a couple hundred years ago. Remember the guys who wanted to shut down the patent office in the late 1800s because everything had already been invented? Ask yourself this: what if this is just like every other time science thought it understood most of everything? Suppose we only know ten percent of the basics? One percent?"

"So what does that mean? Are we just supposed to accept whatever anyone says? Are we supposed to ignore the things we already know are true, and take contradicting claims on faith?"

Ettenmoor laughed. "Those the only options? Toss out science, or ignore anything that doesn't fit?"

"Well they don't seem very compatible to me!" I could tell I was getting too aggressive, but I was unable to stop. "They really can't coexist, can they?"

"Why not?"

"If we start letting in wild claims and experiences, we'll be back in the Dark Ages, we'll be burning people for witchcraft. Somebody sees something in a dream or a vision or on drugs and with no more proof than that some poor guy's tied to the stake."

"Hey, you don't have to let it into court—though some of the things they already let into court are more subjective than the *I Ching*. Character witnesses. Psychologists, for the luvva Skinner."

"What are you saying, then?"

"That these things need to be studied. Carefully, objectively. *Gently*. What I'm trying to do out here. Back to your original topic:

Take Mandy very seriously. She has information. The police confirm that some of it's accurate. You don't have to swallow it whole. But what more do you want?" He stood up, swayed a little, said, "Whoa—wine on an empty stomach. I'm going to step outside. You might want your jacket."

I stood too fast, and wobbled a little. I retrieved my jacket, and Ettenmoor reappeared, pulling on a huge cable-knit sweater. We wound our way wordlessly back down the hallway, past the study, and out the sliding-glass doors. He slapped the light switch on the way out and darkness rushed up around us. I heard his footfalls move out across the rocks. I tapped forward tentatively on each step, my eyes still not dark-adapted, all of me a little drunk.

The cold air cleared the fumes from my brain. I could see Ettenmoor's pale face through the gloom. I carefully worked my way forward and sat beside him on a flat boulder. Through the wide gap in the canyon walls above the stars glittered down with a brittle light.

"You interested in this whole topic?" Ettenmoor asked. "I mean, as a scientist?"

"Sure."

"Said you've got time on your hands. Want to help with a little experiment?"

I pictured myself guessing the numbers on cards. The prospect was unappealing. "What kind of experiment? What would my role be?"

"You'd be the objective observer. The scorekeeper. Talking about an experiment in psychophysics here. Real equipment. Blind testing. The whole enchilada. Take a couple hours of your time on Sunday."

"Sure, why not?"

"Great. Excellent. Might make what you call 'these things' bother you a lot less."

I grunted noncommittally. "One thing that *does* bother me," I said, "is that Mandy was on some kind of psychedelic drug when all this happened."

"Entheogen."

"Excuse me?"

"Not called psychedelics anymore. They're entheogens. *Entheos*, god within, *gen*, giving rise to, manifesting. Letting God come within."

"Whatever they're called, doesn't that kind of undermine her story? Being stoned?"

"Not really. Much the opposite, in fact. Those kinds of drugs tend to bring on non-ordinary experiences."

"But they make you hallucinate."

"Not really. There *are* drugs that make you hallucinate. Not those."

"Have you taken those kinds of drugs?"

He laughed. "Of course. Been a while, though. Haven't you? Not even once? Man, Walker, what did you do in high school and college? Go to one of those religious schools? Raised in Orange County?"

The questions seemed rhetorical, so I ignored them. "Well, don't you think that the fact that drugs were involved lowers the credibility of the whole thing just a little bit?"

"Not at all. No one knows how these guys work. Oh, they know what neural receptors pick them up. That's it. Some people think they act as a non-specific amplifier. Just cranks up the volume of whatever is already going on. Others say the main function of most of our brain is to cut down on the total sensory input. Hard to run from a lion if you're noticing all the flowers, yeah? Those people think that your 'psychedelics' just open up a choke valve. They let what's really out there come in." He leaned back on his hands and looked up at the night sky. "Makes sense. Immensity of everything would crush you if you really took it all in…" I could almost hear his mind withdrawing to some other pursuit.

I hadn't intended to speak, but found myself saying, "I don't know what to believe."

There was a long silence before Ettenmoor said, "Ever read Peter Guyer? Works as a counselor up in Berkeley. Treats people who are suicidally depressed. People who think their lives are big tragedies." He paused, stretched a little. "He writes something like, 'People would rather believe in a tragedy than live with uncertainty. Rather decide once and for all that they're losers than agonize every day over the uncertainties in *maybe*.'"

"I'm not trying to decide things about myself. I'm trying to understand something about reality, about what does and doesn't happen."

"Not so sure there's a distinction... Be a scientist. Approach it empirically."

"Meaning?"

"Let go of your preconceptions. Or pretend you have, and act the part. Stop letting your theories about reality run ahead of your data."

"And how's that scientific?"

"It's an experiment. Watch yourself. Watch everything. Note the results."

"I don't really see how that would help."

"Got something better to do?" Ettenmoor lay back on the boulder, clasped his hands behind his head, and gazed up at the galaxy.

I steered the Jeep down the long driveway, lightheaded with wine and conversation.

Ettenmoor's house stood at the apex of a road that shot straight up from Highway 62 and then glanced off the wall of exposed rocks, deflected to loop down toward the handful of houses on the sloping bajada. I headed toward the main road. There were no streetlamps in the area; the twin beams of my car provided the only illumination.

Headlights showed in my rearview mirror. I was jarred when they drew closer, began flashing like a stroboscope, and then sprouted the spinning blue lights of a sheriff's cruiser.

I pulled toward the edge of the road, expecting the car to zoom past. Instead it followed me over as if we were joined by a trailer hitch. I slowed and came to a halt, slid open the window, and waited.

Someone got out of the patrol car. He switched on his flashlight and shone it toward me. The reflection from the side mirror lanced into my eyes and blinded me, and I heard rather than saw him approach.

"Can you step out of the car, sir?"

I opened the door and swung my feet onto the ground. He shot the beam of the flashlight into my face to examine me, then lowered it. I could barely see his shape though he was only two feet away.

"Can I see an operator's license, registration, and proof of insurance?"

I dug out my wallet and found my license and insurance card, more by feel than sight. I held them out in his direction and felt him take them from me, heard him pin them down in the jaws of a clipboard. He held the flashlight up to examine the cards, and I could see that he held it like a club, the bell of the light chamber butted up against his little finger, the long, heavy battery chamber sticking out a foot from the circle of his thumb and index finger. He tilted the light again, right into my eyes, presumably comparing my face to the license.

"The registration is in the glove box," I said, "let me get it out for you." This is a major sortie in a Jeep Wrangler. I stood on the running board with my left foot, kneeled my right leg on the driver's seat, and leaned far over to brace one hand on the front passenger seat. After the deputy's maglight, the Jeep's dome light was a dim yellow. I dug through the glove box with my free hand. My retinas were still saturated in a few spots from the repeated stabs of the flashlight, and long lozenges of pale colors drifted across my vision, disappeared, and then resumed their march from the other side, like a parade of pastel-tinted fluorescent tubes.

I snagged the registration at last and clambered back onto the pavement. I shut the car door behind me, handed the paper to the patrolman, and waited.

"Is this your current address, sir? San Diego?"

"Yes it is." He continued to use the upraised flashlight to pore over my papers. Either he was a very slow reader, or he was deliberately trying to annoy me. "May I ask why you pulled me over?"

"Were you aware you were driving a little erratically, sir?"

I had expected some minor equipment violation. This took me off guard. "No, I wasn't aware of that. In fact, I don't believe I was."

The shadowy figure nodded. "Have you been drinking this evening, sir?"

"Well—well, yes, I have. A little." Surely I was nowhere near the legal limit. I felt like I could easily walk a line, or stand on one foot with my eyes closed, or whatever it is they have you do.

"Would you please wait here for a moment, sir?"

I didn't get the impression that this was just an invitation. I leaned my back against the car while he went back to his cruiser. I could hear the crackle of the radio, and the muffled sound of his voice.

Looking north I could see across all of the lights of town. Beyond was a river of darkness, but perched on its far shore were the distant lights of Landers, and, just at the edge of perceptibility, a few twinkles from the reclusive houses out past Emerson Dry Lake. Back where I live on the California coast the burdened air itself is a barrier, and the world a mile or two off is always indistinct and blurry. In the desert only something with true mass and substance, like a mountain, can block your vision.

This seemed to be taking a preposterously long time. Why didn't he just come back and breathalyze me, or do something?

Down on the highway a car turned onto the road and came up the slope toward us. How is it that cars have body language? Sometimes you can sense that a car is likely to dart out or swerve, that it is driven by an older person or a teen, by a man or woman. As this car approached, even though masked by its headlights, something about it told me that this was another police car. Had the deputy actually called for backup? I tried to imagine the kind of mind that could see me as a desperado.

The car was unmarked, but it was clearly a cop car. Before it came to us, it pulled a U-turn, one front tire cutting a crescent through the sandy verge. It shifted into reverse and backed up the road until it was parked just in front of my Jeep.

Rick Bolles got out of the driver's seat, bumped the door shut with his hip, and strode over toward me, snapping his fingers. He seemed to have the knack of snapping three fingers on each hand, so that by alternating hands rapidly he made a sound somewhat like a horse's gallop. "Ah, Herr Doktor Professor Clayborne. Happy New Year. I just happened to be passing by and heard the call…guess you've been knocking back a few tonight." He was close enough now that I could see his face clearly. He wagged his eyebrows as if we shared a secret joke.

"I've had a few glasses of wine, but I don't think I'm impaired."

A little chuckle. "Now, we're not always the best judges of our own capacity, are we?" He stuck his left hand into the pocket of his suit pants and left it there. I heard a steady *ching ching ching*; he was cupping keys or coins in his fingers and tossing them up and down inside the pocket. "Normally they'd probably breathalyze you and then either lock you up or let you go. But under the circumstances, I don't think that's necessary, do you? Lot of trouble for everybody, and a big possible downside for you. So let me do you a favor." *Ching ching ching ching.* "I'll drive you home. The deputy can follow in your car. Keep the streets safe, keep you out of any possible trouble…"

I shrugged. "Fine, but I really don't think—"

"No, no, no, don't give it another thought. Safe versus sorry and all that, right?" He opened the door to the Jeep, checked to see that the keys were in the ignition, and shut the door again. He paced quickly back to the deputy up at the patrol car and conferred with him. The deputy set about locking up the cruiser as Bolles came hustling back. "C'mon, Professor," he said. He handed me my ID and registration as he stepped past me. I followed him to his car and got in the passenger side.

As we drove down toward 62, I said, "Curious coincidence that you happened to be in the neighborhood this time of night."

"No rest for the weary." He drummed on the steering wheel with his fingertips while maintaining a grip with his knuckles. "The Thin Blue Line between the public and chaos, you know. Or Thin Khaki Line, in these parts."

We stopped at the highway, and he flipped his blinker for a left turn. The holiday traffic was continuous in both directions. He tapped his fingers lightly in time with the tock-teek of the blinker, and after a few beats drummed them harder, ONE—TwoThreeFour! After a few repetitions, I was sure I recognized the tune, one of the most meatheaded melodies of all time: *tock-teek tock-teek, tock-teek tock-teek, tock-teek tock-teek, MY Shar-ron-a!*

He saw an opening and peeled out to merge with traffic. "It was about time we had a talk anyway, don't you think? Detective-to-detective, as it were?"

"I would scarcely characterize myself as a detective."

"Well, you may not carry the club card or have the secret decoder ring, but I don't know how else you would describe all this nosing around."

"I'm just trying to get a little more perspective on my sister's life, that's all."

"Mmm-hmm. But if you happened to come across any information that had to do with her murder, that would be fine too, right?"

"Well, certainly. I mean—"

"Good. Glad to hear it." He turned right onto Sunfair. "This car's been out here so many times now it could probably find the way by itself, like a good horse. Had any more problems with break-ins? Unexpected visitors?"

"I certainly had unexpected visitors." I outlined the visit from the UWI lawyers.

He nodded. "We've been looking at Universal. They have a rep back east for using strong-arm tactics. But it sounds like they didn't know about Claire's murder."

"Except that the work order your office sent the locksmith specified that he was to open 'an unoccupied residence.' How did they know it would be unoccupied?"

"Boilerplate. We only use the locksmith if the residence is unoccupied. If we get there and folks are at home, we knock just as polite as can be, and send the locksmith on his way. Any other surprises?"

There had been plenty, but none I felt like sharing. "No, not really. Things have been rather peaceful since I last saw you." Which, it occurred to me, had been a matter of forty-eight hours or so.

"Good. It'd make me nervous staying out there after that assault, but..." He gave me a sideways glance; like most of his looks, it was hard to classify. Eyes narrowed and a shining, tight little smirk. "Guess you have nerves of steel, though."

"Hardly."

He turned onto the dirt roads that meandered through the flats. "In any case, it's good to have you there. We went through Claire's stuff pretty thoroughly, but I'm sure you've been spending some time with it. Maybe you have some insights that we don't. Found something we missed."

"Such as? Are you following up on anything in particular?"

He slowed and drove cautiously over the round curb of hard-packed dirt that separated Claire's driveway from the street. "In these parts, homicide usually means sex or drugs." He pulled up to the cottage and put the car in park. "Rock'n'roll usually isn't fatal. Sex or drugs, or both." He shifted to park and turned off the headlights, but left the motor running. He turned toward me, bending his right knee up onto the seat. He rested his left elbow high on the steering wheel, and his fingers reached up and grabbed the visor, gently tugging it up and down as he talked. "In this case, I think we can rule out sex." He gave me a significant look. I guessed he was telling me that Claire hadn't been sexually assaulted. "So, drugs are the next possibility. I'm not suggesting that she was using—her bloodwork was clean—but she sure had contact with people in the drug trade. Have you found anything relating to drugs in her house—any papers or notes?"

"Actually, I've found a considerable quantity of information on that topic. In particular, she seems to have a lot of writings about psychedelic drugs, and shamanistic uses of mind-expanding drugs in other cultures—"

He gave an impatient wave. "Irrelevant. I mean, serious drugs, with serious money involved: cocaine, speed, heroin..." The Jeep pulled up next to us, and the deputy got out and slammed the door.

"There's quite a bit of material on that. It mainly seems to concern counseling for addicts. I would assume it's connected with her job at the prison."

"No, no, no, I mean specific things about specific people, or organizations. She was active in counseling, she was active in some kind of drug-policy-reform organization. I just worry that she might have stumbled across something..." In the dashboard lights, his face had a green tinge to it, like an undercover alien whose human makeup is rubbing off.

I was aware of the deputy looming just outside the door. "Is that all, then? You want me to keep my eyes open for anything relating to hard narcotics in the area?"

"Might help, might help." He sucked his teeth. "I shouldn't really say this, but frankly—if I were staying out here all alone, after all that's happened: I'd get a gun." He turned to face front in the seat. Clearly I'd been dismissed.

I got out of the car. At last I could see the deputy's face, but it revealed nothing: impassive, dark, probably some Indian or Hispanic blood in the family. It seemed as if he didn't like me much. He held out my keys, dangling them by the key ring, and I took them. Without a word he stepped around me and took my place in Bolles' car.

Bolles turned on the headlights and shifted into reverse. Just before he turned his head to back down the drive, he looked through the windshield at me and gave a little wave of his fingers, wagging them at me *toodle-doo* style.

I watched the car pull back out to the street and then approached the front door, key extended. On the rough brown doormat lay one long-stemmed white rose.

10

By morning the white rose was in a crystal bud vase, centered on Claire's coffee table. The previous night I'd tossed it on the kitchen counter, but seeing it dying there in the morning shamed me into digging through cupboards until I found the vase.

The rose nagged at me because I had no idea what it meant. Was it a message for me, or for someone else? Some sort of Sicilian death threat most people recognized?

There was a whole system of flower symbolism in the 19th century, but I'd never paid attention to the details. A background in Romantic poetry would come in handy now, but my colleges never stressed all of the practical applications of Shelley and Keats.

On the other hand, suppose I knew what a white rose symbolized; that didn't mean whoever left it there was familiar with Romantic symbolism. Maybe it was the only color of rose available. Maybe it was the only flower of any sort available.

Hell, maybe the Givens children from the front house left it there for whatever kid reasons they had at the time.

In searching for the vase, I'd found something else: a tiny plaster bust of JFK. These used to be everywhere when I was young; now they are mainly seen in the more traditional Mexican restaurants, the kind where they bring you a basket of steamed corn tortillas with the meal, no need to ask.

November 22nd, 1963, was an eventful day in many ways, but almost all the other happenings, such as the death of Aldous Huxley, were overshadowed by the Kennedy assassination. My mother's labor with Claire began about the time the news was spreading through the hospital—my mother always contended it was the commotion that set off her contractions—but Claire wasn't born until late in the night; if she'd held out another half-hour or so, she would have made it to a birthdate of November 23rd instead. After almost twelve hours of labor—"not what I expected from my third"—I am sure Claire's arrival made an impression on my mother, but no one else seemed to care much, not even our relatives. Edgar and I were staying with Aunt Laura, my father's sister, and Dad's phone calls to Aunt Laura from the hospital began with perfunctory updates on how Mom was doing, but quickly turned to the assassination. At breakfast the morning after, Dad was tired, but not too tired to shock Aunt Laura by observing it wasn't much of a surprise someone had shot the President.

"Why, H.A., I can't believe you'd say such a thing."

"I'm not saying I approve, Laura, just saying it might have been expected. A Boston Catholic gets elected in this country, he should know he's taking a big risk."

"Dad," Edgar asked, "when can we go to the hospital?"

"You know better than to interrupt, boy." He directed his words back to Aunt Laura. "The president represents our whole country. I'd never say anybody should kill him. But if a president had to get shot, I can't imagine a better one. Between him and those 'Hahvad' boys he has all over the White House, I don't know where this country's been headed. The negroes are getting so uppity they'll be asking for a state of their own pretty soon, and Kennedy's done nothing but egg 'em on. At least LBJ'll put a stop to that: no Texas boy is going to put up with the coloreds getting out of line."

I'd only been at Claire's for three nights, but it seemed like weeks. I tried to focus: drugs, churches and cults, past lovers, Universal Waste... Despite my morning-after mind-fuzz from the previous night's wine, I limited myself to a single cup of coffee and left the house by 7 a.m. I drove into Yucca Valley searching for the Church of the Rock. The address was on Chukchee Trail, which intersected 62 in the old downtown strip. I pulled around the corner and checked the street numbers. According to these, it had to be hiding somewhere right in front of my face. Just across the street I saw a plastic banner hanging from an old storefront: *Church of the Rock* in large red letters, and beneath it in smaller type, *An Open Christian Fellowship. All Are Welcome.*

The building itself was from the '40s or '50s. On the stubby overhang supporting the banner I could see where large letters had been unscrewed from the stucco. The sunbleaching of the surrounding paint had created a blurry stencil that still whispered, *Western Auto Supply & Hardware.*

The front of the building consisted of two large show windows that paralleled the street and then angled inward toward glass double doors. There had been no attempt to curtain or wall off the interior from the gaze of the street, and I looked right in at a congregation.

I hadn't expected a service to be in progress on a Thursday morning. The street was parked up, and from the *God Said It I Believe It and That Settles It* bumperstickers, I guessed the church was responsible for the congestion. I drove down the street and pulled the Jeep up in the first available space, right behind a yellow pickup. The truck was a Ford from the '50s, and had either been restored or carefully preserved. It sported a sticker telling me *It's a Child Not a Choice*, as well as a raised stick-on showing a legged fish labeled *Darwin* being swallowed by another fish labeled *Truth.*

I walked back down toward the church, feeling like I was heading to the Scopes trial. Was the Flat Earth Society big out here too?

I examined the church from the sidewalk opposite. The pulpit—no more than a cheap speaker's podium with purple velvet draped down the front—stood at the left end of the storefront. The congregation sat in metal folding chairs facing the pulpit, with their profiles turned to the street. There were a few suits showing in the crowd, but certainly no more than a few.

The pastor behind the pulpit, however, was traditionally dressed, with a clerical collar and heavy black coat. He was a round man who used big, reaching gestures as he spoke. I judged from his demeanor and the steady stare of the faithful that he was probably delivering the sermon. At my parents' church, this would have meant we were anywhere from fifteen minutes to an hour away from the end.

I strolled out onto Highway 62 and wandered the business district until I found a small diner. I bought a bad, acrid cup of coffee in a styrofoam cup and made my way back, wincing at the taste.

By this time the congregation was on its feet singing. "Rock of Ages?" Something traditional. There was a small portable organ in a back corner; no matter how it looked to the eye, to the ear this was any other church.

The song ended and everyone remained standing and bowed their heads. Final prayer, I assumed and hoped. I remembered years of Sundays with inclined head and closed eyes, grateful release was near, the infinite drone of the minister's voice, my mind full of what the rest of the day promised. Often Claire was beside me, much younger, much smaller, surreptitiously poking me or reaching up to tickle the back of my neck.

At long last the service ended and the doors opened. The pastor stood outside the doors, almost on the sidewalk, shaking hands and exchanging a few words with each member as they filed out. The strains of the electronic organ drifted across the street: it was a fair imitation, but didn't have the underlying, boneshaking power of a real pipe organ.

It was hard to generalize about the congregation. Perhaps a third were Hispanic, clashing with my supposition that all Hispanics were Catholic. Most of the rest were obviously poor—it was depressing to reflect these were probably their best clothes—but some seemed prosperous enough, the sort of men and women who owned small businesses and paid dues to the Chamber of Commerce. A surprising number were young, in their teens and twenties. Some sported slightly punk hairstyles, but a handful looked like members of the high-school debate team.

When the crowd thinned I tossed the coffee in a trash bin and crossed the street. The pastor saw me coming and smiled, his round face shiny from his bald head right down to his chin. He seemed two glasses of champagne into a celebration. His hand was out to shake mine before I even stepped up onto the curb. What a contrast with Pastor Ledger of my youth, a dry old bone of a man who scanned your eyes for any hint of impiety before he so much as said hello.

"Welcome, welcome. Ira Bickman, Church of the Rock." He had a big voice and expansive manner, the kind of man who could dominate a large auditorium without a microphone.

I shook his hand. "Walker Clayborne. Claire Clayborne was my sister."

There was no banishing the glow from his face, but his eyes turned sad. He didn't let go of my hand, but placed his other hand on my shoulder. "I'm so sorry. Claire was very important to many of us here."

Ira was about to continue, but a man carrying a stepladder on his shoulder eased between us, stood it up at one end of the banner, and began unhooking the sign. Ira looked past me, spotted someone, and said, "Eddie. Can you give Darnell a hand there?" Eddie went to the base of the ladder and Darnell fed the detached end of the banner down to him.

I moved a little closer to the minister and lowered my voice. "I was wondering if you could spare a little time to talk about Claire. I'm hoping to find out a bit more about what happened to her. I'm sure you're quite busy, but…"

"Not at all. I have a number of things to attend to right now, and we do have another meeting at the end of the day, but we'd be pleased if you joined us for lunch at our house."

I protested I didn't want to intrude, but was quickly overridden. The man with the rolled banner began to edge past us again, and Ira said, "Darnell. This is Walker Clayborne. Claire's brother."

The man with the banner stopped and turned to us. He was slim and whipcord wiry, with sharp, tiny lines in his face from years of outdoor labor. His long-sleeved checked shirt had been neatly ironed. He inclined his head slightly, almost as if he were going to pull his forelock. "I'm, I'm sorry about your sister, Mr. Clayborne. Terrible thing. Just a terrible thing." He didn't make eye contact; he seemed painfully shy.

"Darnell and his wife knew Claire well, didn't you, Darnell?" The man just nodded, still not looking up. "Speaking of Rachel, I didn't see her here today. Is she still with her sister?"

Darnell stared down fixedly. "Her sister's ailing worse 'n we thought. Might be some time afore she gets back."

"We'll remember her in our prayers. See you at evening service, then?"

He shook his head. "Not sure. Aimin' to get the junkheap down at the Ranch loaded onta the flatbed today." He tilted his head down one more time to acknowledge me, and turned to carry the banner back inside the church.

A large van blotched with gray primer pulled up to the curb. Plastic stick-on letters had been pasted to the side, a little unevenly, to spell out *Shackles Torn Asunder* and, below that, *Born to Serve Jesus*. Two denim-clad bikers jumped out and went to the back of the van. Ira ushered me out of the doorway and onto the sidewalk. The bikers began to unload amplifiers, drums, electric guitars. I heard the roar of motorcycles from down the street, and three chopped Harleys pulled up to park behind the van. The three new arrivals dismounted and began to help with the unloading.

The first two carried an amplifier past us. "Mornin' Ira," the first one said.

"Steve, Richie, greetings," he answered.

"Are they a branch of your church?" I asked.

Ira grinned. "No, not really, but they use our facilities."

"So you just rent them space?"

"No, we let them use it. If Christian charity doesn't begin with helping other churches, them I don't know where it starts. And some of our younger members actually attend both services."

Ira described how to get to his house, gave me a phone number in case I got lost, and disappeared back into the church.

More and more people were arriving for the Shackles Torn Asunder service—a few more on motorcycles, but most of them packed into old cars and pickups. Not all of them appeared to be bikers, but those who weren't looked like they had spent their lives on public assistance. Mandy had been right—an abnormally high percentage of this congregation were visibly missing teeth. I decided to leave before Billy and Moonface showed up.

As I pulled back down the street, I looked out the window of the Jeep at the Church of the Rock. *Western Auto Supply & Hardware.* It was at a *Western Auto* that I found my first bike, a red Huffy with fat tires. The place where we bought it was right next to my father's appliance store, on a side street in oldtown Phoenix. When I drove by after Claire's funeral, both the stores had been boarded up.

Our father was always known by his initials, just "H.A.," often slurred by his friends and customers to "aitchay;" one of my boyhood friends thought my father's name was "AJ." It said it on his checks, on the front of his store (*Quality Modern Appliances HA Clayborne, Prop.*), and pretty much anywhere you looked except in his wallet. I don't remember when Edgar or I first discovered his full name; it seemed we had always known, and we were smart enough not to bring it up. It was strange a man who hated his own names so much would saddle his sons with "Lionel" and "Julius."

I don't remember why Claire, about nine years old, had his driver's license in her hands, but I remember the glance Edgar and I exchanged when she said, "Harlan Abraham? How come you never use those names?"

Dad was on the couch, bent over to replace a broken shoelace. He looked up. This was the kind of thing that might set him off, but he must have been in a good mood. He tied the shoe and sat back on the couch. "Because 'Harlan' sounds like some two-bit Southern cracker, and Abraham sounds like some kike."

"What's a kike?" Claire asked.

"A Jew. It's a name for Jew."

"And not a very nice one," Mom said. "Not one I want to hear you using."

"I'm not knocking Jews," Dad said. "Some of my best customers are Jews—though if one of them started up an appliance store in the same neighborhood, they'd be gone like a shot. They all stick together."

"Isn't it good to stick together?" Claire asked.

"Not like that it isn't. They put their kind ahead of everybody and everything else. One for all and all for one. Everybody else can go to the dogs."

Mom didn't like the drift of this conversation. "Come on, H.A., just the other day you were saying the Golds were shaping up to be your best customers."

"Because of my prices. Just like the rest of them—all they care about is money."

Claire frowned. "I thought you said what they cared about was sticking together."

Dad chewed his lip. "Are you getting smart with me, young lady?"

"No sir."

"Well make sure you don't. And don't let me hear you saying 'kike' again, you hear?"

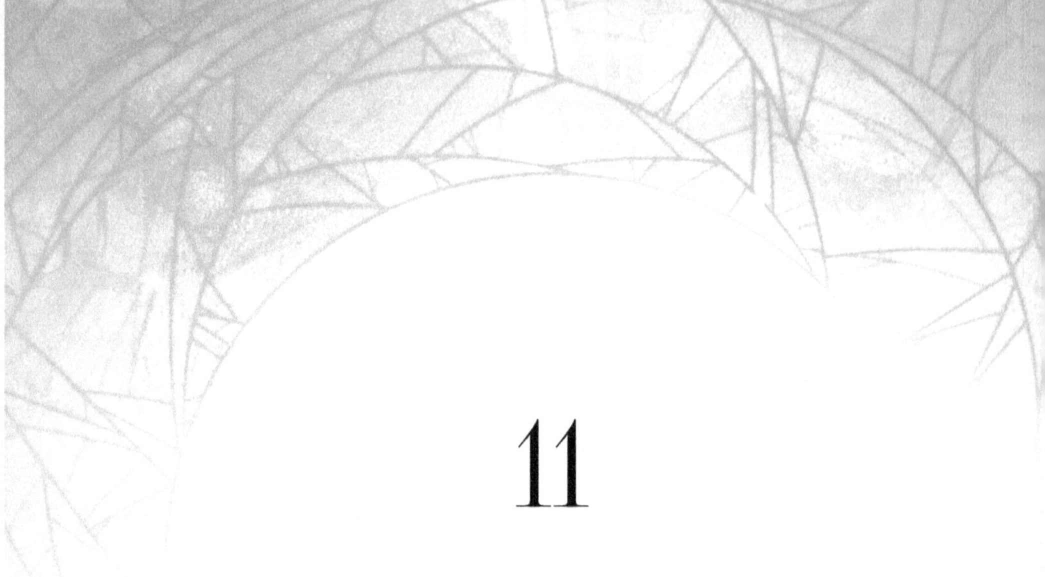

11

Jared's phone message had given me basic information on two of Claire's former lovers, Bryce Childers and Gary Handwerk. Handwerk was a kickboxing instructor who worked out of a downtown studio, but Childers was "some kind of astrologer" who worked out of his home.

I checked my watch: not even 8:30 a.m. yet, and over three hours before I was expected for lunch at Ira's. It seemed too early for kickboxing, so I decided to track down Childers.

I had to visit three phone booths to find an intact phonebook. Childers was listed, and his house turned out to be well north of Yucca Valley, out by itself off Pioneertown Road. I considered calling first, but decided just to drop by. It's a lot easier to give someone the brushoff over the phone than in person, and I didn't care to be brushed off.

His house was a little Spanish-style affair, but a stumpy, copper-domed silo was partly visible in the back. His yard consisted of two patches of sand to either side of the walkway, a shaggy Joshua tree centered on the left, a stand of purplish beavertail cactus to the right.

I knocked. At first there was no response, and then I heard movement. I knocked again.

The door opened a crack and Kirsten looked out. She frowned, then recognized me, and smiled. "Walker. Wow, this is a surprise…"

I imagine it was more of a surprise to me than to her. She opened the door and stepped back, covering a yawn. She was dressed in nothing but a big T-shirt, and her hair was still tousled from sleep. "I'm sorry," I said, "I didn't mean to—"

She waved my words away. "C'mon in, I just finished making coffee. Like some?" I made an affirmative noise and she ambled into the kitchen, raising her voice over her shoulder. "How do you take it?"

"Black."

She came back with two full mugs and indicated the couch with a nod of her head. I sat and accepted the offered mug. She sat in an armchair opposite, folding her legs up into the chair. "It's nice to see you again. How'd you know I was here?"

"I'm really glad to see you—but the reason I came was I was hoping to find Bryce Childers. I was told he used to be close to Claire."

"Oh." She tugged at the bottom of her shirt where it was riding up her thighs. "Well, once upon a time, they were. But that's been over for a while." She squirmed into the cushion of the chair. Her glossy curls were matted on one side, dampened and then dried during sleep, and her lazy posture spoke of a long night of sex.

"I understand. Jared told me Claire and Bryce hadn't been seeing each other in a while. But he also said they were pretty serious a few years ago."

"They were. But she was, well, done with him before I—" She flicked her free hand in the air, trying to knock her words aside. "God. What a mumblemouth. What I'm trying to say is, it's not like I stole him, or anything. I even talked with her about it before I got involved with him…" She laughed. "I don't know why I'm getting embarrassed…"

It puzzled me when I thought about it. Claire was nearly forty, and she had handed on her lover to a friend who was, what, twenty-two, twenty-three? Kirsten had a wide, sensuous mouth that fought furiously to deliver a different message from the cute freckled nose. But she was literally young enough to be my daughter, if I'd had one. Even worse, one of my undergrads. Incest only puts you in jail. Sexual harassment accusations can take away your tenure.

"It doesn't make any difference to me, you know," I said.

"Yeah. It's just—well, Chad once accused me of turning into a Claire Clone. She *was* kind of a role model for me, I guess."

"A role model?" I asked it out of surprise—Claire never seemed to me like someone a young woman would deliberately emulate—but Kirsten took it as a request for clarification.

"She got me involved in all kinds of volunteer stuff out here. She was probably one of the only reasons I stayed." She used her fingers to fluff her matted hair a little. "So I guess I'm a little defensive about hanging with her former boyfriend."

"No accounting for matters of the heart," I said, trying to sound sage.

"Oh, it's not a love thing with me and Bryce. To be honest, it's just recreational." I blinked, unused to women being this frank. But she went right on: "Things were pretty serious between him and Claire, but that was a long time ago. I think he's still kind of hung up on her." She stared into her coffee cup.

"You said Claire was 'one of the only reasons you stayed.' I don't understand."

She frowned, then said, "Oh. Sorry. Sometimes I forget everybody doesn't know me. I'm from Santa Monica, went to USC. About the time I graduated, Perry, my baby brother, had gotten himself into quite a bit of trouble with drugs. You know a place called the Ranch?"

Darnell had mentioned loading up a junkheap at a place called the Ranch. "Maybe. But there's probably a lot of places called that."

"It's a rehab center run by the local church groups. When Perry hit bottom, he got religion and checked himself into the place. My parents, especially my dad, completely flipped out, like he'd joined the Hare Krishnas or something."

"It's a cult of some sort?"

She shrugged. "No more than any other church. I graduated just about the time he joined up, so I figured I'd move out here for a while to be around if he needed anything."

I'd never even bothered to drop in on my sister. "You moved out here just to take care of your brother?"

She laughed. "Sounds pretty noble, doesn't it? No, way more complicated. I'd just finished my business undergrad, Dad was pressing me to apply to law school, become a bigshot corporate attorney like him. I just wanted an excuse to get out of everything for a little bit. I figured I'd be out here a couple weeks, a month maybe… After Santa Monica, at first this seemed like nowhere, but I got to like the place. My parents have a vacation cabin out at the River, so maybe the whole desert thing reminded me of good times as a kid." She looked over my head, past me. "And then I met Claire, and Mandy, and everybody…"

Her eyes were getting misty, and it was way too early in the day for that, so I asked, "Is Perry still in treatment, then?"

"No, not at all. He really got into the program at the Ranch. When his time was up he just stayed. He's part of the staff now. A little over the top, I admit—*I used to be all screwed up on drugs, but now I'm all screwed up on Jesus.*" She gave a lopsided smile; her mouth was large enough that it had a lot of side to lop. "I'm not bitching, really. At least I'm not going to get a phone call some morning telling me he's OD'ed. But he's not the guy I used to be able to joke around with."

"So what did Claire get you involved with?"

"Everything, I guess. She was the one who put me in touch with the *Wild Desert* gig—I'm actually their business manager. Just part-time, you know—not as big a deal as it sounds like. But part-time is good, lets me volunteer for things I care about. It was Claire who made me understand what your life is about isn't necessarily the same thing that pays the bills. She got me involved with the Clinic, the whole Eleusinian Circle thing, environmental activism, anti-drug stuff—"

"Anti-*drug?* I thought you and the Circle were *into* drugs."

"Those are sacraments, not drugs. Anti-drug is a little broad, though. Anti-speed, anti-coke, really—not that anybody around here can afford coke. Claire was seriously down on speed, and after seeing what it did to Perry, I was in full agreement." She glanced beyond me and said, "Shit. I'm going to be late for work." She jumped out of the chair and I stood.

"And where do I find Bryce?"

"Out back in the observatory. Just knock." She hugged me lightly and ran off to the bathroom.

Observatory? And in the daytime? But Jared must have had it wrong; he must have meant astronomer, not astrologer.

Professional astrologer, amateur astronomer, as it turned out. His homemade observatory, a big rotating dome atop a slump-block adobe wall, doubled as an office. Dimly lit; the walls were papered with sheets displaying arcane geometric figures.

"I told her it was a dangerous time," he declared, rapping the screen of his laptop with the backs of the fingers on his free hand, as if this were proof positive of his point. "So what did she do? Took off with some of her LA friends and went boating."

Bryce Childers was slender and blond, probably in his mid-thirties. He had improbably long hands that magnified the smallest gesture. "So, she went boating," I said. "So?"

"So that's when she had the accident." He pointed at the screen, where there were two concentric circles containing peculiar symbols. "Look here. Mars and the Sun conjunct and exactly opposing her natal Sun. Pluto on top of her natal sun, in opposition to Mars in the tenth. Moon opposition natal Neptune, bad for anything to do with water, Saturn smack in the middle of her ninth house at the time of the accident, as bad as you can get for travel—I could go on and on."

I believed his concluding statement even if I didn't understand any of the rest. "I wasn't aware she'd had an accident."

He considered me for a moment and gave a nasty bark of laughter. "She told me you guys weren't close. But I figured even you heard about her accident."

"Well I didn't. So if you'd care to enlighten me…"

"Don't think I will. I mean, if she didn't bother to tell you, maybe she didn't want you to know."

"Maybe it just wasn't important to her."

"Oh, it was important to her, alright. Changed everything. Changed her, mostly. She really just wasn't there anymore after that. Started thinking she was Mother fucking Teresa or something. Started this whole UWI thing." He gestured at what seemed like the world in general.

Why Claire or Kirsten put up with this guy was a mystery. I was tempted to leave, but decided to see if, since the accident was off limits, he was willing to be helpful at all. "And what exactly is 'this whole UWI thing?'"

"A dump, man. Going to be one of the biggest dumps in North America, if it's approved. Right over an aquifer. Biggest section of the dump centered over part of an underground river. One big rain, and the water rises right up into the garbage level. Carries out all the poisonous crap everybody in LA and Orange County have tossed in the trash, and sucks it right down into the desert water supply."

I asked for clarification. Was there a known underground channel there? Weren't there EPA regulations governing such things? Wasn't some of this BLM land, where the government would have final approval?

"Hey, it's Claire that turned me on to all this stuff. Started organizing. She seemed to have the facts."

"I didn't come across any of those facts at her house."

"They keep everything at Hapgood's place. That's sort of the headquarters. Or go to StopUniversalWaste dot org." He fell silent.

I waited a few beats and tried again. "I don't understand anything about astrology, you know."

"Nothing? Come on, everybody knows something about it."

"I've never really believed in it. No offense, but the idea there's only twelve kinds of people in the world doesn't seem to make much sense."

He flicked his hand in dismissal. "Newspaper astrology. Sun-sign nonsense. Positions of the planets never repeat precisely. Natal charts—birth charts—of even identical twins aren't usually the same. The rising sign, the ascendant changes about every four minutes in most latitudes, so unless they're born pop-pop, like coming out of a toaster, twins usually have different charts; sometimes significantly different."

"I don't even recognize the symbols. Well, most of them." I pointed at the symbol for male and female which sat side by side in the interior circle. "I know male and female."

"Mars and Venus. The circle with the pointy arrow off at an angle: that's a spear and shield, for the God of War. Most people think it has something to do with a penis. The female symbol, that's a hand-mirror, for the Goddess of Love and Beauty. I have no idea what most people think *that* is. Mars right on Venus—that's what Claire was all about, for sure."

I myself had carried around a vague notion that the Venus symbol had something to do with female plumbing—unlikely, now that I looked at it—but I saw no reason to explain this to Bryce. "Mars on Venus?" It seemed to be impossible to keep this guy on the matter at hand.

"Mars conjunct Venus in the fifth house, the house of romance. Strong, powerful sex drive. Incidentally trine to my own Venus. So we were pretty compatible physically. And until the accident, we were pretty compatible emotionally too." He seemed absorbed in staring at the chart for a moment. "Afterward, she was gone."

"So you stopped seeing each other?"

He chewed his lip. "We never really stopped seeing each other. Not completely."

"And how did Kirsten feel about that?"

"Doesn't know. I mean, it just never came up."

"Would she care?"

"Oh, yeah," he said, with emphatic nods of his head, "she'd care, believe me."

"Claire didn't have any qualms about it?"

"Claire was—you know, it's hard to explain what a different level she was on these last four years. The old rules didn't apply to her anymore. She was kinder, less angry; but she just didn't give a damn about a lot of things." He rubbed his forehead. "This isn't making sense. It's hard to explain."

"She became inconsistent?"

"Who isn't? No, she became…fearless. I tried to tell her she was going through a dangerous patch over the last few months. She'd say, 'I already know what it is to die, Bryce.' I tried to tell her something was coming after her."

"What? Who?"

"I don't know. I just know what the stars were saying. Mars and Venus conjunct in the sky, not just in her chart, opposing her Midheaven and Moon, passing right over Neptune: passion, religion, things hidden from sight…"

"If by passion you mean sex was a motivation for the murder, the police seem to think there wasn't any."

He lifted those long hands into the air, shoulder-width, as if showing the size of a fish. "Maybe there wasn't sexual assault. But whoever did it was getting off on it, I guarantee you. It's written all over the chart."

"You'll have to excuse me if I don't consider that to be particularly compelling." I was about ready to leave; there didn't seem to be more to be gained here.

He looked at me as if deciding whether I would fit into a coat he had in mind—a very focused consideration, but also impersonal. "Okay. When were you born?" I didn't respond immediately, so he said, "Your birthday?"

"September 14th, 1958."

He leaned forward and double-clicked the mouse, typed. "Birthplace Phoenix, like Claire?" I made an assenting sound. "Do you know the exact birth time?"

I did. 6:14 a.m. But some perverse side of me said, "Eight in the evening."

"Exactly eight? Not eight-oh-three or something?" I nodded, and he typed. A circle plastered with symbols appeared on the screen. He leaned forward to examine it, touched the screen at a few points with his lance of an index finger. He pushed back in his chair, folded his hands on his stomach and looked me in the eye. "Bullshit. Excuse me, let me rephrase that: I don't think you're being honest with me, Mr. Clayborne. Either this date is wrong, or this time is wrong."

I felt ridiculous. "Just testing…"

"This chart shows you have Aries rising. From the way you conduct yourself and from the general bearing of your head, that just couldn't be right. And from the fact you think it's interesting to lie to me about it, I'm guessing either Gemini or Virgo, because you think it's kind of tricky, or Scorpio rising, because you're just plain secretive. Would you like to give me the right info?"

"I'm sorry. The birthdate is right. The *time* was really six-fourteen a.m."

"Okay." He swiveled the chair back, tapped in the new numbers, and waited for the chart to pop up on the screen. "Uh-huh! What did I tell you? Virgo rising, which makes you a double Virgo."

"Which is supposed to mean what?"

"Really want to know?"

I nodded.

He smiled wide without showing any teeth. "Fine. Okay, Virgo's an Earth sign, very practical, but mutable Earth—almost a contradiction in terms. A ton of Virgo in your chart: Sun sign, rising sign, Venus, Mercury, Pluto. Very, very intellectual, but not a deep kind of intellect. A little facile, a little inclined to think otherwise. Libra moon in the first house, which makes you kind of wishy-washy. Mars in the ninth, house of travel and abstract thought, in Taurus: travel quite a bit, probably for practical reasons rather than vacation, kind of hard-headed about abstractions, if that makes any sense."

This was all very general, and my first reaction was to argue this applied to anyone. But it didn't, really.

He continued. "Virgo is kind of prissy and kind of organized. Especially the prissy part. Not the world's most passionate lovers, being the Virgin and all. You're probably the kind of person who takes a shower as soon as possible after getting laid. There's some passionate makeup in your chart—Venus conjunct Pluto—but it's blunted by being in Virgo and by being buried in the twelfth house. Sun, Venus, Mercury, Pluto—all in the twelfth house, the house of hidden things. Not only is a lot of you under the surface, a lot of you is probably hidden from yourself. Probably find you function best in institutional environments; the kind of person who works at a hospital or college; or you could be at a monastery—you'd make a pretty good monk, all in all."

This seemed to be an annoyingly accurate picture of me, as far as it went. I cleared my throat. "Aren't you supposed to make predictions? Tell me that I'll win the lottery or have a car accident or something?"

"Scoff if you like. I can't do a detailed reading just sitting here. But here's the main things going on. Saturn passing over your Midheaven: a career crisis, or a realization that your career isn't fulfilling. Jupiter passing over natal Uranus: weird, sudden changes, finding yourself thrust into new situations, possibly taking new risks; eleventh house, so this has to do with new friends or acquaintances. Mars squaring Venus, Mercury, and Pluto: strange new feelings, an urge to transform, strong and sudden sexual attractions. Plus the very definite possibility of physical danger."

"So I should be careful, or make sure I use the crosswalks, or what, exactly?"

"Way more complicated than that. Uranus, the agent of change, the Promethean force, is opposing your natal Pluto. This all amounts to an invitation to transformation, but it will only work out if you take risks you wouldn't normally consider."

"And suppose I don't accept this 'invitation.' What then?"

"Then the danger is you'll hurt yourself. When God knocks on the door, you answer it. Stay inside and you'll transform anyway, but not in a pleasant way." He smiled again, this time showing big, uneven teeth. "But, hey, you don't believe in any of this anyway, right?"

I stood up to leave. "Thanks for your time." He continued to stare at the screen.

Just before I closed the door behind me, he looked up and raised his voice. "Don't think too long, Mr. Clayborne. Choices will be upon you sooner than you expect."

Bryce Childers was an annoying jerk. And it was even more annoying that so much of his assessment of me seemed undeniably accurate.

12

It was after 11 a.m., but still too early to head to Ira's, so I stopped off at Water Canyon and made a few calls over a cup of coffee. Universal Waste—not the name I would have picked for a company—had two local numbers, the field station and the Morongo Valley office. I rang Morongo Valley, and after a little fencing around, managed to score a short appointment for midafternoon with Vance Whipple, UWI's project coordinator. I identified myself simply as "Walker—," letting them assume it was my surname—a UCSD professor interested in details of the project.

I checked for messages, and then rang Kirsten on her cell and retrieved a few more details about *Stop The Dump*, including the name and number of the organization's coordinator, Augustus Hapgood. My call to him went straight to the answering machine. I identified myself as Claire's brother, and asked him to call back and let me know if and when he could spare some time.

All of this took enough time I could drive to the minister's house without fear of arriving too early.

Ira's house was a boxy little affair which must have been built around the time I was born. It had three small bedrooms, one of them given over to office space for the church. Ira and his wife Barb, as I was quickly invited to call her, were only a few years older than I, but it seemed like they might have been my grandparents. Their house echoed the feeling as well: these might have been the original furnishings.

The couches and chairs had doilies, the curtains had ruffles, and the hardwood floors were interrupted by multicolored ovals of braided rag rugs.

Ira had divested himself of his coat and collar, but still wore his pintuck-pleated black shirt. What remained of his hair rose only a little higher than his ears, making him look tonsured. Barb brought us coffee and then went back to the kitchen. "We live rather simply," Ira said, "but we love it out here. I had a—a falling out with the Presbyterian Church several years ago. I searched and searched for another position, another home, and found a group in Riverside that wanted to expand their ministry. At first I thought that the Lord was making me do penance by coming out here. Now I see that it's exactly where I need to be. It's not a wealthy church, but I've never felt so blessed in all my life."

"And what was Claire's connection with the church? When did she join?"

He sipped his coffee, set the cup back down. "To be honest about it, Claire wasn't a member of our congregation in the classic sense. More like a guardian angel. She helped people who needed help, sometimes steered people to us when they were adrift. Every so often she might attend a service, but it was a rare thing indeed. But she was one of the finest Christians among us."

"I'm a little puzzled by her affiliation with a church, frankly. I mean, no offense, but when Claire was younger she was vehemently anti-Christian, anti-Church."

"It's my word, not hers. I doubt that Claire would ever have described herself as a Christian. But Jesus would have recognized her as one."

"Still, it's hard for me to picture her even entering a church without being dragged in."

"I think a lot of things changed for her after the accident."

Ah. "That's the second time today someone has mentioned her accident. All I know is that it had something to do with boating."

"Oh." He considered for a moment. "There's no reason you shouldn't be told the story. It's no secret. About four years ago, now, I guess Claire was still pretty wild—at least by my admittedly unworldly standards. She ran with a crowd that came out from the coast on weekends to party. Sometimes they'd climb rocks or have bonfire parties out in the desert. Sometimes they'd head for the River."

Barb stepped into the room, wiping her hands on her apron. I couldn't remember the last time I had seen someone in an apron—with the exception of the big *Come and Get It* apron the department chair wore at his backyard barbecues. "Lunch is on the table if you two are ready."

The kitchen boasted an avocado-colored refrigerator and Harvest-Gold tiles around the sink. The table was topped in formica, and stood on tapered steel legs; the chairs had padded plastic seats with an aggressive floral design.

Prayer was inevitable. I went ahead and closed my eyes. Ira intoned, "Thank you Lord, for this thy bounty…" I let my mind drift away. I remembered Claire as a giggling baby, Claire bedeviling me during Church in hopes of making me laugh. Claire as angry young woman. Claire dead on the gurney. Today I was being told about a Claire I never knew existed, a Claire that didn't really sound like the sister I knew. Thought I knew. But, then, who would have seen the angry teen hiding inside the giggling baby? Maybe people evolve into something unexpected, the way insects go through a larval stage and then acquire a whole new shape.

"…and accept our prayers for Darnell and Rachel and her sister, who are coping with the trials of illness—may that burden be lifted soon. Finally, we ask that You comfort our new friend Walker in this time of sadness, and be with him and watch over him in the days to come. All this we pray in the Name of our Lord and Savior, Jesus Christ…Amen."

The food was good, but like Ira and Barb and their house, seemed to have slipped through some time warp. Fried chicken, peas, mashed potatoes with gravy, biscuits with honeybutter. We ate steadily for a few minutes, pausing only to compliment Barb.

"Walker hadn't heard about Claire's boating accident," Ira said to Barb. He turned to address me. "There isn't that much to tell, as I understand it. She and five of her friends were on a boat out at Lake Havasu. Some fool in one of those cigarette speedboats lost control and plowed right into them. Cut their boat right in half. The speedboat flew through the air like it went over one of those ski ramps, and then blew up before it hit the water. Somebody had video of the whole thing, so it was on all the news stations for a while. Surprised you didn't see it."

I vaguely remembered some sort of accident at Havasu, ending with a boat explosion. "Maybe I did. I remember some footage that they kept running with a ball of fire falling down to the lake." Had I glanced at a TV and seen my sister almost die?

"That was probably it. Two of Claire's friends were killed immediately by the force of the collision. The rest of the group was thrown into the water, unconscious."

Claire had almost died and I had heard nothing about it. I knew this was superstitious thinking, but… I thought back on what Ettenmoor had recommended to me, and decided to make an effort. Okay. I admitted it. It *felt* like I should have sensed it.

Ira polished chicken grease from his fingertips with a paper napkin. "By the time rescue boats got there, all four of them had drowned. But they worked on Claire, out there on the lake, and they brought her back. Her heart had stopped, they don't know for how long. But she'd been dead."

Barb finally spoke up. "She made no secret it changed her. Course, we hadn't met her before the accident. She started doing all kinds of volunteer work. Seemed like she was just everywhere, and we got to know her."

Outside there was the sound of a loud car, or maybe a truck, pulling into the drive. Ira and Barb exchanged glances; it didn't appear anyone was expected. The kitchen door opened and Darnell looked in. "Sorry," he said, and immediately dropped his gaze, realizing he had interrupted us.

"No, no," Barb said, "pull up a chair and I'll fix you a plate. Still plenty left, and I think we've all had sufficient."

"Just came 'cause I need the storeroom key. For the hitch. "

"Well don't just stand in the doorway," Ira said. "Come on in while I fetch the keys." Ira left the room, and Darnell stepped inside and closed the door.

He stood by the table, ill at ease, and shook his head when Barb offered a chair. Not quite looking at me, he finally said, "Your sister did a lot for me and Rachel. Sorry I won't have the chance to pay her back as she deserves."

Barb and I both mumbled things that suggested we were sure Claire didn't feel she was owed anything, but Darnell just stared at the bowl of peas. He seemed to have nothing else to say, and remained silent as Ira entered and handed him a ring of keys. "Get these back to me tonight if you can," Ira said, "the office is always losing the extra set."

Darnell took the keys, nodded, and went out the kitchen door. He favored us all with another bob of his head as he began to pull the door closed, but he bent down just a little to look at something on the back step. He moved back a step and kicked the molding at the base of the door—a sharp, sudden impact from the toe of his workboot.

We all stared. Darnell came in, snatched a paper napkin from the kitchen counter, and used it to pick up something from the back step. "Black widder," he said. He held the napkin open and I could see the crumpled, glossy shape. A fragment of the red hourglass winked from the blackness like a traffic reflector.

He folded the napkin double, then doubled it again and again before throwing it in the trash. "It's the females as has all the poison," he said. "The males is most of'em just little brownish things." He stepped outside and this time closed the door.

We were silent for several breaths.

"So he knew Claire well?" I asked. "Would it be worthwhile talking to him?"

Ira chuckled. "If you had a very specific question, maybe. But Darnell isn't much for conversation. What you heard just now probably used up his allotment for the rest of the day."

"Maybe the rest of the week," Barb said.

"Some of our congregation can't afford medical care," Ira continued. "Claire arranged it through the clinic where she volunteered. She also made herself available for counseling for our members—especially if they were having trouble with drugs or alcohol. That's how she got to know Darnell and Rachel so well. Darnell had a drinking problem that just wouldn't go away, and their marriage was barely hanging together. Claire spent a lot of time with the two of them, and Darnell actually cleaned up." I reflected on Darnell's pinched, lined face; I now saw it was weathered not just by the elements, but by years of booze as well. "Now that was a miracle, and all glory be to God, but I don't see how it would have happened without Claire. Rachel just loved your sister. You'll have to meet her when she gets back in town."

The battery of our conversation seemed to have run down. We sat quiet until I asked, "Do you have any idea who might have wanted to murder Claire, or why?"

Barb started to protest no one could have a reason to hurt Claire, but Ira said, "Does murder ever make much sense?" He shook his head, and continued. "Claire certainly might have put herself in harm's way: all her anti-drug activism, all the people that she ran into doing her counseling out at the prison..."

"Is there any possibility that one of the religious groups in the area might have done it?" I described the incident with the Shackles-Torn-Asunder crowd when they had accused Mandy of being a witch.

Ira expressed shock at the very idea they could have anything to do with Claire's death. "Why, some of them loved her as much as we do."

"Then why call her friends 'witches?'"

He sighed. "People get overzealous when they first convert. Despite what our Savior warned, folks are all too willing to hurl that first stone. But the stones are just words, not real rocks."

"Perhaps. But the Shackles folks scared me."

"They're harmless. Drop by one of their services and you'll see. Unorthodox—I still can't picture Jesus as savoring rock music—but not dangerous. They meet every evening at seven, right after my own service. You'd be more than welcome at either."

"I'd be afraid to run into Billy and his friends."

Barb laughed. "Billy's not as scary as he looks. But if that's worrying you, go tonight. Tuesdays and Thursdays he runs evening Bible study down in Indio."

I thanked them for the meal, and they urged me to return anytime, and to drop through the church for services. One last question occurred to me. "So why did Claire decide to—to devote herself to a Christian organization?"

Ira put his big hands down on either side of his plate. "I have to confess that she didn't, not really. Claire worked with anyone. If she decided that someone would be better off at an ashram than at our church, that's where she'd steer them."

Barb looked a little sad. "I'm not sure that Claire ever formally accepted Christ into her life. There's some that say that the gates of heaven are barred to her because of it. I believed that once. But I know different now."

Ira chuckled, but with a fond expression on his face. "I know in my heart that Claire's with Jesus now. But I bet she's real surprised about it. She was a big believer in reincarnation." He shook his head. "Funny thing is, she gave me references to some of the writings of the early Church fathers—ones we didn't read back in seminary—and guess what? A lot of them believed in reincarnation too."

13

When my cell phone rang I was trying to pass a dented panel truck on the steep road down from Yucca Valley to Morongo. My hand patted all over the passenger seat before finding it, and I barely got it before the fatal fourth ring that would have rolled it to voicemail. It was Professor Sam Drexler returning my call from Mammoth, where he was spending a week skiing. He informed me it was cold there—hardly surprising to me, but then, he was in the Econ department—and asked what the hell I was doing interrupting his Christmas break. I asked what he knew about Universal Waste.

"UWI? Not much. Publicly traded, so you can get lots of info from SEC filings and annual reports, but I don't have those with me."

"I meant more generally—big, small…what are they like?"

"Oh. A little easier. They're big, only in the waste business as far as I know, but I don't follow them closely. Why? You got a hot tip?"

"No. Just trying to find out something about a project they're involved in out in the desert."

Sam thought for a while, then said, "I can put you in touch with somebody who tracks them pretty closely. Stock analyst at Dover Securities. Former student of mine…take a look in the old DayTimer… Got a pen?"

"I'm driving. Wait till I can pull over."

"Isn't that illegal yet? Talking and driving?"

I ignored the question, pulled off the roadway at the bottom of the hill, and found pen and notepad. "Okay."

He recited a name and number, New York by the area code. "That's his home phone. Call him there and drop my name."

"I don't want to bother him at home…"

"Trust me, you can't get ahold of him at the office. He won't mind, these guys all pride themselves on working 24/7 these days anyway. Plus he owes me."

"Thanks, Sam. Now I owe you, too."

"Want to repay me?"

"Sure. What do you need?"

"I'd really like to ask your ex out, but I'm afraid you'd get pissed at me."

I laughed. "You're welcome to do whatever you like with Elizabeth…but I should probably let you know, the last I heard she had just gotten married again."

"Oh." Surrounded by the beautiful apres-ski crowd, and he's disappointed Liz is off the market. "Then can I ask you something?"

"Sure."

"Was she as hot as she looks?"

"No." Not with me, at any rate.

I called the number he gave me, got the stock analyst's answering machine, dropped Sam's name, and left my numbers.

UWI's offices in Morongo Valley were modest—unsurprising, since there aren't any plush offices in the High Desert—but Vance Whipple was dressed for the Boston business district. Silver hair, custom suit, expensive manicure: it clashed with the wall full of pictures showing him in hardhat and overalls at construction sites around the world. He seated me on a low couch, and took a seat in one of the nearby chairs rather than sitting back behind his desk. "What can I help you with, Mr. Walker?"

"Actually, Walker is the first name—there must have been some confusion in getting the message to you. Walker Clayborne. My sister was Claire Clayborne." I watched him carefully. Something changed in his eyes.

"Ah. My condolences. We only recently…heard. But surely you're not here on her behalf?"

"In a way I am. I had a rather upsetting interaction with some of your lawyers the other day, and I wanted to find out what some of the facts were."

He nodded, his face suitably sympathetic. "I wish I knew all the facts. It's no secret that your sister was vehemently—I almost might say violently—opposed to our project. And when some of our field-office buildings were burned down—clearly arson according to the fire marshal, by the way, no question of an accidental fire—at any rate, when some of our facilities were destroyed, I'm afraid that certain of our legal staff got a little overzealous."

"That seems like a mild description. They were making all manner of threats out at Claire's house the other day."

He crossed his legs, draping one over the other so that his ankles nearly touched. "I can only offer my sincere apology; they misread the situation, and greatly exceeded their mandates. But I can assure you that all proceedings against your sister and against her estate have been dropped, permanently, at my direction. I'm sure this must be an impossibly difficult time for you, and if there's anything we can help with…"

I gave a not-entirely-untrue explanation of how I was tidying up her affairs, and trying to find out "on behalf of the family" what her charitable pursuits had been. I suggested that her estate, such as it was, might be contributed to charity…which was not a bad idea, now that I'd thought of it.

Whipple gave me a sardonic look. "To be completely candid, I hope the money won't go to *Stop The Dump*. Or have you already made up your mind on the subject?"

"Not at all. In fact, I don't know anything about your project, or about the organization opposing it. That's why I'm here."

"You haven't come here with an agenda, then?" I shook my head. He hummed to himself for a moment as he thought. "In all honesty, your sister was a very difficult woman." He watched me.

"I know that as much as anyone."

"Just so. In any case, your sister was very vocal—and, as I said, almost violent at times—in her opposition to the project. But her grounds seemed to be more emotional than scientific." This matched with my impression of Claire, so it was easy to nod in affirmation. "How much geology do you know?"

"I have a PhD in the subject."

His eyes registered surprise, but he dealt with it smoothly. "So much the better. Too bad your sister didn't seek your advice before making wild prophecies about the dangers of this project."

He led me over to a small conference table, and ran through what was clearly a well-rehearsed overview of the project. It was indeed enormous: if they went to a possible second phase of the plan, it would be the largest single landfill site in the world. Massive quantities of earth would be excavated and dumped in a canyon, with a packed-earth dam to contain it. Complex drainage had been added, and the monster hole in the ground would be packed with bentonite and other clays so that during rain the base layer would swell and prevent any percolation of contaminated water down into the soil. It would be a huge scar on the landscape during the twenty years it was expected to operate—even UWI was willing to admit that much—but they had taken every precaution…

In fact, it sounded like a fairly well-planned operation. "So what is the basis of *Stop the Dump*'s opposition?"

"Other than just rhetoric? They claim we're building directly over an underground river."

"And are you?"

"No. We've done all the test drilling required to satisfy both BLM and EPA, and there's no sign of anything under our site. There is a major hydrologic channel off to the east of our site—that's well-documented—but there's a solid granitic dike walling off our site from that channel."

"Have you run seismics?"

"No need. In this kind of situation, you'd only run seismics to avoid having to do the real drilling. But we spent the cash to get core samples on a tight enough spacing that there's really no doubt.

So I submit to you, sir, that the opponents to this project are basing everything on emotion, and nothing on the facts."

I shrugged. "Claire was no geologist, I can assure you of that."

He favored me with a patrician smile. "That she was not. And as I tried to explain to her, even if there was an underground channel—and there isn't—but even if there was, for the water level in the channel to rise to the point where it would breach the baselayer is so improbable as to stagger the imagination. Based on the channel to the east, our estimates show it would require an enormous rainfall, both here in the desert and up on San Gorgonio. The chances of such a deluge in the next hundred-fifty years are about one in two thousand down here, about one in a thousand up in San Gorgonio. You can figure it as well as I can: the probability of both of these things happening at once is their product—about one in ten million." He held up his hands. Case closed.

I started to nod, but then stopped. "But that assumes the probabilities are independent."

"Seems like a reasonable assumption to me."

"Does it? Does it really? That's saying the level of rainfall here is independent of the level of rainfall just thirty miles away."

"Well—"

"But that's absurd! I can't imagine anything more likely to be correlated than rainfall on a mountain and rainfall directly in its rain shadow—"

He waved a hand to slow me. "Whatever you think about the probabilities, that was just an *example*. There isn't any channel underneath our site. Look…" He stood, pulled over a geology report that measured two by three feet. He thumped it open, turned the pages, searching. He came to the page he wanted and shoved it over in front of me. It was an aerial photo with crosshatchings and drill-log numbers at every intersection of the chessboard. The outline of the landfill margins was drawn on the page.

The drilling plan looked very complete to me, and I said as much.

"Thank God for someone who understands science," he said. "You can't believe how many times I've had to run through this before. I might as well have been talking to the wall."

I thanked him and assured him I was satisfied. It reminded me of Claire all too much, charging ahead with something once she had made up her mind, the facts be damned. She was, to use Bryce's refined phrase, no Mother fucking Teresa.

When I got back to Claire's, her message light was blinking. Augustus Hapgood had returned my call, and was willing to meet with me any time. "I'm retired, so you can find me pretty much whenever you want me…" He left his number, ignoring the fact that I obviously already had it, and gave directions to his house.

I decided it was a waste of time to talk to a crackpot who couldn't accept a decent drilling diagram.

At the New Year's Eve party, Chad had suggested Claire's involvement with the prison and with anti-drug meetings might have had something to do with her murder. Others had disagreed, but what Ira had said today seemed to support Chad's point of view.

I called Mandy on her cell. She sounded pleased to hear from me. I asked what she knew about Claire's anti-speed campaign.

"Not much. I stayed out of most of Claire's activist stuff. You should talk more to Kirsten."

"You remember the other night, when the car almost ran us down on the road?"

"Gosh, no, what car? You know, Walker, I have this tendency to remember almost dying. What about it?"

"Do you think it had something to do with all this? Or was it just a freak occurrence?"

"I don't think there's any evidence one way or the other." She paused. "Are you asking me how I *feel* about it?"

"I guess I am."

"Confused. Remember those magic eightballs? *Answer is Cloudy, Ask Again Later*."

"Some oracle you are."

"If I recall, it was customary at Delphi to bring rich offerings in exchange for an augury. Rather than just being snide."

"How about dinner?"

"Are you asking me on a date?"

"Not exactly. That is, I was planning on going to get something to eat, and—"

"I'd love to, but I can't, at least not tonight. And tomorrow I'm subbing for Rhonda at the Free Clinic…but if you're up for it, you could come by there kind of late, and we could get something to eat after we close up…"

We agreed on this, and signed off. It was a curious thing. None of Claire's circle of friends had much in common with me, and I didn't have much respect for their worldviews. Yet they had made me feel welcome, and I felt comfortable around them—or, at least more comfortable than I was around other people. I was beginning to develop an affection for all of them. Well, all of them except Bryce.

If Claire's involvement in the local drug scene was a factor in her murder, then that seemed to rule out the relevance of the near hit-and-run the other night: why would they be after Mandy or me? On the other hand, if they were after witches, Mandy was a perfect candidate. Ira had dismissed the idea that local Christian groups might have had anything to do with it, but it looked like a leading candidate to me.

I was trying to decide where to go for dinner when my cell phone rang. It was recharging on the kitchen counter, so I had to dance around the couch and then literally leap for it. "Hello?" I panted.

"Umm—Jeff Lukeman for Dr. Clayborne? Dover Securities? This a bad time?"

"No, not at all…I just had to make a dash for the phone."

Jeff Lukeman was the real article. Slightly hyper, overstuffed with jargon, he knew more about UWI than I wanted to hear. He also seemed to worship Sam Drexler's intellect, which gave me a surprising angle on my old acquaintance—I'd always thought Sam was an intellectual lightweight.

It took a while to get him to focus, and longer to get him to give generalizations. If I'd wanted their debt-equity ratio, or the history of their stock splits, I could have had those in the first three minutes, but it took longer to get the big picture. UWI was based in New Jersey but had branches in more than sixty countries. They operated everything to do with waste, not just dumps: high-tech incinerators, hazmat facilities, sea dumping, recycling, lube oils, batteries… "What's your bottom-line question here, Dr. Clayborne? I'm not going to go telling tales. Are you thinking of taking a position, or going short, or selling to them…?"

"I'm just interested in a project they have out in the California desert."

"The one in San Bernardino County? North of Palm Springs?"

Technically, yes, but his geography would have made the Palm Springs city fathers wince. "That's the one."

"One of their linchpin projects. They think the whole future of waste in the US is tied up with huge central disposal sites, rather than a million little dumps everywhere. Numbers make sense, too. What's your position in it?"

"I'm sort of investigating some claims an environmental group has made about the project."

There was a long pause. "Whoa. Hey, are you on the wrong side of that equation. These guys are serious money, heavy money. They usually get what they want."

"I'm just looking at the facts of the matter, not taking a position."

"Dr. Clayborne. Look. Don't fuck with these guys."

"Are you saying they use physical violence?"

"I won't go that far. Maybe. But, man, *legal* violence can be just as nasty."

I thanked Jeff, promised to pass on an effusive report to Sam, and hit the end call button.

I dialed Augustus Hapgood at Stop The Dump and set up an appointment for the next morning.

14

The evening service at Shackles Torn Asunder—in the donated space at Church of the Rock—was already well underway by the time I arrived. Despite the chill in the night air, the door was left standing open so that what I guessed was an attempt to render "Spirit in the Sky" could blare out onto the sidewalk. Ira was right that there wouldn't be a problem with dropping in. The lights were turned low, and with the massed singing and handclapping, the cast of *Star Wars* could have walked in without getting a second glance. There was no need for chairs at this service: the whole crowd was on its feet.

I stepped in, leaned against one of the windows just past the door, and let it wash over me. Well, "wash" is a poor term, since it implies a cleansing. There is a belief among some critics that enthusiasm is enough to lift even poor music to a kind of folk art. They're wrong.

I waited through another song—one I didn't recognize—and was about to take my leave, concurring with Ira that Shackles was harmless, when a man grabbed a microphone and said, "Do you feel the spirit tonight?"

Cries of, "Yes!" and, "Praise the Lord!"

"Tonight we have something special! We have a guest, Reverend Gorston, the founder and spiritual leader of God's Law!" He waited for the applause to lessen, and then said, "The reverend is going to show us his latest educational film—made with only Christian dollars, not one penny from Hollywood!—and then will answer questions."

The lights went all the way down in a cyclone of cheers and applause. A projector in the middle of the room started up, focused on a sheet tacked up behind the pulpit. There was a general shifting in the room as people moved to where they could see the screen; with most people standing, this necessitated the shorter moving toward the front.

What followed over the next twenty minutes would have been hilarious were it not so earnestly meant—and were it not absorbed raptly by the audience. It began with music from a forties horror movie, and a cheesy special effect where Satan seemed to burst through the screen.

It was all done with voice-over narration: "Did you ever wonder why crime is on the increase? Why families fall apart? Why addiction is soaring? Why our leaders are corrupt and deceptive?" The screen filled with the words—also read out loudly by the narrator for the benefit of the illiterate—*A NATION CANNOT TURN ITS BACK ON GOD WITHOUT TURNING ITS FACE TOWARD SATAN!!!*

Few of the shots seemed to have been composed for the film; many seemed to be cut from old movies, and there was no matching of the color tone or photographic quality. But it reviewed its concept of the problems in America: happy, healthy looking school children in the beginning, but then cuts to shots of people exchanging gunfire with the police, of men dancing with one another, of feminists marching, of angry black men yelling, and, as a trump card, planes crashing into the World Trade Center.

Then it rolled back to look deeper at the causes of the problems, and there seemed to be only one: Satanists. Women casting spells in suburban bedrooms, then a scene of school children, then a scene of homosexuals in the park. Carefree young girls buying books on crystals or the Tarot, and, in the next scene, the same girls, debauched and sporting inverted pentagrams on their foreheads. Cut to a photo of Charles Manson, a photo of Anthony Hopkins as Hannibal Lecter, and, weirdly, a poster of Freddy Kruger from *Nightmare on Elm Street.* Fictional characters and real people were wrapped together on the screen as if they were somehow equivalent. In the background, Enya's demanding "Cursum Perficio."

Then the voiceover narration launched into a frothing rant atop a series of grainy photos that seemed to have no relation to the text. "FACT: Arrests of devil worshippers have risen more than 700 percent in the last decade alone!…FACT: The Federal Reserve Board controls the ENTIRE MONEY SUPPLY in America!…FACT: Satanists now occupy over fifty key positions in the FBI—and that is why child pornography continues to spread!…FACT: While in office, Bill and Hilary Clinton invited more than TWO HUNDRED practicing witches to have dinner at the White House!…" In the background— what else?—Karl Orff's ubiquitous "Carmina Burana." At least that was in the public domain.

It was crudely done, utterly illogical, and shameless. And because of this strange hybrid, something like a supermarket tabloid in MTV music-video format, it seemed to mesmerize the audience. When it ended with the questions, "ISN'T IT TIME WE TURNED BACK TO THE LORD? ISN'T IT TIME THAT WE ACCEPTED… *GOD'S LAW*?" the room was silent except for the blaring music.

There was wild applause as the lights came up.

Reverend Gorston himself took the microphone and stood behind the podium, waving to the claps of the crowd. He was slender but with a pronounced paunch, and wore horn-rimmed glasses that made his eyes look huge. Three young men in black T-shirts lined up behind him, arms crossed over their chests and chins upthrust, like bouncers in front of a crowded bar.

"Do you wonder what has gone wrong?" I half expected shouts back from the audience like a Baptist revival, but not a word was spoken. "America is a great country. The greatest there ever was. The finest constitution, the wisest system of laws. Yet it has all gone astray. And why is that?" He searched the room for an answer. "Because the laws of man, even the finest laws of man, are still imperfect! Can man perfect himself?" He searched the room again. "He cannot! Yet we have the tools, we have the recipe, right in the word of God! He has given us the laws! And if the laws of man say that homosexuals have the right to teach our children, if the laws of man say that witches can do the devil's work without hindrance of law, if the laws of man say that children may dishonor their parents, that wives may disobey their husbands, then I say to you, I say to you that the laws of man must be overturned and replaced with the laws that God commanded us to obey!"

Loud applause and cheering. Several of the Shackles musicians I'd seen that morning were clapping with their hands raised over their heads; off to my right I saw Darnell, clapping and almost, but not quite, showing a smile.

A few workers passed through the crowd handing out flyers. I took one of them and slipped out into the cool darkness before I had to hear any more. Under the streetlight, I read: *God's Army—GOD'S LAW. Local Chapterhouse, 2420 Hoot Owl Lane, Landers. All CHRISTIANS Welcome. Chapel. Reading Room.*

When I arrived at Claire's, there was another white rose on the doormat.

15

Two white roses in Claire's crystal vase as I had my morning coffee.

I called Eagle Mountain Prison and explained to the operator I wanted to speak to whoever had worked most closely with Claire Clayborne. After spending ten minutes on hold, I had been transferred to a female administrator who demanded to know precisely what information I wanted and why. Was I connected with the official investigation into her death? No, but I was her closest living relative… I was given to understand it was a strict policy to avoid giving out information about employees or former employees, and that in any case such information would never be divulged over the phone.

Did that mean, then, they might be willing to discuss things with me on an informal basis if I came in person with suitable identification? It did not. In fact, the administrator did not intend to discuss this with me any further. Well, then, could I speak to her supervisor? Certainly. Another interminable wait, and a man came on the line, already in confrontational mode. He didn't intend to argue the matter with me. No he couldn't give me the names of any of her co-workers. If I didn't like it, then I could show cause to a judge and get a court order for the release of records. There were established procedures for such things, and he had no intention of making special exceptions for anyone, particularly not someone who was so rude: and, to my utter astonishment, he hung up on me.

I'm not used to being treated dismissively. I was stupefied, then angry. I would do something about this; I would call someone, contact my state assemblyperson or congressional representative…if I could figure out who they were.

I was obscurely depressed. It was the third of January. Just a little over two weeks ago I had graded my last final exam of the fall quarter, and my bags had been packed for the first stop on my leisurely sabbatical, half fieldwork, and half writing. I knew who I was and where I was going, and my only real worry in the world was that the revisions to my textbook were a little overdue.

At odd moments over the last week I had the feeling you get when you almost trip going down the stairs: something you can hide from those around you, but something which clenches at the base of your belly. I longed for my old routine, but I couldn't get there from here: the previous evening I had sat down to work on the textbook and achieved nothing. Even in a textbook each sentence ought to flow on into the next, but my words lay there dead and flat on the page, as if the laser printer had squashed them when they passed through the rollers.

I was all alone out here. I could blow my brains out and it might be weeks before anyone discovered the body. And if someone did find the body quickly, it would probably be Mandy or Bolles. No one from the university had even called, although I had left Claire's number on my office voicemail. I realized that in truth I had been alone back at the school too: I was surrounded by people, but they interacted with my role, not with me. As long as I published my papers, ran my classes, and showed up for at least some of my committee work, the rest of my life could have reeled out of control without anyone noticing; I could have spent my evenings tied to a bed by a dominatrix or shooting heroin or running up huge gambling debts and no one would pay attention until the day I didn't show up at the expected time.

No one really cared about me. I had believed that Claire isolated herself, working at part-time jobs out here in the desert; but at least there were people who missed her. I had believed I was approaching the apex of an important career—but if I were suddenly gone, the main effect on those who were part of my day-to-day life would be to open up my seat in the Ashford endowed chair. Too bad about Walker, isn't it… Say, do you think they'll go outside to fill the vacancy, or will we have the inside track?

I hate whining, and I hated myself for whining now, and I hated the fact that I wasn't willing to let myself whine without hating myself for it.

I almost rose from the couch to start packing my bags. There was nothing to keep me here, really.

But there was nothing to go back to, either, and if I felt like this when I was back in my familiar surroundings I was afraid it would destroy me.

The phone rang and I jumped. Even though it was within my reach, I didn't answer it until the third ring.

It was Kirsten, just calling to check on me.

"I was planning on calling you," I said. "I'd like to talk to you a little more about the drug trade in the area, and what Claire and you had to do with it."

"You can drop by *Wild Desert*—that's where I am right now."

"Actually, I have an appointment in about forty-five minutes."

"Can you come out to Hidden Valley after lunch? I do a guided tour out there during the Friday lunch hour—well, the lunch two-hour, on Fridays—for the local natural history society."

"Sure. Sounds great."

"Inside the Valley sort of oneish, then. Come late. I don't want to talk in front of you about things you know more about than I do."

We chatted for a while longer; I told her about the white roses, and she thought I should try and figure out who was leaving them and why as soon as possible: "'Honor the symbolic and learn from the random,' she always said. This seems like both."

"Who always said?" I asked.

"Claire."

"I don't recall her ever saying that around me. Was it a quote, or something she made up?"

"I don't know. A lot of the things she said sounded like she was quoting." She paused, and then said, "Walker…we all appreciate your staying out here during all of this. We know you don't need to be here, and, well: thank you."

I was surprised at the tightness in my throat as we rang off.

I spied Claire's little book of quotes where I had left it on her desk. I picked it up and flipped it open haphazardly: honor the random.

If you shut your doors to all errors, the truth will be shut out as well.

—Rabindranath Tagore

Stray Birds

I slipped the little book into my shirt pocket.

As I pulled the Jeep back down the drive, I stopped on impulse and went up to the door of the house out front.

Mrs. Givens answered the door, blinking against the morning light. In the relative dimness behind her were the sounds of morning television and spoons clinking on cereal bowls. "Oh, Professor Clayborne," she said, "come on in."

I shook my head and smiled my best smile. "No, I'm just on my way somewhere. But I wondered: Have you heard any cars drive up to the cottage in the last couple of days, during times that I was away?"

"Well, I don't rightly know. I don't keep track of your coming and going. Though that Jeep you got sounds like a Mack truck."

"Mom! Hey, *Mom*, he's still doin' it!"

"I am not! And she put jam in her cereal again!"

"Hey!" Mrs. Givens snapped her head back toward the kitchen. "You just straighten up and fly right or I'll give you what for!" She turned back and in a perfectly calm tone said, "No, don't think any cars been coming through. But in the late afternoon yesterday, almost sundown, there were a motorsickle."

I pounced on this. "Did you see it? Was it a big motorcycle, the kind that bikers ride?"

"You mean one a them Harvey Davidsons? Nope, this was one of them little things as sounds like a lawnmower. You know, the kind they ride off the street, tearing up the desert and everything."

"You mean a dirtbike?"

"Yeah, I guess so. I ain't no motorsickle enthusiast." This word seemed to please her so much she repeated it. "No motorsickle *enthusiast*."

"Would you do me a favor? If you hear it again, would you try and get a look at it, and see who's on it?"

"Sure." Her eyes narrowed. "Say, is somebody bothering you back there? Ain't something you should be telling us about, is there? I mean, I got the kids to consider."

"As far as I know, there's no problem. But someone has been leaving some rather mysterious presents, and I'd like to try and get to the bottom of it."

"Ah." She nodded her head and looked wise. "A secret admirer. Must be quite some gal, if she goes zooming around on a motorsickle." She winked. "I'll let you know if she's pretty."

There are thousands—well, alright, dozens—of people like Augustus "call me Gus" Hapgood in the desert. They wear the label of "desert rat" like a badge, and spend most of their energy trying to seem eccentric and picturesque. "Yep, ole Gus—he's a real character, that one…" After you've met a few, they get tiresome.

His potbelly hung out over a beltbuckle the size of a hubcap, and he had the requisite amount of turquoise and silver, as if New Mexico were just over the hill rather than 800 miles distant. A white goatee and sunburnt bald head completed the picture.

After the usual condolences about Claire, he started to tell me about how long he'd been in the desert, his years running a small local paper, but I pushed him, none too gently, back to Universal Waste: "What reason did you have to think that Universal's hydrological assessment was wrong? They did a full-up drilling program."

"You're lucky this stuff was all over at the old shop; Universal seized all the files at my house as evidence for some damn thing." Hapgood stood up and rolled a map out on his desk, weighting it down at the corner with what looked liked old assay samples. "Looky here." It was the same aerial photo Whipple had shown me in his office, but it had a meandering pair of red-ink lines drawn across it, trending from the southeast up toward the northwest. "That's where our hydrological surveyor reckons there's a major water channel. Now look at this." He rolled out a sheet of transparent acetate on top of the map, and I stood for a better look. The grid he showed was the same as I had seen at UWI. The crosshatchings were at an oblique angle to the property lines of the site. Not a single point on the grid fell inside the channel. "Obvious why they did their grid at this funny angle, isn't it?"

"The protocols just demand a certain coverage and frequency," I said. "Nothing says you have to lay your grid out in any particular direction."

"Uh-huh." He rotated the sheet so the lines of the grid were aligned with the property boundaries. Five drill centers fell inside the channel. "And furthermore..." He slapped down a long ruler and aligned its edge against two distant points on the grid. In between, one of the other points were slightly off center, the connecting crosshatch lines making a skinny triangle against the ruler.

"You don't have to drill a perfect grid... I mean, there's allowance for spacing based on physical obstacles, or impossible slopes..."

"In the middle of a perfectly flat playa?"

"And how did you get permission to do your hydrological survey?"

"They had to let us. We're legal intervenors in the EPA hearings." Hapgood sat down behind his desk and let the acetate curl itself closed. "Tell you what else," he said, "they drilled a bunch of holes, and then they called the driller back and did a bunch more. Cause they changed the grid."

"You know that for a fact? That they changed the grid?"

"No. But I know they drilled a full set, and then drilled a bunch more after they analyzed the samples." He consulted an address book and scribbled out some information. He handed me the piece of notepaper. "There's the guy at the company that did the drilling. The other's our hydrological consultant. See for yourself."

Sitting in my car without starting the engine, I left a message for Jack Priestly, Hapgood's hydrology consultant, to call me. I also left messages at home and at the office for Alfie Prentiss, one of my colleagues back in the Earth Sciences department.

To my surprise, when I rang RK Drilling down in El Segundo, the phone was snatched up after the first ring. "Channing."

"Mr. Channing, my name's Walker Clayborne, a geologist at Earth Sciences down at UCSD."

"UCSD? My girl's down there, Sylvia."

I searched my memory. "I don't believe I know her."

"Probably wouldn't. Theater Arts, or some such crapola… Anyhow, what can I do for you?"

"I wanted to ask about some core sampling your company did for Universal Waste, out past Landers."

There was a long pause. "I'm afraid I can't discuss the details of that contract."

"I'm not really looking for details. It's just that I've been given to understand you drilled one grid set, and then drilled another. I was wondering why."

There was a long pause. "Listen. Unless you're with Universal, I can't discuss this. Get their approval, and I'll tell you whatever you want. But without a call from Whipple's office, I can't help you."

"Can you at least tell me if it's true that a second set of cores was drilled?"

"You don't understand. It's not that I *won't* discuss this with you, I *can't* discuss it with you. I've been legally enjoined from any further discussion of this project without UWI approval."

"You said *any further discussion*. So I guess you must have admitted this to someone else before UWI set their lawyers on you."

"Conclude whatever you like, Professor. You call again, I better hear from Whipple first." Without further words he hung up.

16

Hidden Valley is deservedly the centerpiece of Joshua Tree National Park. I've seen America's most dramatic geological features, and it can stand alongside any of them. It isn't the garish kind of rock garden you see at Bryce Canyon or Chiricahua or Hell's Half-Acre, with their sunset colors shouting for attention as if a child had its way with the scenery. The only thing comparable to Hidden Valley, in my opinion, is the Hilina Pali area downslope of Kilauea in Hawaii, where giant ropes and cables of glistening black pahoehoe lava overlapped and intertwined as they sped down the thousand-foot slope to the water. Hidden Valley and Hilina are both exercises in form, severe and monochromatic, like the best sculptures, but on a much larger scale.

Back when Joshua Tree was only a national monument you could spend hours in Hidden Valley without seeing a soul. On moonlit nights in the summer you could stroll through and study the geology without the pounding heat of the day, and all you might encounter would be a few stoned hippies, wandering happily lost through the corridors of stacked boulders. Today, of course, the Valley "closes" at sundown, and park rangers patrol to make sure no one is enjoying any unsanctioned solitude in the darkness. National parks now have curfews on their more remarkable features, and nationwide most beaches are off limits after sunset; it may be we are gradually moving toward the outlawing of night.

I was surprised and somewhat appalled at the level of pedestrian traffic channeling itself in and out of the narrow defile—now wheelchair-accessible, of course—that led into the Valley. I was also irritated by the constant shouts echoing off the rocks, and I scanned the area for their source. Rock climbers, of course. The park had always had some, but it now seemed to have turned into a training ground, where more experienced climbers shouted down a continuous stream of instructions and encouragement. When I listened carefully it seemed I could hear different groups of climbers stretching off in all directions, all shouting the same instructions. Ah, nature.

Hidden Valley isn't really a valley at all, but simply a stretch of desert the shape of a stadium, surrounded by concentric rings of stacked boulders, going up a hundred feet or more. Not far to the left of the main entrance, a huge single isenberg rises up a hundred feet, sheer and maybe even undercut. The formation has a number of names, but The Hood is the most common, since it resembles the cowl of a monk's habit, flat in front and reaching up toward a pointed peak.

Back in the mid-70s, when I started studying geology in earnest, I had been out there one moonlit night, field notebook under my arm, and passed in front of that massive tower. From above, I'd heard, "Yow! Hey, somebody else who likes the dark."

Another voice. "Hey, what's your name?"

I looked up. At the very top of the rock was a little overhang and then a hollow, worn by wind. In the little cave sat three figures, their legs dangling. "Walker," I answered. Then, for lack of anything else to say, I said, "And who are you?"

The indistinct voices of teenage boys answered: David, Pat, and David.

"How did you get up there?" I asked.

"Oh, that's easy," one said.

"Yeah. It's getting down that we may not be able to do."

"Hey, down is easy!"

"I meant alive."

"Oh. That's another matter…the way up is easy, just go around over to the side—my right—and follow the path up onto the rock. The only tricky part is at the very top—go left and kind of edge out…"

The path was clear. It led back down a narrow canyon where even the midsummer sun would never penetrate, roofed in places by evergreen oaks and floored with fallen leaves. At length it stopped at the edge of a boulder the width of a small parking lot, curving up at that end to a height of maybe eight feet. But this was like the toe of a short boot: the rock curved up slowly from there, gaining altitude and becoming increasingly steep until it hit the ankle, a hundred yards away, and turned vertical.

I started up the easy slope, which had been smoothed and rounded by years of rain. Crisscrossing dikes, where harder magma had pushed through the mother rock when it fractured, offered ready footholds. Here and there the mother rock had flooded around some inclusion of softer rock and encased it, far below ground; now, exposed to the elements, the soft rock had eroded away, leaving a few deep basins in the surface.

The moon had been bright. The huge rock ended in a cap very like the hood of a sweater, with the face turned away from me. Around the left side of the hood, I could see the three boys edging their way back toward me, their bodies pressed flat against the sheer rock wall. It made my stomach uneasy just to watch. Two of them made it onto the slope; the last one slipped, his arms wide and clinging to the rock, one foot planted firmly, the other reaching down into space. He pulled himself up and kept edging along the rock face.

I met the three of them on their way down. Their pupils were dilated to the point where their eyes were white circles around a black center. They seemed joyously stoned on something, even the one who had almost plummeted into space. "You going out there?" one inquired.

"Probably not," I said. "Just thought I might have a look."

"Oh, you can make it, easy," said one, who wore a sweatshirt that reached to mid-thigh. I peered at the university logo on the front of the sweater; it was a spoof of the University of Hawaii seal, and around the edge it read, *Truth •Knowledge •A Great Tan.*

"Looks to me like one of you just about fell."

"Yeah, sure, but look." The one in the sweatshirt lifted his foot and pointed. "Not the right stuff for climbing." He had on a rubber thong. His other foot was bare. "Hope we can find the one I lost when we get down there."

"Big chance of that," one of his friends said. "Live with it, man."

They headed down, and I continued up. Up near the stony hood of the rock mountain, I could see where a dike of hard material cut through the isenberg, parallel to the ground, forming a walkway perhaps three inches wide.

Another time, I told myself.

Almost every time I have come back to Hidden Valley, I have at least hiked up to the ankle of that rock. There are many larger rocks in the world, but few so generous in displaying their total mass to the eye. And I still think someday I might edge out around the wall…

Today, however, I would have to forego even the hike. About a hundred yards away, I saw Kirsten and a young man, both dressed in ranger get-up, ushering a crowd of about twenty tourists down the circuit path toward the entrance. As I approached she noticed me, smiled, and gestured for me to join the line that was traveling back out the narrow pathway through the rocks. I stepped in to the tail of the line, where her male counterpart was chatting with a pair of old ladies wearing baseball caps.

By the time I made my way to the parking area, Kirsten was leaning on a wall of rock answering a question from a chunky woman who wore a sweater proclaiming, *I Hiked the Canyon!* Kirsten waved me over, and said, "Here's someone who can answer your question a lot better than I can. Mrs. Morris would like to know why we call these rocks 'volcanic' when the lava she has seen before is usually black and shiny."

"Ah. Well, you know the Bowen series?" She looked blank. "Andesitic versus basaltic minerals?" She stared at me, baffled, and I realized I had made things worse. I held my open palms out toward her and waggled them, erasing the air. "Okay. The stuff you are calling lava, the stuff that's usually blackish, comes from deep down in the Earth's core. The stuff you see around here is crustal material—rocks that were up near the surface, and were pulled down, mixed and remelted, and then pushed up again."

"So why are the ones from down deep so black? They come from Hell or something?"

I stared at her, unable to figure out if she were serious or not. "That's—well, that's a hypothesis I hadn't heard before, Mrs. Morris…"

Kirsten's nature-tour partner, introduced as Jace, stood in the open driver's door of an SUV. Kirsten opened the back door, tossed her ranger hat in like a Frisbee, and retrieved her backpack. "Walker'll give me a ride back to work, Jace—right, Walker?"

As we strolled over to the Jeep, I asked, "You're a park ranger, too?"

She tilted a shoulder forward to display her patch: *High Desert Natural History Interpretive Society*. "They like for us to dress this way. Say it gives us 'authority.' The park people like it too, so they can tell at a glance that a mob traipsing through somewhere delicate is under supervision."

We situated ourselves in the Jeep. "So how did you get into this nature-guide activity?"

She began unbuttoning her khaki shirt. "It seemed interesting… and I've learned a lot. I'd pretty much decided to bag the whole law-school thing, and so I was thinking maybe environmental science or something…" She leaned forward, struggling her arms out of the sleeves, and I quickly turned my head to look out the driver's-side window. "In fact, I was thinking I should talk to you about that, maybe you could— Oh, I'm sorry! Am I embarrassing you?"

"No…I just thought you might like some privacy."

"Oh. That's sweet. But I think of you as one of the gang now, and we aren't real shy around each other…" She wadded up the shirt and opened her backpack. I faced forward, trying to be casual, not staring at her but not obviously looking away. Her bra was a faded blue-and-pink floral design, with an unexpectedly lacy edging. She found a purple sweater in her pack and pulled it over her head, dragging it down to her waist and squirming until it was even. Then she fluffed her curls and pulled out her lunch.

I refused to share her lunch, having eaten before I came out, and explained I wanted to know more about her anti-speed activities with Claire.

"Haven't been involved with that for over a year," she explained. "The whole thing was based on stuff a woman did back in Michigan called Safe Streets…hold town meetings, share information: identify the dealers and let everybody know we knew."

"And then what? Turn the information over to the sheriffs?"

She paused to wash down a bite of sandwich with bottled water. "No. Just give it as much publicity as possible. Of course, the sheriffs could hear about it as easy as anybody else, but Claire didn't think putting people in prison for using drugs made any sense at all. And most of the street dealers are just doing it to support their own habits anyway."

"And so they close up shop, just like that? Because of the bad publicity? They see the error of their ways and get respectable jobs?" This seemed dangerous and probably ineffective.

"We're not stupid, you know. These people aren't local homeowners with a wife and kids to support. Make it too hot for them here and it's easy for them to move on to somewhere else."

"It seems like just exporting your problems." I regretted saying this before it was all the way out of my mouth.

Her head whipped up, tossing her short curls. "Hey, we weren't trying to fix the whole world, just the local towns. What would you do?"

"I'm not sure. Probably let the police handle it."

"If they were handling it, there wouldn't be a problem, would there?" She busied herself with her lunch.

I leaned on the steering wheel and paused to let her annoyance ebb. "What can you tell me about the current situation? What do you know about what Claire was looking into recently?"

"Not much." She wiped her hands and mouth on a paper napkin and started putting things away. "Claire was convinced there was a big drug lab in the area. I never saw any evidence…but I stopped working on the whole thing more than a year ago."

"Why?"

"Because I'm a chicken. This guy over in 29 Palms—one we had on our Safe Streets list as a dealer, a bad guy to have in your neighborhood—got murdered and buried in the desert. Turned out he was DEA, and Claire and I both got called to testify in the grand jury inquiry. Creeped me out. Didn't want to have anything more to do with it."

"But Claire kept working at it?"

"Sort of. The Safe Streets thing became kind of self-supporting, so she didn't babysit it much after a while. But I know she kept digging at the whole thing, using her contacts from the prison…"

"So how do I find out more about the local situation? Where do I start?"

"Why do you want to?"

"Don't you think this just might have something to do with Claire's murder?"

"Not really. We were pests, but not the kind of problem that would get you killed. What are they going to do, kill everyone in Safe Streets?"

"Maybe she turned up something important after you stopped working with her?"

"But wouldn't she have told me?" Kirsten paused, and then answered her own question. "Maybe not, not after I told her I was done with it." She laid her hands on her lap, palms down, limp. "I feel guilty about the whole thing. I feel like I let her down."

In guilt terms, she was in kindergarten; I was doing a post-doc. I waited, and then asked, "If I wanted to find out more, where would I start?"

"You could talk to the Safe Streets people. They're in the book. But maybe the best place to start is with Perry. My brother doesn't use anymore, but he always gets new clients fresh off the streets."

"You sound like you think this is a waste of time."

She shrugged. "How should I know? Like Claire always used to say—" She sucked in a sudden breath and then froze for a long moment.

Her hands covered her face and she began to cry. She crumpled against my shoulder, and, voice muffled by her hands, managed to get out, "I miss her… I miss her so much…"

My right arm was pinned, but I tried to comfort her with my free hand. I stared out the windshield, the outer wall of Hidden Valley soaring up just ten feet away from the car.

17

This time I showed up at UWI unannounced. Ms. Benedict, the receptionist, rang back to see if Vernon Whipple would see me without an appointment, and the surprise on her face told me he'd answered in the affirmative.

"Dr. Clayborne…" he said, greeting me with an outstretched hand. "Didn't expect to have the pleasure again so soon." He left the door open and led me to sit at his conference table.

I explained how I had been to *Stop The Dump* headquarters, and had been told that their hydrologist claimed to have evidence of an active water channel under the proposed disposal site.

"Did you contact their hydrologic specialist?" he asked.

"Not yet."

He smiled. "Well, I'd check out the source before I got too excited about all this. But ask yourself what the chances are that any major watercourse would be missed by a drilling grid like ours."

"Hypothetically, low. But if we're talking about a real feature, then the chances are one hundred percent, because it apparently already happened."

"But we aren't talking about a real hydrological feature. We're talking about some last-ditch effort to stop us from completing a project. We build a rail-spur down from just outside Argos, and this facility can handle all of the waste generated in the High Desert, as well most of the growth in LA and Orange counties. It has to go somewhere, but even way out here it's always NIMBY—Not In My Back Yard."

"I noticed that some of your cores are a little off the standard grid spacing, too."

"All within legal limits."

"But why?"

He ran his hand back through his perfectly combed silver hair, and mussed it a little. "I don't know why. I don't second-guess my field crew. Probably staying away from an old gas pipeline or something."

"And did you redrill about sixty percent of your original holes, on a new grid?"

He studied me, and then said, "I don't know where you get these ideas, Dr. Clayborne… No, I misspoke, I know exactly where you get these ideas, from those loonies at *Stop The Dump*." He leaned forward. "I would advise you—no, urge you—to just leave this alone. This has all been vetted by competent geological engineers and hydrologists, and joining up with an ill-conceived, scientifically illiterate coalition of antibusiness activists can only damage your standing in the scientific community."

"My standing in the scientific community is quite safe, thank you very much, and if everything has been so extensively approved by experts, then I can't see why you have a problem with me looking into it a little deeper." I waited only briefly before adding, "You act like you have something to hide, and it makes me want to find out what it is."

He looked at me with a strange smile and stood up. Still with a smile on his face, he yelled, "Are you threatening me?"

It was weird. It was some kind of a put-on, and he wasn't even bothering to act. "I'm not threatening anybody," I said, "I'm just—"

"You can't just come barging into my office making wild accusations and threats!" His voice was still loud and unrelated to the expression on his face. He looked behind me, and I saw Ms. Benedict in the doorway. "Ms. Benedict, you're a witness. Please fetch security."

Ms. Benedict was gone for all of half a second before a burly man in a polo shirt stepped into the room. "Greg," Whipple said, "please escort Dr. Clayborne out of the office immediately, and then please stay in the parking lot until he leaves the premises. Dr. Clayborne, any further contact or trespassing on your part will be dealt with through legal channels."

Greg flexed his steroid-pumped muscles for my benefit before he put his hard hand on my shoulder. "Now."

When in doubt, drink more coffee. I headed over to Water Canyon Coffee and parked out back. There was a lot of trash on the floor of the passenger side, much of it take-out coffee trash from this very coffeehouse. I leaned over and stuffed all of it into a paper bag—I love the economy of consolidating trash inside other trash—crushing the cups flat to make them fit.

I carried the trash to the overflowing dumpster. From behind me, a woman's voice: "You have to make sure it will stay in. They won't pick it up if it falls out." The woman, probably in her mid-twenties, stood in the open screen door of the coffeehouse kitchen. "In fact, in fact, you shouldn't even be putting your trash in there." Her blond hair was frizzed. The expression on her face tightened with each word. "We have to pay to have it hauled away. It's not for the public. So, so, so why don't you just take that right out of there? Right now?"

Having been around a university, I recognized the sure signs of a course in assertiveness training. The naturally assertive simply state their case as a first reaction. Those who are trained sort of wind themselves up, like a broad jumper running down the track, and, like the jumper, once they take off they go as far as they can. I looked at her and considered mentioning that it was mostly trash from her establishment. To hell with it. I pulled the bag out of the trash and carried it back to the Jeep.

I walked around to the front and pushed through the doors. It was a little after three, and the place was deserted except for an elderly woman looking through the shelves of books. I ordered a cinnamon roll and a cup of the house blend. While I waited, the frizzy-haired girl came out from the kitchen, recognized me, and looked away.

At a table by the front windows, I checked my messages. Jack Priestly, *Stop The Dump*'s hydrological consultant, had called and left me the number of his cell phone.

I was baffled by Whipple's behavior. If he had been genuinely angry, I could have accepted it; but the reasons for the way my exit was stage-managed escaped me. It made me want to take a harder look at UWI.

My call to Jack Priestly, on the other hand, made me want to abandon the UWI issue altogether. I found him at a site where he was drilling a well, the whirling thrum of the rotaries behind his voice. The first disconcerting thing I learned was that he had no academic training, and was just a well driller—hence Hapgood's reference to him as their "hydrological consultant" rather than their "hydrologist."

The second disconcerting thing I learned was his methodology. Dowsing. He had outlined the edges of the channel using a forked birch rod. "And it's not a dry'un, either—there's water flowing down there, year-round I suspect." I hardly listened, and when he said he had to get back to work I let him go gladly.

No wonder Whipple had been smiling.

To take my mind off UWI, I decided to check out Claire's former boyfriend, Gary Handwerk—the martial-arts instructor whom Jared disliked so much. He had given me a description of roughly where the studio was located. I found it two blocks east of Ira's church. *Valley CardioKickboxing and Self-Defense.*

It too was in a converted storefront, but one only half the size of the Church of the Rock. Like the church, it had kept the expanse of open glass so you could see in from the street, but in this case it was largely obscured by signs and posters.

I parked and crossed the street to get a better look. The larger posters featured men dressed in judo attire flying through the air in various aggressive postures. Others were schedules of classes, or reprints from magazine articles stressing the apparently limitless health benefits of kickboxing, "The Ultimate Cardio Workout." I peered between the signs. The studio had panels of high mirrors along the back, alternating with various obscure canvas-covered pads mounted to the wall. A few heavy punching bags were suspended from the ceiling by thick chains.

The lights were on inside the place, and I realized there was someone inside. In the center of the mat-covered floor, a man appeared to be squatting and crouched over with his back toward me. As I looked closer, I realized he was not in fact squatting; his knees were on the backs of his elbows, his feet were off the floor, and his whole body weight was balanced on his outstretched fingers. His body trembled slightly as he maintained the pose. Suddenly he launched his legs back and straightened out into a plank as if he were preparing for a pushup. Slow, slow, every muscle on alert, he lowered himself to the mat and then just lay there.

I gave a gentle tug on the glass door of the studio. It was locked, but from the way his head tilted, I could see that the man inside had heard me. He pushed up to kneeling, jumped to his feet, and came toward the door. He was dressed only in loose martial-arts pants; his upper body was slick with sweat.

He turned the deadbolt and pushed the door open just wide enough to accommodate his torso. "Yeah?"

"Are you Gary Handwerk?"

He thought about this. His hair was dark and stiff, his eyes a creamy brown color. "Yeah," he said at last.

"I'm Walker Clayborne, Claire's brother. I was wondering if I could have a word with you."

"About what?"

"About Claire." *What else, you moron?* I added silently.

He considered again for a while and then opened the door. "I'm not just gonna drop everything," he warned me. "I can't lose my burn."

He simply let loose of the door and turned away. I caught the door and stepped inside. He was already several steps away. "Shoes!" he said without looking back.

"Excuse me?"

"Shoes. Take off your shoes before you come on the mat."

I sat down on the edge of the mat and unlaced and removed my shoes. Over by the back wall he was searching through some kind of net filled with equipment.

I left my shoes by the door and walked across the mat toward him in stockinged feet. "Sit down," he offered, gesturing at the floor as if it were a chair. I sat down crosslegged and watched him put on his gear—strange half-boots plus gloves that fit across the top side of the hand and wrist, open on the bottom except for elastic straps. His body was extraordinarily taut and sculpted: not only did his abdominal muscles stick out in sharp definition, as if he had swallowed two columns of tennis balls, but the tiny muscles in the connective tissue between his ribs were all chiseled in full relief.

He stopped adjusting his gloves long enough to stare at me. Although his body was a marvel of lucid anatomy, his face was still soft and undefined, like a young boy's.

His lower lip protruded slightly, and there was a faint blotchiness to his cheeks. He had that sullen, spoiled-brat look so many women describe as smoldering. A guy would describe his looks as petulant.

"What d'ya want? I already told the cops everything I know. Which is nothing."

He didn't wait for my answer, but instead whirled about and leaped at one of the suspended heavybags and kicked it away. He had his feet planted on the ground by the time it swung back, and he caught its full weight with a hard punch and proceeded to pummel it furiously with his fists, leaning back every so often to deliver a smashing kick.

He stopped his assault and turned back, panting with exertion.

Sitting on the floor watching this display of ferocity made my back tense. I was worried I was about to have one of those lower-back episodes where I would have to lay down. "I was hoping you might give me some suggestions as to why my sister was murdered."

He jerked his shoulders forward in what must have been intended as a shrug; it was more like a flinch. "Don't know. Haven't been with Claire in over a year."

He turned to the back wall. There was a long canvas pad attached there with height markings along it in feet. He gathered himself, tossed his head loosely side to side, coiled down a little, then sprang up and slammed his foot into the pad at the five-foot mark. He gained his balance, glanced at me with what I would call a sulky expression, though others might have found it sensual.

"Do you have any idea why someone would want to kill her?"

"Sure. Lots." He squatted down and cupped his fingers under his heels, tugging.

"For example?"

He straightened up, put his head through another long rotation, loosening his neck. "Hey, she was always trying to shut down the meth dealers in the area, nosing around their business. Maybe they offed her."

"Are there any other possibilities that come to mind?"

"Yeah. Interfering in other people's business. Trying to run other people's lives. Jealousy. Sex stuff."

He breathed forcefully for a moment, gathering himself, and erupted off the floor. His foot slammed into the pad above the six-foot mark, and, seemingly hovering there, he lashed out and connected with a kick from the other foot.

This time he didn't land so gracefully. He stumbled, and began to fall backward. He curled a little and caught his weight on the heel of his hand. He sat there as if perched on an invisible stool, leaning back on the arm. Without moving from this position, he looked me in the eye. "Hey, no offense, but your sister was a slut." He continued to hold my gaze as if he had issued a dare.

I was perplexed. Did he expect me to challenge him to a duel to uphold my sister's honor? Like most words that are intended to hurt but miss their mark, it was still irritating because of its intent. I just stared back.

He looked away. "I don't think I want to talk to you anymore, man."

I was back in the Jeep when the cell rang, and I pulled over as I answered. It was Alfie Prentiss, the best hydrologist I know, returning my earlier call. I apologized for interrupting his vacation, and told him I'd thought I had some important questions for him, but that the whole issue had evaporated.

"Come on, Walker, give it up. You tell me to call, tell me it's urgent—then you tell me it doesn't matter. What's the story?"

I recounted a quick outline of what had happened, and then concluded with the punchline: "Dowsing. The whole thing was based on *dowsing*."

There was a silence before he said, "So?"

"What do you mean, 'so?' *So*, this whole thing is based on crackpot logic. *So*, there isn't any evidence at all."

"Nothing you can take to court. But you shouldn't ignore a lead just because it's based on dowsing. I mean, most hydrologists have run across good dowsers every so often, and it's pretty generally acknowledged that there's something to it. The real question—"

"What? *What* are you telling me—?"

"—is how it works. There's a number of theories, some people think it's a sensing of subtle changes in the electromagnetic field, but—"

"I don't believe this."

"—there's a substantial minority who think it's some kind of hypercognition, and the dowser just does some kind of elaborate pattern recognition that lets him subconsciously put together the geological history of the area. My own observations—"

"Alfie…"

"—suggest that it has something to do with the geology rather than just water, because most of them can't find water flowing in pipes. There's a few, though, who—"

"Alfie: Will. You. Shut. Up."

"What? You raise a question, I give you my considered opinion."

"Did I shift into a parallel universe recently? Has the whole world gone New Age while I was asleep?"

"Dowsing is about as Old Age as you can get, Walker."

"Are you telling me—as a scientist—that you'd let a dowser delineate an underground channel?"

"Well, I wouldn't write it up in a journal. But I'd sure use it as a starting point for a more technical survey. Don't ignore something just because you don't have the explanation for it."

I wanted to argue more, but suppressed the urge. "Fine. And what tools would you use?"

"They've already done a core grid. Seismics, obviously. Electrical conductivity. Could fly over and do a gravitational anomaly search…"

"Not exactly back-porch science experiments."

"Nope. Oil company stuff, mostly. Just to do a preliminary workup, see if it's worth bothering with, is probably fifty K or so."

"Yow."

"Don't know what to tell you, Walker," he said. "Truth don't come cheap."

18

"I can tell you what it means when it appears in a Tarot card," Mandy said. "Any time you see a white rose depicted, it means the purified life force. Purified desire. The Will-to-Creation aspect of God manifested in matter. A red rose is the same thing, but at a lower level, one where desire and lust are the major manifestations of that Will."

I tilted back in the rickety office chair. I wasn't sure whether this information was helpful. "The problem is that I have no idea what it meant to whoever left it there."

"True." A light on the desk console blinked. Mandy stood up and walked around the desk to the small waiting area. "Mrs. Hernandez? You can come back with me now."

A gray-haired Hispanic woman rose slowly to her feet. The side of her face wore a large scar shaped like a burst of fireworks. When she bent down to pick up the handle of her purse, it seemed she might freeze there, forever bowed over. Mandy helped her straighten up, took her by the arm, and guided her through the doorway at the right end of the room.

The battered metal desk must have been purchased originally by some government agency, probably back when Eisenhower was in office, but the computer perched on it was a recent model. The chairs backing against the front wall were mismatched. Most were steel with padded seats, but a couple were wood, and one was a white plastic patio chair. With Mrs. Hernandez gone, only one chair was still occupied:

a stringy-haired young woman held a doubled-over *People* magazine with one hand while balancing an infant on her knee with the other. The baby could have been cleaner, but seemed fat and healthy; it stared fixedly at me as it chewed on the wet collar of its jumpsuit.

On the wall above their heads was a sign: *The High Desert People's Clinic.* Beneath the words was a logo of a howling coyote beneath a saguaro cactus—not reasonable, really, as any saguaro around here had been trucked in from Arizona. The coyote sat atop an exhortation to *Volunteer! It's* Your *Clinic!*

Mandy swung her hips into the desk chair but had her fingers on the keyboard before she sat all the way down. "Just a sec." She typed something, made a few mouse clicks, and then sat back. "Okay."

"So do you have some sort of medical training, or—?"

She smiled with one side of her mouth. "Everything I know about medicine comes from the soap operas my mother watched. Which makes me an expert on rare fatal diseases, I guess: the kind that kill you eventually but leave you looking good in the interim. Nope, I just staff the desk sometimes. Same with Claire."

"So which one of you decided to volunteer here first, you or Claire?"

She used the tip of her right loafer to push off the left, brought her bare foot up onto the chair, and hugged her thigh to her body with her left arm. "Dawn's a surgical assistant at the hospital, and she's the one that got us all volunteering here. Then she gets in this big fight with the clinic director, ends up quitting. So here's Claire and Kirsten and me still working at this thing that she dragged us into in the first place." It was hard to keep from staring at her toes. They were almost perfect, like the unmarred digits of an infant, but her little toe bent up high and crooked itself in toward the others. I wondered if her other foot had the same slight deformity.

"So why do you continue to do it?"

"The obvious reasons. Same as Claire. The place needs help, and it makes me feel good to give a little."

"Where do you get your doctors?"

"We don't have doctors every day. But when we don't, we have a nurse practitioner, like today. Most of the time with anything serious the people have to be referred. There are quite a few doctors around who provide free services, but we have to get the patients to them. They haven't got time to do a four-hour shift over here."

Across the room, the baby spit up onto its jumpsuit. The mother went on reading. "I had a number of interesting visits over the last two days," I began.

I told her about my visit with Bryce, and my following meeting with Hapgood and UWI. I reviewed my talk with Kirsten, and my suspicions that Claire's interest in the speed trade might relate to her murder. Then I told her about my visit to the Shackles meeting the previous night, and about the God's Law film.

She shuddered. "I thought somebody was getting the Shackles people worked up lately. They usually aren't so pushy."

I concluded by relating my visit to Gary. When I reached the part where he told me that Claire was a slut, Mandy snorted and interrupted. "Pretty much what any woman gets called if she likes sex better than a given man does."

"He seemed really quite hostile on the subject. And given that he seems to have these violent tendencies…"

"Maybe." She stuck out her bottom teeth and bit her upper lip. "And I'm not surprised that he's touchy on the subject. From what Claire told me, he had what they delicately refer to as 'performance problems.' But its been some time since they were together…"—she frowned—"at least as far as I know."

"Oh." I imagined that if there was any obvious link between Gary and Claire's murder, it would have been looked into already. Jared and Bolles were both immediately suspicious of any boyfriend. "What was she doing with a guy like that in the first place?"

"Eye candy. Hey, boys are attracted to empty-headed bimbos; some of them don't mate with anything else. Girls are like that too, we just wise up faster. Claire spent years going through one 'intense' guy after another. Guess she decided to finally try a Ken doll." She gave a malicious smile. "Barbie may not have anything else, not even nips, but at least she has tits. Ken, on the other hand…"

There are people who claim that males evaluate every woman they meet in terms of desirability as a sex partner within the first thirty seconds of visual contact. It may be true of other men, but it definitely is not true of me. In some cases I can be around a woman for years before I notice she's attractive. As she talked, Mandy suddenly registered on my sexual radar screen. Her small, self-contained body, the precision of her hands, her capable hips, and her peculiar attitude all coalesced to make her desirable—not the unexpected visceral draw I had felt from Melanie, but undeniably a strong pull. But listening to her dismiss Ken made me vaguely uncomfortable, as if I should speak up on Ken's behalf. I changed the subject. "What about the other things Gary brought up?

"Most of it sounds like generalized bitching. Maybe the part about crank dealers bears looking into—"

"Crank?"

"Crank, methamphetamine, speed, ice. Crystal. All basically the same stuff. But I'm inclined to agree with Kirsten and Melanie—the way Claire was killed doesn't sound like organized crime."

"So what do you think I should follow up on?"

"Everything. The way she was killed just felt so, so *personal*—but I'm not going to rule anything out yet. The UWI stuff is weird, the God's Law stuff is downright scary. And drug stuff is always dangerous."

I frowned. "I'm afraid I don't really understand the views that your Circle has of drugs. On the one hand—"

The phone console buzzed. Mandy held up her hand like a policeman stopping traffic and stood, easily sliding her foot back into her shoe as she did so. Some people have astonishing minor motor skills.

Mandy escorted the mother and infant to the back room. When she returned, she made a few entries in the computer, moused her way through a menu, and then pushed the desk chair back to face me. She popped off both shoes and pulled her feet up to sit crosslegged, her denim-clad knees pushed down under the arms of the chair. "I'm not sure this is really a discussion we want to get into,'cause it gets endless. But having an opinion or policy on 'drugs' is like having one on 'machines.' There's all kinds of them, and they do share a few common principles, but generalizing about them is a stupid exercise. I mean, let's say speed is like an assault vehicle, heroin is like a gas chamber, and LSD is like an X-ray machine. All three of them are machines, you can argue that all three have their place—or don't—and all three are dangerous under certain circumstances. But it would be kind of retarded to have a single policy about all three, or to make pompous speeches about machines in general."

"But they do all share the characteristic of being addictive," I noted.

Mandy raised her eyebrows. "No they don't. LSD isn't addictive."

"Well, isn't that what everybody always claims about whatever drug they happen to like?"

"Look, Walker, trust me on this: no one with any scientific knowledge anywhere at any time has ever suggested that LSD is addictive. Not even the fuckwits at the DEA try to claim that. Because it isn't possible. If you keep taking it day after day it stops doing anything. If you wanted to stay loaded on psychedelics for a month— and I can't imagine anyone wanting to do that, since eight hours on them *seems* like a month—you couldn't. The brain adjusts. The stuff has no effect, even at high doses. Its like having somebody pop out of a closet at you: The first time, you jump and scream, but if they do it two minutes later it doesn't do much. Keep it up, it doesn't do anything."

I was stymied by this information. It didn't sound right to me, somehow. I wanted to argue with it, but I had no facts. Unlike most Americans, I don't maintain the belief that I am entitled to my opinion on subjects where I am completely ignorant. I waved the topic away. "You were right, this isn't a relevant discussion."

The side door pushed open and Mrs. Hernandez wandered out. She came over to the desk and held a piece of paper out toward Mandy. "They say I give this to you."

Mandy took it, glanced down to read. "At least nurse practitioners have legible handwriting," she muttered. Then a little louder, to Mrs. Hernandez, she said, "This is a referral. They want you to see another doctor at another office."

The old woman shifted a little and looked over her shoulder. "But is no money for doctor. *Clinico* is free…" She started to glance around the room and a note of urgency entered her voice. "Where is Angel? Angel is for picking me up…!"

Mandy was on her feet and around the desk before the woman finished. "No, no, the doctor is free. Referral is free. *Medico es gratis.*" She put one hand on the woman's shoulder and another on her forearm, and gently steered her back into a seat. She sat beside her and held one of Mrs. Hernandez's hands in both of her own. I expected her to calm the woman and then return, but instead she sat there and they talked in low voices, their heads inclined together like long friends, Mandy nodding as she listened.

Minutes passed. I expected some sort of apologetic glance, but her focus was all with Mrs. Hernandez. I tried to think over the events of the last week: the intruder in Claire's house, Mandy spritzing me with pepper spray, Desert Christ Park, the visit with Ettenmoor, the weird drive with Bolles, Whipple and UWI, the weird God's Law film, the white roses… The longer I stayed here the less sense it all made, and once or twice a day I felt a rising uneasiness. Was I running away from my life and my academic commitments? Or was I facing life squarely for the first time?

I leaned forward in the chair and drove my fists into the small of my back, trying to get the muscles to relax. It had been years since I'd had a full-on episode, and I didn't want one now; they were humiliating.

The side door opened again, and the woman with the baby came out. She stopped in front of the desk, hoisted the baby sideways onto her hip, and tossed a piece of paper onto the desk. She and the baby both stared at me as if waiting for me to do something. Her face was pinched and suspicious, the baby's was round and ready to be pleased. Despite the post-partum heft to the woman's breasts, it was hard to believe they were related. I shuddered to speculate what life would have to do to make the baby's face resemble the mother's.

Mandy raised her voice for a moment. "Walker, can you fill her out an appointment card? They're in the top drawer." The woman with the baby nodded with a tight mouth, satisfied that somebody was making me do my job.

I scooted the chair forward, searched the top desk drawer, found little cards reading *Appointment Reminder. .... has an appointment with .... on .... at.......... am/pm.* I looked at the paper the woman had tossed down. The nurse's handwriting was big and loopy. It has always surprised me how often you can tell gender just from penmanship. I solicited the appropriate information—Tiffany Potts, Dr. Siler, January 17, 10:30 a.m.—and filled the card.

The mother took it from me with an air of moral victory, hefted the baby up against her chest, and went to gather up the bag of infant impedimenta that still sat on the chairs against the wall. The baby continued to stare at me over its mother's shoulder as they pushed out through the glass doors onto the street.

A harried-looking woman came out of the door leading to the consulting rooms. She stopped short and took in the scene between Mandy and Mrs. Hernandez. She noticed me, bustled over, and said, quick and low, "I really have to get. I'm closing down the back and I'll lock up the rear on the way out. You're new, right? Hi, I'm Erin. You guys should shut down and lock up out here, okay?" I nodded, and opened my mouth to tell her I didn't really work there, but she said, "Great, I'll see ya," and almost ran back through the door.

It was nice to know that if the UC ever closed its doors I could pass for a receptionist. The screensaver on the computer monitor was one of those things where fractal patterns build from a single geometrical seed, becoming more and more baroque, until the screen goes black and the process starts again from some other simple form.

Eventually a slender young Hispanic man burst in through the front door like a dancer moving onto the stage. Angel, I assumed. He spotted Mrs. Hernandez and strutted over toward her, the concern in his eyes at odds with the cocky language of his body. Mandy stood and talked to him in hushed tones, pointing at the referral form. He helped Mrs. Hernandez to her feet. As they turned toward the door, Mandy's hand reached out and touched the old woman's gray hair, the merest brush of the fingertips.

Mandy watched until the door closed behind them, then came back and sat down at the desk. She leaned back in the chair and covered her face with both palms, pulling in a long breath of air. She held her breath and then let it out slowly, carefully, as if it were a liquid she were pouring into the narrow top of a bottle. She uncovered her face and sat up. "She's dying."

"Oh." I had been a little annoyed at waiting for so long, but this deflated me. "She had an upsetting diagnosis, then?"

Mandy turned her head toward me without turning her body. Her gaze was flat at first, then seemed to focus sharply, then went flat again. "No. They don't know what's wrong with her. But her heart is going to go someday soon. I could see it."

Her certainty was so great that part of me instantly believed her. The other part wanted to argue with her. I settled for asking, "If you can tell her heart is bad, shouldn't you tell somebody?"

She blinked long and slow, like a cat ignoring a command. "There's no point. Besides, she just had an EKG." Her eyelids batted rapidly, almost fluttering. "You should see somebody about your back, you know. It's mostly fear, but there *is* an old injury there."

"I've never injured my back. The doctors tell me it's just stress. Believe me, I've seen plenty of them."

She exhaled long through her nose and swiveled her chair to face me. Her eyes seemed to grow both darker and larger, as if she were getting closer and closer. She said, "Baseball."

"What?" This was a complete *non sequitur*. "I never played baseball."

"Something with a bat. Grade school. You were batting. Nervous. You weren't any good at it. You took a swing, hard, twisted your back. Fell down."

"Hunh." I was remembering now. Softball, it was softball, the Phoenix sun hot already in the spring, two out, everybody on my team groaning when it was apparent I was next up. The eager expression on the pitcher's face when he saw easy prey. I put everything I had into the first swing.

Mandy said, "Nurse's office. Parents, no, mother, must be your mother…"

"You're right. All of that's right." She could have seen me fiddling with my back, inferred I had back trouble. But how would she know about the softball game when I didn't remember it myself? Wait, maybe Claire had told her. That had to be the explanation. But Claire would have been a toddler when it happened…

I remembered what Ettenmoor had said: Stop letting your theories run ahead of the data. Watch yourself. Watch everything. Note the results. "I remember. And I also remember that the school nurse sent me to the ER, and they said I just pulled a muscle."

"You also hurt your spine, a disc or something. When you get scared your muscles all tighten up to protect that place." She was matter-of-fact now. Whatever had been moving through her was gone.

"If you can diagnose things like this, if you have this…this power, why don't you use it as some sort of a, what's the word I want, a *diagnostician?*"

She was already shaking her head before I finished the sentence. "There's so many reasons why not that I don't even want to go there, okay? But I have to tell you: most people who have this kind of gift or curse or whatever the hell it is, and try to use it, end up fucking it up. Especially if they try to make a living at it. It isn't reliable. So there comes a time when they're on the spot, and they fake it, maybe just a little. It fades more. They fake it more. Pretty soon they're faking it most of the time."

"But still, it seems that if you just used it to help people—"

"I did, just now. But I don't want it to be a career." She chewed her lip. "You don't *understand*, Walker." She leaned toward me, her hands open on her knees as if she were displaying something. "I don't like this. I'd shut it down forever if I could. It feels like I'm contaminated." She leaned back again and flexed her shoulders, trying to relax.

"Contaminated? Contaminated with what?"

"I see people buying these books, *Develop Your Psychic Powers*, and I say, boy, if that works, will *you* ever be sorry."

She turned back to the desk and picked up the paper the young mother had tossed down for me. She said, "Hang on a minute. Let me clean up this stuff. Then we can lock up and go get something to eat."

She began to enter information in the computer as if nothing had happened.

19

Saturday morning. Three white roses in the vase. The first one was wide open and had let fall two petals onto the table; the second bud was beginning to relax its chaste posture; the third, from last night, was still snug and compact. I drank coffee and tried to perk up.

I had already paid my morning visit to Mrs. Givens, who'd told me I'd indeed received a visit yesterday from someone on a green motorsickle, along about sundown. No, she hadn't had a chance to get a good look, her arms had been full of laundry when she first heard it pull in—she couldn't drop everything just to run to the side window, could she?—and in any case, whoever it was had on one of them helmets as covers your whole face. It could have been a boy or a girl, take your pick; a slim little thing either way.

I was halfway through my second cup when I heard cars pull into the driveway, followed by the slams of car doors. I stepped onto the doormat, coffee still in hand. There were two cars—a sheriff's cruiser, and, behind it, a long gray luxury sedan.

The sheriff's deputy reached me first, flanked by the UWI lawyers. Attorney Chiarella wore an expensive, conservative suit, and this time she had abandoned her running shoes for matching pumps, a decision that resulted in a wobbling gait as her heels pierced deep into the sand with each step. Her partner already had his sunglasses on, though the winter sun hid behind the escarpments of the national park to the southeast.

"Mr. Clayborne?" the deputy asked. I answered in the affirmative. He held forth a folded sheaf of papers, and I took them. "I'm here to serve a temporary restraining order, sir. I'd appreciate it if you'd sign an acknowledgment of receipt"—he held out a clipboard—"but this service is binding in a legal sense whether you choose to sign or not." I sat my coffee down on the concrete beside my feet, glanced at the receipt—*I the undersigned, do hereby affirm and acknowledge*, etc.—and signed the form.

Chiarella said, "You can read the papers at your leisure, but let me caution you that, now that you have been served, you are enjoined from any further contact with Vernon Whipple, Universal Waste International, its subsidiaries, or any employees thereof, whether via telecommunications, written word, or verbal interchange; that you are barred from the grounds of facilities owned by Universal, and will be prosecuted for trespass as well as violation of this order; and that you are not allowed to approach Mr. Whipple or any of the employees of the local office of Universal any closer than one hundred yards. Furthermore, any further threats made by you against Mr. Whipple, Universal Waste, or any of its employees, will be dealt with by both criminal and civil actions."

The two men in suits turned and started to walk away. The deputy gave a little toss of his hands—just doing my job—and started to follow. "Hey, wait a minute," I said. "I never threatened anybody."

They turned back to me, and Chiarella said, "If you wish to contest the order, the usual legal channels are available. I suggest that you retain the services of an attorney."

"Did you guys do this to Claire, too? Along with all the other nonsense?"

The silent man finally spoke. "Must be something genetic with you guys, huh?" He smirked and they headed back to their cars.

I went inside and called Mandy to ask if I could see her, but she was on her way out. "I'd like to talk to you later today, if I can," I said.

"My afternoon's shot, and later this morning I have to drive somebody over to Palm Springs." She thought. "You could come along, if you want—I'm just dropping her off over there."

I agreed, and we arranged to meet in front of the High Desert Free Clinic at eleven.

Park Boulevard is the road leading from the town of Joshua Tree to the national park's westernmost entrance. If you turn the other way on Park, toward the flats, it's only a block to the San Bernardino County Branch Library.

The sole remarkable feature of the facility is that it stands on the corner of Park and Commercial, and Commercial is one of those pieces of desert roadway which, for reasons unknown, has been built of asphalt mixed with red cinder aggregate: what looks like a long stretch of dried blood. The library itself is about what you would expect, whitish, stuccoed cinderblock in rectangles. At least buildings like this don't stand out against the desert, like the new strip malls; in fact, if they designed the county buildings right, putting a porous outer shell on them, they could erode down slowly and become one with the landscape.

I spend a lot of time in libraries, especially the Geisel down at UCSD. It's a comfortable place, and the architecture is stunning: it resembles a giant space station that has crashed down and partly embedded itself in the earth. Plus how can you not love a library named after Dr. Suess? But as I entered the local branch library, it occurred to me that this, and the thousands like it, would be a more fitting tribute to Theodore Geisel; these were the kind of libraries where we all learned to read.

It was a large single room, broken up by freestanding shelves. Windows high on the walls let shafts of light into the space. In the back of my mind I knew Melanie might be there, and I was delighted when she looked up from a sorting cart across the room and recognized me.

People are fond of saying an attractive woman has something you can't quite put your finger on. This is typically an evasion; usually you could literally put your finger on it, although you might have to put your finger on several different spots. Beautiful women have extraordinary parts.

But Melanie was something different. She came across the long room toward me, and as she advanced she walked through the shafts of light from the windows. There was nothing special about her gait, no particular thrust of the hips, no extra movement of the shoulders and torso, and yet it all knit together into something exquisite.

It was an unexpected pleasure to be able to study her so openly, without the need for covert glances. She was dressed simply, dark sweater and jeans, her brown-blond hair just touching her shoulders. Her small breasts were nothing more than a suggestion of curve. As she came close she spread her arms and hugged me, not the close embrace she had given me at her house, but a public hug, one that used only the arms and shoulders. She smelled sweet with a faint undertone of musk, but it wasn't perfume; it was something exuding from her pores.

She spoke in a whisper as she led me to a seat. "Walker! What are you doing here?" She sat next to me at the long table and leaned close.

I explained about the white roses and said I was hoping to find some reference materials that would cover the possible symbolism.

She nodded. Her skin was clear and perfect. There was nothing remarkable about her features except the way they fit together. "There's some things that would help you out. But I know flowers and colors pretty well. White roses are spiritual love, love on the highest plane."

"Don't they show up at funerals?"

"Sure. But that's the same symbolism, it's still spiritual love."

"Is there any way that white roses could be interpreted as a threat?"

She chewed her lip. Perfect white little teeth. "About the only negative thing I can think of is that sometimes a lover would send another a white rose as a sign that it was over: I still love you, but I no longer desire you."

"But what about the death connection?"

"The white rose is mourning and resurrection, not death. If I were making a threat, I would send the blackest rose I could find— maybe even paint it. Or better yet, I'd send belladonna or henbane or skullcap."

"Are those easy to come by out here in the desert?"

She smiled. "You just have to know where to shop." She stood. "Let me get you a few books."

This gave me a chance to gaze at her as she went, to observe her searching the stacks, and to stare as she came back. Normally I would have found a magazine or book to fill the minutes, but I could watch Melanie all day.

She brought back four books. The one on top was *The Language of Flowers*. She was about to sit down again when a motherly woman near the rear wall gestured to get her attention. I hadn't realized we weren't alone. Looking around I realized there were about a half-dozen people in the library with us.

There's a collection of behaviors humans have to show that we're trying. There is an apologetic bent-forward, scurrying motion people use when they are in the way, moving in crosswalks or getting out of the way of a photograph. They don't really move faster, they just move differently. Similarly, there is what I think of as "library voice," where the voice is pitched to show the speaker is aware of the need to be quiet. It isn't really quieter, just a little strained and desperate. This is the voice the woman used as she said "Melanie, we need to go over those orders. Jill can handle the desk."

Melanie nodded. She leaned down close to me and said "I have to go do this, and it'll take a while. I think you have what you need here." She leaned closer and purred in my ear, "Good to see you, Walker."

Her breath in my ear left me so rattled that I almost didn't look up to see her go. By the time I did, she was halfway through a door at the rear of the room. She turned her head, smiled at me, and pulled the door shut.

I paged absently through the books. What she had said about symbolism of white roses seemed to be accurate, but I stayed and read for a while longer, not wanting to stand until my erection subsided.

Mandy introduced the woman in the passenger seat of the Saturn as Deb. The woman barely turned to acknowledge my presence in the back seat. She had on a scarf and dark glasses, and it was hard to make out anything about her.

I kept my mouth shut for several minutes of the drive, thinking they might need to talk, but they drove in stolid silence. Eventually I filled Mandy in on the latest developments in what she called 'The War of the Roses,' and then described my visit from the UWI legal team.

"Oh, yeah, I remember that Claire said they were giving her some legal flak with a restraining order a few months ago."

"Well you might have mentioned it," I said.

"She gave the impression it was no big deal. Seemed to think it was pretty funny that somebody believed she could be a threat."

We chatted aimlessly until we pulled into the parking lot of the Palm Springs Greyhound station on Indian Canyon. "You have everything, then?" Mandy asked.

The woman turned her head, and I could see a yellowing bruise on her cheek below the rim of her sunglasses. "Sure. I'm good."

"You've got my phone numbers. You've got my address, and Erin's too, and there's another copy of everything in the ticket folder. Call any time, and call collect…You ready?"

The woman took a deep breath and nodded. They opened their car doors. "Can you hang here for a minute, Walker?" I nodded. She popped the trunk, and they both stepped out and shut the doors.

The trunk slammed, and they walked together toward the terminal, each tilting to the side with the weight of a suitcase. When they approached the glass doors of the station, they sat the luggage down and hugged. Mandy helped her inside, and returned to the car after a few minutes, swinging into the driver's seat. I moved to the front passenger side, and we headed back toward Yucca Valley.

"So why the trip to Palm Springs?" I asked. "There's bus stations all along 62."

"She's getting away from an evil shit of a husband in 29 Palms, is why. Don't want him, or anybody he knows to see her leaving, or have any idea where she's going."

"Friend of yours?"

"Not really. Somebody who came into the Clinic all beat up."

"Oh. I assumed from all the address and phone number exchange—"

Mandy sighed. "We do more of this than we ought to have to. When somebody really wants to get away, we need to stay in touch somehow, so we can send medical records, or forward messages from them back to friends and relatives…"

"Uh-huh. But why your personal address and all?"

"Because about three years ago, we helped this girl move up to Tahoe to get away from some Marine-Corps prick. And he just kept going through the Clinic's incoming mail until he found something from her, and he got the address and drove up there and shot her in the head. That's why."

"Oh. Couldn't you just have them leave off their return address…?"

"Hey, a postmark might be all the clue one of these psychos needs. No. Ever since the Tahoe thing, if somebody does a geographical, we get rid of everything in the Clinic—medical records, the works." She shook her head. "You'd think that if somebody spent their time being so pissed at somebody that they beat the hell out of them, they'd be glad to see them go… This was an easy one. You should see what happens when they have a pack of kids, too."

We drove in silence past the Desert Hot Springs cutoff, and up through the desiccated canyons which carried 62 from the Low Desert to the High. As we turned into the elevated basin of the Morongo Valley, I told her about my trip to the library to check up on flower lore. "Melanie was quite helpful. How old is she, anyway?"

Mandy glanced over at me in an indecipherable way. "Late twenties… No, twenty-nine, to be precise, because her next birthday is the big three-oh."

"And how long have she and Chad been together?"

"Why all the questions about Melanie?"

"I—I don't know, she just seems like an interesting person, and…"

Mandy's smile widened and she burst into laughter. "Oh, shit, oh, oh, I'm sorry Walker—!" She laughed harder and clutched at the steering wheel. She guided the car over to the edge of the highway and fumbled to shift into park.

It's difficult to see someone give a real belly laugh without some of the feeling rubbing off, and I felt the corners of my mouth twitching upward. At the same time, however, I had the distinct feeling that I was the butt of this joke, and I felt annoyed. "What is so damn funny?"

Mandy sat up, wiping at her eyes with one hand, waving me away with the other. "No, no, just a sec… Oh, oh man…" She shook her head, still grinning. "I'm sorry…I'm sorry…but the way you brought it up, all so fake casual, when you're practically panting over her… Oh, man…I should have warned you about Melanie. She's been cultivating a glamour for a couple of years."

"A what?" Cultivating a glamour? "That doesn't even sound grammatical."

Mandy sniffled, and ran her hands through her hair, trying to recover from her mirth. "It's a Wicca thing. It's a kind of spell that you cast on yourself to make you entrancing, desirable, irresistible."

"And this is supposed to work?"

"My God, Walker, be honest with yourself for a second: Didn't it work on you?"

I was tempted to deny it, but Mandy's mention of honesty made it obvious she saw through me. I actually managed a weak smile. "Okay. Whatever it is that she does certainly has an effect…but why?"

"Why what?"

"Why does she do it?"

Mandy shrugged. "I don't know. I'm not really into Wicca. Possibly just a discipline, like yogis standing on their heads. Maybe she felt plain when she was young but always wanted to be a goddess. Lots of people would like to be irresistible."

Accurate enough. Any man I knew would love to be able to overwhelm women the way Melanie had overpowered me: a juvenile fantasy come true. "And you?"

Mandy sniffed, a wet intake of breath that rattled in her sinuses. "I'd rather be invisible than the center of attention, frankly."

"Does she have that effect on everyone?"

"Only people with penises." She fought to suppress a widening smile.

"Great."

"Actually, forewarned is forearmed with this sort of thing. Everybody in our circle of acquaintances knows what she's doing, and so we just kind of sit back and watch it happen. It can be kind of fun to be with Melanie in a restaurant or store…you can almost see little puddles of drool accumulating around the feet of all the guys."

"Isn't that a little dangerous?" A thought struck me. "Claire wasn't doing anything like that, was she?"

"Second question first: No, Claire wasn't into Wicca. First question: Dangerous, as in stalkers or weirdos? C'mon, Walker, you didn't want to hurt Melanie, did you? More like wanting to be her love slave?" She giggled. "To do whatever she wants, just to be able to kiss the nethermost hem of her garment?"

"So does this last indefinitely? Or, now that I'm aware of it, does it just dissipate?"

"Well, being aware of it will let you fight back, but it sure would help if Melanie was really an ugly hag, with the warts and everything. Unfortunately for you, while she ain't Cinderella, there's nothing wrong with her looks. Fished in like a trout. You'll have to watch your step. To use a fine word that's been trivialized, you've been *enchanted*, ace."

"So how does Chad deal with all this?"

"Well, nobody really wants to live with a goddess twenty-four-seven, so he mostly ignores it. But I suppose when they're alone together, he lowers his guard enough to let some of that juice seep through…" She made salacious eyes at me. "I mean, wouldn't you, Walker? Just imagine: all alone with her, that attraction sort of oozing off of her…"

"Oh cut that out." It sounded good to me, and she knew it. "So am I to believe that this is literally some kind of 'spell' she casts? That there's actually some sort of—of stuff, of substance, being transmitted? Wouldn't it be easier to assume that this is some sort of self-hypnosis that changes the way she acts, and that the changes in the way she acts affect those around her, and…?"

Mandy rolled her eyes at me. "Easier to assume? What you just said didn't sound easy to me. I can tell you what's easi-est: Just notice that it works and accept it. Sure, she casts the spell on herself as much as on anyone: If you feel sexy, you are sexy. Everything's magic. Some of it's just more unusual."

20

My grandma, who lived most of her life on the Oregon coast, would have called The Ranch a stump farm, referring to Northwest lowlifes who bought a piece of land and cut all the trees for quick cash, but never got around to clearing the land. As in: "Hey! Whatcha raising there? Stumps?" There were no stumps here, but the rest of the picture fit my grandma's definitions: a scattering of trailers, a handful of what would have been outbuildings if there had been any main building, and tons of scrap in the form of wrecked car bodies, doorless refrigerators, and unrecognizable clumps of twisted metal. Weathering is slow out here, so there was every chance this technological midden would be preserved for archaeologists a thousand years hence.

A little wash ran across the property, and junked appliances filled it rim to rim. If you took every appliance ever sold out of Dad's store and bulldozed them into a ravine, this might be the result. A disturbing number of them were of the right vintages too, gold and avocado, pink and bronze, neither appliance-white nor yuppie steel.

Dad was always of two minds about his work, proud of his business and his success at it, plagued by the feeling he was cut for some finer task in life. I recalled one evening after dinner. Dad had put away a few beers, and something on television had annoyed him enough that he had jumped up and slapped the power button, turning the set off. The rest of us in the room listened to the quiet electrical crackle as the set went dark. He fell back heavily in his chair and snatched up his Miller High Life.

"The damned country is run by damned idiots and the jackasses who run the TV stations are no better. They call it a damned democracy, but if you want to have any kind of power you have to have real money." He pointed back and forth between Edgar and me, two fingers outstretched from the hand that held the beer. "That's why you need college degrees. The more the better." This seemed like preaching to the choir: Edgar had already won a Princeton scholarship for the next year, and I was taking nothing but college-prep classes. "Don't end up being a damned salesman like your old man."

"H.A.," my mother said, "you're not a salesman. You own your own business. And we make a very good living, far better than most people."

"Don't interrupt me, Evie. Point is that the little guy in this country just doesn't have any clout. I'm not John D. Rockefeller, so if they want to be anything in life they'd better get all the degrees they can. That's the only way anybody listens to you any more. And you," he said, turning to Claire, who couldn't have been more than eleven, "don't throw yourself away on some loser because he can throw a football or drives a fast car. Find a husband who has something going for him, a rich boy or a college boy, not some damned fool." He glared around the room. "You all understand?"

Edgar stretched. "If it's any consolation to you, I have never had the slightest intention of getting into sales."

Dad's face changed and he stood up. "Don't be so smug, mister. You got no right to think you're better than anybody else." He moved closer to where Edgar sat on the couch and scowled down at him. "It's sales that got you everything that you have, sales that put food in your mouth for eighteen years, and you got no damn right to criticize me or anybody else." He made an angry gesture and sloshed a little beer onto the carpet. "Do you understand?" He waited. "You understand?" he demanded.

"Yes sir," said Edgar, without meeting his eyes.

"Good." He turned and stalked from the room. Mom jumped up and hurried after him.

Edgar let out a breath that was half whistle. "What the hell was that? *Don't* be a salesman, *be* a salesman…"

"Dad's weird," I said, by way of explanation.

"Mom's weirder," Claire said. "She married him. She's the one that backs him up when he gets crazy."

"She has to," Edgar said, "she's his wife."

"If that's being a wife, maybe I should be something else."

Edgar leaned toward her. "Fine with me, sis," he said. "But let's not bring it up with Dad, okay? And for God's sake don't mention appliances."

Now parked here outside The Ranch, it seemed like someone had dumped a huge section of my childhood into the wash, jumbled about in designer colors. Probably a good place for it. I have been told repeatedly, in childhood, in high school, in college, that I would some day look back on those particular years as the best years of my life. They were all wrong. Life began for me when I graduated and started work.

If Kirsten's directions hadn't been so precise I would have driven on by, because The Ranch didn't look like a human habitation. The trailers looked just as abandoned as the junked cars. But as I idled on the road, I noticed two boys walking along together, stopping to exchange inept martial-arts blows and kicks.

I pulled off of the road and onto the property. The whole area was crisscrossed with dirt drives to the point where even the tough creosote had been pounded away by tires, and only around the edges of buildings, trailers, or car bodies could any signs of green be detected. Since the whole place seemed to be one big road, I headed for the two boys by the most direct route, curving aside around the occasional junked car.

The boys saw the Jeep coming and waited, staring slackjawed at my approach. I pulled up beside them and my trailing dust cloud caught up with us and drifted over them, but they showed no signs of caring, not even to the extent of closing their mouths. I slid open the window. "Yeah?" one of them said.

"I'm looking for Perry Benninger?" I'm not sure why I delivered this as a question.

The taller one stepped forward and tilted his head to the side, like a dog that doesn't quite understand; I half expected his ears to lift and bend. I guessed he was about seventeen. In the bright sun his tangled hair glistened with little flecks of desert sand. Mica, most likely. "Whatcha want with Perry?"

"I'm a friend of his sister."

The boy looked back at his companion in silent consultation. A few yards beyond them, I could see faces peering out between the louvers of a trailer window. I had the sensation I was being watched from a dozen different trailers and sheds.

The boy turned his head back to me and said, "So?"

"So I'd like to see Perry."

He rubbed his tongue back and forth between his top lip and his teeth while he considered this, and eventually pointed over the top of a ramshackle building, as if he was describing the trajectory of an arrow's flight. "Out there in the tackhouse." He rubbed his nose with his knuckles, and by way of encouragement added, "But he's probly busy."

I thought of asking for more precise directions, but decided it wasn't worth the trouble. If I'd believed children were our future, I'd have slashed my wrists right then. "Thanks," I said.

"God bless," he said.

I drove toward the building he had pointed over, steered between it and a silver trailer with primered patches, and found myself at a building older but better-built than the rest. I wasn't sure what a tackhouse was, but I vaguely connected it with horses, so the horseshoes nailed up on the walls made me hopeful.

By the time I shut off the engine one of the big doors on the building was opening. A young man stepped out, and I could see at once that this had to be Kirsten's brother: freckles against a deep tan, his head topped with the same glossy brunette curls, as if their parents had bought them matching caps. He slid his hands into his back pockets and waited until I got out of the car to ask, "Can I help you?"

"I'm a friend of Kirsten's." There were no steps to mount, just hardpacked dirt. I stepped forward and held out my hand. "Walker Clayborne. Claire was my sister."

His face changed from quizzical to somber. "Oh, man," he said. He looked down at my outstretched hand for a moment as if he had never seen such a gesture, and then focused. He shook my hand and then continued to grip it as he turned back toward the building, an awkward pose for both of us. We walked side by side as he laid his free arm on my back to steer me through the wide doorway.

It was dim inside, and when Perry cast me loose I was afraid to move. As far as I could see, the place was the real thing, an old ranch building rather than some modern attempt at rusticity. Shards of daylight cut through knotholes in the old boards, highlighting desert dust slowly boiling through the air, and those sharp fragments of sun made the lightbulbs in the room seem weak, grayish, limp. I fought the urge to remove my glasses and rub at my eyes. Despite the antiquated feel of the room, I gradually took in that this was some sort of an office, with a small desktop computer and a daisy-wheel printer. The monitor on the computer had a twelve-inch screen glowing with amber letters.

"Like a technology museum, huh?" Perry asked. "It's not much, but it's what we have to work with so far." He gestured with an outstretched hand and I perceived a chair behind me.

We sat, and I explained why I was there and how I thought he might help me. Before I had finished he made chopping motions with his hand. "Slow down, slow down, I think you're on the wrong road, man. I was a serious cranker, but I don't know much about the local scene. I'm from Santa Monica, remember? And most of the kids here are from Berdoo, or Riverside, or Barstow—we don't have that many locals. The person you want to talk to is Darnell, he was heavy into the speed scene around here."

"I thought that—rather, I was led to believe that he had a drinking problem, not a drug problem."

Perry leaned forward and a sunbeam fell on his mouth like a spotlight, and with the contrast against the shadows all I could see were his lips moving around the white of his teeth. "Ah, that's the thing. It's not a matter of choose one or another. Most of us out here have had more than one problem. Some of us have 'em one after another; some of us, like me, are efficient and have a whole bunch all at once." He stood. "Come on. We'll go find Darnell."

We stepped back into the daylight, and he led me off to the north, between a trailer and a shack. The door on the shack stood open, and I saw eyes peek out at us. "How many people are out here?" I asked.

"Right now, about seventy. Health department tells us that's about thirty more than we can support, but we don't admit they all live here. Keep saying we need to put in more septic and more running water." We stepped over a jumble of orange extension cords that ran between two trailers. "I'd love to do all that. And if the Lord sent us a swimming pool and a rec room, I wouldn't complain. But like I said, we work with what we've got. More'n a lot of people on this planet have."

Ahead of us was an actual mobile home, in need of paint and rust removal, but a step up from the surrounding trailers and shacks. Perry stopped in front of the door and said, "Darnell and Rachel's place. Used to see Claire out here quite a bit." He knocked, waited, and knocked again, louder. "Yo, Darnell?" He stood a while more, listening. Then he hooked his thumb at the yellow Ford pickup at the side of the trailer. I recognized it from the street in front of Church of the Rock—a late-50s model, from back when the front ends of pickups had curves and bulges, back before Detroit turned truck profiles into threatening boxes. "That's his rig, so he's around. Figured he'd be back here for lunch, but he still must be over at the shop." He turned around and started off to the left. "With Rachel away the man doesn't seem to know what time of day it is."

He guided me off through another maze of tilting sheds and trailers. To fill the silence, I asked, "Are these people all out here of their own free will, or does a court send them here, or what?"

"All the adults are here because they decided to be. That's how I got here. But the juveniles, most of them are here because their parents decided to put them here to clean up. There's some good kids, but some real hardheads, too."

"So some of the kids here aren't here voluntarily?" We passed a shed with some kind of rumbling equipment inside.

He sighed. "You ever hear the term *in loco parentis*? A while back social services decided we couldn't keep kids here unless we had affidavits from the parents that we were acting in their stead. More paperwork every day. Feels like I'm my father. I'm too young for this shit."

"How do you keep them here if they don't want to be here?"

He laughed. "How did your parents keep you at home when you didn't want to be? Guilt, threats, lack of anyplace else to go." He threw his arms wide as if displaying the desert, though in truth we were in the midst of The Ranch's sheds and shacks. "Where they going to run off to out here?"

Ahead was a large shed topped with the kind of fiberglass panels that were popular for patio roofs back in the 1950s: corrugated, translucent sheets of blue-green plastic that yellowed around the edges as they aged. As we approached there was the stutter of an engine starting up, searching for a steady rhythm, and then dying out in a cough. "That's Darnell," Perry said. "Fixes things up and resells them. Genius with his hands."

The big wooden door was on slides, the rusty wheels just nailed to the side of the building. Perry braced himself and used both hands to run the door open. He brushed off his hands, and said, "Darnell. We have a visitor."

The shed was lit by nothing but the sun coming down through the fiberglass. It was plenty of light to work by, but the tint of the panels made it look as if we were all underwater. At one end of the big workbench in the center of the room was an outboard motor, its prop hanging down over the edge as if someone planned to launch the whole table. Darnell stood next to it, wiping his hands on a greasy rag.

"Have you been introduced?" Perry asked. I started to say yes, but Perry went right on. "Walker Clayborne? Darnell Huber."

"We met," Darnell said.

I stuck out my hand. Darnell looked down at his own as if dubious about offering it; every detail of his palm stood out in relief against the dark grime embedded there. He reached forward and gave me a hard, dry clasp. I gave my own hand what I hoped was an unobtrusive glance after he let loose of it, but it was clean; whatever dirt was on Darnell's hand was virtually part of his skin.

I explained how I thought he might be of help, detailing what I knew of Claire's connection with the drug trade in the area, the circumstances of her death. His eyes kept wandering back to the outboard. After no more than a minute, he picked up a screwdriver and began to poke around in the open top of the engine, giving a curt nod every so often to emphasize that he was listening.

I kept waiting for him to interrupt with some sort of reaction. Eventually I tailed off into a lame, "So, what do you think?"

There was no apparent reaction from Darnell, who seemed engrossed in some fine adjustment in the motor. Perry hitched himself up onto a table by the wall. The silence didn't seem to bother either of them.

Darnell finished what he was doing, glanced in my direction, and looked back down at his work before he said, "Makes some sense." He set down the screwdriver, picked up the rag, and scrubbed hard down inside the housing. He tossed the rag back on the table and picked up the screwdriver again, poking at something. Just when I had decided he wasn't going to speak again without a direct question, he continued. "They's a few people dealin' around here…some other people make the stuff. I don't talk with any of them these days. I had sufficient back when."

"Would any of them have wanted to hurt Claire?"

He cocked his head sideways like a robin spotting movement in the grass and peered suspiciously into the motor. His eyes narrowed and he tapped the tip of screwdriver against something, pulled back and then tapped it hard. "Could be," he said. "Could well be."

I was about to ask another question when he surprised me by offering, "That bunch out by Emerson, now. I never bought from them. But Claire had all manner of trouble with them selling to people she was tryin' to keep straight. Know for a fact she bitched'em out about it, pardon my French."

"By Emerson? You mean out by the dry lake?"

"Was. Heard tell they moved to Las Flores." He twisted the screwdriver with force, and then put it down on the table.

"Where's Las Flores?"

He seemed to ignore my question. "'Scuse me." He held the motor steady with his left hand on top of the casing and grabbed the starter cord with his right. It sputtered and roared. He let the cord whip back so the pull handle slapped into its fitting, and reached into the inside top of the engine with his right hand. He found what must have been part of the choke system and adjusted it, and the engine's spastic pulse steadied.

It was far too loud for the confines of the shed, and I had to fight not to stick my fingers in my ears. I noticed Perry had already covered his ears with his palms, so I abandoned any pretense of toughness and did the same.

Darnell reached down with his right hand and picked up the screwdriver, but this time held it like a knife ready to stab. He fit it down into what I assumed was the carburetor and pried at something, apparently trying to bend a part or line into position. Whatever the screwdriver was wedged against suddenly gave, and the force of his levering right arm flipped the whole motor sideways. His left hand flew out to steady it and there was a distinct *thik* as some part of his hand hit against the spinning propeller blade. A few drops of darkness arced up.

He quickly righted the engine and shut it down, then immediately thrust the ring finger of his left hand into his mouth. There was a huge smear of blood on the side of the engine housing where he had grabbed it with his injured hand. Perry and I crowded in next to him, asking stupidly if he was hurt.

He pulled his finger from his mouth and grabbed it with the index finger and thumb of his other hand. He turned his head to the side, taking careful aim between my shoulder and his, and spat a huge gob of bloody saliva onto the dirt floor. Only then did he look closely at his finger. He released the clenching tension of thumb and forefinger and bent the tip of his ring finger back. Before the blood welled out in a long pulse I caught a glimpse of virgin-white bone in the gash. He pressed the cut closed and applied more pressure. Under the green light from the roof, the blood was blackish. "Band-Aids and tape in the toolbox," he said to Perry.

Perry knelt by the workbench and I heard the clatter as he rummaged through the tools, but my gaze was locked on the trickles of blood running down Darnell's upright wrist, the thin liquid lines growing and branching like a time-lapse movie of roots reaching down into the soil. "Out on the old cutoff, Two-Mile Road, over'n Twenty-Nine Palms," Darnell said, apparently to me.

"What?" I asked.

"Las Flores," Darnell said. Perry had dumped Band-Aids, gauze, and athletic tape onto the benchtop, and Darnell studied them for a moment before saying, "Take a length of that tape and pull it round the base of my finger tight as ever you can." Perry scrabbled to get the edge of the tape started. "It's an old motel. All finished now… Tighter'n that, boy… Okay, hold it."

He let loose of his hand, and the blood flowed, but slower. He snatched up a gauze pad, wiped his finger with one long pull, tossed the wet gauze down and wrapped another around the wound. He pressed his finger and the pad hard against the tabletop and grabbed the roll of tape. He stuck the leading edge of the tape to the back of his wounded finger and then lifted the whole affair up and whipped the tape around in a circle. Then, slowly, he wrapped turn after turn, pulling it as tight as he could. "Can't say as they're still there," he added, "not for sure. That line of work, people move house a lot."

"I can drive you to the ER," I said.

He put his hand down on the table and used a carpet knife to cut the tape. "Take it kindly but no thanks."

"That'll require stitches," Perry said.

"Maybe. If it does, Doc Stewart can do'em. Ain't got money for no emergency room."

I almost offered to cover his costs, but decided it might not be taken in the proper spirit. "Fine," I said, "I can drive you wherever you like, then."

His lips moved as if he were going to spit again, but all he did was say, "I can *drive* myself. It's only my left hand." He patted his pocket, heard the jangle of keys. He started out the door, paused, and without turning to me said, "They ain't there anymore, then you ask around for the Ridgecrest Boys. People'll know who you're asking after." He stalked out without a further word.

"The man's got a little too much pride," Perry said. "But the Lord seldom fixes everything at once. When I got straight, I thought everything was all fixed. But, you know? It just cleared things up enough to see what the real problems were. Know what I mean?"

This was one of those questions I would usually have dismissed with a thoughtless agreement, but I paused to ponder it for a moment. "Actually," I said, "I think I do."

I didn't stay long after that. For a change, I wanted to get back to Claire's house well before the sun started down.

21

There was little to do but wait for the enigmatic daily visitor. I tried to read, but couldn't focus. I put on some music—Delibes' *Lakmé*—but when the gorgeous female duet came on, I imagined it piercing the walls and warning people away. In the end, I sat in silence with a cup of tea.

I have been told that in total quiet the ear begins to manufacture sounds, that our auditory nerves are always so poised to fire that if left unstimulated for long they begin to go off in their own strange rhythms, like some timbral form of masturbation. I have spent many days in some of the quietest places on the globe, alone in the great deserts of the earth, and this has never happened to me. It may be the constant chatter of my own mind is more than sufficient to ward off the sensation of too much silence.

Now, however, I was actively listening. Even inside the cottage my ears reached out for the faintest and most distant sounds. It is extraordinary how much you can hear if you pay full attention, and perhaps even more extraordinary just how much damn noise humans have created, even out at the edge of the desert. I could hear the overflights of passenger jets, the distant roar of highway traffic, and what must have been assault helicopters far off at the Marine base in Twenty-Nine Palms.

So it was that I heard the motorcycle long before it turned onto my street, at first just a tickling at the edge of my hearing, then louder and louder, and I waited, each moment certain it would turn aside or somehow transmute into another kind of machine, until at last it turned into the driveway and became intolerable, half bellow and half chain-saw whine. The engine died and I breathed again.

I picked up the baseball bat, slipped the pepper spray into my pocket, and crept out the back door. I pushed it open with all the delicacy I could muster. I edged past the Jeep and worked my way forward along the side of the house. I put each foot down with care, touching heel down first and then rolling the sole of my shoe forward, but despite this attempt at stealth the crunchy sands seemed to squinch in protest at each step.

I reached the corner and stopped to listen. Nothing. I peered around the edge and looked toward the front door. A few feet from me was a lime-green dirtbike perched on its kickstand. Beyond it, sitting on the front doormat with his back leaned against the door, was a young man—a child, really, he seemed. A motorcycle helmet and a backpack were placed carefully by his side. One knee was drawn up high; the other leg stretched out along the ground. Between the fingertips of both hands he held a single white rosebud. His lips moved without sound.

I'm neither sure what I'd been expecting nor what I was planning. I think I had envisioned a more furtive visitor, someone carrying a great secret or dark purpose. I would have leapt out, brandishing my bat like a club, demanding explanations...

I felt a little foolish. I tilted the bat against the wall, stepped from behind the corner, and said, "Excuse me?"

He didn't start at my voice, but merely turned his head and looked. I could see why Mrs. Givens had been unsure whether he was male or female: he was slim, and his face lacked even the slightest trace of a beard. His eyes were a soft blue, and he had that smooth, asexual beauty most of us show only before puberty.

I took a few steps toward him. "Might I ask what you're doing here?"

Without turning his face, he let his head fall back against the door, as if even thinking about answering this question exhausted him. From that position he said, "Just leaving a present."

"For who?"

"For Claire."

"Why?"

"I think she would have liked it." He looked at his bent knee a few inches from his face, studied it as if he had never seen it before, and then turned his face to me. "Who are you, anyway?"

I unconsciously found myself adopting authoritative postures; my hands went to my hips; then I abandoned that, and crossed my arms in front of my chest; this, too, felt wrong, and I let them hang by my side, unsure of where they belonged. "It seems to me I ought to be the one asking who you are, but I'm Claire's brother Walker."

"Oh." He pulled himself up into a squat. "I'm Malcolm. Claire was a friend."

"I haven't heard of you. How did you know Claire?"

"That's a long story."

"I have time. Would you like to come inside? You can put the rose in the vase with the rest of them."

After the slightest hesitation, he agreed. I seated him on the couch, freshened my tea, and brought him, as requested, a glass of water, no ice, room temperature please. I sat in one of the armchairs and asked, "So how did you come to know Claire?"

"She was my substance-abuse counselor. Over at Eagle Mountain." My astonishment must have been plain—were we throwing children in prison now?—because he continued by saying, "I'm twenty-two, you know. And it was my second offense. Mandatory minimum sentence; the judge said she didn't want to give it to me, but her hands were tied."

I shuddered at the thought of what prison life would be like for such a pretty young boy, and once again Malcolm seemed to read my mind. "Everybody left me alone." He narrowed his eyes into a self-conscious, sly expression. "By the end of my first day in the place, I made sure everybody there knew I was HIV positive. Actually, I also got the word out that I had AIDS, since I figured a lot of the retards in there didn't know what HIV was."

"Oh. And everybody left you alone?"

"Pretty much. I mean, look." He put the glass of water down on the floor and then held both arms out toward me, heels of his hands upward as if waiting to be handcuffed. I saw that his elbows bowed a little past 180 degrees, something you don't see often in men. I craned my head forward, puzzled. Impatient, he jiggled his elbows up a little and said, "Tracks. Show a long line of needle marks, and people will believe you in a minute: AIDS, Hep C, whatever. Hel-lo, Mr. Toxic. Look but don't touch. Oh, there was one guy, came to me, said, hey, nobody knows it, but I'm HIV-positive too, so what have we got to lose? I told him that if he so much as looked at me funny I'd tell everybody his little secret, and the guys he'd been blowing in the shower would probably kill him."

"So are you really infected?"

"What do you care?"

"I guess I don't, really."

"In that case, no, I'm not. I shot up a lot of shit, but I always kept it real sterile, never shared my kit with anybody. Makes a good story, though." He picked up his glass from the floor and settled back on the couch. "I've been strung out on one thing or another since I was fifteen. Probably still would be, if not for your sis."

"She cured you, so to speak?"

"No. You don't get cured. Junkies are born, not made. What she did was give me something else to put in the hungry place."

"God, I suppose?"

He smiled like I were an eager but dim child. "Poetry."

"Poetry."

"Yeah. Part of our group counseling, she had us all keeping journals. Sometimes we had to read from them. One day after I read out of mine, she asked if I'd mind if she borrowed it. Well, hell no. Then she comes back, says, Malcolm, I've got some things maybe you should look at." He put his glass down again and hefted his backpack off the floor. He unzipped the main compartment and pulled out paperbacks: Yeats, *Complete Poems*, Stevens, *Palm at the End of the Mind*, Wakoski, *Dancing On the Grave of a Sonofabitch*, Snodgrass, *De/Compositions*. "A whole new world, man. Now if something goes wrong, I don't get loaded, I write about it. And if I feel like I really want a spike in my arm, I write about *that*."

"Did she use this approach with many people? Poetry therapy, that is?"

"Doubt it. Claire did what works, you know; and that's different for everybody."

I thought for a moment. "And the roses? What's the explanation for that?"

He looked down at his lap. "I don't know, man. It seemed like something she would have liked—symbolic, you know." He looked up again and his eyes were wet. "Word got around pretty fast after she got killed. Even when they had it roped off, I'd ride past every day. One day the rose thing just came to me, kind of like visiting her grave." He spread his hands. "I don't even know where she's buried, you know…"

"In Phoenix. Back where we come from."

"Can you give me directions? I'd like to spend some time there. If it's okay."

"Sure."

"Anyhow, I kept wanting to come up to the place—I spent a lot of time here, you know, I lived on this couch for a while—but that yellow tape was up, and one time when I thought about coming in anyway, I saw that prick Detective Bolles was here. So forget that."

"You know Bolles?"

"Sure. Who doesn't? He's a jerk. A scary jerk. For a while, he tried to—"

The phone rang. Intent on Malcolm's narrative, it startled me enough that I didn't reach over to pick it up until the third ring.

It wasn't the last person in the world I would have expected to call, but he could have chatted with the last person from his position in line: J. Raymond Gerrity, PhD, Vice-Chancellor for Administrative Affairs at UCSD. Jay-Ray. I made a gesture of helplessness at Malcolm, and he stood up and walked to the back of the room to pore over Claire's bookshelves.

He offered the usual condolences—something I was getting a little tired of—and apologized profusely for calling over the break, on my sabbatical, on a Saturday evening. He described the trouble he had gone to locate me, and said he would have never disturbed me were it not for the fact that, "We have a little bit of a situation here. Someone in the governor's office, from the economic development group, called me today. And I imagine you already know what it was regarding."

"On the contrary. I don't have the slightest idea what you're talking about."

"There's a major development project out there in the desert—UWI, I believe is the name. And I'm told you're unreasonably interfering in the project. Now I don't know the facts of the matter. But this was from the governor's office. Up in Sacramento."

"I know where the governor's office is, Jay-Ray."

"Well?"

"Well what?"

"Well, what am I supposed to tell them?"

"Whatever you want."

He hmmm'ed and mmmm'ed for a moment, almost as if he was eating something yummy. "The thing of it is, Walker, this is important to Sacramento, and this is a very influential corporation, and…well, they asked me to intercede, and just see if you could, you know, *go easy* here."

"I don't see that I'm answerable to you, much less to them, for what research I undertake. Tell them to go scare somebody who doesn't have tenure yet."

"Uh, well—I don't quite know how to put this, you know, but there are apparently possible questions of moral turpitude, and tenure can be stripped in such cases… I'm given to understand that you've been associating with some sort of radical group out there, and that there's been a complaint sworn out against you for terroristic threatening, even some kind of court order."

"Wait a minute. Let me get this straight. Are you threatening me and my position—"

"No, no, that's not what I meant—"

"—because of pressure from a bunch of politicians and Big Money from Back East—"

"—now, what I was trying to say—"

"—because, if you are, if you're trying to suppress my academic freedom to inquire into a significant environmental problem because of outside pressure, then I can tell you right now, all kinds of people are going to be interested, from the academic senate, to the faculty council, to half the newspapers in California. So just back off, Jay-Ray, or you'll be the one who's out of a job."

"Walker, you're taking this all wrong…"

"At the moment, I'm too pissed off to take it any other way. So let's talk another time."

"Maybe that's a good idea, I understand you're quite distraught given your recent tragedy, and—"

"You have no idea. Don't call me again. If you need to say anything, leave a message at my office. Or better yet: communicate with me through the academic senate."

"Look, Walker, I—"

I dropped the receiver back in the cradle. Malcolm was staring at me with some degree of surprise. "Man," he said, "I can see now that you're related to Claire."

It took some work to convince him I wanted to take him out to eat; took even more work to get him to state a food preference (Mexican); and then when we finally pulled up at Ramona's over in Twenty-Nine Palms, I practically had to drag him inside. "I meant a taco stand, or something," he protested.

"Well, I don't feel like eating at a taco stand tonight, so let's just go in here."

He was ravenous. Where in his slim body he found room for a three-item combination plate was a mystery. He cleaned his plate while I was still picking at my first enchilada, and then sat back, continuing to work at the second basket of chips they had brought.

I brushed aside his thanks and tried to get back to our earlier talk. "Before I left you were about to tell me about Detective Bolles…" I prompted.

"Yeah." He sat up straighter and brushed the hair back off his forehead. "Well, you see, when I got out of Eagle Mountain I hung around the area. I didn't have anyplace to go, really, and Claire got me started trying to get my GED…"

"You don't have a high school diploma?" I asked, amazed.

"No," he said. "I didn't get through high school. It doesn't mean I'm stupid."

"I'm sorry, I just—well, you seem like an intelligent young man, and with the poetry and all, I just assumed— This isn't coming out well. Forget it."

"Anyhow, Claire told me that I was smart enough to go to college, maybe even major in English or something. She was helping me a lot, and letting me crash at her place when there was nowhere else to stay."

"I'm sure you are smart enough to go to college. You seem smarter than most of my students."

"So you're a college teacher?" He seemed awed.

"Sure. Don't look at me like it's such a big deal. Anybody can do it if they don't mind staying in school for an extra eight or twelve years. It's not the brains, it's the endurance."

"Huh." He thought about this for a while. "Anyhow, Bolles knew me from the old days, when I used to sometimes run stuff from Barstow up to the Central Valley. I told him everything I knew about that, which wasn't much, but he didn't seem to care. He started putting pressure on me to get him information on this bunch of dealers out at this old motel. Wanted me to join the gang, give him info. Threatened to find some way to catch me in a parole violation if I didn't play along. Even fake one if he had to."

This was starting to ring any number of bells. "This motel wasn't by any chance called 'Las Flores,' was it?"

"Yeah." He frowned. "How'd you know that?"

"Someone else told me something about it. And was there a guy who ran this operation?"

"Yeah. I never met him, but he had a mean rep. The guy was called Joop."

Joop. The name that Bolles' informer Jesse had mentioned the first day I had been in town. "So what did you do?"

"Only thing I knew to do: I asked Claire."

"And?"

"And I guess she ripped him a new one. I don't know. But she had some kind of a meeting with him, and she told me everything was cool—that if I just stayed straight, Bolles wouldn't bother me anymore."

"And did he?"

"No. I guess he probably got somebody else. But he still makes me nervous, and now with Claire gone…" He rubbed his face with both hands. "God, I miss her. The closest I came to shooting up again was right after I heard the news about her. But then I said, hey, man, that'd be a hell of a way to honor her memory. Why don't you remember her by just staying straight instead?"

"Maybe you could write a poem."

"No. Still way way too recent for that." He looked like he might cry, and I was sure he didn't want me to see that, sensitive poet or not, so I switched the subject to college. He wanted to know everything about college, and became fascinated with the details of being a professor. He wanted to know if professors made a lot of money; his idea of a big salary turned out to be anything over $30,000 annually. I affirmed that I earned more than that, but was too embarrassed to mention that his "big money" figure was about a quarter of my salary. When he asked why I wasn't at school, I explained that there was a long holiday break, and that in any case I was on sabbatical.

"Wow. Let me get this straight: You get more than thirty grand every year, you can't be fired, and you get these research vacations, these whaddyacallums—"

"Sabbaticals."

"Right. Man, that is sweet. No wonder all the smart people become professors. My mind's made up: I'm going to school to be a college teacher."

"Well, it's a lot more work than it seems like."

"Beats loading boxes for five bucks an hour."

I had to agree. I steered him back to the issue of drugs, and he filled me in on the Las Flores gang: "They mainly deal speed, but they do some crack, sometimes some heroin. Pretty much anything that's white and powdery—though some of their smack's that brownish Mexican shit."

"And how do they get their drugs?"

"I'm not sure where they run the stuff in from these days, but I know those guys don't manufacture around here. Somebody cooks shit around here, because some of the crank we used to get up in Bakersfield was sourced out of here—I used to run some of it up. But the Las Flores guys don't seem to be tied into whoever the locals are in these parts. Their speed probably comes from some place in the Central Valley, the other shit probably comes across from Mexico."

"Why doesn't Bolles just raid their motel and search the place?"

"Probably has by now. These guys aren't stupid enough to keep their shit where they live. That's strictly small-time. The guys who work for them, who actually do street retail, they probably keep their stash around the house, but serious guys don't do that."

"So that's why Bolles wanted you to join up with them? To find out where they keep their—uh—merchandise?"

"Probably. Who knows? He's a weird, weird guy."

"Indubitably."

He laughed. "Now *that's* a great word."

Back at Claire's he was flabbergasted when I gave him all of her poetry books. "But I'm sure she would have wanted *you* to have them," he said.

"I very seriously doubt it. And I'm absolutely certain that you can give them a better home than I would. They were meant to be read, not stored."

He gathered some up, and it became obvious he would have to come back for at least another trip, if not two. He started to zip up his newly heavy backpack and paused, a little embarrassed. "I hate to ask for another favor after all you've done…"

I expected him to hit me up for money. Why not? I was feeling generous.

"Back before she— Back before Claire died, she offered to type up some of my poems on the computer so I could have printed copies.

I don't know if she ever got them all typed in. If she did, I'd really like to have printouts…"

"No problem. Go ahead and make them now."

"Well, that's the thing, you see; I've never used a computer. That's why it's a pretty big favor."

"No, it's easy. Do you know the file name?"

He made a face and shrugged.

"Don't worry about it. I'll prowl through her files. If I find it, I'll print it out. If not, well, I'll look a little harder. And Malcolm?"

"Yeah?"

"Can we leave off the white roses stuff now? We're all a little nervous around here these days."

After Malcolm left, I scanned the internet for the number of the *UCSD Guardian*, the school paper. As I expected, there was someone there even over the break—using the T1 line to surf the web, no doubt—and after they satisfied themselves as to my identity, they dug up the home phone for Teresa Hernandez, one of the two news editors. She had interviewed me the previous semester for a story about earthquake preparedness and, although I hadn't given the answer she would have preferred—that we were all fated to die because the school was trying to save a few dollars—we parted on good terms.

Whoever answered the phone—her mother, I suspected—barely spoke English. She said, "'Scuse," and shouted, "Roberto!"

Roberto told me Teresa had gone to the store for ice cream, and was expected back within a half hour. I left my name and both phone numbers.

I was surprised to find it was only a little past seven. I had discovered Malcolm just before dark, but dark at this time of year was well before five. In addition, it had been a crowded day even before dinner with Malcolm: I'd been served with a restraining order, seen Melanie at the library, accompanied a battered woman to Palm Springs, visited Darnell at The Ranch, and told my vice-chancellor for admin to screw himself. I wasn't sure if I was getting anywhere, but I was certainly stirring up a lot of dust.

I stood and stretched, walked back to Claire's study. I was tired, but too wound up to think about sleeping; plus, if I went to sleep now, when would I wake up? Three in the morning? My eyes fell on the flyer from Thursday: *God's Army—GOD'S LAW. Local Chapterhouse, 2420 Hoot Owl Lane, Landers.* Why not at least drive by? I looked it up in the Thomas Guide, and headed out.

There were shorter ways to get there, but not faster. I drove over to 247, headed east on Reche Road, and turned north on Belfield. Belfield collides with Linn Road, and then takes a discontinuous hop to the right. At the junction with Linn, I waited at the stop sign and studied the looming dome of Landers' most famous building, the Integratron. Van Tassel, the Lockheed engineer who had built it back in the '50s, claimed it was a healing center built according to blueprints given to him by visitors from Venus. There were lights on around the structure, and it looked like it had been renovated. Interesting town, Landers: a medieval-minded anti-witch cult within shouting distance of a center designed by Venusian spaceship pilots.

I turned right, swung up onto the continuation of Belfield, meandered back west on a couple of side roads, and reached Hoot Owl. It was easy to find the address; there were only three houses on the street. I parked across from 2420 and killed the motor.

The street was dark, but the chapterhouse was well-lit. It was an old house with a large prefab sun porch attached to the front. The sun porch—all glass on aluminum struts—held a half-dozen tables, each covered with displays of books and pamphlets. Although there were several vehicles parked on the flat area next to the house, inside the bright porch there was only a woman, reading intently at one of the tables. Moths and other night insects hovered around all sides of the glass like an animated fog exuded from the surface. A sign on the door: *God's Law Reading Room and Bookstore. 10 am-8 pm, Mon-Sat. Open to all Christians.* I'd been through catechism and even confirmation, so I supposed I fit with the letter of the admissions requirements, if not with the spirit.

The cell phone beeped. I groped across the passenger seat, found it on the second ring, and hit *talk.* "Hello?" I said.

"Dr. Clayborne? Teresa."

"Oh, Teresa, thanks for calling back."

"Is something wrong?"

"No, nothing, why?"

"Because you're whispering."

I realized she was right. I assumed a normal voice and told her about the controversy over the UWI dump site. She asked a couple of questions, clearly pausing to scribble notes, but didn't show signs of much interest until I mentioned the restraining order. When I related the call from the governor's office to the vice-chancellor's office, and Jay-Ray's call to me, she was simultaneously outraged and delighted. I knew the story had at least some news potential, but she seemed to have visions of Pulitzers in her mind's eye. "Keep me in this—please, I really mean it," she said. "Call whenever you want, day or night. I can be on the ground out there in no time."

I tried to tell her this wasn't exactly Watergate, but she would have none of it: "You don't get it. This is my ticket out of journalism school."

When we rang off I felt less nervous, more confident. It was nice to touch base with a world where I was a real player.

I stepped out of the Jeep and walked across the dark street to the brightness of the Reading Room.

The woman looked up from her book and favored me with a bright smile. "First time here?" I nodded. "Okay. Everything's for sale, unless we're down to only one copy—then you have to wait while we order it. You can read whatever you like while you're here, and you're welcome to stay as long as you want… Oh, and you can have drinks in here, but you have to keep all food outside—there's some picnic benches around the corner. Any questions?"

I had plenty of questions—*Are you a group of murderous fanatics?* came to mind—but I merely thanked her. "You need anything, I'm right here," she said, and went back to her book.

I glanced through the titles propped up on display. The room was a festival of crackpot diatribes, ranging from the 1500s—Jakob Sprenger's *Malleus Maleficarum* and James I's *Daemonologie*—down to more recent and less literate works; my favorites included *Messengers of the Devil: The Real Meaning of UFOs* and *Christ-Killers: How the Jews Abandoned God for Satan.*

I was most interested in finding some of Reverend Gorston's writings, since it seemed like the easiest way to get some insight into the nature of the God's Law organization. Before I could ask the woman about it, the door from the house opened and someone stepped down the stairs into the porch.

I locked eyes with him only briefly, and then looked away, hoping he didn't recognize me, but he moved across the room in a few strides and positioned himself between me and the entryway. Moonface, one of the Shackles crowd that had crossed swords with Mandy in the coffeeshop. I pretended to be absorbed in looking at the book titles.

"What the hell are you doin' here?" he asked.

"Watch your language, Donnie," the woman said.

"Hey!" he yelled back at the house. "We got a visitor here!" In a lower voice, he said, "You get outta here, Sarah…you *get!*"

She jumped up and ran into the house in a swirl of long skirt.

I turned to face him. "Is there a problem here? There's a 'welcome' sign on the door, and I—"

A figure in black hopped down the stairs. "What's the problem?"

"He's a spy, that's the problem. I seen him just a few days ago with that witch-bitch Mandy. You can ask Billy."

The man in black had a weightlifter's build, and sported a large T-shirt on a body that demanded extra-large. He walked toward me, in no hurry. Blond and square-chinned, eyes set much too close together. I was sure he was part of the trio of clones I'd seen behind Reverend Gorston two nights before.

"What *are* you doing here?" he asked, stepping closer.

I tried to keep my voice matter-of-fact, without much success. "I'm just looking at these books. The sign on your door implied—"

"He's one of them, Rafe," Donnie said. "He was right there with her, and she told all kinds of lies, and twisted the scriptures, and—"

"Shut up, Donnie. Send Gabe and Mike out here, tell 'em we got a situation." Rafe stepped so close I could feel his breath; his manner was calm, but his breathing was strangely excited. He waited until Donnie was out of the room, and said, "We really need to talk."

"Fine, I have no problem with that, but I'd like—"

He spun me around, jerked my left arm up behind me in a painful half-nelson, and leveraged it until I was bent at the waist, the upper half of my body flat against a book-laden tabletop. "Look," I began.

"You just lay still for a minute. We're not gonna hurt you unless you deserve it."

I heard rapid footsteps entering the room. Hands grabbed me from all sides and yanked me up off the table, but all I could see was a blur of black to my sides. A rope tied my hands behind me, firm and expert, and then the rope was pulled up my back and looped around my neck. A quick jerk made me stand up tall, choking. "Let's take a little trip outside."

They marched me back out the front door of the sun porch and around to the makeshift parking lot at the side. The light from the Reading Room spilled out as if the whole porch were a giant lamp, and our shadows rushed out at the cars.

They slammed me onto my back atop the hood of a car and held me there, my feet kicking just a few inches above the ground. All of my weight bore down on my tied hands. One of my captors grabbed the free end of the rope and went to one side of the hood, while another grabbed the rope from the other side, just before it circled around my neck. I was pinned down by the rope around my throat, and without a word, they both tugged a little, just to show me they could. I choked. They loosened up and I sucked in a ragged breath.

I could hear footsteps crunching through the sand, as if a small crowd were gathering. "Now," Rafe said, "what are you doing here?"

"I was at Church of the Rock on Thursday night," I said. I swallowed. "I got a flyer inviting me to come."

"And what is your connection to the witch? Why were you consorting with Mandy Cicerone, a known and sworn servant of Satan?"

"She's not a servant of Satan, she—"

They tightened the rope again and I felt a crackling sensation in my throat. They let up and I coughed and choked, fighting to free my hands.

"Don't argue. Just tell us: what is your connection with the known witch, Mandy Cicerone?"

"She was a friend of my sister's."

"And your sister would be…?"

"Claire Clayborne."

"And why were you—"

"Let him up," another voice said.

"You're not in charge here," Rafe said.

"Right now I am." There were sounds of a momentary scuffle and a body hit the ground with a thud. "I said, let him up." The rope went slack, and I squirmed forward until my feet touched the ground. I rolled painfully to a standing position.

Billy, the giant Shackles biker, hulked next to me, but he was looking at the ground about ten feet away, where Rafe lay sprawled.

As I watched, Rafe lifted himself to a sitting position; it was clear the fall had knocked the wind out of him. "You don't know who you're messing with, Billy," he said.

"Yeah I do," Billy answered, "somebody I can slap the piss out of." He addressed the area in general. "Take it back inside, folks, less you want to argue about it." He busied himself untying my hands as the handful of people drifted out of the parking lot. Rafe was on his feet glaring at us. "You know where to find me, pretty boy," Billy said, without looking up. He let the rope fall to the ground, and my freed hands went immediately to rub at my throat.

"You're really Claire's brother?"

"Yeah. Thanks."

"I owe her."

"I'd say that debt is more than paid off, at least from my perspective."

He shook his big hairy head. "No. I mean I owed her big-time. She was my counselor out at Eagle Mountain."

"Well, that was her job." We were alone in the parking lot now, but I knew eyes were watching us from the house.

"More than that." He tugged at the bottom of his beard. "After I got out of prison, I stuck my beak right back in the bag. I was snorting down everything I earned or could steal, even though a condition of my parole was monthly blood tests. I just decided not to show for 'em. Next thing I know Claire's bangin' on the door of my trailer down in Coachella."

"She came and found you? Was she part of your parole supervision?"

"Nope. Just heard about what a mess I was and showed up… Now, not too many people come tell me what-for when I'm coming down from a week's speed run." He shuffled his feet, looked up, then looked me in the eye. "But the Lord put just the right words into her mouth. She said, Billy, big as you are, everybody needs to believe in something bigger than themselfs. We need it, like water or air. You better get straight, Billy. And you ain't gonna do it on your own. You gotta ask for help."

Billy turned and hefted his butt up onto the hood of the car where I had been roped down. His eyes grew distant, a poet declaiming above the heads of his audience. "I told her to mind her own damn business and get the hell out of my trailer. But after she left, I looked in the mirror, and I saw the Devil lookin' back at me. And that was when Jesus came into my heart, and then everything in my life changed."

"If you're a friend of Claire's, then why were you threatening Mandy?"

This seemed to make him a little uncomfortable. "Just cause I love Claire doesn't mean I have to like all her friends."

"You seem to like her enemies well enough."

"What d'ya mean?"

"These God's Law people. The reason I'm out here tonight is because I think they might have had something to do with Claire's murder."

"No. No, that's impossible…"

"Why? Aren't they talking about hunting down witches?"

"Claire was no witch…"

"Mandy's no witch either, but they about strangled me just for knowing her. And I don't know her nearly as well as Claire did. I heard their presentation at the Church the other night. These people are psycho."

"They're only doing as the Bible commands…"

"Oh? You know that line from Exodus, 'Thou shalt not suffer a witch to live?' The Hebrew word they translated as 'witch' was *chasph*, which doesn't mean 'witch' at all, it means 'poisoner.'" I didn't think I'd strengthen my case by mentioning it was Mandy who had brought this to my attention.

He frowned. "Is that true?"

"It is. And here are these people worked up into a panic over something that's a mistranslation in the first place. They're ready to overthrow the Constitution and deal out death based on God's Word, when they don't even know what the right Word is." I leaned against the hood of the car, suddenly exhausted.

Billy seemed lost in thought. At length, he said, "Maybe I've been too quick to make up my mind about some things. And maybe I'm listening to the wrong people."

"Well, I'm not a Bible expert, but I know that it tells us not to judge others, and that vengeance is a prerogative of the Lord." I clasped my hands behind my neck and pulled my head down to stretch it. "I need to get back home. I'm beat."

"I'll see you off."

He trudged with me across the street to the Jeep. "Who are those guys, anyway?" I asked.

"The punks in black? Rafe, Mike, and Gabe. Call themselves the Angels. Don't know their full names."

"They always dress like that?"

"Always."

I stepped up into the Jeep and started it up with the door still open. "Thanks again. If you hadn't shown up, they might have killed me."

"Don't mention it. If there's anything I can do for you, just ask—I owe it to Claire. But they wouldn't have killed you. They were just trying to put a little scare in you."

"Are you sure?"

Billy was still chewing his lip, thinking about it, when I drove off.

I didn't start shaking until I was nearly back to Claire's, but when I did it became so severe I had to pull over. Once in the cottage, I considered calling the sheriff's office and filing an assault complaint. But after thinking it over, I decided it was premature; there might be a more useful way to handle the matter of God's Law. I called Mandy.

"So are you ready for tomorrow?" she asked.

"Tomorrow?"

"The big experiment at Ettenmoor's."

"Oh." I remembered I'd agreed to participate, but I had forgotten tomorrow was Sunday. "Sure. But I was calling about something else." I gave her a quick review of my experience at the chapterhouse that evening, shushing her exclamations of dismay. "Now here's what I'd like to do, if you can figure out how to program it…"

When I finished, she said, "Sure. Not my long suit, but do-able. I probably won't get it done tonight, though—maybe not even tomorrow, with all the prep I have to do for this experiment."

"No matter. And what exactly is this experiment, anyway? Ettenmoor was very mysterious about it."

"Don't think he wants to spoil your objectivity. So I won't either… Walker, are you okay? Do you want me to come over there for a while?"

I did, but found my mouth saying, "No, you don't need to bother. I should probably go to bed."

Which is what I proceeded to do, although I dreamed all night that a mob was in the process of hanging me from a twisted tree that kept changing into a tower of stone.

23

The control room at Ettenmoor's house was directly adjacent to his office. A TV monitor gave a video feed from his study, like an electronic window cut through the wall. The control room could have been a good-sized bedroom but for the lack of windows and the profusion of electronic equipment. You had to step up to enter the room; like a computer center in a lab, it had a false floor with liftable tiles to accommodate bundles of cables.

There were two desktop computers, and also one of the larger Sun workstations. When Ettenmoor led me in, Mandy was tapping away at the keyboard in front of the giant Sun monitor. She held up a warning hand: "Take it somewhere else for a few minutes, guys." Ettenmoor held up a finger—give me a second—and meandered out of the room.

I stood a little closer to Mandy's chair and watched the keystrokes flow onto the screen. An old-fashioned girl, I saw—no icons or little pictures to click on, just a smooth flow of UNIX commands at a sysop level, piping and directing. "Ohhh…kay," she said. She swiveled in the chair. Next to the workstation was a rack filled with generic steel-fronted housings, all lidless, so you could see the snarled innards. The connections to the boards were garish wire-wraps: this was all custom work. She pushed the toggles on the face of a few housings and LEDs winked on, green and red.

The screen popped up a series of lines that meant little to me:
SRM1: 1B53F __LINK12 INTERRUPT: 01001 STATUS: OK

SRM2: 19BE3 __LINK14 INTERRUPT: 11011 STATUS: OK
KRAKEN: OK CELLAR: OK VIDEO: OK
SMPTE STAMP: READY SMPTE BASIS: RELATIVE

Mandy nodded to herself and leaned back in her chair. This was a side of her I hadn't seen; she could have been a smug SuperUser at any EE grad school. I wondered where she would be now, what she would be now, if she weren't plagued by visions.

"Did you build all this?" I asked.

She tilted her head at the equipment rack. "Everything over there. We had to bring in a guy from Boeing to do the hydraulics interface."

"Hydraulics?" I searched the room for any signs of pressure vessels or pneumatic pistons. "What's the purpose of all this equipment in the first place? Ettenmoor hasn't really acquainted me with the details." I sat down in a chair a few feet from her.

"That would be telling, wouldn't it? Part of your role is to be the objective observer—hell, skeptical observer, in your case. Plus we need somebody to press the buttons."

"Any progress on our little research project?"

"I started programming it, but I'll have to finish up tomorrow. Basically it'll crawl out to websites for all of the news sources in SoCal, page back as far as it can, up to six months, and check for violent crimes. It'll bring the text and URL back home, and then I'll have a sort that'll bin it into some categories…"

Ettenmoor's big frame loomed in the doorway. "We set?" Mandy nodded, and made a sweeping gesture of display at the equipment around her. "Good. Big day, probably, but shouldn't anticipate. Stick to the empirical and let the theories sort out later. Right, Walker? Observation is all."

Larry peered around Ettenmoor and said, "Hey, Walker. Mandy." Ettenmoor turned to him and cocked his head as Larry said, "I'm still on the phone. LKI will pump some funds into it if you set it up as a nonprofit with your name attached. Something vague, 'Ettenmoor Fund for Advanced Research' or some such. But you have to sign up for a five-year stint on their tech advisory board, and they get to shout it from the rooftops…"

"They'll be around for five years? Doubt it." They moved a few feet back from the doorway, immersed in business details.

Mandy stood and picked up her long black coat from the table. "I'm outta here. I'll be back in a couple of hours."

I had assumed she'd be staying. "Don't you need to watch the equipment? I don't know how anything works."

"If something goes wrong now, it won't be the kind of thing that can be fixed without calling in the mechanics. The electronics bits work, and they have backups on top of backups."

I hadn't noticed that Ettenmoor had leaned back into the room. "Believe her. And there'd better be backups. Don't feel like trying to repeat this right away."

I must have looked a little forlorn, because Mandy said, "Hey, I'll be back later to check out the analysis. But I hate to be around when this thing runs."

I looked at the two of them standing together. The top of Mandy's head hardly reached as high as Ettenmoor's heart. "When what thing runs, exactly?"

Ettenmoor shook his finger in a mock scold. "Objective observer, remember?"

Mandy said, "Walker, you must have been a pain around Christmas. Wait and see."

The experiment was simple and boring. I watched through the TV monitor as Ettenmoor conducted six twenty-minute Zener card sessions with six different people. Zener cards are one of the oldest tools in ESP research: Each card has a simple figure on the back, like a circle, a trio of squiggly lines, a cross… The putative psychic is supposed to guess what is on each card as the tester selects them. Scores are tabulated.

They've been doing Zener research for decades now. Since it's all statistics, both sides, the believers and the skeptics, are able to claim victory from the experiments. Even when the guesses are correct, there's always the possibility the tester is giving clues, consciously or unconsciously. People do have some extraordinary runs of correct guesses, but this proves nothing: Somebody wins the lottery eventually, even though the odds against any individual are huge.

There was just one difference between this experiment and normal Zener tests. There was a little box, obviously custom-built, with two buttons, one blue and one red. Ettenmoor had instructed me to push one of these buttons sometime during the first ten minutes of each session. "I'd like to get four tests on red. Two blue. Don't demand it. I'd like it. Do three and three if you really want."

"And do I have to do anything else? Log what I pushed and when?"

"Nope. Mandy's got it wired. All automatic. Don't even need to watch or listen if you don't want to."

"Then I don't see why I'm here."

"Observe results. Make sure I don't know what's happening. Check out the post-game analysis."

I listened to the first five minutes of the first session. The subject was a pale, nervous young man dressed all in black. "Cross… Squiggle… Circle…" The camera was positioned so I could look over Ettenmoor's shoulder and see each card as he drew it, and look past the card to the subject's face. The subject's eyes darted back and forth, as if the right answers were floating through the air. If they were, he wasn't reading them well. His rate of correct guesses was abysmal.

I pressed the red button. Nothing apparent happened. The subject droned on: Cross… Cross… Circle… I concentrated hard, trying to see what, if anything, the red button had triggered. I almost fancied I could hear or feel something…but if you strain to hear or feel something, you always think that you do. The subject's guesses hadn't improved one iota. Ettenmoor hadn't given any obvious indication that the fellow was failing the test miserably, but the subject must have known: his forehead was furrowed and shiny.

Apparently the tension of having his supposed psychic powers tested was all too much for him. He gripped the edge of the table, and pushed his torso upright and back. "I—I feel them."

"Them?" Ettenmoor's voice was noncommittal.

"The Watchers. I can tell that the mother ship has returned. Even as we speak, it is in orbit directly over this site. The implant in my brain has been activated. They—they want to speak to me…"

This was really too pathetic for words. Probably one of the subjects today would score higher hits than probability would dictate, and Ettenmoor would try to make something of it. It was sad, really, but not unprecedented; although most historians of science try to whitewash over it, Isaac Newton had devoted most of the late period of his life to alchemy, and he considered his mystical writings to be greater contributions than his theory of gravity or his invention of the calculus.

I turned the volume down to a quiet hiss and picked up one of the books I had brought. An old favorite: John McPhee's *Basin and Range*. I read for a bit, but somehow it didn't engage me. I was on edge, probably with exasperation at this idiot waste of time.

I turned to another book, one of the most-thumbed paperbacks in Claire's library. *The Thursday Night Tarot*. A peculiar book. Excerpts from audience question-and-answer sessions with someone named Jason Lotterhand, a man who sounded more like someone's grandpa than like a mystic.

I checked the time as I browsed through the book. Ettenmoor rose and showed the pale man out. After a few minutes he ushered in a pudgy, middle-aged man who carried himself with an air of supreme composure: Buddha in glasses. I waited through only three minutes of card guessing before pushing the blue button. I went back to *Thursday Night Tarot*, and read an exchange between Jason and one of the questioners on the nature of illusion. The key point seemed to be that everything happening is real, but our interpretations are likely to be illusions.

I wasn't sure I always followed the discussion. Perhaps starting at the beginning would have helped. But none of this fit with my conceptions of how mystics spoke. Lotterhand was earthy, practical, strangely skeptical.

I continued browsing through Lotterhand's book. At one point I came across a marginal note in Claire's handwriting: *Who would have thought that white light is composed of all possible colors? Before the prism, who would have foreseen such a thing?* I continued to track the time and press buttons as required. This book was affecting me in some way, possibly because I was in some sense trapped here with it; a few times I had the eerie illusion the words in the book were being spoken aloud, close to my ear.

At long last the session was done. A little over two hours. Dull, but I had promised myself I was going to take a closer look at some of Claire's books, and this had forced me to take some time. I stood, massaged my low back. Softball, a softball injury. How much of ourselves is buried but still alive somewhere deep inside?

Mandy opened the door and peeked in. "All done? Everything work okay?"

I tilted an eyebrow. "As far as I know."

She came in, pulling off her coat. Ettenmoor appeared behind her. He seemed excited; he bounced on his feet slightly, like a huge child. "Think we got something here. Really got something. Pretty sure I can do the blue and red. Blue on two and five. Other four were red. Right?"

I thought about it. I hadn't paid attention. "I think so…"

Mandy stepped around my chair and sat down at the workstation.

"Don't remember?" Ettenmoor asked. "Good. Even better. You see what was happening?"

"I didn't watch most of it. Why? Did you get a lot of hits? Were the number of correct guesses correlated with which button was pushed?"

Ettenmoor actually giggled, a creepy behavior for someone his size. "Didn't follow at all, did you? Cards were just to have something to do." To Mandy, he said, "Can we watch the tapes?"

I gave an inward groan. The idea of sitting through a second round of this was almost too much to bear.

Mandy tapped at the keyboard. On the TV screen above, the camera view disappeared and was replaced with the earlier view of Ettenmoor leading in the first subject. "In order, or by color?" she asked.

"In order, in order. Differences aren't subtle. Not if I'm right."

"Okay." She tapped at the keys. "I'll forward to the timestamp about thirty seconds before initiation."

The TV went blue and I heard the whine of tape. "We really ought to go DVD on this soon," she said. "Then we could just jump there."

"Would that be hard? Take long?"

"Probably a day or two, max."

"Do it, then. When you get time."

The screen flipped to the pale young man. "Cross… Cross… Circle…" At the bottom of the monitor a timecode began whirring away second by second, 00:05:03, 00:05:04, :05, :06…

A large red dot appeared in the lower corner of the screen. "Now watch," Ettenmoor said.

The man pushed back from the table and said, "I—I feel them." He then launched into his rant about the mother ship. Mandy and Ettenmoor exchanged grins.

"Get the idea? Let's skip ahead. No reason to watch it all."

Mandy tapped a key, the screen blued out, and the pudgy man appeared. His reading of the cards was much slower. "Circle." Long, thoughtful pause. "Umm—wavy, no, no, *cross*." A blue ball appeared down by the timecode. He showed no response. "Wavy lines." Ponderous hesitation. "Cross."

"See?" Ettenmoor asked me excitedly.

"See what? I didn't see anything."

"Exactly. Just my point. Rest of the session, he just reads cards!"

Mandy tapped keys. We forwarded to a hefty woman in a caftan, with huge strands of beads around her neck. It was clear she had consciously gone for the Madame Zola, midway-fortune-teller look. "I see—I see—a cross!" Her voice was portentous. "It isn't clear… It isn't clear yet… No, wait, I can see it, like water, three wavy lines…"

The red ball appeared by the timecode, but she continued in the same vein. "It grows dim, dim, but as the mists part, I see, I see a ball, a circle…" Her eyes narrowed in an inward look, as if she had become uncomfortably aware of a loose spring in the seat of her chair. She held up a hand. "Wait. Wait. There is a presence. Someone seeks to gain admittance. Perhaps someone who has passed on… Dr. Ettenmoor, is it—is it your, your father?"

Ettenmoor must have been closer to the microphone, because his voice on the video was much louder than hers. "Probably he'd use the phone. In Michigan, last I heard. Fishing."

She was paying no attention to him. In fact, her hammy manner was fast disintegrating. "It's— I don't know what it is. Who are you? Who are you? *Are all of you still there?*" She clasped her hands in prayer and pressed them to her lips. Her eyes were shut tight.

Ettenmoor leaned over to Mandy. "Maybe we need a panic button. Some way to turn it off manually?"

"Easy to rig up, but I'm not sure it would help. Once the thing starts up it gets you into a state that tends to persist for a while. Still does it to me if I'm around it too long."

The fourth subject was a thin, almost ethereal woman. When the red ball appeared, she continued to guess cards for a while, but suddenly she sat upright in her chair and began to intone strange words in a deep, hollow voice.

"What language is that?" I asked.

"It's glossolalia," Mandy answered. "Evangelical Christians call it speaking in tongues. It's been studied pretty carefully. Some experts claim it's nonsense, others think it shows some kind of deep language structure, in a Chomsky sort of way."

"Sometimes it's phony," Ettenmoor offered. "Sometimes it has syntax."

We forwarded to the fifth session. "Betting on the blue this time," Ettenmoor said. A blue ball appeared by the timecode. "See? And, now: nothing."

Right enough. Just an earnest young man making a seemingly endless series of guesses at Zener cards.

Sixth and final session. A middle-aged man in a suit, his hair long and puffed up on top of his head to hide the emergence of a bald spot to the rear. Ettenmoor said, "I'm guessing red ball. He goes off a little slow. But watch. What happens first is interesting. Check the cards."

For more than a full minute, the man calmly guessed cards, one after another, and each of eighteen guesses was correct. He couldn't see the cards, had no feedback on his hit rate, but his smug face began to glow with a light of confidence. You could tell he wasn't guessing anymore. He knew, or believed he knew.

Then he stood up. He could have been a televangelist rising for the camera. His formerly nondescript accent suddenly veered in the direction of Georgia. "Sometimes," he said, "sometimes you can feel the spirit descend. And then we get the gifts of the saints, then we can prophesize, and heal the sick, and make the lame walk again. But there can be pride"—he pronounced it *prahhhd*—"at those moments, if we forget that it is *Jesus* who works thorough us. The Evil One is always nearby, even in the same room with our Lord, even *Jesus* could not banish him forever, but only bid him, 'Get thee behind me, Satan!' And when we invoke the name of our Lord—"

"Enough?" Mandy asked. Ettenmoor nodded. The screen blued out and the tape started into rewind.

Ettenmoor turned and hustled out of the room.

I looked at Mandy. "What the hell was all of that? And was that a success of some sort?"

"That was definitely a success. But I think I'll let Ron explain it." She gave a wicked grin. "Hey, Walker, we just may be making history here."

Ettenmoor reappeared with a bottle under each armpit and four champagne flutes in one hand. "Larry'll be along if he ever gets off the phone. Warm enough for a little toast outside? Put these puppies to chill just before the session started. Hubris, I guess." He winked at us. "*Prahhhd.*"

The three of us sat on the table-like rock where Ettenmoor had done his yoga during my previous visit. He seemed swollen to twice his size, a stage actor who finally has his chance at Falstaff. "Champagne *on* the rocks: bad taste. Champagne *amongst* the rocks: nothing better. Here's to it." We raised our glasses and clinked in the gathering shadows.

The champagne was cold yet strangely warming. "Are you two going to explain yourselves?"

Ettenmoor grinned. "Long version? Or short?"

I shrugged. "Suit yourself."

Mandy rolled onto her side like an odalisque and sipped her drink. "Just as well. Ron doesn't have a short version."

He took a big drink of champagne, and I matched him. If I was becoming an alcoholic, would I know it? In the last three weeks I had consumed more booze than I normally swallowed in a year.

He gestured at me with his glass, index finger releasing to point. "What did you see? What happened?"

"Well, if there was a pattern, I suppose that whenever I pushed the red button, whoever was in the room started acting peculiar. But no pattern to their peculiarities—completely different stuff from each person. Sounded like nonsense most of the time."

"Three things got me here." Ettenmoor held up three big fingers. "First thing. Woman wrote this book. Claimed sightings of UFOs, sightings of the Loch Ness monster, and reports of hauntings were all correlated timewise. Different stuff, happens all at once. Found it suggestive. Don't you?"

I frowned. "Three unlikely categories of unconfirmed and probably unconfirmable experiences are correlated with each other? I find it weird that anyone would bother to do the research to correlate them. Suggestive? Not really."

"Walker. Hmm. Don't like mind exercise much? Accept it for a moment." He took a drink, refilled his glass, and topped off mine and Mandy's. "Second thing. Reports of animal behavior prior to earthquakes. Let me show you something." He stood and gestured for me to follow back toward the house. I stood.

Mandy didn't budge. "I'll give it a miss if you don't mind. And if you turn it on, please don't leave it on very long. It's like having a hive of bees in my head."

Ettenmoor led the way toward the sliding-glass doors at the rear of the house, but turned to the right and led me into a narrow alley formed by the wall of the house on the left and the steep rocks of the canyon on the right. He flipped a light switch. Twenty feet in, the alley became a descending stairway carved into the rock. At the bottom of the stairs was a light, for all the world like any porch light, and a door that led under the house.

I followed Ettenmoor down the stairs. He pushed open the door and light spilled out.

The cellar was perhaps twenty by twenty, with a ten-foot ceiling. It had been hollowed out of the solid granite into a boxy shape, but the corners remained rounded. The floor was level except in the center where a large thumb of rock, about four feet high and three feet in diameter, had been left standing—but it wasn't bare. Mounted to the floor on either side were strutted assemblies. What looked like two long pistons protruded from these and pressed against the rock. A third piston came down from the ceiling to press against the tip of the stony thumb.

"Watch your step," Ettenmoor cautioned. I saw that the floor of the room was crisscrossed with four long pistons laid out like the matrix for tic-tac-toe. At the center of each twenty-foot span the pipe was as thick as a tree trunk, but as they headed toward the edges of the room, they stepped down in two stages like the telescoping legs of a camera tripod. Where their round feet pressed against the walls, the tubes were about the thickness of a man's thigh. "Hydraulic press," Ettenmoor explained. "Actual engines to drive the pneumatics are way over there." He waved his hand over his shoulder in a vague direction. "Just pipe the pressure over. Need to keep it quiet here."

A network of pipes ran here and there beneath the pistons and connected into them toward the center. The pattern was deliberate yet asymmetrical; I had the sensation that I was inside a three-dimensional computer chip. If Ettenmoor was losing his mind, he was doing it on a grand scale.

"You know piezoelectricity?" Ettenmoor asked. Of course I did: the electric current you get from compressing a crystal. I just nodded, part puzzled, part impatient.

"Few years back, some geophysicists were measuring crustal conductivity." His voce sounded hollow in this chamber. "Happened to be doing so before a big earthquake. Huge surge in piezoelectric current, hours before the quake."

"I remember that work. The Loma Prieta quake in '89, the one that collapsed the Bay Bridge…but the work hasn't really led to a prediction mechanism."

Ettenmoor flipped open a wall-mounted panel that resembled a breaker box. "Not interested in earthquakes. Interested in what animals and people sense. You pushed that red button, you triggered these pistons." He pushed a switch with a loud clack. There was only the slightest hiss of sound. I felt a strange sensation of pressure around me, and the air seemed to thicken. "Feel anything?" he asked.

"Not really. Maybe. To be truthful, I can't tell."

"Honest man. Sometimes I do, sometimes don't." He thunked the switch back to its off position with an obvious effort. "Any change?"

The air felt lighter, or I imagined it felt lighter. "I really don't know."

"Okay. One: UFOs, Loch Ness monster, hauntings, all tend to happen at same time. Two: animals and psychics get these weird feelings before earthquakes, same time piezoelectric currents are moving through the planet crust. Three—and this is the good bit: I'm up in Berkeley. Friends have this new baby, Milo. Smart kid as far as you can judge."

He shut the breaker box and walked back to the door, stepping high on his way through the pipes and pistons that sectioned the floor. He put one hand on the doorframe and turned back to me. "So. This baby: you can almost see him putting it all together. Wiggle, wiggle, whole body moves when he's trying to move just his arm. Then he gets it a little; can move his arm without moving everything. Eyes are starting to work. He's trying to put together vision and space. Grabs at stuff. And if he gets it, what does he do with it? Puts it in his mouth. Why?"

"Well, babies seem to want to eat even before they're ready for solid food; and I guess the psychologists think that orality is a main stage in development…"

"Yes and no. Deeper than that. His sense of touch is developed. Especially tongue and mouth—those nerves work right from day one. Works or he doesn't eat. He sees stuff. Tries to touch it. Trying to understand space and vision in terms of touch. We get ahold of it, we put it in our mouth. Feel it with our most developed sensory system. Here's the thing, Walker: He's trying to model a new sensory channel in terms of one he has already mastered." He spread his hands out before him as if he had demonstrated a theorem. QED.

He turned, stepped back into the stairway, and climbed out of view. I followed, pulled the door shut behind me, and said, "Excuse me if I'm slow. Can you be a little more precise about the exact content of your hypothesis?"

He stopped and revolved on his heel near the top of the stairway. "Oh. Thought it was obvious. There's some sense we have. Or some people have. Isn't stimulated very often. Don't really know how to work it. So when it's stimulated, we model it in terms of something else. It's not visual, but some people have visions. It's not auditory, but some people hear voices. If you believe in UFOs, you see UFOs. You believe in Nessie, you see her instead. Today we gave some psychics an artificial earthquake precursor. They felt something. Every one of the four who got it thought it was something different. But they all felt it." He turned and left the stairway.

I jogged up the stairs and turned off the lights. He was right. This was a breakthrough. "So hold on," I called after him, "that means there's a perfectly natural explanation for all this. There's a measurable phenomenon, no need to assume supernatural abilities…"

He waited for me to catch up with him. "Nothing's supernatural when you understand it. But that last guy saw every Zener card in sequence. Earth currents we generate stimulate other things. Mandy's opinion too. Haven't solved anything here. But this may be our first leverage point to pry open this box."

The sun was down and only the lights from the windows of the house lit the canyon. From twenty yards away I could see Mandy sitting crosslegged on the rock, huddled against the cold, her hands holding her big coat around her. We drew closer. Something was wrong. She shivered, tiny puffs of steam wafting from between her lips. Her eyes were focused somewhere in the middle distance. Her champagne glass lay on its side in front of her.

We hurried over. "Mandy?" I said. "Mandy, are you okay?"

She shuddered and stared right through me. "Something's wrong…" she whispered.

"Mandy." Ettenmoor's voice was firm. "Let's get inside. You're getting cold…"

"Just stop!" she snapped. She dropped her desperate grip on the lapels of the coat and thrust her hands out as if to fend us off. Her breathing grew deeper. Suddenly she launched herself forward, knocking the glass off the shelf of rock and shattering it on the ground. She tried to scramble off the rock, but fell, right in the glass. "Shit, shit, it's Kirsten, warn Kirsten—!" She tried to push herself up off the ground, one of her hands pressed into the chips of glass. Ettenmoor and I lifted her by her shoulders and stood her up. One long shard of glass stuck straight out of her thigh, a dark stain spreading on her Levis.

"Mandy, you're hurt, don't move," I said. I grabbed the shiny blade of crystal between thumb and index finger and pulled it out. It made a little sucking sound as an inch of glass withdrew from her flesh. She showed no awareness of any pain.

Her hands dug through her coat pockets but her eyes remained fixed in midair as if she were blind. "Fuck it, fuck it, pay *attention*, we have to call her!" She yanked out her cell phone from a pocket.

"But you're bleeding!"

"Goddammit!" Her fingers stabbed erratically at the phone, trying to switch it on. "Call her! Call her now!"

I took the phone, found the power button. "What's her number?"

"I don't know! It's in my appointment book, inside somewhere!"

Ettenmoor let loose of her shoulder and ran back toward the house. Mandy leaned back against the boulder and oscillated her body forward and back chanting, "…ohfuck ohfuck ohfuck ohfuck…"

"Wait, wait!" Kirsten had given me her numbers at at *Wild Desert*. I fumbled at my wallet, spilling credit cards onto the rocks, and found the note. I had to turn it at an angle to catch enough light from the house to read it. "Her cell or home?"

"Fuck, either one—no, her cell, her cell!" Mandy chewed on her knuckles.

I punched in the numbers, squinting to read them, hit SEND. A long pause. A ring. Another ring. A recording: *The number you have called is presently busy. Please press one to—* "It's busy. I'll try her house."

As I dialed Kirsten's home phone, Ettenmoor came pounding back with Mandy's appointment book. I waved my hand to forestall him. One ring. Another. Four rings total, and it rolled to her answering machine. "It's her machine, what do I say?"

"Tell her to get out of there! Tell her to go to my house!"

"Kirsten. This is Walker. If you get this message, Mandy says leave immediately and go to her place. Call us on Mandy's cell." I hung up.

I dialed the cell phone again. Mandy's hysteria had rubbed off on me and my fingers trembled. I punched the wrong number and had to start again. It rang once, twice, and then I heard the connection being made.

"Hello?" It was Kirsten's voice.

"Kirsten. Hi, it's Walker."

I could sense Mandy off to the side, sagging with relief.

"Hi, Walker. What's up?"

"It's hard to explain. Where are you?"

"On my way home." Her voice grew a little suspicious. "Why?"

"Look, I'm calling because Mandy wants to get in touch with you— Hold on." I stopped. "Can you talk to her? It might be easier."

Mandy nodded and held out her hand. "Kirsten... No, just listen, it's important. Just go to my house, let yourself in. Something's happened... Uh-huh...well, just *don't go home*... I *know* I'm scaring you, I'm *trying* to scare you... We'll be there as soon as we can... Yeah, take care...bye."

She pressed the power button and laid the phone on the stony shelf by her elbow. She wiped her palm across her face and left shiny dark streaks from the cuts in her hand. She seemed puzzled at the wetness, and even more baffled when she looked down at her wet pantsleg. Blood leaked across her ankle and into her shoe. "Wow," she said, "that ought to hurt."

24

The entrance to the national park from the town of Joshua Tree is at the upper end of a valley that stretches southeast from the highway to the park boundary. The valley was carved by an ancient watercourse that poured its flood northwest to Emerson Lake, now itself a desiccated playa. Houses are gradually filling the gap, pushing southeast from town along the ancient water channels like fossil salmon fighting their way upstream to some Pleistocene headwater.

The main road changes names as it curves toward the park boundary: Park Boulevard leaving the town center of Joshua Tree, Quail Springs Road as it snakes its way through the newer neighborhoods, Monument Road when it finally reaches into the park. Mandy's house was an adobe-style cottage a half-mile east of Monument Road, set well apart from the surrounding houses.

Ettenmoor and I had dressed Mandy's leg and hand as best we could—a butterfly bandage over the deep cut, and gauze wrapped round and round the thigh. What we may have lacked in skill we made up for in volume of wrapping. She made a strange, iconic fashion statement as we helped her off Ettenmoor's front porch and into the Jeep: sweater and long black coat on top, yellow panties and bare legs below, the bandage an impromptu garter. She sat with her blood-soaked Levis bundled on her lap as I followed the directions to her house.

Although the bleeding seemed to be stanched, I tried to persuade her to drop through the emergency room. She refused, aching to get to Kirsten. We compromised by calling Dawn and asking her to be waiting for us.

Kirsten and Dawn had already let themselves in by the time we arrived. They helped Mandy hobble off into the bathroom, leaving me to wander around Mandy's living room.

It was a long rectangle of a room, with the front door right in the center. To the left was an open arch leading into the kitchen; bathroom and what had to be the bedroom door were on the rear wall toward the left. A real-estate agent would have described it as "cozy;" with everything Mandy had stuffed into it, it was cramped.

The right end of the room was given over to a large window, and there was another to the right of the front door. This must have provided fine views during the day, but Mandy was desperately short of wallspace. Shelves stuffed with books and reports seemed to cover every available bit of wall. Two tall bookcases even stood behind the couch on the rear wall; the couch would have to be moved to get at the lower shelves, but from the papers peeking out, it looked like they were filled. Bookcases stood behind the two armchairs; bookcases were so close to the left side of the entrance that the front door could only swing in to ninety degrees.

A triangular desk fit into the right corner against the front wall. This was topped with a large computer monitor. Beneath the desk were two computer housings set up tower-style; a switchbox showed that the mouse, monitor, and keyboard could be driven from either computer. There were no posters or pictures anywhere in the room, presumably because there was no available wallspace, but above the computer monitor a framed sign had been mounted to the walls, covering the corner. I wondered what deserved this pride of place; it turned out to be a pair of quotes, blown up into 72-point type:

The great question that has never been answered and which I have not yet been able to answer, despite my thirty years of research into the feminine soul, is "What does a woman want?"

—Dr. Sigmund Freud

...and, beneath that:

Oh, a glass of Chardonnay, I suppose.

—Dr. Pamela Blake

I could hear water running in the bathroom, and muffled feminine voices. I scanned the shelves. Horowitz and Hill: The Art of Electronics; Goldberg: Genetic Algorithms; Press, et al: Numerical Recipes; Russell: Odour Detection by Mobile Robots; Clifford: Computers, Pattern, Chaos, and Beauty. I studied the shelf just below. Fortune: Psychic Self-Defense; Regardie: The Tree of Life; Guthrie: Faces in the Clouds; Wilber: A Brief History of Everything. And, of course, the ubiquitous Thursday Night Tarot.

Dawn came out of the bathroom, tossed me an inscrutable glance, and let herself into what I presumed was the bedroom. Doors and drawers rattled open and closed. She returned a moment later with clothes draped over her arm. As she closed the bathroom door behind her, I noted Dawn was dressed in a bright knit top and slacks—out of the scrubs she usually wore at the exact moment we needed her medical skills. Something about her face looked different.

The bathroom door opened, and Kirsten and Dawn stepped out to flank the door. Mandy followed, limping slightly, and passed between them like the guest of honor between two ushers. Mandy went toward her bedroom. Dawn spoke to her back in a no-nonsense nurse's voice: "It's just on the edge of needing stitches. If it bleeds at all, I mean *at all*, you get to the doctor's. I cleaned it as good as you'll get anywhere." Mandy disappeared into her bedroom, and Dawn raised her voice as she came toward the center of the room. "But any puffiness, any discharge *what-so-ever*, and you need to get on antibiotics." She lowered her voice to address Kirsten and me. "Clean cut, and the bleeding was actually a blessing. Plus, if you *must* impale yourself on glass, a glass containing booze is a good choice. Just FYI."

Mandy came out of the bedroom. She had a handgun, huge and heavy in her petite hand.

"Is that a *gun*?" I asked.

Not the question I really meant to ask, and I expected a suitably sarcastic answer, but Mandy just smiled mock-sweetly and said, "It is."

Kirsten and Dawn both seemed to lean back away from the gun, uncomfortable with its presence, but Mandy seemed completely at ease as she picked up her coat and slipped the gun into one of the capacious pockets. She tugged on the coat and said, "Let's go." I realized I'd never seen her with a purse or backpack: the coat seemed to hold everything. I wondered what she did in the summer.

"I wish you'd reconsider," Dawn said.

Mandy shook her head. "What are we going to do—call 911 and tell them that we *imagine* there's been a break-in?" Her eyes glittered. "I'd much rather call them and tell them that we just shot an intruder."

"Are you sure I shouldn't come, too?" Dawn asked.

"No, don't bother. Three of us is plenty. I'm not really expecting someone to be there anyway. Get back to your date." That was what looked different about Dawn—makeup. "Poor guy's probably digging through your panty drawer by now."

"I wish. More likely he's watching sports." Dawn put her hand on the doorknob, and then changed her mind and came back over to hug Mandy. "You call, okay? Even if there's nothing to report."

"I thought you planned to be too busy to answer the phone."

"That's why God gave us answering machines, cutey." She kissed the top of Mandy's head.

Kirsten's apartment was in Yucca Valley, in one of the more built-up areas. Other than location—within walking distance of stores and shops, a rare quality in the desert—the building had little to recommend it: a three-story cinder-block shoebox with wraparound walkways open to the elements.

Kirsten had a first-floor unit, its front door adjacent to the parking lot; we could pull up and park no more than four feet from the entrance, just like a cheap motel.

At Mandy's house, I had lobbied her to leave the handgun behind; on the drive over, I urged her to leave it in the car. I had little experience with guns, and they made me very nervous; from what I read in the papers, the right person was seldom the one who ended up shot. She refused to argue with me about it. When I kept at it, she finally said, "I'm a woman. I live alone in the desert. I have a gun. Unlike most people who have handguns, I bothered to get trained to use it. So relax."

Kirsten unlocked the front door and pushed it open. We all stopped and listened. Plenty of street noise from behind us, but nothing obvious from inside the apartment. Kirsten reached inside and flipped on the lights. Still nothing. Mandy edged around Kirsten and stepped inside, her hand thrust deep in her pocket. Kirsten and I followed.

The building itself might have been grim, but Kirsten's living space was an oasis of comfort. To our left, the living room was filled with couches and chairs piled high with pillows; the wall-to-wall carpeting was mostly hidden by plush rugs. The front window was a riot of green hanging plants that intertwined with each other, and climbed up their macrame hangers to brush against the ceiling. To our right, the kitchen and breakfast nook were spotless but filled with treasures: bits of weathered wood, crystals, water-polished rocks.

We all froze, listening. Something sounded unnatural, but there was no specific noise. Mandy moved forward across the living room and we followed. On the right wall, what had to be the bathroom door was closed. She headed for the door on the rear wall of the living room, which stood slightly ajar. She paused, listened, pushed the door open with her foot. She flipped on the light and looked in, turned back and shook her head.

I was by the bathroom door. In the back of my mind, I heard Claire's voice, saying, "Hey, it's always the bathroom, isn't it? Like *Psycho*?" I shook my head; it was remote and soft, but the vividness of her voice was disconcerting.

I pushed the door open. Somehow I knew there was no one inside. The sounds of the outdoors were louder than they ought to be. I flipped the light switch and looked in. The bathroom stretched to the rear of the unit, ending in a tub with a shower curtain. The curtain stood open, moving slightly.

"I think you should come take a look at this," I said, and stepped into the room.

Mandy and Kirsten crowded in behind me. Above the tub, the louvers in the window had been pried out of their aluminum casings, and the sounds of the night came in through the opening. The slight breeze fluttered the shower curtain. There were black smudges on the rim of the tub where someone had pushed down hard with their shoes.

Kirsten drew in her breath in something close to a sob. Mandy tried to step around me for a closer look, but I blocked her. "We shouldn't disturb the evidence."

We backed out into the living room. "God," Kirsten whispered, "he was waiting in the bathroom..."

Mandy chewed her lip, staring hard at the floor. The she said, "No, no, he wasn't—" She turned and strode back into the bedroom.

"Don't touch anything," I urged, turning to follow her. I heard rollers and a creaking sound. She'd pulled open the slatted bi-fold doors on Kirsten's closet. The hanging clothes had been pushed wide apart to create an empty space in the center; many items had slipped off their hangers and lay in limp piles on the floor of the closet.

I hadn't heard Kirsten come in but now she slipped an arm around me and hugged herself against my side. "Hiding in the closet," she said to herself. "God, it's like a little kid's nightmare..."

We sat together in a large horseshoe booth at a Carrow's coffeeshop. None of us were hungry, but the bright lights and relentlessly artificial surroundings formed a shelter against the strangeness. All three of us had ordered coffee and slices of apple pie. I managed just two bites before I laid down my fork.

The sheriffs had arrived at Kirsten's promptly after we called. I was relieved that neither Bolles nor Wilson had come. One of the uniformed deputies had kept staring at me. I smiled and nodded. He frowned and looked away.

They took a statement from Kirsten, but there wasn't much to relate. She didn't bother to tell them Mandy had warned her off from entering the house earlier. They did note the fact that she was a friend of Claire's, and told her Detective Bolles might be contacting her.

As far as the evidence team could tell, the intruder had worn gloves. The glass louvers were neatly stacked on the ground outside the bathroom window. There were marks of heavy boots in the sandy soil, but there were footprints everywhere around the back side of the apartment; the fellow in charge of preliminary forensics at the site was dubious there was anything useful on the ground.

Kirsten had stuffed a few clothes into a small duffel, and gave the sheriffs her cell number, as well as numbers for Mandy and Dawn. She called the apartment management company and left a message asking to have the window fixed. The message light on her answering machine was blinking. She pressed the button, and my voice came through, against a background of static: "Kirsten. This is Walker. If you get this message, Mandy says leave immediately and go to her place. Call us on Mandy's cell."

"Do you leave your volume on?" Mandy asked. "You screen messages?" Kirsten nodded. "That's why he left, then; he heard Walker's message."

When we had left, the sheriffs were still busy knocking on the doors of neighboring units to ask if anyone had heard or seen anything. Based on the first few responses it hadn't looked hopeful.

Kirsten pushed the pie around with her fork. None of us seemed to have much to say.

Chad and Melanie appeared at last and we scooted in to make room for them, Chad sliding in next to Kirsten, Melanie gliding her hips in next to mine. Chad wrapped an arm around Kirsten's shoulders, crushed her in a big hug. "Jared's down in Palm Springs or he'd be here. We came as soon as we got the message." He left his arm draped over Kirsten, and she seemed pleased; she reached up and gave his dangling hand a squeeze.

As always, I was acutely aware of Melanie. I could smell her beside me, and even fancied I could feel some miasma drifting off of her. Foreknowledge didn't seem to be much of a defense; the fact I knew she was trying to enrapture me didn't make her any less sexy. Maybe the opposite. She patted me on the thigh in what would have to be described as a chummy fashion—nothing lascivious there, nothing anyone could take to court—but the double pat seemed perfectly judged to be just one iota farther down my leg than the tip of my swelling cock.

I steeled myself to take a glance at her. She was looking right back at me, her face inches from mine. Her eyes ebulliated amusement, but also something smokier. She knew that I knew what she was doing, and she was pleased about it. She knew I'd happily get up from the table right then and take her anywhere she wanted to go: Bangkok, Omaha, Patagonia. I suppose I should have been annoyed, even angry, at being manipulated, but I wasn't. I wanted her so much right then that I felt more alive than I had since—well, maybe ever.

I pulled my eyes away and directed them at the table, carefully cutting myself a bite of pie I didn't want. I heard Kirsten's voice: "Walker. I know you've been digging into all kinds of things…"

I looked up. "Excuse me? Sorry, I was thinking about something else." At the apex of the curved booth, Mandy gave me a small, lewd grin, but Chad and Kirsten showed no sign they had noticed my Melanie-induced fugue.

"I was telling Chad that maybe he was right," Kirsten said, "that you were starting to think maybe all this has something to do with the crank dealers in town."

"I don't know what to think," I said. I mentioned that Claire's idiot former boyfriend Gary had speculated the speed trade was involved. I mentioned talking to Billy, whose story about Claire coming to his trailer to slap him into shape seemed to suggest she was willing to move onto risky ground.

I was interrupted by the waitress taking orders from Chad and Melanie. Chad followed the crowd and ordered apple pie and coffee. "What is this, some kind of cult?" the waitress asked. She turned to Melanie. "You want apple pie too, I guess?"

"No. Cherry." She bumped my knee lightly with hers as she said this.

When the waitress left, I told them about my peculiar encounter with Bolles when he drove me home from Ettenmoor's. "He was vague, but insistent that he wanted to know anything about Claire's connection with hard drugs. Like he had some suspicion he wouldn't share with me. He's cagey about everything."

"I warned you about him," Mandy said, "the guy's a control freak."

Chad was nodding his head steadily. "I *thought* this had something to do with either drugs or the prison or both. It's the place in her life where Claire came in contact with violent people; I mean, violence happens, but the convict crowd jacks up the probability about a zillion percent. Now maybe somebody's after Kirsten too: that seems to clinch it."

"Wait a minute," I said, "there's other strange things. First off, there's what Kirsten calls the Uber-Dump." I filled them in on my talks with Universal Waste, my gradual discovery that there really did seem to be something weird with their hydrological survey—capped by their calls to Sacramento and their service of a restraining order.

"Something like that happened to Claire, too," Melanie said. "I remember her laughing about it." She bumped my knee again.

"You're not suggesting that UWI had Claire killed, are you?" Chad asked. "And what's the connection with Kirsten? I mean, she's handed out flyers and things, but she's not a major player in *Stop The Dump*."

"I don't know what I'm suggesting. I just know that the longer I'm here, the weirder things get. But I've saved the best for last." I told them about the presentation Reverend Gorston made during the Shackles Torn Asunder service, and then told them about my visit to the chapterhouse and my near strangulation.

With the exception of Mandy, who already knew, that stopped them dead. Melanie even ceased teasing me.

"On behalf of Dawn," Mandy said, "who apparently isn't checking her messages at the moment, I guess I should say 'toldja so.' She's always thought this was some religious nut. Somebody almost ran us over on New Year's Eve—maybe coincidence, maybe not. But if it isn't, why would somebody who's after Kirsten and Claire bother with me and Walker?"

"Maybe because Walker's her brother," Chad suggested.

Mandy dismissed this with a shake of her head. "Weak. From a practical point of view, we know that Kirsten's in danger, but we should assume that any of the rest of us might be, too—all of us here, and Dawn, and Jared, and maybe even some of the folks who aren't quite as close to us. Be paranoid."

"You don't need to tell me that," Kirsten said. "I'm not staying by myself in this town until this is over. Whatever this is. Dawn's got two bedrooms, she's always saying I could share with her. Starting tomorrow, she's got a new roomie."

We all sat silent for a moment. I avoided looking at Melanie, deliberately glancing over at a large family that had pushed two tables together to accommodate the whole group. Father, mother, seven children. The kids ranged in age from a three-year-old boy to a preteen girl. All of them bore a striking and somewhat unfortunate resemblance to the mother, variations of her snub nose and close-set eyes stamped on every face. Some people think it's cute when everyone in a family looks so closely related. To me, it always smacks of some medical experiment gone awry.

There was some discussion of whether I should go to the police about the assault up at the God's Law chapterhouse, but Mandy and I squelched it, saying we wanted a little time to do research first.

We paid our bill and left, with the usual mingling outside the restaurant doors. I concentrated on keeping my eyes off Melanie. The few times I darted a covert glance at her she was looking right at me, smiling. Chad hugged everyone, and so did Melanie, but she saved me for last. She was subtle about it, but she pushed her coat open with a casual downward brush of her arms, so that we embraced blouse-to-shirt rather than through her coat. A brief contact, chaste enough to onlookers, but one that left my body humming.

I drove Kirsten and Mandy back to Ettenmoor's place to pick up Mandy's car. Mandy's leg was still a little sore, so Kirsten took the keys and followed us to Mandy's house. As we drove, Mandy said, "I think maybe this Melanie obsession is good for you, you know. You seem a lot more lit up when you've been around her. Kinda makes a believer out of you, doesn't it?"

"Shut up, Mandy," I said, and she laughed.

I saw Mandy and Kirsten settled into Mandy's house for the night, and drove back to Claire's. It was nice not to find a rose waiting on the doormat.

25

The dream had been vivid and repetitive, like when a fever first comes on, and I had understood something clearly. It was so obvious…but sitting in Claire's living room with my first cup of coffee, I couldn't remember a single detail. "Stop grabbing at the soap bubbles." It seemed to be a whisper of Claire's voice again. "You'll pop them."

I'd read that hearing voices in your head is one of the surest signs of serious mental illness, and hearing the voice of a dead person had to be even nuttier. I'd had the feeling a number of times that Claire was communicating with me through things I read in her books or in her notebook, but the tiny, whispering voice seemed to start after the previous day's experiment at Ettenmoor's. Maybe I was mildly sensitive to that piezoelectric field. Just a minute of it had set Mandy off into her vision of Kirsten being stalked…

That was it. Ettenmoor's apparatus. I'd been dreaming about using it…

I dialed his number, and Larry answered. I pleaded with him to put Ettenmoor on the line.

Ettenmoor seemed pleased to hear from me, and thanked me for pulling him off the other call he had been on.

"Do you have any idea," I asked, "how far away the currents from your instrument can be sensed?"

"Not really. Drops off fast initially. Mandy doesn't get the 'bees in the brain' thing after she's about half a mile away, so we had all the volunteers during the experiment stay a mile away until it was their turn…"

"I meant in terms of physical measurements."

"Did some readings early on—have to get the frequency established. Use a probe, and a Fourier filter, look for just the frequency in question—long ways, no doubt, but you have to amp it up at the receiver. Gone out maybe twenty miles and we could still get it… Say, there's an idea…"

"What?"

"Could use it to transmit info through the ground—frequency modulation, FM, just like radio. Huh. Might have some application. But what? Mostly military, I suppose… I'll have to think about it. Thanks. I'll let you go now."

"Ron, *I* called *you*."

"Hmm. So you did. Thanks anyway."

"You still have your probes and filters?"

"Probes? Anything'll work, anything conductive. Filters? Probably. But Mandy could whip one up in an hour anyway. She made the ones we used."

I thanked him and rang off. I freshened my coffee and made some more phone calls.

I don't know what the hell I was thinking. I crouched down around a crumbling stucco corner, listening for footsteps, afraid to breathe. I could almost hear my father asking that same question—*What the hell were you thinking, huh?*—repeating it two or even three times before he slapped the side of my head and concluded, *You didn't think at all, did you? Did you?*

Perhaps he'd been making an important point all those years. Great. Now Claire had company in my head.

After I'd finished my coffee, washed dishes, and showered, I had decided it was time to take a look at Las Flores, the place both Malcolm and Darnell had pinpointed as the speed-dealers' headquarters for the area.

It had been easy enough to find—an old Mexican-style courtyard motel set well back from the road. The neon sign looked as if it had been dead for decades, but the long border of oleanders that enclosed the establishment on three sides was still flourishing, impossible out here unless someone watered it.

I'd parked on the road. The old cutoff from Highway 62 runs just north of a crumbly low hillock which is quickly becoming one with the valley floor. From there the ground slopes down to the north and levels out as it heads toward the Marine base, but up on the road, the slope was steep enough that I looked down on the motel. A small office and residence at the rear and five standalone units on each side, coming forward to form a horseshoe. All were roofed in cracked red tiles. The stucco had been painted yellow long ago, but where the topcoat had not already fallen away the sun had bleached it to a sand color.

It had seemed utterly deserted. There were no cars or motorcycles, no signs any rooms were occupied, no sounds. I'd sat in the Jeep and watched for fifteen minutes before I trudged my way down the drive.

I'd reached the middle of the horseshoe when there was a noise from somewhere inside a room. Without thinking I ran to my right, between two of the units. That, I suppose, was my first mistake; it would be easy to explain wandering around the place, but hard to explain hiding. No, come to think of it, that wasn't my first mistake; my first mistake was going there at all.

I should have brought a camera. Cameras can provide an excuse for anything.

For a while I had thought maybe it was just nerves, that there had been no unusual sound. But then I heard a door open, and I slid down into a crouch. So, as Dad would say, *What the hell was I thinking?* Too many movies, I imagine. People always go places in movies for no better reason than to check things out.

Right. But they go with a gun, or a badge. Or at least a plan.

I heard running feet coming in my direction. I straightened up and faced the courtyard. Never tell lies when you appear to be hiding from the person to whom you are lying.

Boys. Two of them, probably ten years old. Both had baggy pants which might or might not have been selected out of fashion considerations. One had a camouflage hunting shirt; the bigger one, who must have cut his own hair, wore a T-shirt that read *Offspring*. Both of them looked right at me.

"Hey, man, whattaya doing?" the bigger one asked.

"I'm just—that is, I'm a, a herpetologist, and—"

"A *what?*"

"A herpetologist, I study reptiles, and I thought that I saw a rather rare species of snake slither over between these two buildings, and so I—"

"Mom!" the kid in camouflage yelled. "There's a snake! There's a snake out here!"

Herpetology might not have been my best bet. The kid in camo hung back, but the other came right between the buildings with me, scanning the ground. "Where'd it go? Did you see where it went? What kind of snake was it?"

"Umm, a hog-nosed snake." Those existed, I was sure, but they might not be rare. "A *Great Basin* hog-nosed snake. Very uncommon." I turned and pretended to search the ground with him.

I heard more footsteps and I stood up to see a woman appear in the opening. She was dressed in jeans and a dark vest, her thin arms bare. She was young, maybe very young, but looked weary. "A snake? This time of year?" She studied me as if she had never seen anything like me before.

"He's some kind of snake guy," the kid behind her said.

"Yeah?" She hitched her thumbs in her back pockets. "Well what you doing on our property?"

"I apologize. I didn't realize I was trespassing. It's just that I happened to see—"

Two more figures crowded in behind her. Men, one with a gray beard, one clean-shaven. The beardless one stared at me and I stared back, and for that long moment we shared the mental state where you recognize someone's features but cannot remember from where.

He remembered first. "That's the guy!" He pointed at me with both hands clasped together and it took a second for me to realize that what he really pointed at me with was a gun. "That's the guy I was telling you about, that's him, man!" His hands shook with excitement, or maybe something chemically induced. At that moment it seemed there was a very good chance that he would shoot me.

It was Bolles' informant, but the name only came back to me as the other man said, "What guy?" Jesse. Jesse, the nervous guy from the parking lot at the diner.

"The guy who works for Bolles. The guy I keep *telling* you about."

Once inside they patted me down with embarrassing thoroughness and took my keys and wallet. The bearded man tossed the keys to Jesse. "Where's your car?" he asked me.

"Up on the road."

He addressed Jesse. "Check it out before you go up. If nobody else is around, drive it down here and park it out back. Then I want you to stay outside, out of sight, and keep an eye on things."

"Aww, c'mon Joop, I wanna—"

"Good, good, use my name, *Jesse*. Should we give him my driver's license, too?"

"Hey, I figured—"

"What makes you think he's by himself? We need somebody to keep lookout. Who you want me to send, Arlinda? Now get out there and stay out there until I'm done here. You got that?"

Although he must have been in his thirties, Jesse complied like a sulky teenager, throwing me an accusing glance as he closed the door behind him.

We stood in the kitchen of the manager's residence. It was a cramped room which must not have been updated, or even painted, since the 1940s. I found myself staring at the wall socket above the tile counter; the refrigerator was plugged into one of those gadgets that allows you to connect a three-prong plug to a two-prong outlet.

"Sit," Joop said. I saw that he was pointing to a kitchen chair pushed up against the small breakfast table near me. I did as I was told. He grabbed another chair, spun it around and straddled it backward, one muscular forearm resting on the chairback.

"Jupiter," he said. I must have looked puzzled. "My name. Nobody ever calls me that. Sixties parents. Lucky I didn't end up being called Rainbow or something." If he was born in the '60s, then he was prematurely gray, but nothing else about him looked elderly: he was broad and slab-sided, and it didn't look like any of him was fat. "Hey, Arlinda?"

The woman answered from what I assumed was the living room. "Yeah?"

"Get the kids back outside. Just in case I have to do anything they shouldn't see." I heard her voice competing with whining protests from the boys as they were directed back outdoors. Joop studied me, in no hurry about anything, and my bladder felt as if it would spring a leak.

Either his parents had been foresighted or his whole form had bent itself to the appellation, for he was well-named: his perfectly groomed gray beard stood out like a fan surrounding his broad face, but his brow was surmounted with stormclouds of unruly hair. He seemed Jovian enough, his round, leonine face made to burst out in mirth…but if I recalled correctly, the King of the Gods was also ruthless over small matters.

"I've done you a big favor already," he said. Arlinda came into the room and sat down on the far side of the table. "I got Jesse the hell out of this room. He's a really jumpy guy." He turned his head at the sound of a match striking: Arlinda was lighting a cigarette. He gave a little sigh. "I thought you were cutting down. What is that, seven, eight already today?"

"I'm nervous, Joop. Guy snooping around here and everything."

"Yeah, sure. Any excuse, right?" He let that big head turn back to me, like a planet revolving on its axis. "Anyway. I've done you a big favor. Now I want you to do me one."

"What's that?" I asked. My voice sounded thin in my ears. I ached with the need to urinate.

He blew out a weary breath and put the palms of both hands down on his thighs. "Just tell me what the hell you're doing here, okay? And tell me one thing—just one thing—that isn't true, and I guarantee you: I *will* fuck you up."

I couldn't stand it any longer. "Fine. But I really have to— I need to use the bathroom."

He scrutinized me for a long moment and then let the slightest hint of a smile appear. "Scared the piss out of you, huh? Okay…but leave your shoes."

"What?"

"Take off your shoes. Just to keep you from trying to do anything silly, like leaving through the bathroom window."

I unlaced my shoes, wincing at the pressure bending put on my bladder. I kicked them off and stood up.

"Just for good measure," he said, "leave your pants, too."

I opened my mouth to argue, then changed my mind. He didn't seem armed, but both of us tacitly agreed he was in complete control here. And the longer I delayed, the longer before I got to the toilet. The watcher in my mind, the part that always remains outside the moment, asked me what underwear I had put on this morning.

I dropped my pants and stepped out of them. Light-blue boxer shorts, nothing too ridiculous. "Show him where it is," Joop said to Arlinda. Clad in jacket, polo shirt, undershorts, and black socks, I followed her meekly through the living room to a small bathroom. Before I shut the door, I heard Joop again: "And don't forget Jesse's still outside."

Though full to bursting, I couldn't start. I tried to relax. I tried to squeeze. Finally I inclined myself forward until my brow touched the coolness of the gloss-enameled wall, and at last, tilted across the bowl like a mop leaning on a bucket, I shuddered with relief as I emptied myself. The poets sing of the relief and pleasure of satiating hunger, of slaking thirst, of bursting into orgasm, but are any of these more exquisite than a really urgent piss?

I rinsed my hands, avoiding my own eyes in the mirror over the sink, and realized there were no towels. I wiped my hands dry on my shirt, opened the door, and followed Arlinda back into the kitchen.

Joop gestured for me to sit down. I bent to pick up my pants, and he said, "That's okay. Just leave those off for now." I sat down, and he said, "Talk."

"Before I start, I should probably tell you that a number of people knew I was coming here today." Not exactly a lie, as I figured that Malcolm, Perry, and Darnell could probably work it out if I went missing.

Joop waved this away. "Skip the implied threats. Talk."

"All right. My name's Walker Clayborne, and I teach college—"

"Says Lionel on the license, but I know all that. Been through your wallet. So skip the plantation cottage you grew up in, and tell me why you were snooping around here."

I did, in some detail. When I described the part where Bolles hassled Jesse with me in the car, Joop gave a bitter chuckle. "Sounds like Bolles. Keep everybody involved off balance." Arlinda lit another cigarette, and Joop shot her an exasperated glance.

I described my growing suspicion Claire's murder might have something to do with the drug trade, and Joop suddenly sat upright. "Hold it. Full stop. You mean Claire, the woman from the prison? *She* was your sister?"

"Yes." I started to elaborate, then thought the better of it and sat silent.

"She was a royal pain in the butt, you know. But basically okay."

"Yeah," Arlinda said. She took a deep drag on her cigarette, and through the exhaled smoke, added, "Least she didn't take sides. And she got the kids into that clinic."

"You know what we're talking about, don't you?" Joop asked.

"Not really."

He stood up suddenly, and I shrank back in the chair. He went to the refrigerator, pulled open the door, and came back with a quart of buttermilk. He took a big drink, wiped his mouth with the back of his hand, and then put one foot up on his chair and leaned his arms forward on his knee, elbows crossed. For some reason I was fixated on the buttermilk carton in his hand. He noticed. "Ulcers. Listen. Two things. First of all, if you are messing around in the drug business, you should get your shit together a little better. Suppose you had been right? Suppose we'd killed Claire? Why the fuck wouldn't I kill you too?" I relaxed a little at this, since it seemed to suggest executing me was not on the agenda.

He continued. "Second. My dad used to raise hounds. Every so often you'd get one whose nose wasn't worth ten cents. Neither's yours. You're chasing after a possum and thinking it's a stag."

He took another long drink from the carton, poked the carton closed with a forefinger, and sat it down on the table. "I *am* a drug dealer. Make no apologies for it. People don't want the shit, they don't have to buy it. I admit, Claire gave us a hard time, pushing us to take our business elsewhere, but that's nothing compared to what we get from the competition. We sell a little crank, and the cops are on our backs like the fat kid at the pony rides. But the Association has meth labs all over the area, and they never get popped. Not once. Any kind of conflict between us and them, we get the shaft. We defend ourselves, we end up in jail on assault charges. They've blown away two of our guys in the last couple years, the cops just throw up their hands—another unsolved murder. So that ought to give you some kind of clue what's happening around here."

"What do you mean?"

"I mean the deck is stacked against us, and it's that sonofabitch Bolles that keeps it that way. I guarantee you, none of my people would ever have messed with Claire. Would have been the perfect excuse for them to bring us up on murder charges. Gets us out of the way, gives the Association more leg room."

"Are you suggesting Rick Bolles is actually working for some kind of drug ring?"

Joop combed his beard with the fingers of one hand. "Don't know what the story is. But I do know that when I told Claire about all this, she got interested. Real interested. Then, a few months later, somebody kills her…"

"How do I find out more about—did you call it the Association?"

He nodded. "That's what they seem to call themselves. It's not like they're in the Yellow Pages or anything." He sat back down. "Look, Walker, you seem like an okay guy. Are you sure you want to mess around with this?"

I took the time to think about this. "Yes."

"Why?"

"To tell the truth, I don't know."

"Good answer. Okay. I don't know who the big guys in the Association are. I know some of their mules who run shit up to the Central Valley. And damned if I can figure out why they keep after us down here. I mean, we're in competition with them on the street in places like Bakersfield and Fresno, but they don't deal down here—too close to the real goodies. But you can't just walk up and say hi to one of their couriers; the low-level guys are all a bunch of nervous freaks like Jesse."

Jupiter seemed to be enjoying our talk in some strange fashion. If Jesse and Arlinda were exemplars of his daily company, he was probably desperate to speak with someone he thought of as an equal. I decided to act like we were having a consensual discussion. "Okay. What would you do if you were me?"

"I'd get the hell out of here and go back to my family."

"Claire was my family. Almost all of it."

He thought for a while. "Well, if you're sure you want to get into it, there's one place you could start. Find somebody from their side who's gone straight."

"Can you put me in touch with somebody?"

"I can't give you an introduction. They're the enemy, remember? But there's a few guys around town who've found Jesus—Jake Stern is still around, and Billy the Mountain…"

"Billy the Mountain?" I knew who he had to mean.

"Yeah, like the song?" I gave him a blank look. "For somebody who's supposed to be educated, you don't seem to have much culture. Anyway, big guy…"

"Big fat guy with a beard? Some kind of a biker?"

"All of them are bikers, and a lot of bikers are fat guys with beards, but yeah, that would be him." He pushed his fingers back through his hair. "Unbelievable. Billy as a Jesus freak. Like George Bush in a garter belt and heels."

We sat there in silence. Arlinda lit another cigarette, and he said, "Jesus, woman, you are totally strung out." He stood up. "Well, put your pants on and get the fuck out of here." He started to leave the room, and then stopped. "Maybe I should walk you out to your car. Jesse would just love to shoot your ass."

As I zipped up my pants, he added, "By the way, the snake thing? Stupidest excuse I ever heard."

26

It took me an hour sitting around Claire's to settle my nerves after the Las Flores adventure. Mandy would have gone with pepper spray, at the minimum; Whipple would have gone with a phalanx of lawyers; anyone sensible would have at least gone with a plan. "But it worked out okay, didn't it?" Claire's voice whispered.

I made a sandwich and sat down on the couch. I had taken a single bite when there was a knock on the door. I opened it just a crack.

It was Malcolm. "Sorry to bother you, but…"

I slapped my forehead. "But you were wondering if I'd printed out your poems yet." I swung the door full open and led him in. "It completely slipped my mind. But I can do it right now."

He protested that he didn't want to put me out, but I carried my sandwich back to Claire's desk and had him pull up a chair next to me. "Let's see what we can find…"

As Windows 98 loaded and played its theme, I reflected I was a pretty poor detective. I had done a cursory look through the computer when I first went through Claire's filing cabinets, but maybe there were more clues lurking inside. WHOMURDEREDME.DOC, or something.

During the interminable boot sequence, I asked, "So, back when you were running drugs out of Barstow, who exactly were you working for? Not the Las Flores bunch?"

"No, those are the Ridgecrest Boys. Tell the truth, I'm not sure who I was running them for—I was just a little mule, lowest of the low. But there aren't that many major sources. The Brotherhood is pretty much history. Coming out of anywhere between here and Barstow, probably the Diablos or the Association."

The Association, Joop's nemesis. "Any other details?"

"They always handed off to me back of a burger joint. Big Mexican guy, real *cholo*. I mean, not Mexican Mexican. Local Mexican. Drove this giant red pickup, the kind with two sets of seats up front. Name of some health-food company on the side."

"Health food company?"

"Yeah. Rockland, Rock City, something like that."

I thought about this for a while, even though Windows was done setting up the desktop. "Do you know anything about how methamphetamine is made?"

"Not me. I'm no cook."

I knew who probably would, though I was reluctant to call her. I flipped through my address book, dialed her on my cell. "Give me a minute, Malcolm," I said. He stood up and started browsing through Claire's books.

Jerry answered. He tried to be pleasant and make conversation, but I didn't rise to the occasion. He sat the phone down and yelled, "Hey Liz…" Then, as the receiver was lifted, said, "Your ex."

"Walker." That inimitable voice, the Ice Queen herself. "Glad you called, I have news. We're pregnant."

I detest the plural when applied to pregnancy, but ignored it. "Do you know much about the manufacture of methamphetamine?"

"Hard up for cash?"

"Ha ha. *Do* you?"

"Lots. Anyone with a background in organic does now days, it's all over the journals—mainly because of the environmental damage it does in sloppy garage labs."

"So what do you need in the way of ingredients?"

"A number of things, but a benzene ring with a single hydrocarbon branch is the main starting point. Lots of ways to get that. The whole amphetamine family is pretty simple, based on common stuff. That's why they'll never stamp out clandestine manufacture—you'd have to outlaw just about everything organic."

"If there was a health food company, would they have the starting ingredients?"

"I don't know. Depends on what line of health stuff they were in. What's this about, Walker?"

"About Claire's murder, I think."

"Oh." She paused for a while. "Well, the commonest way to go at it is with ephedrine-based building blocks, so if they had a lot of decongestants...or, a health food store might carry ephedra, the herb—Chinese call it Ma Huang. In principle, you could make it out of Mormon tea, but you have to have bales and bales of the stuff."

"So the answer is...?"

"The answer is, you tell me what kind of stuff they sell, maybe I can say yes or no."

I thanked her, and even congratulated her on her pregnancy.

Malcolm sat back down as I rang off. "You figure something out?"

I shrugged.

I launched Windows Explorer and hunted around. Under the subfolder C:/Writings/Misc there seemed to be a lot of documents. I clicked the MODIFIED button to sort by the last date.

There it was, second in the list, MALCOLMPOEMS.DOC. December 9th, 6:15 pm. But it wasn't at the top. The top file was NEUTRINOS.DOC. And it had been modified on December 20th, 11:48 pm.

Five days after Claire had been murdered.

Mandy studied the screen. "Did you open this file?"

"No. Once I saw the date, I just left it alone. I left everything alone. Told Malcolm he'd have to come back in a few days."

"Good boy. Okay, want to see something stupid?"

"Oh, by all means. My specialty."

"You've got serious competition from Mister Gates. Watch this: I right-click. Menu comes up. Click *Properties*. This dialogue box comes up. Click the *Statistics* tab…"

Created: Thursday, August 8   6:23:08 pm
Modified: Friday, December 6   11:48:42 pm
Accessed: Monday, January 6

"That's great," I said. "It gives you a complete log…"

"Notice any problems with it? Like the fact that the last access is right now? There used to be this jerk in the EE department where I went to school. If you said, 'Can I ask you a question?' he'd say, 'You just did.' Well, this is exactly like that guy. You ask, 'When was this file last accessed?' and it says 'Right now.' Zero information."

"So we can't tell when it was last accessed?"

"Not from this, we can't. There's ways to read the information off the header. But what's weird is that somebody modified it… I'm going to go ahead and open it up." She double-clicked NEUTRINOS. DOC and Microsoft Word started up, and, after the typical whirring and blinking, displayed a poem by John Updike titled, "*Cosmic Gall*," which did indeed appear to be about neutrinos.

The poem went on for twenty-some lines. It became more and more amusing, but if there was a clue here it escaped me. "I'm baffled. Why would anyone…"

"The poem looks complete, and there's nothing out of place. My guess is that someone was looking at it—not just looking at this poem, but looking through Claire's documents. They must have screwed up when they opened this one, accidentally hit a key or something, and then panicked and saved the changes. Or maybe they didn't panic; maybe they were just sloppy."

"So the only reason I noticed anything was wrong is because somebody hit the wrong key?"

"Hey, my friend, unless we assume your particular sperm was a real sprinter, the only reason your DNA got to Momma first was because about a billion others stopped to check out the scenery or buy gum. Little things add up."

She leaned over and dug through a satchel she had brought. "This doesn't necessarily mean anything, you know. The sheriffs probably went through her computer files looking for clues." She pulled out a compact disk, slid it into the CD drive, and waited while the install window took over the screen. *ALPHA-OMEGA PRO UTILITIES*. She clicked rapidly through the license agreements and install locations and started it loading.

While she waited, she kicked off her shoes and put her feet up on the desk, nursing her mug of tea. I was pleased to finally know that her feet were mirror images: both had that crooked little toe.

When the installation was finished she put her feet on the floor and leaned forward. "Just for fun, before we start, let's look and see if anything's been deleted lately… Recycle bin's empty… Let's take a look at the disk stats…"

"Sonofabitch." She put her mug down on the desk, hard. "Look at this." She tapped the screen, which showed:

You last defragmented this drive   17 day(s) ago.

"And that," she said, "was about the same date that file was modified."

"I don't understand."

"Well, I think I do. Hang on for a minute or two. I need to check something out."

She started the Alpha-Omega Utilities and a series of dialogue boxes came up on the screen demanding search criteria: FAT/Other, Header Code, Hex/ASCII/Both…

I went to gaze out the back window. Maybe Malcolm wasn't being truthful. Maybe he really did know how to use a computer, and had broken in here while the police still had it closed off, and—

"Think I got it," Mandy said. "Or rather, I think I see what's happened here."

I sat down by her. "And?"

"And we're shit out of luck. Somebody ran WinWasher on this machine…and then, in complete overkill, they defragmented the hard drive too." She sat back in the chair and made a steeple of her fingers. "Now why do you defrag a drive?"

"To speed up access times."

"That's one reason. Another reason is to overwrite old files. Windows security is pretty lax. If I delete a file, all it really does is eliminate that address in the FAT. So the information is still out there, even if you've emptied the recycle bin. And it's pretty easy to go out there and recover the goodies, even if the whole header is gone. But if you defrag…"

"Then it repacks the disk—and writes over all of the supposedly unused spaces."

"Right." For a moment I thought she might pat me on the head. Or toss me a fish. "But it looks like they ran WinWasher in bleach mode, so the defrag was unnecessary… WinWasher cleans out everything—all the little clues and entries and logs, all the bits from the deleted files. The NSA itself couldn't recover any evidence from this computer. Kick-ass program."

"Does it come with Windows?"

"Of course not. Third party." She swiveled the chair and opened and slammed the drawers of the desk, one after another. "Didn't the woman keep backups? This CD drive is read-only… Have you seen any boxes of floppies around here?"

"No."

"Damn. Damn." She stood up and walked around the room, dragging her hair back into a ponytail with both hands and then releasing it, over and over again. "Okay. Right. Either she didn't keep backups—not likely—or somebody took all the disks. Somebody *must* have taken all the disks, everybody has *some* flops around…" She walked into the living room and threw herself back onto the couch.

It was quiet for a long time. I walked over carefully and looked down. Her hands were crossed beneath her small breasts as if she were lying in state, but her ankles were crossed too, which detracted from the dignity of the pose. She stared into the nothing a few feet above her face, as if waiting for something to coalesce from the dust of the desert air. "Are you okay?" I asked.

"Shh!" she said.

I went back to the rear window to watch the creosote tremble in the breeze.

Eventually Mandy rolled off the couch with a sigh and went back to the computer. I heard her fingers rattling the keys, the occasional louder *thak* as she hit *Enter*. After several minutes of this, she said, "Damn! I hate Windows! Hate Macs too." She lifted her feet from the floor and pushed hard against the edge of the desk with her hands so the chair wheeled back several feet to the center of the room.

"So we're not getting anywhere?"

"It's hopeless. I'm a UNIX girl, not a Windows jock, but dead is dead and gone is gone."

"So we don't know anything more than we did before, really."

"Hey, wake up, Walker. We know a lot more. Somebody erased some files, stole the disks, and did it like a pro. Well, a semi-pro, at any rate. Does that sound like a random junkie breaking in? Does it sound like some sex-crazed stalker?"

"But it might fit with the theory that this is tied into some sort of drug organization."

Mandy stood. "Maybe. I still don't think much of that idea."

"Why not?"

"Doesn't feel right. If it's a mafia sort of thing, it seems like they'd shoot you in the head and bury you in the desert. And steal your whole damn computer."

"But maybe they wanted the body to be found. As a warning."

"What good is a warning if nobody gets the message? I don't think this drug thing is the answer." She clasped her hands behind her back, straight-armed, and then lifted her wrists toward the ceiling, groaning as she stretched the muscles in her shoulders. "God, humans are weird."

"Pardon?"

"It's just bizarre what we can adapt to. Have you listened to us for the last couple of minutes? 'Maybe they wanted the body to be found,' 'shoot you in the head and bury you in the desert.' We're standing here in Claire's house talking about her murder like it's some kind of brain-teaser."

"You mean we should be more respectful, or shouldn't follow up on this, or what?"

"None of the above. I was just noticing: humans are weird."

I couldn't quarrel with this observation, but I didn't see how it moved us ahead. I took off my glasses and polished them on my shirt. "So what do we do now?"

"We should check and see if my little web-search program is done running. If that doesn't give us anything, then, based on what you told me from this morning, we should probably go find Billy."

"What?" I pulled the wire earpieces of my glasses back behind my ears and let them settle into their accustomed grooves in my flesh. "I thought you just finished telling me that you didn't think the drug trade was the solution to this whole thing."

"I don't. The important thing sometimes is to keep things moving."

"But it seems to me I was reading in one of Claire's books the other day that one step in the right direction is worth more than a thousand in the wrong direction."

"Sure. But we're at the bottom of a hole here. I figure any direction we head now is up."

We leaned forward to peer at the monitor on Mandy's computer. "Wow," she said. "I wasn't expecting this many hits…there's more than five thousand things reported in the press that fit our general criteria in the last six months. Violent place. Of course, a lot of them are probably duplicates. Let's look at the sorted stuff…"

She opened another window on the screen. "This should be the smallest category, because it's most restrictive—multiple assailants, strangulation, reverse chronological… Lord, still 153 hits. A lot of these had better be dupes, or I'm moving to Nebraska."

A lot of them were. The first forty-six were all about the same case, the New-Year's-Eve gang-rape and murder of a college student in Orange County. Mandy scrolled past these, found three hits on the attempted murder of a prostitute in Los Angeles by a gang.

"How about this?" she asked, eyebrows raised. She knew she had it this time.

December 30. Three assailants. The victim: Reverend Geoffrey Tilson, an openly gay minister in Palm Springs. Beaten and in the process of being lynched outside his church when a car pulled into the parking lot, and the assailants fled. He was listed in guarded condition at Desert Regional Medical Center.

"So why isn't Bolles on top of this?"

"It's a man, not a woman; it's a lynching, not a chain around the neck; it's Riverside County, not San Bernardino."

Mandy jumped to the web page for the *Desert Sun* newspaper and we moved forward in time. There were articles decrying this outrageous hate crime, but no announced leads from the police…

Mandy punched a few numbers into her cell phone, waited, punched some more, and then sat it down. "Paging Dawn," she said in answer to my expression.

Coverage in other papers was similar. The *Sun-Telegram* had reactions from the man-on-the-street. A Riverside paper had interviewed members of his congregation.

The phone rang, and Mandy snatched it up. "Dawn? Hey, do you know anybody at DRMC? …Yeah? Well here's the deal…" She filled her in on the assault, and asked her to see if she could dig up more details about the man's condition.

Then we paged through the rest of what Mandy was calling our Greatest Hits, the multiple assailants plus strangulation sort. Grim reading, but nothing immediately detectable as likely work of God's Law and their little Angels. "Maybe I should have searched to see if anyone was burned at the stake," she said. She leaned her head on my shoulder. "God, this is ugly stuff."

I stroked her hair for a moment. "What now?"

"Let's go for a walk somewhere—get out on the rocks. Then maybe some dinner."

Dawn called Mandy while we were at dinner. Tilson was still in the hospital with internal injuries, but he was expected to make a full recovery with the possible exception of his voice. His larynx had been badly crushed in the near-lynching, and at present he couldn't speak at all. He was allowed visitors, and his congregation kept up a flow of well-wishers that the hospital found almost unmanageable.

After she flipped the phone shut, she said, "Do you want to try doing this tonight?"

"No. It'll be too dark. Maybe Jared can handle it in the morning. Plus I need to go up to Ettenmoor's, and then get up early tomorrow."

"What for?"

"I'd rather not tell you in case it's a complete flop."

"Is it dangerous? Another Las Flores kind of venture?"

I laughed. "No. I think I'll leave the Sam Spade stuff to somebody else from now on. No, this is more in the nature of a scientific expedition."

"Be mysterious if you want. Shall I call Jared, or do you want to?"

I turned up my palms. She hit a speed-dial button and a digit, and waited. "Jared? ...Yeah, it is. You have one of those big telephoto lenses, don't you, the one you used for those raptor photos...?"

28

As agreed, Teresa Hernandez was waiting for me at the Joshua Tree Visitor's Center at seven in the morning. "Sorry to make you drive out here so early," I said, "and then make you meet me somewhere on top of it. But finding my sister's house is really hard."

"Right. You're just afraid of a sexual harassment charge if you have a female student at your house unchaperoned."

"Yep, that's the problem, alright. Especially female reporters."

We drove back through the center of Joshua Tree, and I said, "I need to make a quick stop to check on something." I pulled down a side street, and there it was, just like in the yellow pages: *Rock Garden Health Products*, the closest match I'd found to Malcolm's *Rockland? Rock City?* I wandered over to the office. It didn't seem to be a retail establishment: more like a small office connected to a slightly larger manufacturing plant. I peered through the window, shading the glare of the glass with a palm over my eyes. Office furniture. I looked around the side of the building. A stocky man was loading cartons into the back of a large red pickup with a King Cab. He noticed me, but didn't seem the least bit guilty or nervous. "Help you with something?"

"Oh, I—I noticed that you're a health food place, and—"

He grinned. "No, we get that a lot. We just manufacture, we don't retail."

I tried to look suitably disappointed. "What do you make?"

"Protein powder. Amino acid mixtures. Body-building stuff. Really only about five different blends."

"Where can I find it?"

"Just about any health food store. Some gyms. All under Rock Garden. We don't relabel for other outfits, the way some do." He went back to hefting cartons.

"Any luck?" Teresa asked.

"More like a dead end, I think. Really wish I'd taken more organic chemistry back in college."

"I've always heard that you older people got kind of wise about life. Here, let me write that down—more...organic...chem..."

"Leave me alone. It's early, and, as you just pointed out, I'm ancient."

Bob Beaumont met us at the gates of the proposed UWI disposal site. The cigarette butts outside the window of his BLM truck suggested he'd been there a while. He stepped down from the cab and stretched. "Walker," he nodded, "long time." We shook hands, and Teresa and I carted the equipment from the back of the Jeep into the bed of his truck while he unlocked the gate. We drove through, Teresa in the middle of the truck's wide seat, and Bob jumped out and locked the gate behind us. "Don't know what they think they're locking up here anyway—sand?"

It was a three-mile drive, slow and bumpy, and Bob and Teresa used the time to get acquainted. He had been a little put out by my pleading he join me on this early-morning expedition, but the opportunity to blab to Teresa seemed to make up for it.

We crossed a border marker that showed we were back on BLM property, though it was land UWI had a lease option on. We piled out of the truck, laid down compass bearings for due west, and started to work.

With a five-pound sledge, we drove a four-foot length of thick rebar into the soil until only a foot protruded. I took the handheld console, wrapped the leads around the rebar and turned on the power. Then I called Ettenmoor. "Is it on at your end?" I asked.

"On. I'm not, though. Wouldn't get up this early for just anyone." He read off the resonant frequency he was seeing in the control room. I punched in the numbers and flipped the *filter* switch. The display read 0.000793, so I hit the x10^4 gain button and it jumped to 7.931002.

"Think we've got you," I reported.

He yawned. "What frequency tolerance you set for?"

"Three percent."

"Fair enough. I'll have Larry call you if it drifts more than one-point-five at this end. Going back to bed now."

Teresa stopped me as I locked down the vise-grips. "Explain one more time? One sentence, in language suited for those of my readers whose touchstone is the sports page?"

"The bar acts as a sort of antenna to pick up currents in the ground that are generated by—well, generated somewhere else, at a particular frequency. The bigger the current, the more conductive the underlying medium. So, if there is something really conductive down there, we'd expect to get a stronger signal as we pass over it."

"C-minus, Professor. I understand just fine, but I can't write it down like that. Plus the assignment was 'one sentence.'"

It seemed easy enough at first: crank the rebar back out of the ground with a pipe-wrench and vise-grips, carry it twenty yards west, drive it in again, wrap the leads, note the sample number, GPS position, and signal strength on a clipboard. Then crank it out again…

Except that under the sandy surface, the soil varied more than expected. In places, the rebar started to bend before it was three feet in. In others, it drove in, but we couldn't get it back out. Bob and I were both experienced field workers, so we had brought a dozen lengths of rebar, but I started to worry even that might not be enough.

Teresa took a few photos and chatted into a handheld recorder. By midmorning we were no more than halfway done, and we were soaked with sweat despite the cool day.

"Looks like someone's finally noticed," Teresa said. Glad of an excuse to break off, Bob and I sat down on the sand, and Teresa jogged off to fetch the truck, now hundreds of yards distant.

"Land Rover?" I asked, squinting at the dust cloud, still well over a mile distant.

"Maybe."

Teresa pulled up in the truck, and we opened the cooler and popped out cold drinks. Bob frowned at the approaching vehicle. "Too flat. Not tall enough for a Rover… Think it's a Humvee."

I whistled in appreciation. Bob said, "Hey, that's the private sector for you."

At length, the vehicle turned off the dirt track and came straight for us, cross-country. They came at about twenty-five miles an hour, bouncing hard, and I winced on behalf of their internal organs. "Wide wheelbase, though," Bob continued. "Know it makes things more stable, but on a lotta the Jeep trails out here, that thing would have two tires hanging over the side of a cliff."

The Humvee stopped about twenty feet away and the engine shut down. After the interminable grind of the motor, the two men inside stepped into what seemed an echoing silence, their forms vague in the dust cloud that had overtaken them. Teresa covered her eyes as the dust passed us too.

It might have been Greg, the UWI security guy who had thrown me out of their office. Whoever it was, he said, "This is private property."

Bob sucked his teeth a second, and said, "Nope. That back there is private property. This here is government property. And as you can see from the truck"—he hooked his thumb back at his rig—"we're from the BLM, and we have a permanent easement over that road you just drove down."

"What are you doing out here?"

"Don't see that's any of your business, but we're doing a survey."

"I'm afraid I'll have to ask you to discontinue your work until we can talk to the office."

"You don't have to be afraid."

"Huh?"

"You said you were afraid you'd have to ask us to quit. Don't be afraid. But the answer's no. We're going to keep right up with our work here, and if you interfere, we'll just send for the Federal Marshals, okay?" Bob turned around as if the matter was closed, and we went back to cranking a piece of rebar out of the ground.

The guard made dialing motions to his companion back at the Humvee, and the other man leaned into the Hummer and picked up a car phone. I wondered if people would understand that dialing gesture in another twenty years.

By the time the second UWI vehicle came through the gate, about four miles distant, we were on the last hundred yards of our transect. It was purely a formality at this point: after a series of random readings all morning, the display had jumped from the six-to-eight range up to fourteen, thirty-six, one hundred sixty-two, then fifty-eight, twenty-nine, twelve…then back to seven…six…eight…seven… We kept going anyway. There is something to be said for completeness, and the technique we were employing was probably novel enough to be publishable.

The Humvee with the two guards had paced us this whole time. We only had two more samples to go when Whipple's own Humvee pulled up next to theirs.

Whipple had traded his usual elegant suit for a safari look, but he was still creased and pressed. He strode over, flanked by the guards, and said, "Clayborne. You're in violation of a court order by crossing our property."

"Not clear. I was on a BLM easement."

"You also aren't allowed in this kind of proximity to me or my employees."

I swung the sledge down on the tip of the rebar. "So arrest me."

He turned to Bob and Teresa. "Who are you two?" I kept driving the rebar, taking breaks between swings to watch.

Teresa identified herself simply as "a journalist," not mentioning she worked for a campus paper. Bob said, "I'm Bob Beaumont, the survey supervisor, out of the Barstow BLM office."

"Benny Palumbo's office? I know your boss real well. Maybe I should give him a call."

Bob shrugged. "Free country, despite what your guards seem to think."

"Good idea," Teresa said. "In fact, Mr. Palumbo has offered to let one of our reporters listen in to any calls he gets from you today. They're all waiting for you."

"Got some good news for you, though," Bob said. "Think we've found water under your property. Wouldn't have expected it, would you? I mean, no offense, but it's like a *desert* out here."

"Based on what evidence?" Whipple demanded.

"Major—I mean *May-Jorr*—conductivity spike back there a ways."

"That doesn't prove there's water under there."

"True enough. Could be a buried power line that isn't on any charts. Could be a buried alien spacecraft. Hell, could be a street paved with gold, and we'll all be rich. But I'm pretty sure that our office and the EPA will both want to be sure just what it is before any permits are issued."

I had wrapped the leads and had a new reading. "Seven-point-three-three-nine-two," I said. Bob noted it down on the datasheet.

Whipple came over to me and spoke in a more confidential tone. "Dr. Clayborne, what's this all about? What good does this do anyone? I can understand that you're in a state of grief—who wouldn't be?—but we weren't responsible for what happened to your sister."

I turned off the unit, pulled on my gloves, and started cranking the pipe-wrench round and round. "Can I have a hand here?" I shouted over at Bob, who was chatting with Teresa.

Whipple persisted. "What good will this do? Just eliminate jobs in the area, drive investment elsewhere… It won't bring her back."

I sat the wrench on the ground and straightened up. "True. And it's too damn bad.'Cause you know what?" I wiped the sweat from my forehead. "I think she would have gotten a real kick out of this."

In the dream, Melanie was in bed beside me, facing away. We were both naked, but I couldn't work up the nerve to reach for her. At last I did, and she turned my direction, and it wasn't Melanie at all, it was Mandy, and I realized it was Mandy I really wanted. I clasped her body, but she simply reached up and stroked my forehead, pushing the hair back…

As I opened my eyes, Mandy turned blurry. I blinked, and realized she was really there, sitting on Claire's bed, stroking my forehead. "Can you wake up? It's kind of important…" She wasn't nude, though, and she was only fuzzy because my glasses were off.

I'd said farewell to Bob, driven a euphoric Teresa back to her car, and then come back to Claire's, showered, and clambered into bed in midafternoon. Judging from the light, it was near sunset.

"Jared's got pictures," she continued, "and visiting hours end at seven."

"Okay," I said.

She stood up. "Well? Are you getting up?"

"I can't get up with you in here. I don't have any clothes on."

Mandy laughed. "Is it that you're shy, or that you don't want to shock my girlish eyes?" She went back to the living room, pulling the door shut behind her.

Jared did indeed have pictures—blow-ups of each of the individual Angels, from a number of perspectives. With a flourish, he produced his masterpiece, the three of them together, stalking their steroid-laden bodies across the chapterhouse parking lot. "Huey, Louie, and Dewey, Junior Woodchucks all in a line."

"Aren't you too young for Donald Duck?" I asked.

"My mom insisted education should be focused on the classics. Hell, I can even name the cast from *Gilligan's Island*."

The hospital in Palm Springs was pretty upscale for the desert, but I should have expected that. Visitors were limited to four at a time, so we had to talk our way to the front of a line of people waiting to see Reverend Geoffrey Tilson. Jared handled it with aplomb; despite his Gen-X looks and dress, he managed to give everyone the impression we were on some sort of official business.

Seeing Tilson was more upsetting than I'd expected. One eye was still swollen shut, and his lips were torn and stitched where his teeth had been driven through them. The lumpiness under his blankets hinted at further damage I tried not to imagine.

Whatever had been done to him, it hadn't affected the sharpness of his mind. Jared handed him the photos without any preamble, and Tilson immediately became aroused, holding the photos in one hand and slapping at them with the knuckles of the other. In his excitement sounds came from his throat, and they were broken, grunting sounds it was horrible to hear.

"Why me?" Bolles asked, leaning on the wall of the hospital corridor, tapping his foot. "Why not the Palm Springs PD?"

"I assumed that you'd do whatever was appropriate with the Palm Springs authorities," I said.

"This crime may have been committed here, but they live in *our* town," Jared said. And who knows what they've done over there, already…"

"What can I say? Good work, guys." He looked back over his shoulder at Mandy, who stood down the hall, visibly distancing herself from us. "And you too, Amandinea."

"Give me a break, Rick," she said.

"I have everybody's numbers. I'll let you know what the story is as it happens. But don't spread this all over town, okay? I'd like to hit these guys without any warning."

He started off down the hall, one hand in his pocket, jingling change. He stopped. "Oh, and by the way: these guys had anything to do with Claire, I'll see that they fry. One way or another."

It was ten by the time we made it back to Claire's, and Jared jumped in his car immediately, late for some kind of function back in Yucca Valley. Mandy seemed like she might want for me to invite her to hang around for a while, but it was more than I could cope with at that moment.

Increasingly I felt myself drawn to Mandy, and it was increasingly uncomfortable for me. In fact, I found I liked all of the Eleusinian Circle, but they made me feel aged and awkward. In academia, forty-four isn't old, but people like Kirsten and Jared made me feel antediluvian. And even Mandy—I probably only had five, maybe ten years on her, but she made me feel like I was from another era.

I planned on going back to bed, but couldn't sleep. I remembered there was still unfinished business from the morning. I booted Claire's computer, started her internet browser, and found the Hall of Records for San Bernardino County.

Under "Fictitious Business Names," I found A.T. Avery as the registered owner of Rock Garden Health Products, with a home address in Desert Hot Springs. For what it was worth, I wrote down the name and address.

Out of sheer nosiness, I searched to see if there were any other businesses registered to Avery. There was one: SkySights Fireworks Company, in Landers, California. Same owner, same home address. Nothing more on Avery anywhere on the net, unless he was the same

A.T. Avery who raised registered bloodhounds in Georgia, or the A.T. Avery who was an accountant in Watertown, Massachusetts.

I shut down the computer and went to look in the refrigerator for something to eat. I realized I hadn't eaten since breakfast. I pulled out the makings for a sandwich, but paused when I thought I heard Claire, way way back in my head. "Psst! Lionel…try looking at what's in front of you…"

I shook my head. If I ever returned to San Diego, I planned to see a psychiatrist and see if I needed some kind of medication.

For no apparent reason, I remembered walking in Desert Christ Park with Mandy on New Year's Eve, remembered it vividly…and the sound of the loudspeaker on a sheriff's cruiser, crackling out:

"All fireworks—are illegal—in San—Bernardino—County."

What the hell? I found my address book and dialed the Ice Queen, found myself in her voicemail. "Elizabeth? Walker. Can you give me a call? Kind of an important question…" I gave her my numbers, and said, "Call first time you get a chance. Please?"

30

I'd asked Elizabeth to call "the first chance she got," so I couldn't really complain when I had to stumble out of bed at five-thirty in the morning. I had, blissfully, forgotten how early she got up; she had probably already done her Jazzercize tape and eaten breakfast. "Sorry I didn't get back to you last night, Walker. Big departmental shindig."

I sat on the couch, settled my glasses on my nose, and tried to kick-start my logy brain. "M'kay. I found out what that health food company makes. Protein powder, amino acid mixtures…"

"There's certainly the right ring structures in some of them," she said, "but that's not at all what I was expecting." I heard her tapping at a keyboard. "They don't make any kind of 'pep pills,' or decongestants…?"

"Not as far as I can tell."

"Let me page through a few structures, here…"

"Another weird thing. The guy who owns the health food operation also owns a fireworks company. And fireworks aren't even legal around here."

She started laughing. "There you go, then. Definitely a meth lab."

"Are you being serious, or sarcastic?"

"Serious. Think about what fireworks are made of."

"Gunpowder?"

"Lots of things, really, but one of the bulk components is red phosphorus. Same red stuff that's on the ends of paper safety matches."

"So?"

"So? So, you need two main things to make amphetamines: a likely starting compound, and a reducing agent. Lithium aluminum hydride is great, but hard to get unless you're a legitimate chem lab. But with red phosphorus and iodine, you can whip up hydroiodic acid in seconds. I guess lots of it's made that way—someone from the DEA was talking about making safety matches illegal."

"Safety matches?"

"Yeah, lots of small-timers tear off the match heads to get the phosphorus…"

"But that's ridiculous!"

"Think that'll slow the DEA down? …Here we go. Plenty of routes, but I'd go with phenylalanine—you know: *Notice to Phenylketonurics, this product*… I could be from there to methamphetamine in four steps with red phosphorus, and there might be an easier route…"

"I don't need a good synthetic procedure, I just needed to know what was happening."

"You do now. Fireworks, no big deal, amino acids, no big deal, both together, definitely a large-scale operation. This isn't kids tearing off match-heads and crushing up Contac."

"Phenylalanine…?"

"Probably. But could be from one of the other ring-based aminos… Are we done here, Walker?"

"I guess so."

"Good, because this pregnancy stuff isn't as much fun as I thought it would be. I think I need to go throw up for a while."

Initially I was excited by my talk with Elizabeth, and assumed I was up for the day, but as I contemplated what to do with this information I became so drowsy I leaned over sideways on the couch to shut my eyes, just for a few minutes.

The sun was well up when the sounds of a car in the driveway awakened me. I went to open the door, using my hands to push my hair into some semblance of order.

A big yellow pickup, and Darnell, carrying a cardboard box. He put it into my arms. A blender, teflon frying pan, assorted kitchen implements. "Told you over at Ira's—few things we borrowed from Claire. Thanks."

He started to turn away. I noted the ring finger of his left hand, where the rotor of the outboard engine had chopped it, was bandaged around two aluminum splints. "How's the finger doing?"

"Well enough." He stood, still half-turned, and didn't look at me, but rather at the doorframe.

"You know, I appreciate your bringing all this back, but I don't need it. I have my own place, back home... I'm sure Claire would have wanted for you and Rachel to have it."

"Loan's a loan. Wouldn't be right." He turned and headed back to the truck.

I thought about arguing some sense into him, but settled for saying, to his retreating back, "Well, talk it over with Rachel when she gets back, and see if maybe you wouldn't want it after all. I'm sure it's what Claire would have liked."

He looked back as he opened the door of the truck, and just nodded in acknowledgement—pleasant enough, but with an expression that said, *I don't think that's too likely*.

As I carried the box inside, the cell phone rang from back on Claire's desk. I sat the carton on the couch and ran for it.

"Walker, are you okay?" Mandy asked. "You sound out of breath."

"Jumped to get the phone."

"Has Bolles called you yet?" When I answered in the negative, she said, "Well listen, then—'The sheriff's department and the Palm Springs PD had raided the God's Law chapterhouse early that morning, arrested the three Angels, and held everyone else who was on the property. They'd found a cache of automatic weapons, some explosives, and a huge stockpile of dried foods hoarded up against the Last Days. Most important of all, they had found a List of the Damned—a sort of hit list of area residents and their crimes. Tilson's name was on it, against the accusation *Sodomite*. Mandy, Kirsten, Chad, and Jared were all listed under *Witch*.' Ironic, isn't it? Melanie's the only one who's a practicing Wiccan, and she isn't listed." Fifteen members of a local Buddhist commune were listed as *Satanists.*

"Was Claire on the list?"

"No. I asked. But that could be—"

"Because they already killed her."

"Exactly. Bolles said his first priority was to get in touch with everyone on the List. The fact they call it a chapterhouse suggests there might be other chapters… Hey, Walker: We did good."

I agreed we had indeed done so, but then told her about my new information regarding Mr. A.T. Avery and his health food and fireworks businesses.

"What do you want to do about that?" she asked.

"Nothing, until we find out more. But I'd like to talk to Billy. Want to come?"

"I don't think he likes me much, Walker. Maybe you should go by yourself."

"I suspect he may have had a change of heart. And I'd really like to have you along."

"I can't go right now, I have a piece of code I have to crank out ASAP."

"Later this afternoon? I have things to work on too."

"Do you mind? I'll call you."

I was deep in two versions of the same paper about our piezoelectric survey out at the UWI disposal site—one as a memo to BLM, one for *Geophysical Research Letters*—when Bolles finally called.

He was even more manic than usual, flying high on a major police coup, and he thanked me as effusively as his strange manner allowed. "There's just one piece of bad news, though."

"That would be…?"

"I'm not ruling out the involvement of God's Law in your sister's murder, not at all. But she definitely wasn't killed by our three little Death Angels, because they have a great alibi. They were in jail up in Bakersfield on assault charges when she was killed. They didn't get out until the end of that week."

31

Finding Billy hadn't been as straightforward as I'd expected. I called Ira to find out where Shackles Torn Asunder was headquartered, and he volunteered that on Wednesdays they were usually at Church of the Rock for their version of choir practice. We drove there in Mandy's car, and found a roomful of men with electric guitars and women with tambourines. Perhaps there is some biblical injunction against women playing real instruments.

If rock music has any merit—a debatable proposition—it must lie in a spirit of rebelliousness and freshness, and Christian rock seemed designed to eliminate even these meager virtues. We waited through the overamplified roar of some song arguing that God is good—had there been some question?—and then inquired after Billy's whereabouts. He had indeed been there; he was off at "Phil and Ellie's," and wasn't coming back. After following some rather confused directions to "Phil and Ellie's," we were informed by a presumptive Phil that Billy had gone back to the Church of the Rock; but when we returned there we found he had gone to Water Canyon Coffee.

Probably where we should have gone in the first place; it seemed to be what passed for a cultural hub in Yucca Valley. When we stepped in, we saw them immediately: four bikers sitting against the westernmost wall, heads bowed in prayer. We sat down at a table near the entrance. Mandy massaged her temples for a moment, and then said, "I'll get us some coffee. When they decide to show off their piousness, it can take quite a while."

Contrary to Mandy's prediction, their prayer ended after only a few more minutes. Billy noticed me, and I gestured for him to come over.

His manner was meek enough, but the way he bulked so large over my table still made me nervous. "Mr. Clayborne," he said.

"Can you give me a few minutes?" I asked.

He was back in his elevated mode of speech. "I can give you as much time as you want. Let me tell the others, so they might continue with their studies."

Billy went back and conferred with his crew. While he was gone, Mandy returned with coffee—three full mugs, I noticed. She sat beside me, and pushed one of the mugs over to the opposite side of the table.

Billy was surprised to see her, and he eyed her with an enigmatic expression before sitting down. "Thank you for the coffee," he said to both of us. Then he addressed Mandy: "I just want you to know I didn't have anything to do with it. I know—I know I've said things that may have made you think I hated you, but they were—well, they were just stupid things. But I didn't know anything about the List, and I have asked those in our church who knew to go and pray on it, long and hard."

"We aren't here to talk about that…" I began, but he kept right on going.

"I'm ashamed, deeply ashamed, to say that some of the members of our congregation knew all about the List." He glanced over his shoulder at his three companions, and turned back. "And were picked up for questioning by the police."

Mandy leaned forward. "Billy. Focus. We aren't here for that. We want to ask you about speed."

No, he'd never had anything to do with a fireworks factory or a place that manufactured health food. A red truck? Yeah, sure…it said something on the side, but he couldn't remember what. But he had always picked up the stuff he ran north direct from the cooks, out past Amboy. No, he couldn't give us addresses—did they even have addresses out there?—but he'd be happy to take us there if we didn't mind the drive…

Billy had to put the passenger seat in Mandy's Saturn so far back that one side of the back seat was obliterated. I ended up in the back on the driver's side, thankful Mandy was so short.

"Out past Amboy" was the most precise description that Billy could offer, so we drove through Twenty-Nine Palms, east through Wonder Valley—"because you *wonder* why anyone would live there," one of my grad students used to say—and headed north on the Amboy Road. I found I was drowsy.

From the front seat, I heard Billy continue their discussion: "But Jesus and the disciples all prayed together…"

"In private, maybe, like at the Last Supper. But Christ was very specific about it. Read Matthew 6, verses five and six. You aren't supposed to pray in public. There's no other way to interpret it. In the King James Version, it says you should pray 'in your closet,' other versions say 'where none can see you.' You're not supposed to make a big display of how religious you are."

"But can't you even give thanks for a meal when you're in a restaurant?"

"Sure. Just don't make a big production of it."

"But I want to show God that I'm thankful—"

"Are you telling me he can't see what's in your heart? Clasping your hands and shutting your eyes and talking out loud—that's stuff for other people to hear, not the Creator. I mean, you aren't even supposed to perform charity in public, you're supposed to drop your alms in the poor box when no one is looking. Everything else is pride, Billy, showing off how much more religious you are than everyone around you…"

I fell asleep.

When I woke we were passing by the outlandish mounds of tailings that surround Bristol Dry Lake, lined up in rows and accidental patterns, like some barren-land version of crop circles. I stretched as we turned right at the T-junction on old Route 66. We drove east on the road toward Cadiz, passed the turnoff for Kelbaker Road, and then came to the defunct Roadrunner's Retreat Restaurant, once a landmark on 66. "Slow down up here," Billy said, "there's a place over on the right…"

We passed a trio of old date palms and a big propane tank. "Whoa," Billy said. "It was right there…" The site he indicated was nothing more than a blackened concrete slab with a few pieces of charred wood scattered about. "Must have had a little accident. Stuff is explosive. Poison, too."

We continued on past the Trilobite Range and pulled up over the pass that descended to Essex. Just outside town we stopped again, this time near a driveway which led to three silver trailers. Mailboxes, but no cars. Mandy wrote down the numbers. "And now?" she asked.

"That's it, as far as what I know," Billy said. "I'm sure there's other labs around, but they didn't want any of us to know much. The guys who are serious about this stuff, they don't use it, you know; and they don't really trust anybody who does." He was silent for a moment and then laughed. "Good thing, too; I wouldn't have trusted me!"

Mandy laughed too, and pulled into the driveway to turn around. I slumped down in the seat, prepared to go back to sleep if I could; it seemed to me the whole drive had been a waste of time, but maybe Mandy could make something of the information we had acquired. It was out of my hands.

When we approached the junction with Amboy Road, I sat up a little to look out at the dome of Amboy Crater, one of the few sites in the Mojave where the lava came out in the glassy black form most people associate with volcanoes. On my right I glanced at the old Amboy Café and Motel, one of the standbys before the Interstates killed Route 66. I was pleased to see it had been refurbished, and seemed to be thriving as Roy's Route 66 Café. The gas pumps were still working, too; for many years, that was the only part of the place which was kept in repair. As Mandy started her turn, something about the change in angle caught my eye. "Stop!" I said.

Mandy jumped on the brakes and the car lurched forward and rebounded. "What?" she demanded. We were still parked in the middle of old 66.

"Sorry. It wasn't that urgent. But can we go back to the service station over there?"

"Sure." She studied the rearview mirror, and then cranked the wheel hard right, pulling us across a long flat dirt area and over onto the parking lot. She stopped the car. "What's the story, you need to pee?"

I clambered out and looked at the place. It seemed like an eon ago I had found Claire's packet of photos, but I was certain of it: some details had changed, probably because of ongoing renovation, but this was the service station that had looked so strangely familiar in one of her snapshots.

I slammed the door. "Claire has a picture of this place, with a bunch of people standing around talking in front of it."

"People she knew?"

"I don't know. But it looked like a really lousy snapshot, like the people didn't know she was there."

"And?"

"I don't know. But I think it means something."

Mandy turned in the seat and inspected me. "You know, Walker," she said, in apparent seriousness, "if you aren't careful, you may start trusting your instincts."

"Aren't detectives supposed to have magnifying glasses?" Mandy asked. "Haven't we got anything like that around here?"

I looked around Claire's cottage as if I might spy one lying about. "I can't think of anything that will work as a substitute. But I'd swear that's the famous red pickup—Malcolm's truck, Billy's truck, Mr. A.T. Avery's truck."

She handed the photo back to me. "You'll need to have that enlarged if you want to read the license. But the guy in the suit has got to be Rick Bolles." She flipped through the other pictures, stopping at the one where Claire posed bare-bellied with her hands on her hips, staring straight into the camera lens. "God, what a woman," Mandy said. "Enough to make me wish I'd been a boy."

She shuffled further, then found one of the pictures of a rundown shack with a trailer parked nearby. "I'd swear this is that place we were at today before it burned down. I mean, picture it without the trailer there, and then mentally burn down the house…"

This was a feat that was beyond my mind's eye, but I was willing to accept her theory. "So, our next step is to talk to Bolles."

"What?" she asked. She stood with her butt leaned against the back of Claire's couch, still wearing her coat; with her black hair, black coat, black eyes, and smooth skin, she looked like she was in monochrome while the room around her was in color. "That's not what I expected you to say, Walker; not at all."

"Well it seems logical to me. Give him a chance to explain himself…"

"Give him a chance to shoot you in the head and bury you out around Kelso, you mean."

"There could be a logical explanation, you know."

"And you could be sticking your head into a noose. You should really think about this."

"I am. And I can't imagine that Bolles would do anything to me. It'd look a little suspicious, after Claire's murder, wouldn't it?"

"If this were a movie, this would be the part where I would run over to you and say, 'Oh Walker! Please be careful!' But as you may have noticed, this isn't exactly Hollywood country out here. So instead, I'm going to stand right here and say: Walker. Do what you want. But don't be a fucking idiot."

"It may be too late to do much about that."

"Well, I hate to tell you to be logical, because it's like telling an alcoholic to have another drink, but think about it. If a sheriff out here decides to kill you, who is going to be in charge of investigating it? Hmm?"

After Mandy went home, I took the photo to Walmart and made three 8x10 enlargements on one of their self-serve photo machines. Just for good measure, I made copies of the rest of the stack of photos, though most of them were just Claire and friends at the River.

Back at Claire's I sealed one of the photos in a manila envelope, addressed and stamped it. I was trying to decide whether to mail it then or wait until the morning when the phone rang. It was Chad, inviting me to come to a little get-together at his place. "I called earlier, but you were out. Left a message, though." He had: the light was blinking. I heard voices across the line; it sounded like the rest of the Circle was already there. "This is partly a celebration of the God's Law arrests, partly to have a chat about what happens next."

I told him I'd come over as soon as I did a few things. I grabbed the envelope and a basket of dirty clothes: Claire didn't have a washer, and I thought I'd look for a late-night laundromat on the way back from Chad and Melanie's.

The Jeep was headed down the driveway when a sheriff's cruiser pulled in, blocking my way. I half-expected Bolles, but it was a uniformed officer. He came over to the window. "Walker Clayborne?" I agreed I was. "I'll have to ask you to turn off the engine and come with me. You're under arrest."

32

Coxey, the lawyer Ettenmoor found for me, sounded like a real legal wizard, with a basketful of possible actions he could recommend against Universal Waste, some criminal, some civil—malicious prosecution, harassment, threatening, defamation of character, obstruction of justice—just about everything except soliciting prostitution and speeding. And he assured me Universal was a pocket worth thrusting our hands into: he could get me six figures easy, maybe seven, and all on contingency.

What he couldn't do was get me out of jail until the next morning. I gave him numbers for the members of the Circle and asked him to let them know what was going on, and reassure them it was just a formality. I also assured him I would think about his proposal for a whole host of countersuits and criminal complaints, and that I would gladly guarantee he could represent me in any actions I might undertake.

With that, he left me to my bunk. It wasn't so bad here: quiet, clean, surprisingly private. I felt relaxed in a way I hadn't felt in ages, maybe ever. "Always safer in a cage, isn't it?" I heard Claire whisper.

"You said it," I murmured, and fell into a sleep so sound I wouldn't have noticed if Armageddon came and went.

Coxey was as good as his word: The hearings officer commenced proceedings at nine in the morning, and I was on my way out by nine-twenty. An unexpected feature was the appearance of Bolles as a friend of the court, which he had apparently cleared with Coxey. Bolles noted I had been an important help to the police in a recent assault case, that nothing suggested I had ever been accused of criminal conduct, and that Universal had filed restraining orders against about a dozen other law-abiding citizens, my sister included. The judge released me without any bail requirements, and suggested that, on the basis of what he had heard, pursuing legal remedies against the company might be the wisest course of action. My trial date remained to be set.

I caught Bolles in the hallway, after telling Coxey to stay put for a moment. "I need to talk to you," I said.

Bolles turned up his palms. "Talk."

"It'll take a while. And I'd like some place more private. Private but public, if you know what I mean—people around."

He raised an eyebrow. "Disneyland?"

"Hidden Valley," I said, with sudden conviction.

"Now?"

"Sure, why not?"

"Because, happy as I was to put in a good word for you, I'm only in the building because I have to testify in a case in about fifteen minutes. You sure we can't just do this now?"

"No. I mean, yes, I'm sure we can't. How about noon?"

"Hidden Valley, High Noon? Should I bring my six-shooter?"

"This is important, Bolles."

"Well, I'm just wet with anticipation. You got it, buckaroo." He cocked his thumb and shot me with his index finger.

Coxey dropped me off in Claire's driveway, where the Jeep remained parked halfway down the drive. I finished pulling out, and drove off to find a mailbox.

When I returned there were messages from everyone in the Circle telling me to hang tough, and a message from Kirsten that implored me to call as soon as I could.

"Walker," she said. "I was afraid I was going to miss you. Are you going to be around for a while?" I told her I needed to leave at a quarter till noon, and she told me to stay put.

Twenty minutes later she came through the door and gave me a long, hard hug. "I wanted to say goodbye."

I sat in the armchair, she on the couch. "What's this about goodbye?" I asked.

"I need to get out of here for a while. Ever since Claire…well, even before, really." She pushed her hair back into a very short ponytail, squeezed it, then let the curls spring free. "I don't know what I'm doing out here, really…it was supposed to be temporary, and then I just kind of stayed. And I like working with Wild Desert, because I like the animals, but my part of the work is mainly business stuff, and I hate it… And Bryce…well, I'm just not Claire, you know. Claire could sort of use men for sex, and they never seemed to mind. I admired that, but I always end up getting used instead, you know?"

I didn't, but I nodded wisely.

"When I found out my name was on that list, you know, it was just too much to take. I know that sounds stupid. I mean, somebody broke into my apartment looking for me, and I could live with that, but I can't handle being on this list?" She puffed up her cheeks and blew air through pursed lips. "God, listen to me. All I know is I need to get out of here for a while, and I didn't know if you'd still be here when I got back, and I wanted to make sure I saw you."

"I'm glad you did. I like you. I like all of you."

She grinned. "Especially Melanie, right?"

I gave an embarrassed smile. "We all know what that's about, though, don't we? No, if we get past the pure lust thing…" I said this without thinking, and noticed Kirsten was giving me a strange look.

"Mandy?" she asked. "Are you getting interested in *Mandy*?"

"I—uh…sort of."

"Cool." The smile on her face grew wider and wider in tiny increments. "Go for it. God knows nobody else can handle her."

"What do you mean?"

"She tends to give boys the creeps, cause she's so…"

"Spooky? Mouthy?"

Kirsten just smiled. "You know the term 'Ipsissimus?'" I shook my head. "It's a high occult grade from the Greek Mystery Schools. It means 'He who is most himself.' Claire was like that too. Both of them are about as 'them' as you can get."

"That's not what men want?"

"As far as I can tell, men want somebody who looks like a movie star and acts like a porn star half the time and a virgin the rest. And I look like me, and end up acting like somebody else, and I've decided to save that shit until I find somebody I actually like."

"Do you realize I have no idea what the hell you're talking about?"

"Good. I'd just as soon you didn't."

We sat quiet for a few moments, and I said, "Where are you going?"

"I'm not sure yet. Maybe out to our family's place at the River for a while. Maybe back to Santa Monica, and sponge off Mom and Dad for a bit. Maybe look into whether I can get into a college program somewhere doing something I like… You're not off the hook, here, y'know—you're a professor, and I plan on using you any way I can, if I ever figure out what I want. And I'll be back, at least for a while; I'm not taking all my stuff. Claire said, if you ever live out here, you'll always be back."

I gave her a skeptical look. "Cumulatively, with all the fieldwork and everything, I've probably lived out here three or four years. But I'm perfectly happy down in San Diego."

Kirsten laughed. "But look: here you are anyway."

I sat on a boulder by the parking lot of Hidden Valley and flipped open Claire's little quote book. This was becoming a reflex with me, the way I suppose some people cast the *I Ching* or read fortune cookies. The discipline involved was to open it randomly, and not allow myself to read more than one at a time.

> To think is easy. To act is difficult. To act as one thinks is the most difficult of all.
>
> —Goethe

I studied the wall of rocks on my right as tourists pushed past me. I was startled when I heard Bolles' voice say, "Professor. Gary Cooper here yet?" He was slouched against a rock wall a few feet on my left, his suit jacket hanging over his shoulder from two hooked fingers. He twirled his key ring around the index finger of his other hand. "Shall we go on in, or you want to talk right here?"

I gestured down the path.

Once inside the valley walls, Bolles pointed to a group of boulders on our left. "That do?" The stack of boulders came up through the sand like a small island, an impression reinforced by the way pinon pines and junipers clung to the rock crevices but shunned the surrounding soil. I shrugged my agreement and we plodded over there together through the rough sand, all of it fragments shed from neighboring rocks in the last few thousand years.

"Hang on a second," he said when we neared the rocks. To my surprise he faced me and slid his hands inside my jacket, running his open palms across my chest and down my sides. "I assume you want to talk frankly. I can't do that if I think you might be recording me."

Bolles selected a waist-high boulder in the shade of a tortured juniper and carefully laid down his jacket. He turned, put the heels of his hands on the rock, and jumped up to sit there. He loosened the slide on his bolo tie, undid the top button on his shirt, and pulled open the collar a little. "Okay, shoot. Not literally, of course." He grinned in a way where the corners of his mouth showed teeth, but the center of his lips stayed pressed together. "I hope the cowboy fixation hasn't made you come armed."

I stepped toward him and pulled out the rolled manila envelope that protruded from my jacket pocket. I handed it to him like an arrest warrant.

He raised his eyebrows high but took it. He opened the flap and pulled out the full-page enlargement of the photo. He looked it over casually, then sat it and the envelope down on top of his jacket. "Okay. So what's the question?"

"Do you deny that's you in that picture?"

He frowned and grinned at the same time, as if he didn't understand the punch line to some joke I had just told. "Nooo…" he said. "Why would I deny that? Admit it's not very flattering, and I need a haircut…"

"That picture shows you meeting with known drug dealers, known criminals. And I believe that Claire took it without anyone's knowledge."

"Ah. So that's what this is about." He drummed the fingers of one hand on his knee, not the usual nervous drumming that many people do, but in alternating sets of two fingers, thumb-middle, index-ring, middle-little, like some piano exercise.

I had a hard time lifting my gaze from his busy fingers to his eyes. "That's not all. But before we go any further, I should tell you I've sent copies of that picture, and a short statement, in an envelope to my lawyer, with instructions that it be opened in event of my death or disappearance." This I had in fact done. I imagine my lawyer, who mainly did my taxes, would be puzzled when he received the letter.

"Walker, Walker, Walker. You don't mind if I call you that, do you? It's really hard to say 'Dr. Clayborne, Dr. Clayborne, Dr. Clayborne.'" He leaned back on his hands, and kicked his legs forward a bit, tapping the toes of his black wingtips together. "Sometimes I wonder what it would be like to be in law enforcement where everybody's ideas didn't come from the movies. But I guess nowadays that would have to be on another planet… Okay, what do you think you have? I'm sure this picture isn't all."

I ignored his amused expression and pretended I was lecturing to a class. I even started to walk back and forth as I did so, wishing for a screen and some viewgraphs. I mentioned his unusual interest in any information I might have found at Claire's about the drug trade; my information about Kirsten and Claire pressuring various parties to shut down operations in the area; my conversation with Joop, wherein he accused Bolles of being in league with the Association. I didn't bother to mention that the latter conversation had taken place with my pants off, after I had been caught skulking around Las Flores.

His only reaction to what I felt was a damning indictment was to say, "So Jesse's playing both sides of the fence, huh? Thanks for the tip—though I'm not surprised. This time maybe we'll send the little weasel-dick someplace where he won't get paroled so fast." He noticed one of his shoelaces was undone, and pulled that foot up onto the rock to reknot it. He took his time, adjusting the length of the loops on the knot just so, and then put his leg down and let both feet dangle. "Anything else?"

I just stood there. This hadn't gone anything like I had imagined. A family of tourists peered around the edge of the rocks looking for some place to picnic, saw us, and withdrew. Across the valley, I heard a climber shouting down, "No, left, left, left—*my* left, not your left—oh, sorry..."

I regathered myself and said, "I wouldn't think I needed anything else, but yeah—I think I've found out about Mr. Avery and his meth labs, how he gets his raw materials. Things the authorities—other authorities—might be interested in."

"So why come to me? Why not go to the DEA, get Mr. Avery busted, and light a fire under my ass with internal affairs? Why are we having this conversation?"

"Because that's not what I'm interested in. I've become convinced that you know more about Claire's murder than you're telling me. In fact, I'm beginning to think you're covering up for some of your friends."

"Hmm. Okay. Now you're starting to piss me off." He jumped down off the rock, made a sweeping maître d' gesture to his former seat. "Let's trade places. C'mon, sit down."

I went over and hoisted myself up onto the rock. While he waited he clasped his hands behind his back and stood on his heels, clapping the inner edges of his upraised shoes together, slowly drilling his heels down in the sand. When I was situated, he stepped forward, leaving two small pits behind him.

"Okay." He rubbed his palms together. "I swore I wasn't going to listen to lectures ever again when I graduated from college, but I find myself making exceptions for the Claybornes. Is it a family thing with you guys? Anyhow, just a few months ago I had to listen to damn near the same shit from your sister, except she wasn't accusing me of covering up a murder."

"What was she accusing you of, then?"

He waved his hands like an umpire signaling *safe*. "No no no. Me talk. You listen. This will all be on the exam, so you may want to take notes. First of all, if you think that proving that I consort with known criminals worries me, let me point out to you that it is *my job* to consort with known criminals."

"It's not part of your job to look the other way while they deal drugs, is it?"

He exploded across the sand, a sudden jump that landed him about a foot away from me. I recoiled. If I hadn't been seated, I would have fallen over backward. "Hey!" he said. He held up his hands on either side of his face in karate-chop position, and then turned the palms to face me. He curled three fingers down on either hand so that his index finger and thumbs formed *L*s, and then he pushed his chin between them as if he were framing his face. "Did I interrupt you?" He gave a nasty little grin. "Then don't interrupt me. Save the Q&A."

He dropped his hands and backed off a few feet. I saw that the slide on his bolo tie was a heavy silver casting of the scales of justice, the tray on one side supporting a cabochon of turquoise, the other side one of fire agate.

"I'm going to tell you essentially what I told Claire. Most of what you say is true. I do cooperate with the Association. And they play by my rules. I stay off of their case, and they do three things in return. One. They don't deal drugs, ever, anywhere in this county. They may cook 'em here, but they ship them out. Two. They help me drive out, arrest, or generally fuck up anybody who's dealing around here. Three. They keep me informed about all kinds of other things. I can't tell you how many people have been put away for burglary, rape, even murder because of the info those guys feed to me. They make their money and otherwise keep their noses clean; I leave them alone. They step over the line, and I put them away just like anybody else."

He paced back and forth, one hand in his pocket jingling loose change. "Claire and I had all the obvious discussions—pretty much this discussion, really. She was weird, your sister; thought you could pressure people into her idea of proper behavior. So she was harassing some of the people in the Association; she was harassing me to harass them. I didn't get it. Still don't. What difference does it make if they move someplace else and manufacture, or cook it here and send it somewhere else?"

"Is that a question? Because if it is, it doesn't seem like you evade moral responsibility just because you don't let them sell it locally."

"Yeah?" His eyebrows wagged. "This is about ethics, then? What do you know about DDT?"

"Huh? It was a pesticide. Messed up the shells of birds and damaged wildlife in other ways. They made them stop manufacturing it back in the sixties."

"Au contraire, Professor. They made it illegal to use it in the US. But we're still the world's largest producer. Ship zillions of pounds of it around the world to places where it's still used."

From atop a tall rock about forty feet away, a man in climbing gear shouted, "Belay that! No! Over there!"

"Hey!" Bolles turned and yelled, much louder than I thought possible. "You want to keep it down a little? Other people can't hear themselves yelling!"

The man turned and looked at us, and I thought he was going to shout back, but instead he shrugged and turned back to whatever he had been doing. He did stop shouting.

"There's going on two million people in this county, now. Fifteen hundred sheriffs. Fifteen thousand violent crimes every year. Lots of them the city cops pick up, but you'd be amazed at how good people are about getting out of town to do their dirty work. Not to mention the constant stream of losers from LA running out to the River every time there's a long weekend."

The wind picked up some strands of his hair and laid them down on his forehead. Without pausing in his speech, he pulled out his comb and smoothed them back into place. "Ever hear of that famous judge, Learned Hand? One time he said to somebody who was bitching about what was fair, 'Young man, this is not a court of *justice*, this is a court of *law*.' Well, I get his point, but it doesn't work like that out here. Justice is what we all deserve, and laws are just a half-assed attempt to get there."

He pointed at me with his comb. "You know the difference between places like America and places where there's complete chaos on the streets, like Columbia or Brazil?" I knew dozens of differences right offhand, but I assumed the question was one he planned on answering himself. "If you look at it, their laws, their constitutions aren't much different than ours—hell, they're mostly *based* on ours. The difference is how they're enforced, what happens on the ground, not in the courtrooms."

"Criminals and cops always have to work together. Down there, the cops work for the criminals, get paid to look the other way. Out here, it's the other way around. I tolerate certain kinds of lawbreaking. Cross that line, and I will take you down—with the assistance of other criminals if needed."

He strolled over and leaned one arm on the rock, uncomfortably close. "I like you, Walker. You're not half bad as a detective, either. But I do what I do so people like you can go about their business. Let me tell you something confidentially: I was really worried for a while that Claire threatened somebody in the Association one too many times, and they iced her. I was afraid I might have to take down one of my own people. But I would have done it without a second's hesitation. You got that? Not a second's hesitation. Yeah, I work with creeps. But I'm on *your* side." He put the heel of his free hand against his chin and snapped his head to the side; I winced at the machine-gun cracking from his neck, as if he had shattered his cervical vertebrae. He tilted his hand, and did the same thing in the other direction. This time there were fewer cracks. "Never works as good the second time: body tenses up." He rolled his head loose on his neck a few times, like he'd succeeded in breaking something vital. "Okay, you can ask questions now."

What I wanted to ask was who the hell he thought he was—Only Law West of the Pecos? But there didn't seem to be much point in arguing with him. "Is there anything else I should know? Anything I've overlooked?"

"One little mystery I can clear up—and keep in mind I don't need to be telling you this. Remember the night when you moved into Claire's and someone attacked you? Well, that guy was from the Association, some low-level clown who thought he could score points with the bosses by finding anything that Claire had on them. Silly little fuck."

"So why don't you arrest him? I'd love to press charges."

"He doesn't work around here anymore." Seeing my look, he said, "No, he's not dead, just probably back in the Midwest. But he'll have to use his left hand to pick his ass for a few months. There go the piano lessons."

"Shouldn't you have given me the chance to decide what to do with him?"

"No. In fact, I was hoping he'd scare you off."

"Why? Are you afraid of what I'm going to find?"

"Walker." He put his hand on my shoulder. "You don't pay attention. I already said I like you. You keep poking at things, whoever killed Claire is liable to come after you too."

"Are you trying to scare me into leaving?"

"A little bit. But in some ways you make my job a lot easier. You're like a big fat piece of bait, just waiting for something to try and take it."

"So you need me, as bait if nothing else?"

"No. Listen, ace: I *will* get to the bottom of this: and this God's Law bunch may be what takes me there. And when I know who he is, Claire's killer is going down. Maybe prison, maybe a grave out in the desert." He leaned a little closer, as if there was some chance of being overheard. "Want to know one of the best-kept secrets of American law enforcement? There aren't as many unsolved murders as the statistics claim. It's just that sometimes you can't make a case. But there's a lot more frontier justice than anybody thinks."

"Hence the bolo tie," I said.

"Huh?"

I pointed at the silver scales of justice at the notch of his collarbone. "That?" he said. "Nope. The wife got me that 'cause I'm a libra."

We walked back out to the parking lot, each busy with his own thoughts. We said goodbye and split up to head to our cars, but something occurred to me. I turned back, looking for him, and saw his car backing out. I stood in the road and he pulled up next to me.

The window whirred down. "Yeah?" He squinted, trying to make me out against the sun behind my shoulder.

"Just one more question. Did you do anything to Claire's computer while the house was cordoned off?"

He made those manic eyes, widening them, and then closing them quickly, wincing at the glare of the sunlight. He peeked out more cautiously. "Well aren't you just Miss Marple? Yeah, as a matter of fact, we looked through it pretty thoroughly. Standard procedure nowadays, you know."

"Did you also delete a bunch of files and then defragment her hard drive?"

He whistled appreciatively. "You're in the wrong business, Professor. Yes indeedy, that's exactly what I did. Or, actually, had someone else do. I'm not a real computer buff, you know."

"Why?"

A car pulled up behind him and honked. Bolles waved his arm out the window for them to go around us. They honked again. "Jesus Thelonius Christ, what is it with people?" This time he held his arm out the window dangling the leather folder that displayed his badge. The car slowly pulled out and drove around behind me at about five miles an hour—the speed that everyone was really supposed to maintain on this bit of road.

Bolles folded the wallet and tossed it on the seat. "Why? Because I couldn't open them. They were locked. And my computer guy told me the FBI themselves can't break that kind of encoding. So rather than wait for someone who might know the codes to pop them open and find who-knows-what, we scrubbed them."

"Did you make copies?"

"No." Something about how he said this made me think he was lying.

"And did you by any chance carry off her box of backup diskettes? As evidence, maybe?"

"No." He raised his eyebrows and showed his teeth. "Didn't see any floppies anywhere. CDs with installation software, but no backups." Another car pulled up behind him. "Have you found any?"

"No. Not a single diskette anywhere."

"Well, call me if you do." The car honked. "Hey, keep it in your pants!" he yelled out the window. "We done here?"

"I guess so."

"Okay. Let's do this again sometime. It's so nice to get out of the office." He blew me an elaborate kiss, glared back at the car behind him, and drove off.

The car pulled past me slowly, the driver a jowly man who narrowed his porcine eyes as he frowned out the open window. "Hope that was important, faggot," he said as he passed. From the back seat his kids roared with laughter, his wife snapping at them to settle down.

33

After Bolles left, I wandered back into Hidden Valley. It was technically a long while before sunset, but twelve thousand feet of San Jac and San Gorgonio stood between us and the coast, and the ground was darkening with shadows even though the sky was still bright. I was almost alone in heading into the Valley, but there was a steady stream of people leaving: bickering families, obstreperous rockclimbers loaded with equipment, who seemed to think anyone not there to climb was interfering with God's plan for the place, and sunburnt frat boys from back east trying to decide whether they needed to drive all the way to Palm Springs to find a decent bar.

Without thinking I followed the little path back under the trees, up onto The Hood, and step by step, up to the edge of the high cap. Everything was exactly as I remembered it, but the little walkway formed by the dike was perhaps more worn, maybe from the elements, more likely from the passage of feet. Almost without thinking I set my left foot out there and leaned my body in against the rock. The air was cool, but the pinnacle of the rock had hoarded the sun's heat, and it felt warm where my coat hung open and my chest hugged against its grainy texture. Large grains: that meant that under the surface of the earth, when the magma first rushed up from the deep to form a huge bulge beneath the soil, it had cooled slowly, so slowly the molecules had time to migrate into crystals of like type, seeking their mates in the molecular chaos that gradually froze them all in place.

I edged out farther until both of my feet were on the stubby dike, toes pointed in opposite directions like a dancer practicing turn-out, my arms splayed on the surface, trying to hug something infinitely too large for my embrace. I tried not to think of the hundred-plus feet of empty space beneath my heels.

Another sliding step, another dragging reach of my left arm out along the rock wall. My fingers tickled the air for a moment, then curled in to reach around the lip of the stone.

There was no way to swing myself around the lip of the cave, and then sit down: the sloping roof of the space was at diaphragm level. It had to happen in one single motion.

I had now reached so far around the corner that I had no leverage to swing my body back to the right. I had to complete my journey, or see exactly how long I could hug this rock.

It was easy once I stopped thinking and just let it happen. The stone roof cracked hard against the back of my head, but the weight of my body did the job of spinning me completely around, so that I sat down hard, my foot shooting out from under me.

I'd wanted to get to this spot for about twenty-five years, and now I couldn't remember why. I still trembled, but the fear was gone, replaced with a quivering kind of exaltation that brushed aside the questions rising in my mind. How would I get down? It didn't matter. I'd climb down. If I lost my nerve? I'd just stay here until the park service pulled me out with a helicopter. It wasn't a problem. Or, it wasn't a problem for right now.

It grew dark, but the moon's crescent was nearly a half-disc. *C for Coy, D for Daring.* The bright side was on the right, so the moon was still plumping out. Hidden Valley is so white that even a half moon gives plenty of light.

Only a few days ago, I had grasped a profusion of threads I was certain would lead to a solution of Claire's murder.

And her boyfriends were indeed strange. God's Law truly was a creepy association of murderous zealots. Universal Waste was in fact a deceptive, bullying corporation that would do anything for a buck. A.T. Avery genuinely had built a drug-lab empire behind straight businesses in the area. And Rick Bolles even admitted to working hand in hand with organized crime.

Yet this handful of threads was just that: a jumble of strings leading to many places, but not to the truth behind Claire's murder.

"Fingers pointing at the moon," Claire's voice whispered. "Look at the moon, not the finger."

"Are you really there?" I asked aloud.

Far-off laughter in my head. "Define 'really.'"

"Claire…?" I said.

Silence. A long silence, where I drifted away.

When I came back to myself, the moon had moved a hand's width across the sky. I pulled myself into a crouch, took one last look at the view, and then swung my body back around the lip of the cave. I scrunched my way along the wall, the edges of my feet on the hard little dike, and in four long, scissoring movements was back atop the long slope of the isenberg.

My car was the only one left in the parking lot—with the exception of the park service truck parked next to it. The ranger seemed to be in the process of writing me a ticket. I waved and walked over. He still had his hat on, even though it was dark.

"Are you aware that this area is closed after sundown?" he demanded, when I was close enough to hear. He was young, probably fresh out of some BA program. "This is a day-use-only area."

A lot of things rose to my lips: I was coming out here before you were born, where does the government get off deciding I can't be out here at night, how can humans decide natural features have curfews, and what the hell does it mean for a pile of rocks to be "closed?" But I said none of these. Instead, I answered, "Sorry. Couldn't find my way out."

"Oh. How long were you lost?"

I pulled out my keys, dropped them, scooped them up again, and unlocked the door to the Jeep. "Seemed like years," I said. "A lifetime."

"How do you know if you're becoming an alcoholic?" I asked, holding up my glass of Zinfandel.

"When did you last have a drink?" Mandy asked.

"I'm not sure. Recently, though."

"I wouldn't worry about it."

Ettenmoor hefted his bulk from his low seat, grabbed the bottle from the coffee table, and poured himself another glass. "Me, I know. Can tell you with precision: Last night, night before that, night before that… Me, we should worry about." He clunked the bottle back onto the tabletop and then crouched down carefully until his haunches touched the chair. "Told you about a friend in Berkeley? Counselor? Says alcoholics never ask, 'Am I an alcoholic?' Either admit they are, or have some great reason why they aren't. Never just wonder."

I'd called Mandy's cell phone as I was leaving the parking lot at Hidden Valley. She had been working through the afternoon with Ettenmoor, and they invited me up. When I arrived, the wine already sat open on a coffee table in the giant front room. A space had been cleared for the bottle, and it sat amidst circuit diagrams and calculations like a tiny rocketship surrounded by its design specs.

They had listened as I described my meeting with Bolles, neither of them interrupting. I left out any reference to my foolhardy climb on the rock. Running out of forward inertia at last, I'd interrupted my own monologue by wondering if I were an alcoholic.

"So if I wonder, then I'm not?" I said, in response to Ettenmoor. "Doesn't seem like much of a criterion. Wonder, and you aren't; one day you stop wondering, and then you are? Maybe they'll have a test for it some day; I've read it's supposed to be mostly genetic."

"Medical science," Mandy said, as if just uttering the name was enough to condemn it.

"Dogmatic wankers," Ettenmoor said with a pleasant smile.

"When I was a little girl, it was, 'The only important exercise is pushing away from the table.' It was, 'Even swimming the English Channel only burns off the calories in a single cheeseburger.' It was, 'Oh, don't eat that, that's nothing but carbohydrates!' Now it's, 'Make sure you exercise at least three times a week, cut your fat intake, make sure most of your caloric intake is complex carbohydrates.' But if you look at the leading edge of the research going on, they're starting to say, 'Gosh, people with high carb intake seem to develop diabetes, and, hey, look at this guy who ran every day and dies of a heart seizure...'"

I chuckled at her summary of the last thirty years of nutritional science, but said, "Well, it's complicated, and there's new developments all the time..."

Mandy waved her free hand in the air. "Hey, I don't mind that. What I mind is the fact that at every step they are so damn sure. And the fact that they lecture us, telling us how stupid we were to believe all the things they themselves were telling us just a few years ago. Remember how everybody always makes fun of nineteenth-century medicine for letting blood? Damned barbarians. Now it seems that maybe losing blood is good for you, stimulates the immune system, pulls iron out of the artery walls, probably waxes floors and extends the life of your car battery. Now they're recommending you give blood at least a few times a year."

Ettenmoor pulled his head sideways with one arm to stretch tight muscles. "They going back to traditional methods, too? Good time to buy stock in a leech farm?"

"Not with HIV and everything," she said. "Unless they have single-use leeches."

"Push the demand up more than multi-use leeches."

"So, what do you think?" Mandy asked.

It took a moment to realize she was addressing me. "About what?"

"About what Bolles said. Does it feel like he's telling the truth?"

"How would I know? Sorry. I guess it felt mostly true. There's something about the guy that makes me think he really believes that he's the right hand of God."

"Told you: Wyatt Earp. Earp was a scary guy, too."

I took a big drink, as my sense of futility flooded back. "I feel like I've gone down one dead-end street after another, and I was so sure that this one was the way out. And—" I lifted a closed hand and then opened it, empty palm up. "Nothing. One more cul-de-sac."

"So where do we go from here?" Mandy asked.

"Well, I was thinking about that on the drive up here." I began my carefully prepared preface. "I don't have to tell you that the things

I've been through over the last few weeks—not least of which are my talks with both of you—have shaken up my preconceptions about what is and isn't possible." Mandy was nodding sympathetically, but Ettenmoor's eyes glittered as if he saw exactly where I was headed. "At this point, I don't think legwork will get us anywhere. We need something more: if not a miracle, then at least inspiration. And I thought about the ancient Greeks, how they took their problems and questions to the Oracle at Delphi. And then I thought, perhaps that's it. Maybe the best thing would be for Mandy to do something to precipitate one of her visions, like sit here while we turn on the hydraulics in the basement…"

Before I even finished my sentence Mandy had leaned back in her chair, way back, as if she were afraid of getting splashed by my words. "Oh, no. No way. You don't have any idea what you're asking. No way. I'm never going to be within five miles of here when that machine's on. Never again. Do it yourself."

Ettenmoor was amused. "Should have seen that coming, Amandinea. Logical next step. But he's been around when it was on. Six, no, seven times. Only gives him the slightest buzz. He *can't* do it."

"I don't care if it's the logical next step. I'm not going there. Forget it."

"Well." I leaned forward a little. "There is another possibility. That potion your circle uses. You seem to take that willingly enough. Why not try another session with that?"

"Two words, Walker: Unh-uh. It may be years before I'm ready for that again." Her expression changed just slightly, moving from defensive to a little sly. "But there's no reason that *you* can't."

Ettenmoor was chuckling. "Your turn: should have seen *that* coming. Hey, whose petard is this? Gosh, looks like mine…"

"I was serious," I said.

"I'm serious too," Mandy answered, but her face showed suppressed glee. "Why not, Walker? You're free enough about signing me up for it. Try it yourself, if it's such a great idea."

"What good would that do?" I said. "I'm not the psychic around here. It would just be a big waste of time."

"Not so sure of that," Ettenmoor said. "Might be a good idea. Shake some things loose."

"Yeah, shake my brain loose."

"You didn't seem too worried about *my* brain," Mandy said. "Why? You think it's already scrambled?"

"Okay, I'm sorry, forget it, it was a bad idea."

Ettenmoor leaned back and crossed one leg over the other. "No. Best idea I've heard in a while. Do it, Walker."

Mandy looked at me with a mock-sweet smile. "At least don't try to get other people to try what you're unwilling to do yourself."

"What are you afraid of?" Ettenmoor asked.

"I'm not afraid," I said, and then stopped. Why was I lying, and lying with such facility? "No. That's wrong. I am afraid."

"Ask you again, then: of what?"

"What if I lose my mind and never come back? What if— What if I like this drug so much I can't stop doing it?"

Mandy giggled, and caught Ettenmoor's eye, and he was already chuckling silently, and I looked back and forth between them as they started laughing, their interlocked stares egging each other on like five-year-olds. Ettenmoor shook so hard his wine slopped over the edge of the glass and onto his white pants, and he looked down at that and laughed harder. Mandy pressed a hand against her low belly like she had menstrual cramps, and her hand bounced along with her spasmodic mirth.

With the possible exception of yawning, laughter is the most contagious human expression. I was a little offended, maybe blushing, but despite that I had a big grin on my face. Mandy saw me, and gasped out, "Oh Walker, we're not laughing *at* you, we're laughing *about* you…" This set them both off into one more burst of merriment.

Finally Mandy stood up, sniffling, wiping at her nose. "Oh, Lord, that made me need to pee…"

"What exactly is so funny?" I asked. "The idea of me on drugs?"

"No. No." Ettenmoor's face was blotchy red, and now he really looked like he had just stepped out from under the Big Top. "The idea that you might like it too much. Oh, man."

"It's like not getting pregnant," Mandy said, "because you're afraid you might enjoy labor too much. Trust me, Walker: *that* won't be the problem." She headed off for the bathroom.

Ettenmoor hoisted his bulk up off the chair, looking down at the purple stain on his pants. "Need to change my clothes…"

"A quick question first. Ever since the experiment the other day, I'm hearing voices in my head—Claire's voice."

"All the time?"

"No. Rarely. It sounds far off, indistinct, yet very vivid. And I wondered if your geological piezoelectricity might have triggered it, and if you think it's—well, real."

"Might have triggered it. Real? Wrong way to frame the question."

"Give me a way to think about it, then."

"Most people would prefer to assume Claire's spirit talking to them. For you—well, assume there's a program of sorts called 'Claire.' You knew her so well that now you're running part of that program on your own brain's hardware."

"Is that what you believe?"

"Only a model. And a model is true to the extent that it's useful. Back in a minute." He sat his glass down on the tabletop, scooting diagrams out of the way. I sat by myself for a while, and then my hand went to my breast pocket like a smoker reaching for his cigarette pack and drew out Claire's quote book. I flipped it open, poked my finger in like I was tossing a dart, and read.

Those who operate most effectively, those I respect most, simply are not afraid… Everybody has a fear level, when you've gone as far as you can go, but you do have to go that far.

—Jim Aubrey

in The Club Rules

Ettenmoor appeared, having exchanged his white trousers for gray sweatpants, but went across the room to the wine rack and opened another bottle before coming over to me. "Drink up," he said, "drain the glass. Something special, honor of your historic decision." He waited while I swallowed, and then filled my glass. "1978 California Cab. Back when California wines mostly came in jugs. Or boxes."

Mandy came back into the room talking on her cell phone. "Umm-hmm. Well, can you check around? Okay. Well, I'll find out, and call you back."

"Drain your glass," Ettenmoor ordered.

She picked it up from the table and looked dubious. "I don't think I want to chug this much."

Ettenmoor took her glass, emptied it with one big swallow, handed it back, and refilled it. "Okay. Here's to maiden voyages. Losses of virginity. Graduations. First stamps in passports." He glanced at Mandy. "Anything else?"

"Waking up in the morning."

"And waking up in the morning. Cheers."

We all sipped our wine. I was too nervous to notice any special quality in the vintage, if indeed there was any to notice.

Mandy and Ettenmoor sat down, and she said, "That was Jared. He's willing to pull it all together if you want to do a ceremony, but it has to be on a Friday to fit his schedule. So that's either tomorrow, or a week later."

I wanted to delay it as long as possible, maybe even talk myself out of it, but Ettenmoor said, "Do it sooner. Like a high dive. Don't stand there and think."

"It's not one-hundred-percent sure we can put it together. We have to have at least five people—"

"Why five people?" I asked.

"The Quintessence. This is sacramental, you know. I'll come—" She saw my look. "No, I'm not partaking. But I'll come and keep everybody company. It's like Communion, you don't have do the wine-and-wafer thing to be in the church... So, you, me, Jared, that's three, Dawn's been saying she needs to purge herself, so that's four..."

Her phone rang. "Hello...yeah. Oh really? Oh, I think I can almost say 'yes' for certain, but let me make sure." She covered the mouthpiece with her free hand, and said "*Melanie* says she'll come if we do it tomorrow night..." She gave me a contrived, prurient little smile. "So do I say yes? Hmmm?"

I rolled my eyes in exasperation, but the prospect was not unpleasing. "Sure, sure. Say yes."

"Thought that'd get your attention." She spoke into the phone. "He's on board… Yeah, I'll explain about those things. And you can get him oriented on the drive… Well, that's up to you. Call me in the morning to tell us where and when we leave… Yeah. Love ya."

She snapped the phone shut and turned to me. "This will require that you go through an initiation rite—one that you may not care for. But it's something all of us have been through. No exceptions. And no backing out."

I figured that something Kirsten or Melanie could handle wouldn't be too tough for me. "Fine."

"Okay. I'll call you in the morning to make final arrangements, but there's some things that you need to do. Do you have a pack, like a hiking pack?" I nodded. "Good. We'll need the pack, but don't pack it. You'll need to bring something you value, something important to you—we make something called a mesa, an altar, that acts as a focal point, and everyone contributes something to it for the night. You'll get it back."

"Like what?"

"Heirlooms, wedding rings, a favorite rock, lucky rabbit's foot—"

"First journal article," Ettenmoor chimed in, "favorite rock hammer, flavored condoms—"

"Shut up, Ron," Mandy said in a mild voice. "You'll also need to make some kind of sacrifice. Eliminate something. Doesn't have to be obvious, but has to be significant to you. Doesn't have to be permanent. Some people give up meat for a month, or drinking."

"Give me a suggestion."

"Thought I just did. Okay. Eat a really big breakfast tomorrow, and then nothing else. Take a shower, and wash every part of yourself until it stings. And bring two coins, any denomination, doesn't matter from where or when. Coins you're willing to part with, by the way. Don't plunder your coin collection."

Most of this seemed to make sense, but… "Why the coins?"

She smiled at Ettenmoor. "If you want to cross the Styx, you have to pay the ferryman."

Ettenmoor lifted his glass to me. "Bra-vo," he said. "Here's to science."

34

When I'd arrived home from Ettenmoor's the previous night, I found Malcolm loitering out front. I greeted him by saying, "Shit. I forgot to print them."

"Hey, no big deal, I just wanted to check…"

"No, I really am sorry. Can you hang around, or come back in a couple of hours?"

"Have to go unload some trucks."

"You're working tonight… Are you free tomorrow, noonish?"

"I can be."

"Let's meet for coffee." Malcolm made a face. "Well, tea, Coke, water…"

I'd started the file printing, and then went to bed.

In the morning, I scooped them into a folder. I hadn't been invited to read them, but I couldn't help glancing at the top sheet.

BONE OF TREES

Bare they stand now dry

Do they recall the days of rain? The

   gray times the dim times, wrapped in cloud caressed by fingers

of water yearning in channels now so barren

Hungry memory of sky as breast…

I was no judge of such matters, but this seemed no worse than many. Seeing as he had no training, I'd been half-afraid it would all be modeled on a "roses are red" rhyme scheme. But in that case, I suppose Claire wouldn't have encouraged him.

I packed as instructed—not much, other than a sleeping bag—and ate a huge late breakfast.

I left early, and took my time driving to Water Canyon Coffee. I felt strange: as if this might be my last day on Earth.

I drove past Valley CardioKickboxing, saw a morning class in session behind the cluttered glass windows. I cruised by the Church of the Rock. Ira was inside, helping someone move a table.

I let myself in. When the door shut behind me, Darnell looked over and then dropped his end of the table. "Sorry," he said, his voice almost inaudible.

Ira greeted me with his usual enthusiasm. I interrupted to ask if he'd heard about the incidents connected with God's Law.

"I have," he said, "and I've informed the leaders of Shackles Torn Asunder that they are not allowed to let any other groups use this space without my prior approval. I had no idea a group of murderers would be invited into our church to hold a rally."

Darnell mumbled something.

"What was that?" Ira asked.

"I said, it's just the three of'em. Ain't shown nothin' against anybody else."

"Well I'm not having them in my church."

Darnell gave a sulky jerk of his shoulders and said, "Gonna go load that stuff." He turned and pushed heavily through the back door.

Ira looked at me. "I think sometimes he's been drinking again. With Claire gone, I fear for him and Rachel. Him and Rachel, and any number of other people." He hoisted his bottom up onto the table they'd been carrying. He looked like he was in pain.

"Are you all right?" I asked.

He massaged his forehead. "I think sometimes that's the real reason God holds forth against murder and suicide. No person's life is that important to themselves, really, no matter what they think. There's always an afterlife. I think what the Lord wants to protect against are the consequences for everyone left behind. Whoever killed your sister caused unimagined damage: a whole web of hurt and sadness spreading out to all those she had touched."

Malcolm tried to be companionable, but he kept opening the folder to admire the look of his words printed out on the sheets of paper. I tried a number of conversational gambits, but none caught his attention until I mentioned I still had to make some kind of a sacrifice before going through the ceremony planned that evening.

"Sacrifice, sacrifice. Nice word. What kind of sacrifice?"

"It doesn't matter, really. Doesn't have to be expensive, or permanent. Just have to give something up. What would you do?"

"If I were you, or if I were me?"

"If you were me, obviously."

He chewed his lip as he considered me. "How long have you had the beard?" he asked.

I arrived at Jared's a little early and borrowed scissors and a razor. He applauded when I emerged from his bathroom bareshaven.

The back seat of Jared's old Datsun was filled with split, stacked firewood. "That's an enormous pile of wood."

"Yeah. We'll need it. Probably be up all night." He slammed the trunk and opened the driver's door. "All set?"

As we drove, Jared cautioned me we'd be spending the night in unknown territory, as there wasn't time to drive to one of their usual ceremonial sites. "I'm thinking maybe Sheephole Valley Wilderness. You know it?"

I grinned, and it felt strange on my nude face. "Oh yeah, I know it in distressing detail. I've crisscrossed every inch of the place. Even written a few articles about it."

"Cool. So why don't you pick the ideal camping spot?"

I asked for parameters, and he listed them. I knew a spot I was sure would work.

We swung by Mandy's house and her Saturn pulled out to follow us. I could see Dawn in the passenger seat, and could just make out Melanie in the back.

We hit the central set of traffic signals in Twenty-Nine Palms on a red, and when the lights changed he turned north onto Adobe Drive in the downtown strip.

Twenty-Nine Palms, An Oasis of Murals. There certainly were plenty of murals, on the sides of buildings that would otherwise have been bare cinderblock facing bare parking lots. The murals were a good idea, but the phraseology bothered me. I wasn't sure of the collective term for murals—Herd? Flock? School? Buncha?—but I was fairly certain "oasis" was not one of the possibilities.

"So," I asked, "would you like to start my orientation?"

"Sure. There isn't really all that much to say. The potion we'll be taking—"

"I have a question already: What exactly is this stuff?"

Jared dug at the corner of his eye as if removing something. "That's hard to explain. Know much botany?"

"Hardly any."

"Okay. Well in that case, the most I can tell you is this is a kind of tea made from a mixture of two different plants. The interesting thing about it is that neither of them has any effect without the other."

"And this is safe?"

"Things like this are never safe, but neither's hang-gliding or bungee-jumping. Definitely not for everybody. But there aren't any physical dangers. Use of this stuff goes back probably three thousand years."

"And is it legal?"

"Ah, there you've got me. According to some people at the DEA, it's illegal to swallow, smoke, snuff, or otherwise ingest any goddamned thing other than alcohol for 'purposes of becoming intoxicated.'"

"Is there a law stating that?"

"DEA doesn't need laws. The existing law lets them issue whatever guidelines they like. On the other hand, there is some legal use of entheogens in religion in the US, but we're the wrong color."

"Sorry. What are you talking about?"

"The Native American Church uses peyote as its sacrament. It's the only organization allowed to do so. And it is illegal for white people, or black people, or anybody else to do likewise, even if they are following the same doctrine."

All of this was news to me. I said, "I guess there's some kind of special allowance for them to follow their traditional religion…"

Jared laughed. "That would make sense, but you're wrong. It isn't traditional. The Native American Church is a Christian church. They pride themselves on being the *real* Christians. Qanah Parker, one of the founders, said, 'The White Man goes into his church and talks *about* Jesus, but the Indian goes into his tipi and talks *with* Jesus.'"

"But in any case, what we're taking tonight isn't peyote."

"No, it isn't. And one of the components of these plants is dimethyltryptamine, DMT, which is a Schedule One dangerous drug, a federal crime to own in any form or preparation whatsoever."

"So what we are doing *is* illegal, then."

"Maybe. But something to think about: they've discovered that DMT is a naturally occurring molecule in all mammalian central nervous systems. So, under federal law, it's now illegal for you to have a brain."

"You're joking."

"No. I'm not. But my point is that the laws are totally confused."

"Great. And you're getting me involved in this?"

"You asked, I didn't offer. But we're small fish. No money, no bribes, we don't even get our stuff through dealers. I mean sure, we could go to prison…"

"Why do you run this kind of risk? This seems crazy."

"Because: It's my religion. People are always persecuted for practicing their faith when it differs from the faith of the majority or the faith of the State. That's just how humans are. We've got it easy: We could be Christians in ancient Rome, or non-Christians in Medieval Europe, or Baha'i in modern Iran, or non-Muslim in Saudi Arabia."

"How comforting." We turned east on Amboy Drive.

"The most important thing to know is that, whatever is happening: it will pass. Time may seem to dilate greatly. Two or three hours into it, you may not remember any other state of being. It will pass."

Past a cluster of old houses and homesteads, the road turned north and began to climb. Jared added, "You should know there can be lots of nausea. One too many cheese puffs. You may want to throw up. Amazonians—and the Native American Church, too—say vomiting is a cleansing process. More experienced folks seldom get the nausea. The Indians say this is because their bodies have been cleansed of the badness."

"Seems like the theory that they develop an increased tolerance would work just as well."

"Sure. Whatever." We neared the top of the pass, and rocks began to close in on the sides of the road. "Where should I pull over?"

"Just beyond the crest. There's an old Jeep trail there where you can get off the highway."

Jared flipped on his blinker and slowed down. "Over there?" I affirmed he should pull off onto the dirt, and he eased the car over the sandy shoulder and onto the firmer dirt of the old trail. About sixty feet in there was a vertical plastic rod in the center of the road, white letters on a red background: *Wilderness Area, No Motorized Vehicles Past This Point.*

He killed the motor and watched the rearview mirror as Mandy's car jolted through our hanging dust cloud. "Two other things to watch for. The Wah-wahs—everything may get real Twilight Zone for no reason: just sit it out. And the Cosmic Insight. You may feel like you understand everything. Great. Try to keep it to yourself. If it's real and profound, it'll still be there later. If not…then it's better not to talk about it."

I took a lot of teasing about my newly bare face, so I encouraged everyone to hoist their packs as soon as possible and follow me up two miles of canyon to the proposed campsite.

On the saddle where two low, rocky hills connected, there was a broad, flattish area ringed by high boulders. The net effect was to create a sandy basin, about twenty by thirty feet, with a pair of haystack-sized boulders inside the southwest edged of the ring. Jared stepped out of sight behind these, and then re-emerged. "Perfect. Even a vomitorium and latrine."

We unloaded the sleeping bags, water, and food from our packs, and then shouldered the empty packs and returned to the cars to load up with wood. By the time we returned, shirts damp with the effort of lugging the fuel, the sun was out of sight beyond the mountains.

Jared took his safety-orange trowel and excavated three small pits in the designated latrine area: one, farthest in, for excrement, the next for urine, and one longer trench close to the entrance for what he described as "any reverse peristalsis." Mandy and Melanie busied themselves gathering small rocks for a fire ring and a mesa.

Dawn climbed up onto a high sloping boulder and stood there looking out in the direction of the sunset. I clambered up beside her and sat.

"Always an adventure," she said.

"How often have you done this?"

"This ceremony? Fifteen times. Entheogens? I'm not sure. A hundred?"

"That many? I thought this kind of thing wasn't habit forming."

She squatted down next to me. "I'm forty-six. I first took acid when I was sixteen. So that averages out to, what, three, four times a year? Not much of a habit."

"Why do you do it?"

"To stay in touch with my better self. Cheaper than seeing a therapist… The interesting question is, why are *you* doing it?"

"I'm not sure. Maybe I'm blocked, stuck, see no way forward. Maybe I want to understand what Claire saw in it—what all of you see in it. Maybe Mandy and Ettenmoor kind of shamed me into it. I really don't know."

"That's a good answer." She took my hand in hers. "Don't be afraid. We'll take care of you."

We sat there as it darkened, until she said, "We should go down."

The fire ring was built and already filled with kindling and wood. Our sleeping bags were folded into squares and arranged in a circle around it. Along the north rim of boulders, a low platform, no more than a foot high and three feet long, had been built from fist-sized rocks.

"Time to set up the mesa," Mandy said as we approached. "Gather round." She waved us over to the small platform of rocks. Dawn dropped to her knees on my right, so I did the same, and Melanie smoothly folded into a crosslegged pose on my left. Jared dropped down on the other side of Melanie, and Mandy squatted down in front of the little altar, facing us. "I'll start." She took both hands, fished down under her collar, and drew a necklace up over her head and let it dangle for us to see. It was a silver chain with a small pendant I couldn't make out. "Claire gave me this." She rotated on her heels, set it down carefully atop the mesa.

Melanie reached inside her jacket and pulled out a book. She handed it to Mandy. "*Drawing Down the Moon*. Claire. Of course."

Jared handed over a sealed envelope. "I'd just as soon not make a statement."

Dawn handed over a packet of envelopes tied with ribbon. "Letters Claire wrote me when I was back in Ohio. When Mom was dying."

I felt inadequate. "A picture," I said. It was the snapshot of Claire at the River, midriff bare, hands on hips, looking like she'd live forever.

Mandy took it, gazed at it, and passed it around the group. When it came back, she placed it on the altar, and then weighted down all of the lighter items with pebbles. "Jared? You're the ferryman this evening."

"What I brought was something from Claire too. Even though there was no plan for this, she's foremost in everyone's thoughts tonight. So let's be mindful of her; let's let our thoughts drift back to this altar every so often; and if things seem bleak or bad—reach out to her memory."

We sat in silence. At last, Jared said, "I've found a High Road in for everyone, and found a Low Road in for our initiate—even cleared it out a little. Is everybody ready?"

"Outside of the fact that it's getting too cold," Melanie said.

He led us up over the rocks at the edge of the basin, and down onto the south slope of the hill. In a sandy clearing there was a shapeless bundle on the ground. Straight overhead I could see the moon, a perfect half-circle that seemed to shed more light as the last of the sun fled the sky. "Does everyone have their coins?" he demanded. "Hold them in your left hand." I dug in my pants, found the two shiny quarters I had selected.

Jared reached inside the bundle and emerged with long strips of dark cloth. "Time to abandon vision for a while." He blindfolded us one after another, me last of all; before he did, he took my glasses from me. "Now undress carefully. Everything. Even shoes. Everything but the blindfolds. And don't drop those coins."

This was impossible! I'd had no idea…and it *was* getting cold out here. But all around me I heard the sounds of disrobing, shoes and clothing dropping down on the sand. Reluctant, clumsy, I obeyed nonetheless, nearly toppling in the process of removing shoes and socks. It was no simple matter to unbutton shirt or trousers while clutching the coins in my hand. I could tell I was the last one undressed; by the time I finished, no one else made a noise.

"Good," Jared said. I could hear him doing something— folding up our clothes, I had to conclude. Then I felt his hands on my shoulders, marching me backward a few feet and bracing me into position. Then he moved someone in at right angles to me, so my left shoulder touched her right shoulder. From her height, I thought it was Dawn, and it felt good to touch flesh when the rest of my body was clad only in chilly night air. Someone moved into position on my left, and I knew immediately it was Melanie: something permeated me, and the touch of her arm against mine was like the tip of a needle poking at me through velvet, soft and slightly painful. Then I heard steps, but felt nothing; it was obvious we stood like the four walls of a very small box, facing out at the four cardinal points of the compass.

"Stay," he said. I heard him gathering up our bundles of clothes, and then listened to his steps disappear upslope. On my left, Dawn's fingers interlaced with mine; on my right Melanie's did the same. My cock stiffened a little in the rising breeze. I pictured us here, in box formation, six breasts and one penis pointing off into the dark with no one to see. At least I assumed there was no one to see. Maybe this was like some hazing ritual, and everyone else had removed their blindfolds. For all I knew, they were having a hard time suppressing their laughs…

"Lion, shut up and pay attention." Claire: vague, distant, but very real. I tensed, and Melanie and Dawn both gave my hands reassuring squeezes.

I heard steps at last. Noises suggested to me that Jared was retrieving something else from his blanket bundle. Then I heard his voice behind me, deep, resonant, like a stage actor: "Amandinea Cicerone?"

"Yes?"

"Pay me for safe passage."

The clink of coins.

"Now follow as best you may."

BOOM boom boom BOOM boom boom…

He had a drum—an enormous drum, from the sound of it. I could barely hear the crunching footsteps beneath its throaty roar. Presumably that was Mandy being led away, presumably naked, presumably unshod… The drum grew more and more distant. Melanie shivered and snuggled a naked hip up against me.

At long last the drum stopped. Eventually footsteps. "Melanie McKinney? …Pay me for safe passage."

The same routine, except this time she squeezed my hand before she left, following the same loud drumbeat. I and Dawn were left standing orthogonally, holding hands.

Then Dawn was taken away, paying her coins and following the drum, and I was left, naked and blind and alone in the dark. The drumbeats receded, and there was a long silence.

Maybe they weren't coming back for me. Like a snipe hunt, where you are left holding a bag into which the snipe will be herded, while all the brave snipe herders leave for someplace more interesting. Leaving you holding the bag, I believe is the phrase…

What the hell was wrong with me, anyway? These were some of the kindest people I'd ever met. It was cold. My erection, thankfully, was subsiding. It seemed like I could hear something far away, but I wasn't sure what, maybe the wind, maybe cars, but it sounded like voices… I didn't need drugs to attain an altered state, just strip me, blindfold me, and leave me alone for a few minutes—or a half-hour, or however unconscionably long it had been…

At last, the sound of footsteps.

"Walker Clayborne."

"Yes." I shuddered with cold.

"Pay me for safe passage."

I reached out my hand and let the coins drop into his.

"Now no harm can come to you, unless it comes to me first." His hand set down on my shoulder and I jumped. "Listen. What we are about to do, you have done before. At least twice in this life alone. Third time pays for all. The others had an easier route tonight, but you have to follow a harder path. We've all been through this before." His lips came close to my ear. "Follow the drum," he whispered, "climb over things, crawl under them, do whatever you must do, but as you value your soul, don't touch the blindfold."

He stepped back. BOOM boom boom BOOM boom boom…

After so long standing still my first step was more of a stagger. I moved in the direction of the throbbing sound, my arms outstretched and brushing through the air, my feet tapping forward tentatively.

It took forever. At first there was just sand, but soon there were rocks to stub my toes on, larger rocks to bark my shins and trip me, and then rocks that I had to climb over. It was horrible, infuriating, and, even though I could rip the blindfold off at any moment, frightening. I had never imagined what it would be like to be blind in a place like this, where the scenery was bizarre enough to the eye, but utterly incomprehensible to the sense of touch. I climbed up the slope of a boulder and then fell, scraping my knee and the heels of my hands. I stumbled, staggered, fumbled my way forward, sometimes reaching down and feeling my way on hands and feet together, like a toddler who fears to stand, and every time I hurt myself anew, standing became a more frightening prospect. I was cold and trembling and exposed and it felt like any moment something unseen might gash some exposed body part. My genitals retreated in fear, trying to climb back up inside me. It was a sharp, hard, cold world, and I was soft.

The tone of the drum changed in some way I couldn't understand. I groped forward and felt a sheer rock face. The drum was somewhere on the other side of it, muffled. I felt back and forth, up against an apparent wall. Nothing, not even a handhold for climbing.

I pat right and left. Just more high, flat stone. Even though I am blindfolded, the fact I don't have my glasses has me on the edge of panic. Calm down, breathe, breathe, this isn't an emergency, even though it feels like one…

Calm down…down. Down. Reach down. Exactly. There is a gap under the rocks, where two boulders come together. Squat, paw at the passageway. Is it big enough? It seems like it. The floor feels like smooth sand. I hear the drum, still booming away, and it is louder the closer I lean my head to the hole. So it must go through. Doesn't mean I can, though.

Try. You can always back out. Probably.

I lay down flat on the sand and start to drag myself through the gap. It's bigger than it seems, bigger until I get toward the center, where it chokes down and I have to pull myself through. Did Jared come through here with a drum? How? My shoulders scrape against the sharp crystalline grains in the rocks, that's right, slow underground cooling, the mineral crystallization sequence, just pull yourself along…

I drag myself through, and maybe I am bleeding.

The drum stops. Hands lift me to my feet, a pair of strong hands. I am embraced by what I realize with dull shock is Jared's naked body. I have never touched a naked man before. "Welcome home," he whispers in my ear.

He takes me by the hand and leads me across the sand to what I realize must be the fire ring. I feel thick softness beneath my feet, and he gently spins me around and lowers me into a kneeling position. I sit back on my heels and try to relax, but the shaking seems to possess my whole body.

Then my blindfold was removed. My eyes, light-deprived for so long, saw the moonlight on the surrounding rocks as jarring brightness. Jared handed me my glasses, and I slid them on.

The women were all seated around the dark fire ring, each on a folded sleeping bag, and they were all still nude. Jared sat down on his own mat. I was still so off-balance I could hardly take it in. Who needs drugs?

"I vote that we get dressed before we go any further," Melanie said. "I'm freezing." There was a general murmur of assent, and we all rose to our feet. They all turned immediately, knowing their clothes had been laid behind their mats. None of them seemed the least bit self-conscious, and for good reason, I thought: none of them were classically formed, but they all seemed beautiful.

The usual male standard of female beauty, if you can judge from beer ads and centerfolds, is something overripe but still virginal. It isn't a look I object to, but it isn't a look I demand, either; I like to be surprised by the ways people can be put together. Melanie had a taut-skinned, youthful look, slim and nearly breastless, but the virginal effect was somewhat undercut by the fact her crotch was shaved, except for a carefully edged triangle that pointed like an arrowhead at her labia. I tried not to study her too long or too obviously, but as always she managed to catch my gaze and smile.

Dawn's body would never be in an ad: even in the moonlight I could see stretch marks on her hips, and her breasts were soft and shapeless. Yet her body was gorgeous because she so clearly enjoyed living in it, and years of use had given it a comfortable look. It was a well-established garden but not one that took a lot of prissy tending.

Mandy was Mandy. In the moonlight her hips were water-polished stone, the whole of her small body dense and self-contained except for her nipples, which in the cool night air stuck out like messages from God. By standard measures, her hips were a little too wide, her waist a little too short, her breasts too small. She was perfect.

Jared too was out of proportion yet proportionate. He was slim and wiry, his chest a little sunken but muscular, his legs a little too short for his slender frame. Beneath his steel-wool pubic hair his cock was unable to choose between waving in the breeze and tightening down against the cold.

So why should any of them be self-conscious? But their comfort with themselves made it even worse for me, as by comparison I felt only half-formed, a clay model the sculptor had toyed with before moving on to the real thing. It didn't help that I'd found Dawn was two years older than me; without that knowledge I could have explained them all away by blaming age.

I struggled to my feet. Facing away from the circle I found my pants and pulled them on, doing the usual one-legged hop-dance that happens when I try to get my trousers on too quickly. I tossed the rest of my clothes to the side of my mat and sat down to finish dressing.

Once we were all dressed and seated again, Jared said, "Dawn?"

"Gratitude," she answered. "I suggest we take a few minutes and meditate on all the things we're thankful for."

The others all closed their eyes, and after a moment's hesitation, I followed suit. At first, nothing came. *Come on, Walker.* There was plenty to be grateful for. I was grateful I didn't have cancer, that I wasn't born in some poor jungle village, that I wasn't deformed or retarded or crippled or blind…but those were all negatives, things I was glad hadn't happened. I felt a stinging on a raw part of my back that I had scraped. I was grateful my initiation ordeal was over, and grateful I had seen it through and hadn't humiliated myself in front of everyone. I was grateful I had my clothes on again, and I was grateful a few moments later when I heard one of the others stirring, so I could open my eyes.

"Amandinea?" Jared asked. "Since you aren't partaking, will you do the honors?"

"Happy to," she said, and rose to her feet without using her hands.

Mandy dug through our impedimenta stacked against the rocks and came back with a bottle and a pottery cup. She went first to Melanie, knelt beside her, poured liquid into the cup, and waited while Melanie drained it. Melanie winced, apparently at the aftertaste, but this being Melanie the wince itself was a work of art.

She poured out libations for Jared, and then Dawn, and finally came and knelt by me. "You're doing good, Walker," she whispered. "I'm proud of you." She poured me my dose and held out the cup. "Try to down it all at once: it's hard to take a second drink."

I took the cup from her hands, breathed in and out, and then gulped down everything. It was bitter and strange and my throat tried to close up and resist it. The aftertaste was indescribable. Green dirt. The smell you get if you dig your fingers into the forest floor.

I sneaked a glance at my watch. 7:14 pm, Friday, January 10.

She took the cup back and corked the bottle. "Welcome to the Styx, Dr. Clayborne. Don't get your feet wet."

35

Everyone else seemed content to sit crosslegged and stare at the ground in front of them. I was agitated. I had just done something irrevocable. And now…

Nothing. I was afraid at first that something too powerful would overtake me. I'd heard about drug users waiting for "the rush." Where was it? Maybe this didn't have it. All in all it seemed like I hadn't received a very full orientation. Maybe I should have asked more questions.

Maybe everybody else's minds weren't chasing their own tails. I looked at my watch. 7:25. It had only been about ten minutes. Everybody else was so calm. Maybe this wasn't as overwhelming as I thought. Perhaps this was a more subtle, kind of meditative thing. I tried to slow down, concentrate on my breathing, deeper, smoother…

I had never received any training in meditation, but I tried to do what I imagined yogis must do, stilling myself and looking inward. But when I turned my gaze away from the outer world of illusion, what I found was that my stomach was becoming distressed. This wasn't just nervousness; it burbled a few times, and I felt queasy.

I sat there feeling wretched for what seemed like a half-hour before I said, "I don't feel so good…"

Mandy and Jared came over and squatted next to me. Jared's ankles were a bit wobbly. "Do you need to throw up?" Mandy asked.

"I don't know."

"Do you feel like you might?"

"Yeah."

"Okay." They helped me to my feet. Each took an arm and they steered me over toward the haystack boulders.

"Sorry," I said. Moving made me feel even more nauseated.

"Happens to most everybody the first time," Jared said. "Happens to some people every time." They led me around behind the boulders, and helped me kneel down by the trench Jared had dug. "We'll give you some privacy, but we'll be right on the other side of the rocks if you need us."

I don't vomit well. Whenever the flu came through my childhood home, the first sign was usually Edgar or Claire running for a bathroom or demanding the car be stopped. I fought against it, even though Mom always said I'd feel better.

"She was right," I heard Claire say. It was startling. I could tell it was in my head, but it was still a perfect reproduction of her voice, and there was no more distant whispering; she might have been right beside me. Perhaps there was something in this potion after all… My stomach spasmed and I leaned forward on my hands and gagged.

I remained like that for a moment, fighting it, and then I vomited, and when I did I saw stars. Not stars like the glitter you get from a sharp blow to the head. The stars were in the stream of vomit that shot forth. I heaved again, and this time it was like I vomited forth fireworks. I looked down in the trench and stared at the viscous, stringy mass of what I had brought up, and it glistened in the silver moonlight, and seemed to shift and show forth hidden depths and colors, like the changing light through a stained-glass window on a cloudy day. This was ridiculous. Hunched over contemplating the coruscating beauty of my vomit. "It *is* beautiful," Claire insisted. "Pull the stick out of your ass, Lionel."

I felt a hand on my back, a touch to let me know someone was there. Melanie knelt down beside me. "Mind if I join you?" she asked in a weak voice. I glanced over at her. Her forehead was moist. She made a tiny smile, said, "Excuse me—" and doubled over and threw up. This set me off again and I joined her for one more productive heave. This was a queer kind of intimacy, something I had certainly never shared with anyone before. I choked a few more times, but realized there was nothing left inside me.

I sat back on my heels. Melanie wasn't done yet. She was on her knees, supporting herself on her left arm, her right hand holding her hair back in a ponytail. Her whole body heaved with effort. I put my hand on her back and stroked, feeling the spasmodic clenching of her muscles as she emptied herself.

She sat up and dug through the pockets of her coat. She unwrapped a premoistened towelette and began wiping her face, then stopped long enough to hand me one. I had a hard time tearing the package; my fingers had become clumsy. "Aren't you glad you shaved the beard?" she asked. Her voice was shockingly loud.

I rubbed at my face with the wet towel and an overpowering scent of lemon burst up into my sinuses. She took the towel and wrapper from me and dropped them into a plastic bag. Then she took out a small bottle of mouthwash, poured some into her mouth, swished, gargled, and spit it out into the trench. She handed it to me.

"You think of everything, don't you?" I asked. My voice sounded hollow. I took the bottle and imitated her. The smell was almost too much, but it did a thorough job of banishing the taste of my stomach acids.

She slipped the bottle back in her pocket. "Yeah, well…this happens to me every time."

I took off my glasses and cleaned them on my shirt. Even if I was feeling clumsy, wiping my glasses is built so deep in my reflex arc I could probably do it even if they removed most of my brain. I put them back on and looked over at Melanie.

She had an embarrassed smile on her face. We stared at one another for a long time before I realized what had changed: there was no longer that cloud of sex charge, that miasma that had swamped me every time I looked at her. She seemed smaller now. Just a little girl, and an insecure one. "I really do like you, Walker," she said.

"I like you too." Color tones shifted across her smooth skin, pink being chased by green, the same elusive transitions that run across the scales of a fish when it is first pulled from the water. The image disturbed me. A fish pulled from the water is in panic and pain: why should it produce such sublime colors?

"It was kind of fun," she said, "having you think I was the most beautiful thing in the galaxy." How did she know it was gone? Could she see inside my head?

I watched the play of light and dark on her face. Her pupils were black circles outlined with a fine ring of blue. "I still think you're the most beautiful thing in the galaxy," I said. "Even though it's different now."

"Walker, you're really stoned." She scooted over so she knelt right at my side and hugged me, and I wrapped my arms around her, and we sat there, content. I let my head fall back and looked up at the sky, and realized I had lied. The moon was the most beautiful thing in the galaxy. It ravished my soul. Or maybe the stars… I chuckled.

"What's funny?" she asked, her face against my chest.

"Ranking things. Deciding what's good, better, best."

"True. Pointless." She stayed there quiet a little longer, then said, "Can we go back? I really want a fire."

She rose with her grace, but I swayed up like a heavy mast hoisted by a crew of drunken sailors. I hoped their ropes held. It was a long way down to my feet.

Melanie held my hand and led me back to the main clearing.

Everything was changed, but everything was the same. Except more so. I could see why Jared had warned me about Cosmic Insight, because this trivial thought seemed profound. We sat around the circle. Melanie wanted to light the fire right away; Dawn wanted to look at the stars for a while first. They kicked this around without rancor as I lay back on the sleeping bag and stared up at the night sky.

The only way I can put it is to say everything was more three-dimensional, which is ridiculous. Everything is already three-dimensional. But I could feel the distances as I looked into space, and suddenly I had the You Are Here insight: I wasn't on the flat surface of California, but could actually perceive I was laying on the side of an unimaginably huge ball, plastered down flat on my back by its fierce gravity, hurtling through space, and the world was spinning around the sun, and turning on its own axis, and I could see the moon orbiting around the spinning Earth…and I knew all this already, I knew it in much more detail than most people, but I had never really grasped it before.

It was all too beautiful. Beautiful. A limp word, an insignificant word. But not just too beautiful for words, too beautiful to tolerate. I sat up and the rush of changing input as I altered the position of my eyes and ears relative to the things I perceived flooded me with too much sensation. I understood how dogs feel with their noses stuck out the window of a speeding car, a bursting dam of news from the world, input, knowledge, sensation, right through the sensitive organs of perception and straight into the lower reaches of the brain without passing first through the filters of thought.

I looked at the boulders ringing our camp and could feel their looming presence, their age; I knew now what so many people meant by the power of a place. I saw the others sitting, Dawn and Melanie talking quietly together, Jared crosslegged with his eyes closed, Mandy leaned back on her hands and looking at the moon. It was extraordinary to be alive—extraordinary if we were put here by some higher power, extraordinary if we weren't; I wasn't sure which was the stranger possibility.

And then I knew this was always here. What I was seeing was always there to be seen, just people, places, nature, the sky. Yet I spent each day without really seeing.

Why hadn't anyone told me all of this?

"They did," Claire said. "Everything you're realizing now has been said a million times, everything you're thinking is a cliché, everything you're pondering as profound is sophomoric. But all true."

I shut my eyes and she was there in my head. I could still feel my body sitting on the ground, but Claire was there in my mind, more vivid than she had ever been in life. She was dressed in the same bare-midriff and shorts outfit as in the photograph that lay ten yards away atop the mesa. "Am I really talking to you?"

She threw her head back and laughed. "Am I inside your mind, or do I only seem to be inside your mind? Are you having a powerful experience, or do you only think you're having one? Are you having these feelings, or do you only feel that you feel? C'mon, Lionboy, give it a rest!"

"But are you a ghost, or alive somewhere…?"

She sprouted white feathery wings and a halo appeared over her head. "This?" The wings vanished and a sheet dropped over her, with eyeholes scissored out. "This?" The sheet blinked out of existence, leaving her back in shorts and midriff. "There's only so much time. I only had four years." She smiled, sad, amused. "Don't waste it on quibbles."

"But Claire…"

She transformed into something shaped like a giant kidney bean, covered with multicolored geometric ripples that ran back and forth, back and forth. It felt like this thing was looking at me. A hole appeared in its center and it sucked itself into its own form and flowed out in another place, this time looking something like a bejeweled lobster.

I opened my eyes. She was right. There was only so much time. Another vitally true cliché. Just tonight I had been unable to find things to be grateful for, when I ought to be grateful just to be able to see, to breathe…

One last whisper from Claire: "Nothing's ever really gone…"

I cried. I cried for myself and the wasted time of my life. I cried for Claire. I cried for my parents and the sad wreck they had made of their lives, and for Elizabeth who had tried to love me and for the junkies and the injured and the dying and the lonely and for all the pain in the world, all the pain past and all the pain yet to come and it felt like the weight of it all would crush me down—and I, so hollow, with nothing to support the pressure. All the unshed tears came now, came so hard I thought I must be dying.

There were arms around me, rocking me, murmuring calming things. It was my mother and father, when I was so young they could still love me, before I became a person. No, it was Claire; it was Elizabeth.

It was Jared and Mandy. "Oh God," I whispered, "I'm sorry, I'm sorry, it's all just…so *sad*." They stayed beside me, holding me, rocking me.

After a long blank time I shrugged my arms free and took off my glasses to wipe the tears from them. To my surprise, I could see just as well without them. "I can see."

"That happens to some people," Jared said, "but you should probably put them back on. If you focus very long without them it'll give you a mother of a headache tomorrow."

"I saw Claire," I said.

"Me too," said Mandy. "Did she grow wings and make like an angel for a minute?"

"Yes…" I turned and looked into Mandy's face. When our eyes locked, something happened I still don't understand. Her face seemed to bulge and twist a little, and I could feel my face moving too, like big thumbs were pressing on the outer edge of my eye sockets. Both of our faces twisted until our eyes were in perfect alignment, as though we were staring down tubes of force. Her black eyes were holes into her head, and I could almost see her mind moving inside her—but even more, I knew she could see me, that she was in my head, the most intimate, personal, embarrassing, touch I have ever felt, a proctoscopy of the mind. I surrendered to it, and let her move inside me.

At last, she said, "You're okay, Walker. You're really okay." She closed her eyes, and turned her face from me.

I was washed out, wiped out. I had thrown up everything in my body, and then cried out all the tears. I felt so light it seemed like I might drift into the air. "I feel good. Is this almost over?"

Jared snorted. "Look at your watch."

I did. 8:22 pm. What time did I take it? "How long?" I asked.

"How long what?"

"How long ago did I take it?"

"A little over an hour."

"How long does it last?"

"It will keep getting stronger for another hour or two, then start to ease off. Eight hours total before you're down enough to sleep."

An hour in. Seven hours to go. This was taking forever. I felt good, clear, in fact wondrous, but how long does one want to feel anything that intensely? "How long do you orgasm before you want it to stop?"

"Huh?" Jared and Mandy asked at once.

"Nothing. Doesn't matter."

They started the fire. Everyone else seemed more at ease using their bodies while on this stuff, so I just sat and let it happen. My thoughts were going so fast now, and down so many different branching lanes, that I could only grasp at them as they flew by.

I understood now how fire had been worshipped in past ages, how the ancients had asserted it was a principle in and of itself, one of the four basic elements. It moved, grew, withdrew, reached out: it was more animate than, well, animals. Animate. Anima. Animus. Animals: literally, things with souls.

The firelight changed the whole nature of the rock-ringed basin; the juddering changes in the light levels made it seem like vision had been cut up into a series of still photos shown in quick succession, each taken from a slightly different angle in contrasting lighting. I tried to relax, and for the first time found that controlling my breathing had profound effects. I could feel energy being drawn from the universe with each breath, racing through my body, transforming, and being exhaled. But that's what's really happening, I realized: oxygen, lungs, blood, cell walls, mitochondria, the Krebs Cycle, cell walls, blood, lungs, carbon dioxide…

"That and more," Claire said.

"Are you there?" I shut my eyes. I didn't see her now. Instead, a field of radiating streams of light, morphing into a series of geometric patterns that seemed to form portals. One grew larger. Larger and I was inside it and then it grew darker and darker and very warm and I floated.

Blood. Blood and cold gleaming steel. "There it is…" Claire whispered.

It was very dim, warm, impossible to see anything. A voice said, "I was all alone in a small, dark world." It was an adult voice, female, but speaking in childish tones. "I was *all alone* in a small, dark world." My mother's voice, reading something…

I went away for a long time, floating in a private sea.

When at last I opened my eyes, considerable time must have passed, because the vermilion embers had piled deep in the fire ring. They seemed to ache and pulse, and they looked a little like hard candy waiting to be sucked. Dawn, Melanie, and Jared were sitting close together on the other side of the fire, deep in some discussion. Mandy sat alone to my right. She looked relieved when I came back to awareness.

With immense effort I stood. My legs had both gone to sleep, but the pins-and-needles sensations were not painful, just a strange stimulation. I walked away from the circle of firelight. Above the rocky hill at the west end of the little basin, the sky had a diffuse yellowish cast. The glow of Los Angeles, more than a hundred miles distant. So much energy, everything roped together by power lines, postal systems, roads, phone lines, the Internet.

The Internet. Networks. Connections. Something was hiding here, just peeking around the corners of my mind, possibly even sticking out its tongue at me. What?

"Yes," Claire said, very faint.

"Speak up," I said aloud.

I waited, but heard nothing.

I walked back toward the fire, watching the weird leaping shadows. I suddenly understood this was what firelight really looked like, but usually our brain smoothed out the sharp changes in light and contrast, interpolated to give us a sensation of steadier light and greater continuity.

I then saw that this same phenomenon happened every time I blinked. The mind froze the image on the retina, continued displaying it during the closure of the eyelid, then moved on to the new input. And if you became aware of this, as I did now, what the world really consisted of was view—total darkness—view (fractionally different angle)—total darkness... It was jarring, jumpy, somewhat horrific, and it was what the external world really looked like before the brain knitted it together into this seamless illusion.

This was fascinating, but I was ready for it to stop now. *Don't think about blinking, damn it, focus on something...*

I did. On the snake crawling slowly away from my mat. Absurd. As Joop and Arlinda had so eloquently pointed out to me, it wasn't snake season. But it was there, and showed every evidence of being real. A Mojave Green Rattler, to be precise.

"Umm, excuse me…!" I said loudly.

Everyone looked up.

"Umm, maybe this is a hallucination or something, but I could swear I see a rattlesnake." I pointed. "Right there."

They all peered at it, and then rose to their feet and came around to my side of the fire. "That's there all right," Jared said.

"Amazing," Mandy said.

We must have built the fire close to its den; the heat must have driven it first out of hibernation and finally out of its burrow. It was sluggish, and interested only in getting far from the fire. It paid no attention to us as we lined up along its path, neither turning aside nor stopping to coil and threaten. Its tongue flicked as it searched ahead. About fifteen feet from our fire was a little outcrop of rock in the sand, and the rattler tongued its way to a crevice and then slid down and out of sight, the nine segments of rattle protruding for a moment as if cut off from its owner.

We searched the area under our sleeping bags, and found the likely den entrance. Mojaves are not known to be communal denners like some rattlers, but we saw no reason to take chances: we wedged a rock in the hole, agreeing to remind each other to remove it in the morning.

After we settled back down, Mandy sat beside me and said, "What's happening, Walker?"

"I'm still very, very stoned. Maybe even more than a while ago. I think I'm just getting used to it rather than coming down."

"Probably. It hasn't been that long."

"I'm hearing Claire," I said. "Sometimes, with my eyes closed, seeing her. "

"And?"

"And something else. It's important."

"Well?"

"Blood. Blood and steel. In a small, dark world."

36

I never fell asleep that night, but spent hours in that hypnogogic state just above the level of true slumber, where vivid images parade past without even the tenuous web of relationships we can expect from dreams.

By seven everyone was getting up. We made a quiet breakfast of fruit, all of it chilled by the night air. At one level it felt as if we should be talking about the previous night, but what was there to say? There was now some sort of bond between us that could be expressed by the merest exchange of glances. I wondered how long it would last.

We buried the ashes of the fire in our makeshift latrines, scattered the rock ring with charred faces down, and freed up the entrance to the rattlesnake den. By the time we hiked out, only the piled rectangle of the mesa, bereft of our offerings, showed we had been there.

Hiking out we had no wood to carry, little water, and less food. We lingered for a while around the cars, dirty with dust and woodsmoke, but lazy, companionable, and washed-out inside. Since Jared was heading all the way back to Yucca Valley, Dawn and Melanie rode with him, and I went with Mandy. I hugged the other three goodbye, initiating the embraces myself. I was amazed to see how Melanie's spell had evaporated. I rather missed it. She gave me a smile that was just a little bit sad and, to our mutual surprise, I kissed her.

I was no longer stoned, but the world looked new. It sounded new: Mandy put in a CD, and it was like nothing I had ever heard, electric guitars interlocking in a complex, growing architecture like Bach gone jazz. "What is this?" I asked, raising my voice above the music.

"*The ConstruKction of Light*," she said, loudly. "King Crimson circa 2000."

This meant nothing to me, but I closed my eyes and let the golden traceries of guitars weave unbalanced tapestries in my mind. Networks of yellow lines in the dark. A small dark world…

"Turn it off," I said abruptly.

She switched the player off. "You don't like it?"

"I like it. I just thought of something. I need to make a phone call." I looked at my watch. 10:42 a.m. I did some quick math, counting on my fingers to be sure. I dug out my wallet and found Edgar's phone numbers on the little card where I had written them. It was around the end of the day in England, so work or home were equally likely. I flipped open my cell phone and bet on his office.

Two rings, and he said, "Clayborne."

"Edgar. This is Walker."

"Walker, what's wrong?"

"What makes you think anything's wrong?"

"You sound strange, and the connection sounds like you're on a mobile. Plus you didn't start out by calling me Julius."

"Just a quick question. Do you remember Mom ever saying anything like 'I was all alone in a small dark world?'"

"Are you sure you're all right? What kind of daft question is that?"

"Just answer it. Please."

"Fine. Sure, I remember that. It's from some children's book."

"Do you remember the book?"

"Christ, Lion. Something with a rabbit, or some such rot."

"The title? Do you remember the plotline or anything?"

"Lionel, why on earth? No. It was just some kids' book. You're really starting to worry me, sibling mine."

"Sorry. I'll explain some other time."

I closed my conversation with Edgar and flipped the phone shut. We pulled up to a stoplight in Twenty-Nine Palms, and Mandy gave me a sideways glance from the wheel. "Care to share?"

"Something from last night. I'd try to talk, but it doesn't make any sense."

"Try me. Free associate. I don't have the authority to have you committed."

"There were things last night. Claire was showing me things—or Ettenmoor might say that my mind was showing me things and choosing to model them as coming from Claire. There's something from a children's storybook, and something with blood, steel, darkness. And something else with networks and postal systems and transport and the Internet…"

"Do you use the Internet a lot?"

"Not recreationally. I use e-mail a lot, I use the Geosciences Superhub…"

"What's that?"

"A site where we can exchange data, post papers for comment, even store big banks of files for backup, keep them as open and closed databases…"

"Shit." Mandy stepped on the brakes and we decelerated sharply. I swiveled my head looking for the problem.

"Did we hit something?" I asked.

"No. No, sorry. You may be onto something." She accelerated back to her former speed.

"As you just asked, care to share?"

"Just a peculiar hunch. I'll check it out back at your place." She chewed her lip. "Claire's wings just fluttered past my cheek."

At Claire's she stalked straight to the computer and switched it on while I was still fitting myself and my backpack through the door. She made a quick trip to the bathroom while the system booted, and then went back to the desk. "Okay. This is a long shot." She sat down at the computer and I came over. She had started Windows Explorer again and was searching against various strings filled with wildcard characters.

"What are you doing?"

"Looking for macros,'bots, scripts…something that would give us a clue to any automated backup. What's this?" She double-clicked a file name, and a media player started up; she closed it before it loaded. "Nope…nope…ahh, maybe, maybe. Come to Momma…" An icon popped up on the screen.

"What is it?"

"Some kind of a'bot for FileWizz. With a little bit of luck her account info is still out there in Internet Explorer…"

She connected to the web via a server I hadn't seen before, the modem giving the usual crackle and hiss before it settled down to the clear high song of a clean connection. "Say a little prayer, Walker…" She surfed over to FILEWIZZ.COM and clicked *Log In*.

"I don't understand what you're doing."

"Just like you leave your data out on the Superhub, some people back their stuff up on the Internet. Not a bad idea. If your house burns down, your backups don't get toasted with your computer."

Hello, MISTRESS CLAIRE. Current Usage is 26 MB. Current Limit is 50 MB. Last Visit: Dec 12. Upload: 3.23 MB. Download: 0 MB.

"Mistress Claire?" Mandy minimized the browser. "What's that, her S&M handle?" She double-clicked the new icon, and a dialog box popped up bearing two tabs: *Backup* and *Restore*. She chose the *Restore* tab, and a series of check boxes appeared. She checked *Compare/Update*, checked *By Name*, unchecked *By Date*, and clicked *OK*, and sat back. "This might take a while, depending on how much stuff has been deleted. What it's doing is comparing all the file names on this computer with all the names of the files stored in her account on the net. Anything that's been deleted on her system but is still stored out there, it'll bring back."

Under *Files Compared* a counter was whizzing along, but it was some time before it printed:

MY_DEAD.DOC   Downloading…

And then, after the counter whirred along for a bit more, in rapid succession it yielded:

CONTACT.DOC   Downloading…
DESOXYN.DOC   Downloading…

Done.

"That's it," Mandy said. "DESOXYN. Very funny."

"Funny why?"

"Oh, that's one of the trade names for methamphetamine back when they used to market it for depression, weight control, or just that quick pick-me-up busy Americans need to get going in the morning. So let's open it up…" She jumped back to Explorer and double-clicked the file name.

Microsoft Word came up, along with a little dialogue box that read *Enter Password to Open File*. Mandy typed. It answered *Password is Incorrect. Word Cannot Open File*. "Damn." I looked away as she fidgeted and cursed, clicking and typing. Finally she sat up straight, stretched her arms above her head, and waggled her shoulders to relieve the tension.

"Well," she said, "the good news is we've got the files that were deleted; the bad news is that they're all key encoded. We can't open them."

"Isn't there some way of getting around that?"

"There's rumors that Microsoft left a tunnel so the government can peek in, but I'm not sure I believe it. Maybe, just maybe, the NSA can crack this nut by doing combinatorials on their banks of Crays. But not us. Without the right word, we're screwed."

"Try 'Bolles.' Try 'Association.'"

She tapped away. "Nope." She tapped some more. "Not 'Danger Rangerette' or 'Mistress Claire,' either."

"I can't believe that there's no way to open this. It seems like there'd be some kind of utility…"

"Believe me, there's no way—at least, not any way that isn't top secret."

I dropped my hands to my sides. "So we're no better off than before."

"I wouldn't say that. We know one of the files that was deleted has a name suggesting it's related to the meth business."

"So what do we do now?"

"See if we can think of the magic word."

"Our Sunday School teacher always said 'please' was the magic word."

Mandy typed, hit *Enter*. "Your Sunday School teacher lied."

She tried a few more combinations and then yawned with her whole body. "Man. I'm beat. You can keep on trying if you want, but I need to use the bed for a couple of hours."

She wandered off to the bedroom and I took her place at the desk. After a few tries, I couldn't come up with another guess. I decided to drop the password problem and instead explore the images and voices that kept arising in my mind.

I did a search on the Internet: [Rabbit OR Bunny] AND Children's AND "all alone in a small dark world."

This gave me fifty-three hits at forty-two different sites. The description of the first two of them suggested they were some kind of B&D sex sites; I decided not to contemplate why these sites gave hits on *rabbit* AND *children's*.

The Golden Egg Book sounded more likely. Was this the story of the goose that laid the golden egg?

No, it certainly was not, the children's librarian at the main branch in San Bernardino informed me when she finally answered her extension. It was the title of a 1947 book by Margaret Wise Brown, and *Golden* referred to Golden Books, the children's publisher. It was considered a minor classic of sorts, and she was pleased to tell me it had just been reissued in 1999 if I wanted to buy a copy.

"Can you summarize the story?" I asked.

"Would you like me to read it to you?" she asked. "Technically speaking, story hour is over, but it must take all of six minutes to read…"

She went away for a few minutes. It took more time for her to retrieve the volume than to read it to me. "I was all alone in a small dark world" was a little less existentially challenging than it sounded: it turned out to be the narrative of a duckling still in its egg. A lonely bunny kicks the egg around, rolls it down hills, eventually tires and falls asleep next to the egg. The egg hatches, "And nobody was ever alone again."

I remembered the story now. It had been read to all three of us by our mother. But what the hell did it mean? I thanked the librarian effusively, and she said, "Oh, you're welcome, sweetheart. And if you can't sleep, just call back and I'll read you *The Tawny Scrawny Lion.* There's a bunny in that one, too!"

Wonderful. I was sure it all meant something, but doubt was beginning to creep back in. I went over and lay on the couch to think.

In the dream I was back in my clubhouse near the arroyo, but I was an adult, and when I stood the mesquite branches scratched my head. The door to the clubhouse swung open and Claire stood just outside, about six or seven years old, but dressed in a child's version of the clothes she had worn in the photograph. She held up her hand and beckoned me to follow, her face solemn.

We were on my old street, and I was having trouble keeping up with her, and then she started to run, across our lawn, around the side of the garage, out through the backyard to her clubhouse in the old paint shed. She whipped the door open, turned in the doorway and stuck out her tongue at me, and then slammed the door behind her.

I arrived out of breath and tugged on the door. "Claire!" I hammered on the door, big adult fists. "Let me in! …I'll say it! I'll say it as much as you want…"

I woke up, sat upright on the couch, and for the first time in my life, actually slapped myself in the forehead. I fumbled for my glasses and made it into the bedroom before I had them on my face. "Mandy," I whispered. I shook her gently. "Mandy, wake up."

She pushed the hair out of her face and squinted. "What? What happened?"

"I think I've got the key. I think I've got the password."

She tossed off the covers and rolled out of bed, dressed only in her T-shirt. "God, I need to brush my teeth…" She stepped around me and made for the door, rubbing her eyes. "Okay, wonderboy, what's the magic word?"

I followed her. "*Stupid boys.* Or something like it."

She sat down at the desk, waggled the mouse to wake the system. "One word or two?"

"No idea."

She waited for Word to launch. "May I ask from whence…?"

"Secret password for her clubhouse."

She loaded DESOXYN.DOC, popped up the password dialogue box, typed "Stupid Boys."

Invalid entry…

She typed "StupidBoys."

A page of twelve-point Times New Roman appeared on the screen.

DESOXYN.DOC was a detailed point-by-point expose of the methamphetamine trade in the area, with names, addresses, and dates of transactions all spelled out. Moreover, it included dates when Rick Bolles had been present during transactions, and also listed the names of people inside Eagle Mountain who would be able to testify as to the facts of all the listed events in exchange for early parole.

"Jesus," Mandy said, "I don't know much about this sort of thing, but this looks pretty damning to me. Still believe that Bolles was essentially telling the truth?"

I held my head in my hands. All alone in a small dark world. Bryce Childers had said the murder was somehow sexual. All the weird impressions of the previous night: none about drugs. "It doesn't mean that they killed Claire."

"Walker, get real! This looks like evidence to me."

I shook my head. "Now who's being overly logical? It doesn't feel right. Does it feel right to you?"

She took a deep breath. "Maybe not." She rubbed at her neck. Without thinking I stood behind her and began massaging her tight shoulders. I suddenly became aware of what I was doing: I hadn't done something so forward since the ineffectual groping dates of my teens. But she groaned, and said, "Keep that up. Let's look at these other two."

MY_DEAD.DOC was a journal that began: "More than two hundred years ago in England, I murdered a farmer and then raped his wife…"

"What the hell is this?" I demanded.

"Just what it looks like. A journal of Claire's past lives."

"Claire was a murderer and a rapist? And, presumably, a man?"

Mandy scrunched her shoulders forward and said, "Lower… There's a big business in bullshit past-life stuff, where you find out you used to be Cleopatra, but most people who have profound experiences have something more modest, and frequently disturbing. A lot of people who are victimized recover memories of being victimizers."

"My, that's tidy. And how exactly does the population ever increase, with so few ancestors to go around?"

"My view? I don't think we just get dumped from body to body like water poured from bottle to bottle. I think everything that's ever been experienced is floating around out there, and I think we tap into things that are congruent to our own fucked-up situations. Why are we talking about this?"

"I don't know. Does this help us? Does this have something to do with why she was murdered?"

"No idea. Maybe. It looks like it's more than fifty pages long. I bet it was just password-protected because it's so personal."

"We should print it out and look at it. What else?"

The last document read in full:

TEMPORARY AND CONTACT:

Abigail

1412 Spanish Mine Road

Baker, CA 92309

(909) 777-2432

NEW:

63 Vernor Court

Searchlight, NV 89046

I let loose of her shoulders and sat back down in the chair. "What do you think of that?" I asked.

"What do *you* think?" She turned. Our gazes linked and I felt the same tugging pressure at the side of my eyes I had felt the previous night.

"We both think this is important, don't we?"

"Yeah."

"Why do we think that?"

"I don't know. Maybe because Claire obviously did."

I called the number and reached a recording: The number you dialed has changed or has been disconnected. Please check the number again before dialing, or—

"Disconnected," I said. "I think we should go there."

"Now?"

"Sure. Why not?"

"Because I need to go home first, and shower, do some things…"

"You can shower here."

"Walker: call it a chick thing if you want. I need to go home first. After that I'm with you all the way, but give me an hour."

I printed all three documents, stapled all but the one-pager, and put them in a manila folder.

Mandy dropped me at the Jeep, which was still parked at Jared's place. I drove it back to Claire's, and Mandy headed back to her house to shower and change.

I took another nap, but awoke with a jolt. Why had I let her go off by herself? I glanced at the clock. 3:13 pm. She'd been gone over an hour already.

I tried to calm myself. Did it *feel* wrong?

What was I doing asking questions like that? Claire had almost died—had died, technically—in a boating accident, and I hadn't felt anything. Why would I suddenly be able to intuit things?

Because you have a connection to these people now. Because you're different now.

I was different, perhaps, but not that different, not yet. I took a quick shower, telling myself over and over that it was okay. I changed clothes and sat back down on the couch. I breathed relief when I heard her pull into the driveway. She had changed clothes, but was already wearing the invariable black trench coat. She had the Thomas Guide in her hand. "Just in case you don't know Baker well. I sure don't."

I pulled on my jacket and grabbed the folder of printouts. Since we had no idea where the quest might lead, we decided to take the Jeep. I opened the rear door and checked my desert supplies: five gallons of water in plastic totes; a five-gallon gas can, filled; first aid kit; emergency rations; a piece of carpet; a foot-long two-by-four; a folding shovel.

"Carpet?" Mandy asked.

"Between that and a two-by-four, you can get out of any sand this side of the Sahara."

I started the engine and pulled down the driveway. I stopped. "You know," I said, "things still look a little…funny to me. Can you drive a stick?"

"Does the Pope shit in the woods? Move over, ace."

37

In the excitement over guessing Claire's password, I hadn't mentioned my research on the "small dark world" to Mandy. I filled her in on my session with the librarian as we drove.

"What does it mean, then?" she asked. "It seems to be a childhood memory, but relating to what?"

"It's tied up with the whole blood thing somehow."

"Blood, small dark worlds, eggs: sounds like a womb thing to me. Birth regression thing? It happens, you know, reliving your birth."

"Someone told me once that memory of birth was impossible because the brain's neural sheaths aren't myelinized until well after birth."

"Did they explain how myelin has anything to do with memory?"

"No…"

"Didn't think so. Flatworms have memory. Their nerves don't get myelinized."

Mandy drove the Jeep fast but competently. The seat didn't adjust for height, so she had it pulled so far forward the lower rim of the steering wheel nearly touched her belly. As soon as the shadows began to lengthen, she turned on the lights.

The quickest route was the most deserted: out through Amboy, up Kelbaker Road past the elegant, abandoned Kelso rail station, and then veering slightly west for Baker. Total population along this two-hour drive, probably about seventy-five people. In late twilight we passed

Kelso and crossed the long slow rise of the Cima dome, a swollen cap of magma ten miles in diameter which had lifted the ground, but never poured forth.

Either the effects of the substance I had imbibed the previous night still lingered, or my brain—or, as Ettenmoor would have insisted, my mind—was permanently changed. I knew the history of the terrain outside the windows, but for the first time I could envision how it must have been fifteen thousand years ago, when this was the wet edge south of the great ice sheets, covered with grasslands that gave way to huge shallow lakes, a soggy world that supported untold millions of ancestral ducks and geese, some of them with teeth hidden inside their hard beaks. Herds of mastodons and mammoths shared the plains with tiny proto-camels and horses the size of terriers; in the river valleys lived beavers the size of grizzlies. All of it gone now, even the grass.

I dozed off and didn't awaken until I felt the Jeep slow as we pulled into Baker. I felt much better and more alert, and was sure I could drive, but Mandy seemed to have committed our route to memory, so I just let her take us there.

Spanish Mine Road was a small, dead-end spur off of Silver Lane, and there were only three houses. 1412 was an old place, a few scraps of scrollwork bracing on the posts of a full front porch. The porch light burned bright as if someone were expected.

We walked onto the creaky floorboards. I knocked, and noticed one of the curtains moving. Someone must have peeked out when the car first pulled up.

The door opened just wide enough to frame the woman's suspicious face. "Can I help you?" The voice was countrified California, probably transplanted from Oklahoma or Arkansas; the face was a tired fifty, hard from years of sun and work.

"This is a little difficult to explain," I began, "but we're looking for someone named Abigail."

She apparently didn't conclude we were from the state lottery, because she said, "What for?" She glanced Mandy up and down. Usually having a woman with you sets people at ease, but her expression suggested she found women in black trench coats a little offputting.

"As I said, it's rather hard to explain. My name's Walker Clayborne. We found your name and address in some of my sister's papers…"

"And who might your sister be?"

"Claire Clayborne. She was—"

"Claire? You mean the counselor lady as worked at that clinic?"

"Yes, that would be her."

"Well why'n'cha say as much?" She opened the door wider, and I saw her lean something out of sight against the doorframe. "I'm Abigail Mothersall. Your friend'd be?"

"Mandy Cicerone," Mandy said.

"You can come on in for a spell—" Abigail began.

"Mrs. Mothersall," Mandy said, "we may not need to impose on you. But can you tell us how you know Claire?"

"No secret there. But if he's her brother"—she tilted her head to the side—"how come you don't just ask her?"

"My sister…died recently."

The woman's face showed genuine shock. "Oh. Oh, Lordy, I'm sorry. But she was so young…"

"We're trying to find out some things," I continued, not wanting to face a long discussion on the topic of Claire's murder unless it were germane, "and we found your address listed as if it was important, along with another address in Searchlight, Nevada. We tried to call first, but it said your phone was disconnected."

"Changed, you mean. We're unlisted now. That damn Darnell was calling up drunk, demanding to know where Rachel got off to. Furthest away from him as possible, I told him. He even come up here a few times; Porter run'im off with a twelve-gauge last time."

"You mean Darnell Huber?" I asked.

"The same. Mean as a damn snake. I been telling Rachel to leave him since the first month she married him. She kept saying he'd change, that he was laying off the bottle and them damn pills or what have you—but I say that once a damn drunk, always a damn drunk, and a man that beats a woman once'll beat her again as soon as the mood takes him." She stared at us, challenging us to disagree.

"And what's Claire's connection with all this?"

"Claire brung her up here in early December. Darnell had been hitting on her, hurt her bad somehow, something with her insides. Claire knew 'em both. She got Rachel to a doctor, got her patched up, then brought her up here. But Rachel was still in a bad way. Your Claire, she told her straight out to get the hell away from that man, same as I'd been saying for years. But my sister Rachel, she—"

"I can't believe," Mandy interrupted, "that Claire would leave Rachel up here if she were really suffering from a serious medical problem."

Abigail set her mouth a little, certain now that her initial negative assessment of Mandy was right on target. "Well, Claire kept sending us letters and stuff, things she was getting from some doctor down there, and she even sent prescriptions. Two times she came up and took Rachel over to Barstow for some kind of tests. So if that ain't a serious medical problem…"

"Where is Rachel now?" I asked.

"Soon as we could we got her set up over in Searchlight. Real nice little town, got more jobs and things."

"That would be a place on Vernor Court?"

"The same."

"Do you have a phone number for her?"

"Rachel's got no phone. Don't have that kind of money yet."

"Is there any way we can get in touch with her?"

"Short of driving on out there, no way I can tell you." She frowned back and forth between us, and finally decided my sibling connection outweighed Mandy's presence. "Porter'll be coming in for supper pretty soon. You're both welcome to stay and have a bite with us…"

I declined as gracefully as I could manage, saying we should get out to Rachel's place before it got too late. In fact, my stomach was tight, too tight to swallow anything.

I took the wheel for the next leg of the drive. Something was making me agitated, and I wasn't sure I could sit as a passenger and do nothing for the hour's drive to Searchlight.

I pulled onto Interstate 15 and headed east. It was Saturday night, so the Friday flood of cars pushing from LA to Vegas was already over, but the volume of traffic was still bewildering after the lonely drive up from Joshua Tree.

"So," I said, "I guess Claire was helping Rachel in sort of the same way you were helping that woman we took to the bus station."

"Sounds like it."

"Still doesn't explain much. I mean, murder'd be going a bit far…"

"You don't know what you're talking about, Walker. You have no idea how fucked up some of these guys get. And the law's practically on their side. In most states until recently, a husband raping a wife was a legal impossibility, even if she'd been hiding from him for years. In one of those southern states a few years back, some guy tracked down what was still legally his wife and he raped her with—well, I'm not going to go into what all he used on her, but it's amazing she lived. And you know what they ended up doing? Law said it wasn't rape; hell, they weren't even sure it was assault. So what'd they prosecute him for? An 'unnatural act' under the state's old sodomy laws. So his lawyer argued that they engaged in this act together, and it must by definition have been consensual, since anything between a husband and wife by definition was consensual, so they couldn't prosecute him unless they prosecuted her too…so they put her on trial and convicted her too. Suspended her sentence, but still…"

"Okay. I'm sorry, already." I paused to let her cool down. "And I can believe that Darnell might have done something horrible to his wife. But it seems a little far-fetched to suggest that he killed Claire just because she wouldn't tell him where Rachel was."

"I'm not so sure—" Mandy started, still wound up. Then she stopped for a moment, and said, "No. I'm sorry. You're right, it doesn't really fit." Then, as an afterthought: "But people have done weirder things."

Maybe I have an especially sick mind. Or maybe I just have a male mind. Or, just possibly, I have a mind with a normal human imagination, and we all think this way. But as we drove in a rather uncomfortable silence, red taillights stretching off ahead of us in a continuous line, I felt my mind drawn back to the subject like our eyes are drawn to a car accident. It was that line she had said: *Well, I'm not going to go into what all he used on her...* Like what? *But it's amazing she lived.* What on earth? Are some people drawn to inflicting genuine injury during sex? Drawing blood...?

Blood. Blood and steel. I was all alone in a small dark world. The duckling in the egg...

"Oh, shit..." I said involuntarily. I let off on the gas, and I could feel Mandy start.

"What? What? Hey, Walker, this is our exit here..."

She was right. We had whipped past Wheaton Springs, and the Nipton exit was just ahead. I flipped on my blinker and steered the Jeep down the offramp. I turned onto Nipton Road and drove a half mile before pulling to the side.

A minute before we had been thundering along in a high-speed parade of metal, all aimed at Vegas like a million sperm fighting their way through the cervix. Now we were all alone, no streetlights, no other cars.

I pulled on the handbrake, but left the motor running. "At the clinic, you guys didn't perform abortions, did you?"

"No. No we didn't, but we referred people out for them... Walker, what is it?"

"I don't..." I massaged my face with my palms. "I think all this blood, steel, eggs, womb imagery has something to do with an abortion. Or a miscarriage. I know that sounds stupid, and I have no real reason to believe it, but..."

"No." Her hand touched my forearm. "No." I felt her shudder. "No, you're right about this, something feels right..." She patted me. "We should go."

I pulled away from the shoulder, and then stopped in the middle of the road. "The package! God, I'm a moron!"

"What package? What are you talking about?"

"When Mrs. Givens found Claire murdered, she was bringing her a package or something, from UPS or somebody. What the hell was it? Does she still have it? Why didn't I think of this the first day I was there?"

"Walker. Walker." Her hand stroked my thinning hair. "Calm down. Just calm down. Do you want me to drive?"

"No." The steering wheel gave me something to hang on to.

"Then go ahead and drive. It's still thirty miles or so. I'll try and get her on the phone."

Mandy popped out her cell. "Hope this works." She called information and asked for Givens on Ironwood in Joshua Tree. She apparently let them connect her automatically for a charge of thirty-five cents, because the next thing she said was, "Okay. I'm going to let you talk."

She handed me the phone. I listened to the rings. Finally she picked up. "Mrs. Givens?" I said. "This is Walker Clayborne—"

"Oh, Professor." I heard a brief roar of static. "You're kind of hard to hear. I was going to come back and see you today. That kid on the motorsickle? He's been here a few times since we last talked, and—"

"I know. Thank you. I wanted to ask another question. Do you remember that when you found Claire's body you were taking her a package of some sort…?"

"How could I forget? I'll never—" Crackling radio waves had cut into our channel. "—and in any case, I—"

"I'm sorry, what did you say?"

"I said I'd never forget that day, if I'da come earlier, mighta been me there with her."

"Uh-huh. Do you happen to remember what the package was?"

She was getting fainter. "I wouldn't say as it were really a package. More like a real big envelope."

I gave up. If we went farther, we might lose her altogether. I pulled to the side. "Do you remember who the envelope was from? Did the police take it? What happened to it?"

She sounded a little put out by this barrage of questions. "Well, the sheriffs took a look at it and gave it back. I gave it back to the UPS man when he come through next. Don't remember who it was from. Some doctor down in Palm Springs."

I covered the mouthpiece. "Doctor in Palm Springs?" I whispered to Mandy.

"Shit, there's two or three who did volunteer stuff for us… Ask if it was Selby."

"Does the name Selby sound familiar?" I asked over the static, loud, as if I were talking to a deaf grandparent.

"Might be. Don't rightly remember. Say, what's all this about, anyway?"

"Unsettled business. Mrs. Givens, thanks, I have to go. I'm starting to lose the line." I started up the car and then, as we drove forward, did lose the line.

"Maybe," I said to Mandy. "She isn't sure."

"He's the only ob-gyn we used in Palm Springs. But he didn't do abortions, usually. He was more of a pregnancy-complication specialist…"

I slowed way down as we passed through the tiny town of Nipton, California. Almost a ghost town back in the '70s, it was now a thriving little tourist destination, with a refurbished B&B hotel and a new campground. If there was going to be a CHP in the middle of nowhere, this is where he would park. But there was nothing…not even cell-phone reception on Mandy's handset.

We drove on grimly through the darkness, past the *Welcome to Nevada* sign as Nipton Road changed to Nevada 164. We could already see the lights of the town of Searchlight ahead across the desolation. Out here you could see forever, and Nevada towns always give off more candlepower per capita than other cities.

Searchlight had boomed in a modest way through the '80s and '90s, not just as another gambling mecca, but as a town that could boast a dammed-up section of the Colorado River for boating and watersports. Until the lake was created, the city was known mainly as the hometown of Clara Bow, the first US-cinema sex symbol. Personally, I preferred Theda Bara, but…

I slowed down to the posted speed limits when I reached the city limits. We were back in cell coverage, and Mandy was back on the phone to the High Desert Clinic. "Hi, Suze. Can I talk to Erin? Well, I know, but it's really important…"

We waited, and I threaded my way across the town. Searchlight wasn't big, but its relative extravagance after beginning the evening in

Joshua Tree and passing though Amboy, Kelso, and Nipton made me feel like a farmboy with five bucks in his pocket on Saturday night.

"Erin? Can you check on records for Rachel…Huber?" She looked at me for confirmation, and I nodded. "I know. I know the rules… Well, to be frank, it's a domestic-abuse case, and—okay." She rubbed the fingers of her free hand back and forth across her thumb as she waited. "Uh-huh… Can you tell if—oh. Oh, I see. Do you have a number for him? Hang on." She dug through the magic bottomless pockets of her coat and found paper and a pen. "Okay…uh-huh. Shit. Listen, Erin, this may be nothing, but tell everybody to be careful, okay? No. No, I don't know any more… Well I'll tell you when I do… Yeah, thanks…bye."

Mandy pulled her chin down onto her chest with both hands clasped behind her head, tugged hard repeatedly, and let loose. "Damn. Tense." She looked around. "Are we there yet?"

"Getting close. What's the story?"

"Alright. Yes. Rachel was there. Was treated for some kind of a 'fall' down stairs. The quote marks were there in Erin's voice. You'd be amazed how many 'falls' down stairs women have around Yucca Valley. Really amazing considering there's really only about five stairways in the whole damn town… Referred to Selby. And even more, *transferred*… that's our fancy jargon for somebody who works there becoming the point of contact. In other words, like I'm doing with Deb, someone other than the clinic started getting all the correspondence. In this case, presumably Claire."

Vernor Court was off Hobson, well past the point where 164 crossed 95, the main north-south artery along the California-Nevada border. There wasn't much there: the street looked like it was slated for redevelopment, and there were a half-dozen concrete slabs where small houses had been ripped down. Derelict plumbing still reached up from the slabs like fingers trying to claw their way from the grave. The street was unlit, but the lights of the city center spilled down from the northwest, creating long and spindly shadows.

At the end of the street was a mobile home—a '50s model, small, in the evolutionary period where trailers with hitches mutated into mobile homes with skirts of redwood slats, hiding the fact that they had once moved down the road the same way former streetwalkers might fabricate a job history. It had been set up on the slab of a former house and tied into the pre-existing plumbing and electrical hookups.

Since it was the only intact building on the street, it wasn't surprising the crooked steel letters on the mailbox read, *63*.

The place was completely dark. I switched off the engine, stepped out, and immediately stumbled on a chunk of broken concrete. The whole street was like a demolition site. Plastic grocery bags and wadded sheets of paper stirred in the night breeze.

I walked across what passed for a front yard, littered with shingles, broken wood, and more wadded papers. There were two steps up to the front door. I tapped on it. It wasn't locked. In fact, it wasn't even shut. But when I pushed on it, the door bumped against something.

Mandy was right behind me. "Maybe I should get a flashlight," I said. She pushed past me and reached her hand inside the door, groping along the frame. She found a switch, and a light came on inside the house.

She pushed on the door, and said, "Shit." She put her shoulder to it, and pushed it open. Then she stepped in, stepped over something.

I stood on the top step and looked in. I assumed it was Rachel. One of her legs had been blocking the door from opening.

I had no idea how long she had been dead. I thought that the dead bloated and rotted after a few days, but this was the desert. I could feel the breeze from all the open louvers. Her skin was stretched tight and dry.

A chain was wound so tight around her neck that some of the links seemed to be missing under her paper-thin skin.

I stepped back, and before I realized what I was doing, I was back on the asphalt, next to the car. Mandy was right beside me. "We need to call the police…" I said.

"No." Mandy glared at me. "Not yet." She snatched up one of the plastic grocery sacks that quivered on the ground and then headed back up the steps.

"Hey…" I said. I followed her. She went right back inside. I was on the steps. "Mandy, you shouldn't disturb the evidence… We should get the police…"

She knelt next to the body. There was a little leather pouch on the floor, done up with a thong at the top. She looked up at me. "Just like Claire." She held down one side of the bag with a knuckle, and, wearing the grocery bag like a glove, undid the thong. She picked the bag up by a corner and tilted it. Dimes spilled out onto the floor.

"Dimes," I said stupidly.

She frowned for a moment and then straightened up. I realized the inside of the trailer was filled with torn-up and wadded paper. She stepped over the body and set about smoothing some of the sheets down to read them. "Mandy," I pleaded, "we really shouldn't mess up the evidence. Let's just call the police…"

She jumped to her feet. "Christ, Walker, will you shut up for a fucking second!" She stepped toward me, found Rachel's leg blocking her way. "Do you care about me at all? About Kirsten? Dawn? Any of us?"

"Of course," I said. And then I was jarred by the realization that these people meant more to me than anyone else in my life, past or present. "Of course I do."

"This freak may be after all of us. We don't have time to spend ten hours in a Nevada police station. We need to know what the hell is going on." She started to turn back to her papers, but stopped. "We both knew this was what we were going to find, didn't we? So stop acting so shocked."

I walked down off the stairs and stood in the empty street. The whole of Vernor Court was a wrecking yard, but a few miles away, Searchlight's little casinos shot their million-watt smiles up at the black desert sky.

I steered the Jeep slowly out of Vernor Court, avoiding pieces of two-by-four that might harbor tire-piercing nails. "You were right on target," Mandy said. "It looks to me like Selby did an emergency abortion. It's listed as 'emergency mid-term termination after trauma to womb; non-viable fetus and danger to mother's life.'"

"Which means?"

"I'm not sure. Could be we really had a dead baby in there; could just be cover-your-ass jargon for doing an abortion so late on an injured mother. But there's other papers that relate to hemorrhaging after another 'fall-related trauma.' Plenty of blood for your 'small dark world.'"

She had her cell phone out, but suddenly said, "Stop!"

"What?" My nerves were jangling.

"I need to go back. Just one second."

Reluctantly, I wheeled the car in a tight corner, and drove back to Rachel's last address.

Mandy flung herself from the Jeep, ran across the yard and up the steps, and flipped on the light. She disappeared inside for perhaps a minute. Then she killed the light, and came running back to the car.

"Go," she said as she slammed the door. I turned the car around and made my way back to Hobson.

"And?" I asked.

"Guess how many dimes."

"I don't know."

"C'mon, Walker, guess. I did."

"One hundred."

"One hundred? What does that have to do with anything?"

"I don't know. You told me to guess."

"Well, the answer is thirty." When I didn't get it, she said, "Thirty pieces of silver."

She punched numbers into her cell phone and listened. I asked, "Where are we going?"

She waved her hand for silence as she listened and scribbled something on a piece of paper. "Message machine," she said. "You better pull over."

I pulled over and watched her in the vague glow of a streetlight through the windshield. She dialed another number. She waited, and then said, "Sure. Sorry to bother you, but we had a patient under Dr. Selby's care, and… No. No, I hadn't heard; I'm stunned… So sorry… Sure, goodbye."

She flipped the phone shut. "Last week somebody shot Dr. Selby in the head with a rifle. Right in his fancy-assed Palm Springs driveway."

"But—but that doesn't make sense. A rifle? How does that tie in with strangulations?"

"I'll tell you how it ties in," she said, as if it were my fault. "Somebody who doesn't have the guts to face up to another man, but who gets off on hurting women, up close and personal. Fuck."

"We should tell somebody…"

"Damn right." She asked for the number for the San Bernardino county sheriff, Yucca Valley substation, and let it ring through. "Detective Bolles, please… Well, yes, it *is* an emergency. A family emergency… Tell him his Auntie Mame." She drummed her fingers and waited. "Rick. Mandy Cicerone. Give me a call on a non-official phone… Damn right it is." She rattled off her cell number and ended the call.

It rang again in a few seconds. "Mandy…uh-huh. Because this is an anonymous tip, that's why, and I know you guys have caller ID on anything that comes through the switchboard. We know who murdered Claire. Darnell Huber—yep, same one. We just dropped in on his wife, at 63 Vernor Court in Searchlight, Nevada, and she was killed in the same way as Claire Clayborne…down to the smallest detail, including the bag of dimes… Well, wouldn't you like to know? I told you the truth the first time I talked to you. I think he may be after me, Kirsten, Dawn, Erin Adams, anybody who worked at the clinic… Okay. I will. We'll talk."

She ended the call and said, "He wants to know if you believe him now. Do you?"

"That he didn't murder Claire? Sure. That he's some kind of saint? Not really."

Mandy held her address book out by the dashboard lights as I drove back down Hobson. She punched in a number and waited. "Hi. This is Mandy… I know, but where did she go?" There was a long pause, and she said, "Is Darnell around? …Okay, well look: if Darnell Huber shows up tonight, you find some excuse to— What? …Oh, fuck. Oh fuck." The agitation rolled off her in waves, and I pulled over. "Okay. Okay. If you do then keep him there. Shit."

She clenched her arms around her head with her fingers clasped behind her head, her elbows pressed together in front of her eyes. It seemed like she was trying to crush her own head.

"Mandy," I said.

"…fuck fuck fuck…"

"Mandy. Tell me what the problem is…!"

"Get over to 95 and head south. Get us to Needles. Now."

I obeyed, but once we had gone the two miles to 95 and turned left, I insisted. "What the hell is going on?"

"That was Perry. Kirsten is out at her parents' cabin in Needles."

"So? We knew that she was going there. Or back to Santa Monica."

She breathed for a moment. "So does Darnell. He and Perry were just talking about it this afternoon. The two of them go out there fishing sometimes. He knows she's there. He knows where it is."

"Well, Jesus, Mandy, call the cops! Call Bolles!"

"We're closer than he is. We'll get there faster."

"So what? He can call out the police in Needles! They can be there faster than anybody!"

She just sat there, rocking forward and back like an autistic child.

I stepped on the brakes and steered toward the side of the road. "Goddamn, Mandy, if you don't call I will—!"

She waved her hands as if clearing away fog. "Okay, okay. I'll call. Just keep going."

She held her address book to the dash again, punched in numbers, waited. "Bolles. Mandy again… Yeah…Kirsten is in Needles, Darnell knows she's there… Sure. It's forty-five forty-five Edgewater… Good. Warn them that we're coming too."

She snapped the phone shut. "Drive fast," she said.

38

We made it from Searchlight to Needles in about three-quarters of an hour. Mandy was silent most of the way, rocking ever so slightly in her seat. When we hit Interstate 40 she seemed to wake up. "Take the Broadway-River Road exit. Here. Here."

She guided me down the off-ramp, but immediately had me spin back north on River Road. When I heard about Kirsten's cabin, I had assumed it was remote, but it was just to the north of town proper, close to the water.

Edgewater itself was a nearly deserted street, parts of which might have been paved in the remote past. Sad ironwoods stood in dark, undeveloped lots. "Stop here," Mandy said. I pulled over. "Shut it off."

I obeyed, but said, "Why? There's nothing right here…" but Mandy had already opened her door and stepped out onto the soft shoulder.

I jumped out my side. "Mandy, what's up? There's nothing here."

She said, "Shh!" and pointed to the lights of a house largely hidden by a grove of trees, about thirty yards away. She started to move that direction.

I caught up to her. "Where's the police?"

"Be…quiet!" she hissed.

"But why aren't the police here?" I whispered.

She kept moving, stealthily but fast, and I hustled along next to her. "I don't get it," I whispered.

"I lied," she said.

"What?"

She stopped. "I lied. I didn't make that second call to Bolles." She stepped over the shoulder of the street and into the grove of ironwoods and christmasberries which passed for a yard. I saw her pull something out of her pocket and realized it was her pistol.

"The gun?" I asked, meaning when did you get it, why do you have it, and what are you planning, all at once.

She stopped again and this time faced me in the shadows of the trees. "Getting this is the whole reason I went home to shower. I thought it might come to this."

"Mandy, this is crazy…"

"Walker: either shut up or go away." She turned and moved off through the trees.

I hesitated and then followed.

Past the little desert forest was a small, probably one-bedroom house—perhaps a "cabin" by the standards of Kirsten's Santa Monica parents. All the lights in the front rooms were on, and the curtains, if such existed, were open, letting a blaze of light out into the night. I could hear a radio playing, and when I listened attentively, I made out the strains of Hank Williams, singing of a lonesome whippoorwill.

It seemed innocent enough, but Mandy crept up to the window to the right of the front door and peeked over the sill. I crouched low and snuck up behind her, but as I did I noticed the bed of an old Ford pickup sticking out around the right side of the house. In the contrast of light and dark, I couldn't be absolutely certain what color it was.

We were looking into a sparse living room with two doors, probably bedroom and bathroom, on the rear wall. To the left of the front door was a dining room and kitchen, but the table and chairs had been smashed into a pile of kindling. In the far corner, where the back wall and kitchen counter met, sat Darnell in an armchair he'd dragged back there. He sat in a pair of grayish boxer shorts, legs splayed apart, eyes closed. A fifth of Jim Beam stood on the floor by his feet. The radio we could hear stood on the kitchen counter, a few feet from his head.

Before I could react, Mandy moved over to the front door. I almost tried to grab her, but realized this would cause a commotion. She glanced back at me and pointed to something near the door handle. I bent down and duckwalked my way over.

The door seemed closed, but it had been kicked in, splintering the frame. Mandy poked with her finger and it gave a little. "Wait…" I said.

Mandy responded by kicking the door open and stepping inside with the pistol extended in a double-handed grip. She stomped forward and stopped. Against my better judgment I stepped in behind her.

Darnell was wide awake but drunk, and he stared at us with red-rimmed eyes. "Aww, shit, look what we got here. Little girl with a big gun. And who's'at with ya?" He squinted. "If it ain't the goddamned brother. Hardly knowed ya without the beard."

"Where's Kirsten?" Mandy demanded.

"Who the fuck're you to be asking questions?" There was a big butcher knife laying on the counter, and he lifted his arm in that direction.

Mandy took two steps forward and shot the radio. Darnell and I both jumped. The sound was more like what I expected from a cannon than a pistol. "Give me an excuse to shoot you, fuckhead," she said. "If Kirsten's dead, you're dead already."

He threw up his hands and leaned back in the chair. "Your little friend's still alive. Shouldn't be. But I saw as we was all alone, and I said, why'nt you show her a last good time?"

Mandy trembled as she stepped closer, about ten feet from him. "You *fuck…*" she said. I thought she might shoot him, and from the look on his face, so did he.

But the moment passed, and he sneered. "Shoot me. It's you witches as ought to die. You're the murderers." His face contorted, and a tear ran down out of one eye. "Killed my baby boy. My only baby boy. Waited my whole life, God promised him to me, just like Abraham, all them years childless…" Drunken tears flowed down both cheeks now.

I felt a bizarre mix of pity, fear, and revulsion, but Mandy seemed to share none of these feelings. "You killed him yourself, you stupid sonofabitch, by hitting Rachel when she was pregnant."

"The Lord would have preserved him, would have preserved both of them. A man is meant to *lead* his wife, and to correct her how he chooses!"

Mandy exhaled long and hard. "Walker. Come." I moved up next to her. "Take the gun. If he moves an inch, kill him."

She pressed the gun into my hands before I could argue, and the only response I could think of was to level it at Darnell's face. Mandy almost ran through the living room, jerked the bedroom door open, and disappeared.

Darnell looked at me for a long time, and then very slowly bent forward and picked up his bottle of Jim Beam. He sat back, unscrewed the top, crossed his legs, and took a big drink. "Your sister'd be mighty disappointed, me back on the sauce like this…but it's her fault more'n anybody's. Pretended to be my friend, Rachel's friend. Then she rips up my family. Takes Rachel away, kills my baby boy…" He wiped the back of his hand across his cheeks. From the bedroom I heard sobbing, and Mandy's voice talking low and urgent.

Darnell took another drink. For a moment his face looked sad—not the demented self-pity he had been putting out, but just sad and defeated. But then a smile appeared at one side of his mouth, and he said, "So, you aiming to shoot me? Over your sister and all?"

I didn't answer. I could hear things happening in the bedroom, water running in the bathroom, closet doors, footsteps…

"Don't seem like you, now. That murdering witch with you, she'd kill me soon as look at me…but you…"—another big drink—"I ain't sure you got it in you, shoot an unarmed man."

I wasn't sure if I had it in me to kill someone no matter what the status of their armaments might be, but he was making me so nervous that I was afraid I might shoot him by accident. He seemed to see this, and said, "Whoa, there, steady, boy. You sure you don't want a drink? No. Well, I don't mind if *I* do…"

The bedroom door creaked open and Mandy stalked out, leaving it open behind her. She veered toward Darnell and threw something at his head, hard, a stiff overhand pitch. It caught him just above the eyebrow and then thumped heavily to the floor. He and I both looked at the missile. It was a leather pouch heavy with coins.

He carefully screwed the cap back on his bottle and put it on the floor before he felt at his forehead. His fingers came away wet with blood. This pleased him. "Whoo-eee, what a little firecracker! Sorry that warn't you tied to the bed all afternoon! We woulda had us some fun…"

Mandy didn't even look at him after she threw the pouch, but came straight over to me. "Give me the gun back."

Her voice was so flat there was no doubt in my mind what she intended. Darnell had the same idea: his hilarity vanished and he shrank down in the chair.

"Just calm down, Mandy," I said. I was trying to maintain a soothing voice, but it sounded thin and reedy in my ears.

She stood right next to me, and said, very quietly, "Give me the gun."

"No. Just take care of Kirsten and then get the cops here."

She tried to take the gun out of my hands, and I wouldn't let her. She had the advantage: she was trying to pry my fingers off the pistol, and I was trying to hang on to it, and watch Darnell, and keep from accidentally firing. She was surprisingly strong, but still no match for me, and I managed to keep the gun in my hands and pointed in more or less the right direction.

By this point Darnell had recovered his uncouth poise, and was showing an open grin at our struggle. I could see him eyeing the knife on the counter and wondering if it was worth a try. "Dammit, Mandy…" I hissed.

Darnell turned his eyes away from the counter to look in the direction of the living room. I glanced that way and froze. Mandy felt the change in my body and stopped struggling.

Kirsten was there. She was wearing a man's bathrobe, thick blue terrycloth, several sizes too large. Her hands were in the pockets and her arms were hunched forward as if protecting her breasts.

Mandy let loose and turned toward her. Kirsten was about ten feet from us, ten from Darnell, a perfect equilateral triangle. Kirsten's glossy curls were damped and flat atop her head, and her face had angry red marks along one side. But it was the eyes that showed the injury, some kind of dark hurt back there I couldn't begin to understand.

"Kirsten," I said. I was afraid that Darnell would somehow get ahold of her.

"Kirsten," Mandy said, moving toward her.

Kirsten took two wobbly steps, and then with shocking strength ran forward and raked her fingernails across Darnell's face. Darnell shrieked, but jumped to his feet, grabbed a handful of Kirsten's hair, and spun her around in front of him as his right hand groped across the counter. Mandy flew forward straight at Darnell and blasted pepper spray into his eyes pointblank, and at the same moment Kirsten twisted in his grip and rammed a pair of scissors into his windpipe.

She yanked the scissors back and the blood spurted from his severed carotids. One hand clutched his throat, but the other clawed at his blinded, burning eyes. He staggered forward, and then fell flat on his back, gurgling and choking on his own blood.

Mandy pulled Kirsten out of the way, for a moment, but Kirsten hurled herself onto her knees at his side and, raising the scissors high, stabbed him again and again, at first in the belly, but then in the crotch. When he stopped moving, she curled down into a ball and lay on her side. Her shoulders moved up and down convulsively, but I heard no sound. The blood continued to well up from Darnell's throat and run out across the floor, and Kirsten's robe soaked it up.

"Deuteronomy twenty-two, you sonofabitch," Mandy whispered.

Through all of this I stood there with the pistol aimed at where Darnell had been sitting.

Mandy tried to get Kirsten up off the floor, but she just stayed there in a ball. "Put down the gun and help me," Mandy said.

Between the two of us we pulled her to her feet, but when Kirsten saw my face she recoiled in horror.

Because I was male, I suppose.

Mandy led her back into the bedroom. I heard the shower start up. I wandered aimlessly around the room. Mandy came back out. "I found some Vicodin and gave her too many." She opened the refrigerator, studied the contents, and pulled out a large bottle of Coke. She opened cupboards, found a large glass, filled it halfway with Coke, and then stepped over the pool of blood where Darnell lay as a centerpiece. She topped up the glass with Jim Beam.

"Is that for Kirsten?" I asked.

"No, I realized I was being a bad hostess, and made you a drink."

"You aren't supposed to drink when you take painkillers."

"You aren't. Kirsten is about to show you why."

I waited. I looked around for a phone, realized there wasn't one. The shower stopped. I heard voices from the bedroom, and Mandy came out, closing the door but not pulling it shut, the way parents do with small children.

"Now I *will* make you a drink." She poured out two bourbon-and-Cokes and went into the living room and sat on the couch. She waited until I joined her, and then handed me my drink.

"I imagine even you will agree that it's time to call the cops now."

She frowned. "I have no intention of calling the police. Ever. The only question is what we do with the body."

I was stunned. "How on earth—"

"Look. Walker. Think about it. We went looking for this guy. He killed your sister and my friend. He killed his own wife. He raped Kirsten, and did things to her she may never get over."

"Exactly. Which is why, if we just explain what happened—"

"There's a bullet hole in the wall, the guy has been hit with pepper spray, stabbed in the throat, and had his genitals mutilated. You think that's going to look like justifiable homicide? Or will it look like we tracked him down, held him at gunpoint, and then tortured him to death?" She took a drink, muttered, "Not that he didn't deserve it."

"I'm not so sure…"

"Walker, I'm begging you. Think about it, just really think about it for a minute." She sat her glass on the floor and went back into the bedroom.

I did think about it, then, and despite my best efforts it looked to me like Mandy was right. With one possible exception. When she came back, looking worn, I asked, "Isn't Kirsten going to need medical attention? And won't that alert everybody to the fact she's been raped? And then they'll investigate…"

"Kirsten's hurt, but she'll be okay, physically." Then, almost to herself, she said, "Hope the fuckhead didn't give her a disease or get her pregnant. That'd just be too much to take. But we can use Dawn and the clinic to keep things confidential."

"Will Kirsten *want* to keep things confidential?"

"The problem is usually that women don't want to talk about it. It isn't that they can't keep from blabbing. She killed somebody, admittedly with our assistance…I think she'll be more than content to leave that alone."

We sat in silence for a while, and Mandy said, "I'm glad we killed him. And you won't admit it, but I think you are too… So do we dump him in the river, bury him out back, or what?"

I thought for a while. I hadn't been much use so far.

But this part I could do.

The only hitch was Mandy insisted that we take Kirsten with us. There was no way that a sleeping Kirsten and a dead Darnell would fit conveniently in the back seat of a Jeep Wrangler, and there wasn't a trunk. The only workable solution would have been grotesque: sit Darnell's body up on the seat and lay Kirsten's head on his lap. But leaving Kirsten at the house, drugged, traumatized, and alone wasn't a pretty idea, either, so we hunted down the keys to Kirsten's Toyota.

We trussed Darnell up in a blue tarp from the carport, wrapped tight in duct tape. We loaded all of the bloodstained clothes into garbage bags, and then mopped and swabbed the floor as well as we could. With the volume of blood he had poured out, any serious forensics examination would find plenty of evidence anyway.

When we finished the cleanup, Mandy called Dawn, gave the short version of the events of the night, and told her to drive out as soon as she could. We lugged Darnell and the trash bags out and stuffed them in the trunk.

Mandy needed my help to dress Kirsten. I was worried Kirsten would see me and panic, but after Mandy let me into the room I was more concerned Kirsten would stop breathing: the booze and pills had done their work. It was dim in the bedroom, and this let me try not to see the marks on her body. Moment by moment I was feeling better and better about Darnell's death.

I carried Kirsten out to her own car and laid her in the back seat, while Mandy raided the little trunk of the Jeep for supplies. As I suggested, she came back with the five-gallon can of gasoline and my emergency kit.

We left an unlocked—indeed, unlockable—house, with most of the lights on.

It was a short drive up River Road, one of the darkest stretches of highway in the world. The blackness of the River looms off to the east, and the Dead Mountains rise up on the west. Glimmering lights from houses across the river just make it seem darker.

Most people think the Dead Mountains are so-called because they are barren, but by desert standards they are teeming with life along the canyon bottoms, including the northernmost stand of crucifixion thorns, and a few pools of standing water. No, the Dead Mountains are where the local tribes cremated their deceased for millennia, and ancestral spirits must be so thick on the ground there by now that you can't sit on a rock without pushing someone's relatives out of the way.

Despite the high population of ghosts, the Dead Mountains are relatively unspoiled because the whites couldn't figure how to squeeze much out of them. There's a single decent mine, Deep Horn, and it only produced for a few years in the 1870s before it too was a ghost. Lots of little holes were dug in the vicinity, but the one big vein was apparently a freak. The Dead Mountains are now a seldom-visited wilderness area, with a long cherrystem road running in to the mine, still open to such vehicles as might care to work their way in.

I had been to Deep Horn many times, one of the few deep cuts in this area, but in the dark I almost missed the little Jeep trail that led inward. I edged the Toyota off the friendly, trustworthy asphalt, and onto a road that was an easy drive in a Jeep, but called for white-knuckle concentration in a two-wheel drive car with a low clearance. "Keep your fingers crossed," I said.

"It's okay," Mandy replied, "I've got triple-A."

It took us thirty minutes to go three miles. I could imagine us getting stuck here, with little surrounding cover and a corpse in the trunk. At one point we bottomed out hard, and Kirsten moaned and moved in the back seat. I was glad to have confirmation she was still alive.

I finally parked beside the huge tailings spill below the mine entrance. We locked the car—I'm not sure why—and popped the trunk. We wrestled Darnell's body out and then dragged him up forty feet of loose tailings, sliding two feet back for every three feet we pulled him along. We were both exhausted by the time we stumbled to the top; we sat next to his tarped corpse and panted in the dark.

We went down again for the flashlights, and started the long process of dragging Darnell into the mine.

Deep Horn is a strange mine by High Desert standards. Most of the mines in the Mojave start in the side of a hill and run in, branching out as the miners chased the veins, but not gaining or losing much in elevation. Deep Horn runs in about one hundred feet, with a couple of minor side-tunnels, and then opens into a sizeable chamber, about twenty by twenty. At the rear of this chamber the ceiling is heavily braced, and the tunnel suddenly turns into a pit, not going quite straight down, but inclined at about eighty degrees. It is steep enough that the only way down is a long wooden ladder held to the side by spikes. It runs down 214 feet. The last time I had gone down, I had counted seventeen missing rungs, but all in all it was well-preserved for a nineteenth-century operation. It pained me a little to vandalize it, but most of the powers-that-be were all in favor of shutting off old shafts in any case. Just doing my part for current bureaucratic theories.

We left Darnell laying there like a low-rent King Tut and went back to get the bloodstained clothing, the gasoline can, and the emergency kit. After lugging Darnell all that way, it felt like we floated back up the tailings and into the heart of the mine.

I used a pocketknife to cut him out of the tarp, rolled him onto the floor, and kicked the bloody tarp down the shaft. I piled Kirsten's blood-soaked robe and our cleaning rags next to his body and used a half-gallon of gasoline to soak the cloth, also splashing Darnell liberally. I dragged his head to the top of the shaft, and then walked around and lifted his feet. His body was beginning to stiffen. I pushed him forward like a wheelbarrow, and then let loose as he fell.

I shone my light down the long ladder. About fifty feet down, Darnell's arm had caught over a rung. I made Mandy hold a flashlight as I climbed down. I had never been thrilled by the climb at Deep Horn, but this time I was so annoyed I forgot to be frightened.

Somehow his forearm had gotten between a rung and the wall, and his whole weight hung from his elbow. I stood on the rung just above it and stomped with all my might. Nothing. I stomped again and again, hammering my foot down on the rung and his arm both. When it finally gave way, I slipped a little, enough to make me remember that I'm not brave. His body jarred against rung after rung, until I heard a satisfying thud and then silence.

We gathered such loose wood as we could find, soaked it in gasoline, and then tossed it down the shaft. I used the rest of the gasoline to soak all of the posts and pilings around the shaft, splashing it as high up the beams as I could.

Last of all, Mandy threw her pistol down the shaft.

We walked back to the opening to the chamber, and maybe fifteen feet down the entry tunnel. I handed Mandy the car keys. "You should wait outside."

"Hey, forget the hero stuff. I can stand here just as good as you can."

"You're always telling me to think. Well, think: if something goes wrong and we're both here, Kirsten's doped up in the back of a car with no keys. Get out at least to the top of the spoils heap."

She nodded, touched my arm, and then ran down the tunnel, the beam from her flashlight bouncing crazily.

I had two flares. I lit one, listened to the initial snaps and pops change to a long steady hiss, and then threw it hard. Too hard: it hit the back wall of the chamber. But it fell down the shaft anyway.

I hadn't reckoned with the power of gasoline vapors in an enclosed area. I heard a distinct, far-off *foomp*! and, about ten seconds later, a pillar of fire roared up out of the shaft. I wouldn't need a second flare, so I dropped it and ran as hard as I could. I had visions of flames racing along behind me.

There were no flames behind me when I hurtled out of the minemouth, but I could hear the crackling of the fire amplified to a trumpeting roar by the tunnel. I grabbed Mandy by the hand and pulled her off to the side of the tailings heap and we slid down about ten feet before our rumps went down hard on the slope of shattered rock.

We turned over on our bellies and watched the smoke come out. After a few minutes, there was a trembling in the ground, and a cloud of dust and smoke shot from the mouth of the tunnel like a waterspout from a blowhole.

It took twenty minutes before the sounds stopped and we convinced ourselves it was safe to venture in. Just as we started down the tunnel, there was one final crumbling fall of rock.

It was still a little smoky, and maybe not as rich in oxygen as might be preferred, but we picked our way back to the main chamber. Or, rather, what was left of the main chamber. The ceiling along the back wall had given way completely. The main shaft was choked with tons of rock, and the ceiling was now a good twenty feet higher. I shone my light up on the newly exposed rock, and saw the snowy glisten of freshly opened quartz. I laughed. I was certain that, if I had the equipment and I dared climb up there, I would find the thin traceries of gold running through the whiteness, running up and up.

"What's funny?" Mandy asked, and coughed.

"Geology joke. Don't worry about it."

I was happy to get out of the mine. Destabilize a support system and things usually continue falling, often over a period of years.

Mandy turned wordlessly and hugged me, her face pressed against my chest. I held her, and we just stood there, atop the spoils heap. I would have been happy to stay in the moment forever.

39

Back in Needles, Kirsten was still so solidly asleep I could pick her up like a child; she weighed nothing after lugging Darnell. Mandy shut the car door behind me and ran ahead to push open the front door.

I felt something wasn't right the moment I stepped inside, but I wasn't sure until I heard a sound from the bedroom. *Ching ching ching*…and then, whistling in time to his jingling change:

Dashing through the snow ching ching ching
Inna one-horse open sleigh ching ching ching
O'er the fields we go ching ching ching
Laughing all the way ha ha ha…

Mandy stared at me in bafflement and fear. For once in my life I was a step ahead of her; I knew who this was.

I pushed open the bedroom door with my foot, and stepped around him. He kept jingling the change in his pocket, but stopped whistling. I laid Kirsten down on the bed, smoothed back her hair, and said, "She needs her sleep. Let's go into the living room."

Bolles nodded, and led the way out. I turned off the light and pulled the door shut behind me.

"Mandy," he said, with a tilt of his head, as if they had just bumped into one another at the county fair.

"How'd you find us?" she asked.

He made a mock-pained face. "I may not be Nancy Drew, but I do have my methods. If I'm looking for Darnell, I go to the Ranch, if

I go to the Ranch, I see Perry. Even us civil servants can connect three or four dots."

"But what are you doing here?"

He sat down on the couch and leaned his arms along the back of the couch, expansive. "Just keeping an eye out for the citizens of this great county. Here, for example, we have some honest citizens who take off without locking up their houses. Don't even lock their Jeeps. Who knows what might have happened if I hadn't dropped through to prevent possible burglaries?"

To my horror, I saw he'd brought the printouts from Claire's computer; the folder lay open on the couch. He followed my glance, and said, "Interesting reading. Yeah, yeah, don't tell me, a copy has been sent to your lawyer, blah blah." He peered at me. "Good look for you, without the beard. Must help with dating these younger women, huh?"

He jumped up from the couch and balanced on the balls of his feet. "You know, sometimes I think nobody really loves me…because love is based on trust, and it seems like nobody trusts me." He made his trademark wide eyes at me. "Everything I told you out at Hidden Valley that day was true. But you still thought, oh, maybe old Rick's on the take, maybe his criminal flunkies offed my sister. Now that hurts, Walker. I really thought we had an understanding…plus now you know for sure it wasn't me."

"So what are you going to do?" I asked.

"Me? Me, I was going to take my cue from you. Probably I'm not going to do anything but drive back and issue an APB for Darnell Huber. Of course, if you go waving around wild accusations like in those printouts—well, in one of those printouts—then it might make it hard for me to do my job."

"And what's your job here, Rick?" Mandy asked.

"Just making sure everybody's all right out here. Looks okay to me. Kirsten's a little sleepy, but she's a growing girl. House is a little messed up, what with a bullethole in the wall, and sacks of dimes laying around, and a chain in the bedroom. Ropes around the legs of the bed, too, but hey—not my job to probe into your sex lives."

He put his hands behind his back, and walked back and forth. "Course, if there were to be a bunch of wild accusations made about me, we'd probably have to look into things a little closer. Don't really see how that could be avoided, do you?"

"Assuming," I said, "just assuming there's no wild accusations made, what then?"

"I go back to minding my own business and you go back to minding yours. And, of course, everybody in the country looks for Darnell. Too bad nobody knows where he is."

"And that's it?"

"And that's it."

Outside a car pulled into the drive. Bolles looked quizzical as the car door slammed, and then gave a tight smile as the front door opened. "If it isn't Dawn. You know, kids, maybe we should just all move out here together. It's the only time we all see each other anymore."

Dawn stood stupidly in the doorway clutching her nurse's bag. Mandy grabbed her by the wrist and led her back into the bedroom.

Bolles gave a long stretch, arms up high overhead. "Well, I'd love to stay and chat. By the way, that's a nice truck outside. A real classic. Can't be too many yellow '54 Ford pickups still on the road in these parts."

"What's your point?"

"I'm kind of a general law enforcement buff, you know. Like, just the other day, I was reading about how down in Tijuana at the crossing into Mexico, with it being a free trade area and all, you can just drive right across the border. So people steal cars and take them down there."

"And?"

"Now the border patrol has these automatic cameras that record every license plate that crosses, and they stop any car listed as stolen. But it also means we can now see who's leaving the country. Oh, we don't get instant feedback; but you can check and see if a particular set of tags crossed the border."

"I'm not following you."

"I'm saying that if, for example, Darnell drove his truck across the border anytime soon, then after we sent out an APB, we'd know he'd gone to Mexico. Off to Ensenada. Up to the Federales to find him."

"And what would he do with his truck once he got down there?"

"I'm sure I don't know. But you're from San Diego, so I bet you've heard how careful you have to be when you park in TJ. Leave your keys in the car by accident, and in no time the thing is gone, and cut up for parts. Been to Tijuana lately?"

"Not for years."

He opened the front door. "You should really visit. After all, it's right by your home, isn't it?" He waggled his fingers. "Toodle-doo."

I opened the door to the bedroom and peeked in. Kirsten was groggy, but awake. When she saw my face, she rolled her head away and shut her eyes.

I closed the door and sat down on the couch. It was almost one in the morning. Twenty-four hours ago I had been on drugs out in the Sheephole Valley. Twelve hours ago I had been racking my brain to find Claire's password. Six hours ago I was looking at Rachel's body. I was tired, but I knew I needed to steel myself to stay up another eight to ten hours minimum.

Dawn and Mandy came out. "She's sleeping again," Mandy said.

"Why does she hate *me?*" I asked. The way she shrank from me hurt my feelings far more than I would have imagined, and was surprising given I was one of her rescuers.

"Don't take it personally," Dawn said.

"How should I take it? Generically?"

"Yes, actually," Mandy said. "You're a man. This doesn't happen to you guys. It happened to her. Don't expect her to be mature about it just a couple hours afterwards."

"C'mon, Mandy," Dawn said, "men get raped all the time. If you include prison rapes, way more men than women get raped every year. And they almost *never* report it."

"Fine," Mandy said. "But how often do women rape men?"

"Can't argue with that," Dawn said.

Neither could I. "To change the subject, I'm afraid Mandy and I need to take a long trip." I explained about the truck.

Mandy looked at Dawn. "Will you be alright here?"

"Sure. What's happening now is ten percent physical, ninety percent mental."

Dawn hugged us goodbye and went back into the bedroom.

"We need to stop and get some large coffees before we leave town," I said.

"No shit." Mandy leaned up against me, slid an arm around my waist. "I didn't mean to sound like I was blaming you for what happened to Kirsten just because you're a male. If they were all like you, the world would be a better place... Weird, really freaking weird, but better."

I drove the truck fast, but always under the speed limit. Mandy followed in the Jeep. We stopped at a coffee shop in Escondido around dawn and ate breakfast, a silent and hoggish meal. In total it took a little over six hours to get to San Ysidro.

Mandy pulled the Jeep into one of the big tourist lots near the border. I idled on the road until I could see where she had parked.

I was too tired to be nervous. I steered Darnell's truck into the stream of morning traffic. We moved faster than usual. I thought the border had become more efficient until I realized it was early Sunday morning: little trade-zone traffic, and too early for the tourists. When I pulled by the guard booths they glanced curiously at the classic truck but incuriously at my bland face.

I drove through the main interchange as cautiously as if I were in a retirement village; I couldn't afford even the slightest accident. I swung west onto Calle Tercera Cabrillo Puerto, crossed Avenida Revolucion, drove two more blocks, and headed north.

The neighborhood was a ten-minute walk from Tijuana's busiest tourist area, but it was a place I wouldn't want to be at night. At seven in the morning, the same people who would turn into predators by late afternoon merely stared, their juices not yet flowing.

I parked the truck with the keys in the ignition and for good measure rolled down the windows. I slammed the door. My butt was sore from the drive, and my back gave a little twinge of soreness. Softball. Who would have thought?

If you ever need to get out of Tijuana quickly, the way to do it is on foot. Up Avenida Revolucion, cross the bridge over the Via Oriente, and you are at a large tourist plaza devoted mainly to discount pharmacies and dentists. From there an enclosed pedestrian walkway takes you over the freeway and guard stations, and devolves you directly into the US Customs inspection station. It can take two hours for a bus to fight its way across the same distance, and a private car can take even longer.

Since I had no purchases I expected to breeze through, but security measures had been increased. The agent frowned at my driver's license. "You look different without your beard. Where are you employed?"

I tossed him my faculty ID and he examined it.

"Okay." He handed everything back with a wink. I must have looked thoroughly debauched. "Hope you had a good night of it."

I walked the quarter mile back to the parking lot, took the driver's seat from Mandy, and headed for my apartment in La Jolla.

My condo is nice enough: clean, bright, spacious. My balcony looks down three stories onto a pool and spa, and out over the cliffs to a gorgeous view of the Pacific. But it's a lifeless place, white walls, tan carpet, unobtrusive art. It had only been two weeks since I was here last, but it felt like a diorama in a museum: realistic recreation of American apartment circa 2000, with many actual artifacts from the period. Only my office in the spare bedroom had anything of me in it, the stacks of books and reports, the jumble that accompanies even the most organized life in academia.

Mandy looked around, and said, "I liked you better back in the desert."

"I liked me better there too."

Mandy went to shower, and I sprawled sideways on the couch, drained. Eventually she came out in a cloud of steam, one towel wrapped around her, and another tied up in that turban that all women seem to know how to make.

I took her place in the shower. I soaped and scrubbed, soaped and scrubbed, trying to wash everything away, trying to purify myself.

I dried, wrapped a towel around my waist, and walked into my bedroom. Mandy stood naked in front of an open drawer, pulling out one of my T-shirts. "Sorry," I said, and started to back out of the room.

She turned in my direction. "C'mon, Walker, you've seen me naked before." She pulled the shirt up over her head and arms and let it fall like a sail running down. "For that matter, I've seen you crawl naked through a hole underneath some rocks. You still have scratches, in fact." She used her thumbs to toss her damp hair out of the collar of the shirt. "What's the big deal? Do you object to it?"

"Not at all. I just didn't want to embarrass you."

"Embarrassing is finding out I had spinach in my teeth, not admitting that I have skin under my clothes." She crossed over to the bed, yanked the covers down, and climbed onto the bed. She yawned and stretched her arms out over her head. "Oh. Man, sometimes there isn't anything better…"

I headed toward the door as she pulled up the covers. "Hey," she said, "where are you going?"

"I'll get some blankets and make up the couch."

"Don't be silly. Don't we know each other well enough now to sleep in the same bed? Does the idea bother you?"

Now that Melanie's spell had vanished, literally, I found myself admiring Mandy more and more, not just for her looks, but for her everything. "No," I lied, "it doesn't bother me."

"Then drop the towel or put on whatever you sleep in, and come to bed. I can't stay awake any longer."

I took off my glasses and sat them atop the dresser. I pulled out a pair of boxers and, staying turned away from the bed, dropped the towel and stepped into them. I almost stooped down to pick up the damp towel and take it to the bathroom, but then decided to hell with it. I slid into bed and pulled up the covers, just in time: my cock had stiffened like a teenager's. This was ridiculous. We were both frazzled with exhaustion. Moreover, I didn't know Mandy's rules. This might seem like a romantic situation to me, but that didn't mean the possibility had even crossed her mind.

Mandy was on her side, faced away from me, that astonishing upslope of female hip jutting up beneath the covers like a swollen volcanic intrusion. I turned on my side and edged over closer to her.

Without turning she said, "You probably really don't want to sleep with me, you know."

"What do you mean? I thought that was exactly what we were doing here."

"Fine, be coy. I mean you probably don't want to fuck me. Or get otherwise romantic. Is that more precise?"

I was glad she was turned away so she couldn't see the blush rising on my beardless face. I was in bed discussing sex with a woman I'd never even kissed. I decided to say what I thought. "And here I thought you were psychic. You couldn't be wronger. Might not be the best time for it…"

"I certainly agree with that."

"…and I know you probably don't feel the same way I do…"

She turned her head and shoulders toward me, peeked out of one dark eye. "Oh, on the contrary, you're a prime candidate. We've gotten stoned together, killed somebody together and torched the body, and just this morning committed grand theft auto. How much more intimate can you get?"

"I don't know…vomiting with Melanie was a moment I don't share with just everybody. There was something special there."

"Well, I'll be happy to barf with you sometime. What I meant is that getting involved with me doesn't usually work very well. Especially the sex part. I mean, it usually works fine for me, but the guys don't like the way it lets me inside their head. It's like I'm fucking them back, and they usually don't care for it. If you really want to be naked…"

"Is that an invitation?"

"Jesus, you're relentless. More in the nature of a rain check. But you've been warned. Most guys don't like it much after they've had a taste of it."

"Most guys aren't as mature as I am. I'm forty-four. Probably too old for you."

"My driver's license says thirty-eight, but I assure you, I'm about ten thousand. And I'm going to crumble into dust if I don't go to sleep in a second." She grabbed my arm and pulled it over her shoulder as she turned away, reeling me over against her like a cable onto a spool. "Sleep," she said.

I relaxed, at least from the waist up, and snuggled up against her. She adjusted her hips a little and chuckled when she felt my erection. "We'll work this all out later, okay?" she said. "Not that it isn't flattering…"

It felt like if I pressed the issue she would respond. At that moment sex and sleep both seemed equally attractive, but I could always sleep. What if this were my only chance?

"There'll be plenty of chances, you know," she said. Her breathing became more regular, and I was sure she was gone.

I hugged her a little closer and let myself relax into a warm haze, smelling the clean dampness of her hair.

I felt something move on the bed and I opened one eye. It was Claire, who had pulled herself onto Mandy's side of the bed, sitting crosslegged. She smiled at me, and I smiled back, happy in my little dream. She looked down at Mandy's head burrowed against the pillow, and she reached down and softly stroked her hair.

"I feel her too, you know," Mandy mumbled. She pulled my arm tighter around her.

Then we went to sleep, just the three of us.

THE END

David T. Isaak (1954-2021) was an American author of both fiction and nonfiction.

Dr. Isaak held a BA in Physics and MA and PhD degrees in resource systems. His professional work spanned the globe, taking him to over forty countries. He co-authored three technical, nonfiction books on oil and international politics, and wrote numerous papers, monographs, and multiclient studies.

David had an eclectic life. His first major in college was music, and he played piano and flute. He was a certified Bikram yoga instructor, an accomplished vegetarian cook, a creative mixologist, and an avid reader of fiction and nonfiction alike. He was driven by great characters and story, original voices, and especially by his love of the craft of writing, all of which are reflected in his own writing.

David passed away in April 2021. The five novels he left behind are as diverse as his life. These novels form ***The Isaak Collection***.

Sign up here to stay in touch and receive regular updates about ***The Isaak Collection***:
https://theisaakcollection.co/IWillFollowYou

If you enjoyed this book, please consider leaving a review wherever you purchased the book. Thank you.

Keep reading for the first chapter of
book 4 in **The Isaak Collection**

EARTHLY VESSELS

The Isaak Collection
David T. Isaak

1 | East Coast People Are Weird

The guardians of the traditional religions might not admit it, but the key to the meaning of life, to the *Mysterium Tremendum*, is real estate. Location, location, location. Everything that exists has to have somewhere to be. Even space takes up space.

Yet any realtor can tell you that the value of real estate changes with time. In 2031 BC, for example, the most coveted property on Earth was the huge flint mine in Britain, the mounds and tunnels now known as Grimes Graves. Jump forward to 1348 AD, and the most jealously guarded holding on the planet was the island of Murano in Venice, home to the fabled Venetian glass industry.

A little time changes everything. By 1969, despite the fact the farmland had been covered by concrete and the oyster beds ruined by pollution, despite the lack of any deposits of valuable minerals, despite the absence of any strategic industries, despite the distinct proximity of New Jersey, the most prized piece of land anywhere on Earth was the island of Manhattan.

A puzzle, but not one that concerned most people. Nor did they much care it was 1969. "The Sixties" was a misnomer: the period where America came unglued, when anything seemed possible, when bones bent and walls flexed, began with the release of *Sgt. Pepper's* in 1967, and ended with Nixon's resignation in 1973.

Hendrix, Morrison, and Joplin were still alive and going strong. The Beatles' album *Abbey Road* swamped the airwaves, individual tracks taking all the top slots. Despite the scorn of the critics, all over America people in highly altered states lined up to see *2001: A Space Odyssey*. When Armstrong walked on the Moon, the main reaction was, *Hey, what took so long?*

1969 wasn't the end of the sixties. It was the crest of the wave.

If 1969 had been awarded a coat of arms, Crystal Keeling would have been engraved upon it. Glossy straight black hair and radiant skin: at the end of a decade of perms, flips, bangs, and Dippity-Doo, she was a vigorous seedling pushing her way through a crack in the concrete to stand upright in the sun, glowing with natural health. Her only concession to makeup was a daily touch of Slicker gloss, leaving her lips wet as though she'd just taken the first bite of the forbidden fruit.

With her friend Sheila, she'd hitched from San Diego to the Big Apple by way of New Orleans: a six-month-long detour where they'd lived in a garage with three musicians as the trio groped toward the jazz-rock blend that would become Fusion.

Sheila's friend Skazz had promised them a place to stay in the Village, but by the time they finally arrived in New York he was in the process of getting evicted. They spent a couple of nights in sleeping bags on his floor—he'd already sold his furniture—and then Sheila and Skazz piled into his van to head for a commune in Vermont. Crystal was invited along, of course; but she decided to hang around the big city for a while.

Spring had just touched the Village, but you could smell Washington Square Park for a mile in any direction, the blend of pot and patchouli overwhelming even the leaded-gasoline fumes of the Yellow Cabs. With her good looks and California Love Child attitude, Crystal was welcome in every cluster of guitar-players, pot-puffers, or wide-eyed acidheads; she'd been passed so many bomber joints of low-potency Iowa ditchweed that her throat was getting raw before noon.

She bought a hot chocolate from a street vendor and sat down on a bench, trying to sense the rays of the struggling Manhattan Sun. The flap pocket of her pack held a secondhand paperback copy of *Cat's Cradle*. She opened it to the latest dog-ear and tried to get back into it.

"So you believe in Sexual Liberation?" a voice asked.

She looked up. The speaker was a middle-aged man, portly, wearing clothes that suggested the aliens had landed at last: a wide-lapeled three-piece suit in light blue, with a paisley Apache tie.

Things sure were different Back East.

She smiled. "Sure."

"Well, howabout sharing some of it with me?" He flushed as he said it, and then added, "There's fifty bucks for you in it."

Crystal shook her head. It was insulting, sure, but the desperation in his eyes ran so deep that, for a brief moment, she considered going somewhere with him and giving him a decent charity fuck.

At least until he said, "A hundred, then."

She stood up and slung her backpack over one shoulder. "Man," she asked, "what is your *trip*, anyway?"

Crystal stalked away, and found a place on the steps by the Arch where she could lean against her backpack and read. She was pondering the pronouncements of the Books of Bokonon when she realized that her butt was freezing off against the cold concrete.

Her eyes sought the Sun with an accusative squint. She'd read that the Aztecs had torn out the hearts of hundreds of sacrificial victims each year when the Sun was at its weakest, using the blood to feed the Sun, to encourage it to bloom again.

Hell, that was in Mexico City, not far from the tropics.

Good thing the Aztecs didn't live in New York. They would've needed millions of sacrificial victims each winter solstice, an assembly-line of heart-gougers, a regular Detroit of cardiac surgeons.

A handful of antiwar protestors marched through chanting, "Ho, Ho, Ho Chi Minh," the ones in front carrying a banner that she couldn't read. Around the park fists rose in solidarity, and there were whistles and hoots of support.

"A *granfaloon*, I fear," a male voice behind her said.

She turned to look up at the speaker. It was impossible to tell his age—he might have been thirty, he might have been fifty. His black hair was slicked down; his dark beard was trimmed in a neat goatee. Despite the hint of a Midwest twang, Crystal thought there was something European about him.

He sat down beside her and gestured at her paperback with an elegant hand. "I couldn't help noticing…" A heavy lace cuff dangled from the sleeve of his Victorian jacket.

"You're right," she said. "I was just reading about it. They're a *granfaloon*—even if I'm on their side." She chewed her lip for a moment. "But, I guess all organizations are *granfaloons*, aren't they?"

He gave a sardonic smile. "No, though one might be forgiven for thinking so. No, for those who can see a little deeper than the common run of man, the real connections become clear. And you, my dear…" He interlaced his fingers with hers and sat her hand down in his lap, patting it with his free hand. "You, my dear, just might be part of something very real indeed."

That was how Crystal came to Anton Reginald LaMarr and The Children of Pan.

The Children lived together in a soaring townhouse off Abingdon Square. And, although most of them dwelt four or even five to a room, Anton gave Crystal—a Guest, rather than a Child—a room of her own, high up against the gabled roof.

Crystal was never initiated into The Children, and her understanding of their theology remained fuzzy. What she understood was that, like her, they were launched on a spiritual quest, and that they shunned traditional, husband-wife, ownership relations. There seemed to be a deep undercurrent of nature worship in their ceremonies, and Crystal wondered at this; New York City seemed a strange venue for a nature cult.

For their part, The Children treated her sweetly, with an attitude that verged on deference. They understood she too was a seeker, and though their code forbade drugs, they didn't judge her; when she came home from parties with her pupils wide, smelling of pot and wine, they merely smiled. The strangest feature of life with The Children was that no one, neither male nor female, approached her sexually; and when she made overtures toward a few of them, they retreated like dogs shying from being petted.

She tried to help in the kitchen, but someone always eased her out, taking over whatever chore she attempted. She offered to clean up around the house, or even get a job and chip in some rent, but she gradually came to understand that her help wasn't wanted. So she read—*Cat's Cradle* (wonderful), *The Glass Bead Game* (curious), *The Harrad Experiment* (laughable)—partied at other Village houses, and deepened her meditation practice.

When Anton finally asked if she'd be willing to play a lead role in The Children's fertility rites, she felt she owed them something; and when she discovered it involved no more than a little friendly semipublic sex, she was happy to oblige. As the old world crumbled around her, Crystal was clear on the trends: By the year 2000, men and women would be equal in every way, race would matter no more than eye color, and sex would be something that happened all the time between friends.

Sort of like a decent back rub.

"I agreed I'd ball him, not that I'd shed all my fur," she said as they shaved her legs. The attention was fun: she'd been massaged, bathed, wrapped in hot towels, cleaned, and polished down to the tiniest crevice. But she had no desire to lose her leg hair—never plentiful, in any case—or the meager bushes under her arms. "It itches when it starts growing back…"

The three female Children attending her laughed like—well, *children*…and went right on trimming, soaping, and shaving. By the time they started on her pubic hair, the sensation had become intriguing. What the hell: sure, she'd spend a week scratching, but in the meantime why not enjoy it for what it was worth?

By the time they were done she was hairless from the neck down, and the very molecules of the air were tiny Ben-Wa balls, dinging against her skin. Talk about naked…

"Far out," Crystal said.

When they started painting symbols atop her chakras, it began to seem ludicrous. Crystal had done body painting before—had even made love with a San Diego artist whose canvases were nothing more than the trysting sheets where he and his lover of the moment writhed, coated in poster paints. But The Children were so damn serious about the whole thing…and the sigil they inscribed around her belly button tickled.

As for the indigo sickle of Saturn on her perineum—well, come on.

The Children's communal dining room—undoubtedly a ballroom in the heyday of the townhouse—had been cleared of furniture. The walls were festooned with fresh-cut pine boughs that wafted their resinous scent through the room, and a pentagonal platform eight feet across had been erected at the end of the hall, opposite the great double doors.

By the time two strong Children carried Crystal into the room, their arms crossed beneath her buttocks to form a chair, the room was lit by the flames of a half-dozen oil lamps suspended from the stamped-tin ceiling by long chains. To either side of the impromptu aisleway, The Children stood—a greater crowd than lived in the house, a hundred or more. Their shapes were wreathed in muslin shrouds, men and women indistinguishable in the shadows.

An insistent drumming started somewhere. Crystal's bearers carried her to the platform, turned to face the crowd, and then lifted her, standing her upright to look out across them.

In the next moment, they whisked away her robe.

Her first sensation was the cold of air on her naked, shaved body.

The next was one of heat, as she felt hundreds of eyes upon her.

Kind of a turn-on, really.

The drums stopped. Then, like a wave passing across the crowd, the onlookers peeled back their muslin shrouds. A hundred bodies stood there, naked to the waist—black or white, breasted or hairy, every chest rising and falling with arousal.

Maybe these Children know how to party after all, Crystal thought. And then the crowd sprouted a forest of a hundred upraised arms, each fist clutching a short whip, and in unison The Children lashed them down upon their own backs, a soft hiss ending in an ugly, reverberating smack.

Way too weird. Crystal stood and watched the self-flagellation as the flails rose and fell, rose and fell, and she found herself counting in sick fascination.

Thirty-two. Thirty-two, or maybe thirty-three.

A palate-tickling smell of blood fingered its way through the room.

Then the drums started up again, and there was a sigh of anticipation as the Hornéd One entered through the double doors and strode down the hall.

Halfway to the altar he threw aside his robes and lifted his arms high into the air, and the crowd roared approval.

The maneuver reminded Crystal of pro wrestling on TV, but she knew what was expected. She lowered herself to the top of the altar and lay on her back, waiting.

The goat-head mask loomed over her as the god clambered onto the altar.

The audience quieted as he positioned himself atop her.

Without pause, he thrust himself easily into Crystal's waiting body.

When she responded with a yummy sound, it seemed to disconcert the Hornéd One, who'd perhaps expected more amazement from her.

She was sorry to disappoint; but if he'd wanted her to be less prepared, he should have jumped her about three hours before. And maybe skipped all the massages, and the whole shaving scene.

Whatever the Hornéd One was thinking, he decided to make the best of it, and, supporting himself on his arms, he drew back and thrust deep once more. Crystal hummed, lifted her legs wider, and, as he drew back, reached around to grab onto his buttocks to pull him down harder.

The goat-headed man survived this treatment for a half-dozen thrusts before he groaned and pumped his sperm deep inside her, making a dying sound with each spasm.

The crowd roared its approval.

Crystal had learned to be philosophical about premature ejaculation; there must have been a dozen over the years who hadn't even gotten all the way in before they came. It was easy enough to get them up again, usually…though she hadn't tried it in front of an audience.

She was wondering what to do next when the Hornéd One slid out of her with a grunt. Strong hands seized her, and four men hoisted her up to shoulder level and carried her away from the platform.

For a moment this was both scary and exciting—she didn't know what they had planned, and in her state of mind, she might have gone along with just about anything…

But they just carried her back to her room and left her there.

Hours of preparation, and then no orgy?

For a moment, she thought about just doing herself and then going to sleep; but the more she thought about it, the more pissed off she became.

Popping off prematurely: hey, it could happen to anybody.

Popping off prematurely and not giving a shit: bad manners.

Popping off prematurely and having her carted off to her bed when it happened in front of a roomful of aroused people, male and female, any number of whom would probably have been happy to leap into the breach: now that was just plain fucking selfish.

Talk about feeling used.

Come to think of it, she wasn't sure she'd had anybody bang her in a decent, considerate, hot, nasty way since she'd crossed the Mississippi.

She paused, trying to figure out which side of the Mississippi New Orleans sat on. She shrugged, rooted through the wad of clothes in her backback, and pulled on an Indian print top and a pair of elephant bellbottoms. She hoisted the backpack over one shoulder and pushed open the door.

One of The Children, the guy called Will, stood outside.

"I'm sorry, Mother," he said, "but I can't allow you to leave."

"*Mother?*" she said.

"You will be the Mother to the god; and then, you will be Mother to us all."

"I'm not going to be 'Mother' to anyone," she said.

He shook his head, smiling. "The seed entered you tonight. Didn't you feel it?"

"I didn't feel much, actually. But maybe I stopped paying attention for the, oh, *ten seconds or so* that it took."

He refused to acknowledge her tone. "I am honored to be the one sent to watch over you, as you grow heavy with his seed."

Crystal dropped her backpack to the floor. "Are you saying I can't leave?"

"Not until the Promised One comes, Mother. I am here to serve you. But I cannot let you leave."

She leaned close. "Listen. I'm not pregnant, if that's what you think you mean. I'm on the fucking *Pill*. So there's no way that I got knocked up tonight by Mister Speedster. No way."

Will tilted his head back, smiling beatifically. "Still. It has happened. Nothing anyone does now can interfere with it."

"Nothing can interfere with it?"

Will shook his head, a wide, happy grin on his face.

"And, other than letting me go, you're here to serve me?"

He nodded, still smiling.

Crystal reached out and grabbed him by his collar. "Then I'm sure you won't mind," she whispered, "coming in here and fucking me until my nose bleeds."

In point of fact, her nose never bled. And, in point of fact, on his first pass, he didn't manage to stay with her any longer than the Hornéd One.

The second time around, he stayed with her long enough that she started to have some fun.

The third time took forever—long enough that Crystal started to worry that Will's shift might end, and he'd be replaced.

They worked through a good third of the extended version of the Kama Sutra before he gave out, but Striking With the Flat of Hand While Sitting on Hams did him in.

He snored as she dressed. She had just lifted her backpack by one strap when he spoke.

"Crystal?"

"Yeah, Will?"

There was a long pause, as if he'd fallen completely asleep again; and then he said, "I love you…"

"I love you too, Will," she whispered.

She stepped into the hallway and, with all the stealth she could muster, raised the window in front of the fire escape.

When her feet hit the bottom flight, where the last stairs of the escape needed to swing downward to allow egress, there was a horrendous screeching of iron as hinges rusted in place broke free.

She ran to the street, her thumb out.

Her first ride only intended to go crosstown, but instead he drove her as far as an onramp in Brooklyn in exchange for her phone number.

Well, for *a* phone number.

It took her two more rides to get out of New York City.

Larry, the third one who picked her up, was headed back to the Rockies. "You ever been to Boulder?" he asked.

"No. Is it cool?"

"Mindblowing. There's these *huge* rocks, and they're just…well, *huge*." He shook his head as if clearing it. "Spent too long here. Need to get back home."

"Tell me," Crystal said. "East Coast people are weird."

When it happens at all, conception typically comes between twelve and forty-eight hours after the Greek Fleet of ejaculate sets sail toward Troy.

Twelve hours is about the minimum swim time; and forty-eight hours is about the maximum survival time for sperm, intrepid little sailors who set forth on their journeys without packing a lunch.

Several variables affect the length of this voyage, not least of which is Helen's smile itself: during a woman's orgasm the cervix comes alive, dipping its head down into the pooling semen and dilating slightly, swallowing hundreds of thousands of sperm at each gulp. A few decent contractions can cut the needed swim time by more than half.

The woman's cycle also affects the trip; as estrus approaches, the mucus in the cervical channel thins to a watery consistency. Earlier or later in the month, traveling through the cervical canal can be like struggling through a bowl of congealing oatmeal…but time it just right, and it can be like diving into the pool at the Tropicana on a hot summer day.

Then, of course, they say sperm motility is critical. Fertility researchers place great weight on sperm motility, like fishermen searching through the bait tray for the liveliest worms. The fact is that, until recently, almost all fertility researchers were men, and men just had to believe their manly vigor has something to do with the whole thing, that sperm had to be, if you will, spunky.

The real truth is, it doesn't matter whether the sperm charge out with all the enthusiasm of a high-school production of *Oklahoma!* or sulk in their tents like Achilles. The process is like swimming the Pacific, and success has more to do with the condition of the ocean than with the conditioning of the swimmer.

Forget about sperm motility. Just get over it.

A final factor, which all women instinctively understand, is the cussedness of the universe.

If pregnancy is unsought, inconvenient, preferably even disastrous, then it happens readily and almost instantaneously. If the woman is only thirteen, or is having a secret affair, or has finally received a long-desired promotion to a high-pressure job, or has just won the 400-meter race in the Olympic qualifying trials—under any of these conditions, the woman in question can become pregnant even while menstruating, despite using six different forms of FDA-approved contraception simultaneously.

The cussedness factor—known to researchers as OSNNS (Oh-Shit-Not-Now Syndrome) or the OSNWHC (Oh-Shit-Not-With-Him Conundrum)—continues to baffle scientists.

The cussedness factor may account for the fact that, snoozing in the passenger seat on Interstate 80, Crystal conceived, a mere six hours after the ceremony in Greenwich Village. Had she known at the time, she would have been righteously pissed: How can you get pregnant on the Pill?

The Children wouldn't have been surprised.

The lucky single sperm adhering to the oocytic cell membrane dropped its tail, saying farewell to everything but its packet of DNA. Once it began to fuse with the cell membrane, the egg's thick coat of the zona pellucida suddenly began to granulate and swell, straightarming all other suitors back into the waters of the womb. *Closed, Cerrado, Out of Business. Try one of our other fine locations.*

Textbooks love to say we acquire half our biological traits from our father, half from our mother. This is usually described in two words: *Equal Inheritance.*

Here's two better words: *Phallocentric bullshit.*

From our fathers, we inherit half of the DNA in the cell nucleus.

From our mothers, we inherit our mitochondria, our ribosomes, the cell spindles, the nuclear walls, the Golgi bodies, all of the transport structures built into the cell walls, and our entire Starter Set of metabolic proteins and enzymes.

And, oh yeah, the other half of the nuclear DNA.

You can't even say we inherit half our DNA from our fathers. Just the *nuclear* DNA. Mitochondria, the powerhouses of the cell, have their own DNA, and reproduce like independent little organisms inside the enormous cells of our body.

Dad contributes some mitochondria to the reproductive process at first: they sit there in the tail of the sperm, running the waving flagellum like the motor of a powerboat.

But these are discarded like used Band-Aids when the sperm drops its tail: *Nuclear DNA Only Past This Point.*

So what was growing now in Crystal's belly was mostly Crystal. Mostly Crystal, but with something special added.

As the nuclei of egg and sperm fused, occultists all over the Northeast of the US felt a trembling pass through them, and those that were abed came suddenly awake.

In the Olympic Mountains of western Washington a dozen mountain goats, hunkered down in a snow drift, rose suddenly and peered about, their shaggy white coats bright against the night sky…

In a radio studio, rehearsing for the next day's broadcast, a famous evangelist was afflicted with such a sudden and rampant erection that he threw down his headphones and ran for the bathroom…

In a basement of an Alphabet City tenement on the island of Manhattan, Gary Masello decided not to kill himself, and put the revolver down on the floor beside his mattress. There was something he was supposed to do…

In the house of The Children of Pan near Abingdon Square, Anton Reginald LaMarr raged and threw things, and ordered The Children out into the night to search for The Mother…

…but Crystal snoozed her way across Pennsylvania. She ate pancakes at an IHOP outside Akron, Ohio; bought four fingers of decent pot at a truck stop near Chicago; and she kept on heading west when Jerry, her ride, dropped her in Boulder.

She was in San Francisco when Gary Masello made the papers by breaking into The Children's townhouse and shooting everyone he could find in the top-floor bedrooms.

She was at a concert in Ashland, Oregon, when an arsonist set a fire that raged through The Children's townhouse in the night, killing a dozen of them, and gutting the building.

She was living in a treehouse near Mount Angel, Oregon, by the time that Anton Reginald LaMarr disbanded The Children and went into hiding.

Treehouses were awesomely cool, living up among the leaves. When Crystal found she was pregnant, she was more than a little irritated; but she couldn't imagine a better place to have a baby.

She wasn't sure whose baby it was—maybe Will's? Larry's?—but the whole fatherhood thing was so property-based anyway.

She was confident that, by the year 2000, nobody would care about the paternity thing anymore.